THE WUHAN RBG VIRUS

DR. PHILIP EMMA

The Wuhan RBG Virus
Copyright © 2022 by Dr. Philip Emma

ISBN
978-1-957378-79-4 (Paperback)
978-1-957378-78-7 (eBook)
978-1-957378-80-0 (Hardcover)

Table of Contents

Prologue

Pardon! Pardon!
Ladies and gentlemen, forgive me for appearing alone.
I am the Prologue!

Since the author is putting on the stage again the old 'Comedy of Masks,' he would like to revive some of the old customs, and so sends me out again to you. But not to say as of old: 'The tears we shed are feigned! Do not alarm yourselves at our sufferings and our torments!'

No!

The author instead has sought to paint for you a scene from life. He takes as his basis simply that the artist is a man and that he must write for men. His inspiration is a true story.

A horde of memories was one day running through his head, and he wrote, shedding real tears, with sobs to mark the time. So you will see love, as real as human beings' love. You will see the sad fruit of hate. You will hear agonies of grief, cries of rage and bitter laughter!

So, think then, not of our poor theatrical costumes but of our souls. For we are men of flesh and blood, breathing the air of this lonely world just like you. I have told you his plan. Now hear how it is unfolded.

Come: Let us begin!

(Prologue from "**Pagliacci**"; opera by Ruggero
Leoncavallo – English translation)

Dr. Grouchi, in his capacity as the Chief Medical Advisor to the President of the United States, was visiting the Wuhan Institute of Virology in the Hubei Province of China. Dr. Grouchi was funding certain classified research being done at the Wuhan Institute. It was all very hush-hush.

Dr. Grouchi was there visiting his longtime friend and research associate, Gao Fu-Yousef, the Director-General of the Chinese Center for Disease Control. The two had worked together throughout their illustrious careers, and Dr. Grouchi had arranged for funding to the Wuhan lab to do a very unusual study. It had to do with a certain virus found in the guano (excrement) of rabid bats. This piece of research was code-named "RBG."

The "RBG" moniker stood for "Rabid-Bat Guano."

"Fascinating," Grouchi said. "You're telling me that the guano contains a new virus – a mutated bacterium – that will cause people who are infected to crave blood. But other than that, it has no symptoms?"

"As far as we've been able to determine," Gao said, "there are no other symptoms."

"I've never heard of a virus like this before," Grouchi said. "What good is it? Why would we care whether people crave blood if they're healthy otherwise?"

"I don't know," Gao said. "We probably don't care. But we're still studying it."

"This sounds like useless research," Grouchi said. "As the person who is funding it, my suggestion is that you simply write a paper or two, and then move on to something else."

"I understand," Gao Fu-Yousef said. "Let me show you some other work that we're doing."

The two of them toured the lab, and Gao introduced Dr. Grouchi to many of the people that worked there.

As they were finishing the tour, Gao gave Grouchi the Chinese fist and palm salute. He made a half-fist with his right hand, and put it into the palm of his left hand. He raised his hands to his brow, lowered them back to his waist, and did a slight bow.

"Dr. Grouchi," he said. "Would do me the honor of coming to my home for dinner tonight?"

"It would be my honor, Gao Fu-Yousef," Dr. Grouchi said, and he returned the salute.

"Come at about 6:00," Gao said.

They bowed again, and Dr. Grouchi left the lab.

That night, Dr. Grouchi took a taxi to Gao's home. He'd brought a small gift with him, which he'd bought in his hotel's gift shop. They'd wrapped it for him.

It was a large house. Dr. Grouchi rang the bell, and Gao answered the door. Dr. Grouchi entered, took his shoes off, and handed Gao the gift that he'd brought. Gao brought him into the kitchen where his wife was cooking their dinner, and introduced the two of them. Dr. Grouchi did a slight bow.

There was tea waiting, which Gao poured for all of them. He saw all of the prep work that Gao's wife had done: lots of chopped vegetables, some chicken, and some fish. And the rice-cooker was on, cooking their rice.

New to Dr. Grouchi were the bats. Gao's wife had some bats soaking in a pot of water. They were going to be part of the dinner. He had never had bats before, but was eager to try them. He'd been told that they had the flavor of mutton and the texture of chicken. He found that hard to imagine.

Gao invited Dr. Grouchi to come sit in their living room while his wife finished making their dinner. They sat and talked and drank their tea. When dinner was ready, they all went into the dining room.

Gao's wife spoke a little bit of English, but wasn't fluent. Gao was. And Dr. Grouchi spoke a little bit of Mandarin. With Gao there to interpret, they all had a nice dinner and a pleasant discussion. Dr. Grouchi enjoyed his dinner very much. While he thought that the bats had an interesting flavor, he wasn't going to put them high up on his "favorites" list. As he'd been told, they had the flavor of mutton with the texture of chicken. Even having now tasted it, that was still hard to imagine.

After dinner was over, Gao and Dr. Grouchi went back into the living room, and Gao poured them a couple of glasses of very good brandy.

"Ganbei," they both said, bowing toward each other. ("Ganbei" is a Chinese toast that means "dry cup.") They did not down their drinks in one swallow as would usually be the custom with this toast, since you'd never do that with a good brandy.

They sat and chatted some more until Gao's wife came to join them.

After another brandy, Dr. Grouchi got up, thanked them both, and said goodnight.

1. The Rabid-Bat Virus

The morning was a morning like every other morning. And then I turned on the TV.

In addition to all of the news stories about what celebrities were sleeping with what other celebrities, there was a new story about a virus that had come here from China.

So far, no one was sick. It sounded innocuous. *So what? A virus? We've had them before*, I thought.

The anchorman assured us that there was nothing to worry about – yet. We should all carry on as we had carried on yesterday, and the day before, and the day before that.

A spokesman from China assured us that scientists there didn't know where the virus had come from. They thought that perhaps it was a disease that had effected a large colony of bats. And the Chinese eat bats. Apparently, they're yummy when cooked right: they're even better than tuna eyeballs, or chicken testicles.

The part of Wuhan that they were reporting from – Wuhan, was the city in China that first saw the disease - was right where their open markets are, and bats are one of the many delicacies that are sold there. Those, along with bee pupae, wormwood dumplings, chicken feet, cicadas, and sea slugs.

While they said that disease affected bats, so far there was no evidence that it affected people in the same way, nor was there any evidence that it was either deadly, or communicable. We really had nothing to worry about. It really shouldn't even be a story.

So why was it a story?

It was true that Wuhan had a biological laboratory in the neighborhood that adjoined their open markets, but the spokesman assured us that the disease hadn't come from that laboratory. That laboratory abided by the highest standards when handling viruses, and this particular virus – the bat virus – had no relationship to anything being studied there.

So why they had bothered with this story? A disease that didn't affect people that was local to the bat-market in a city in China? A disease that wasn't deadly or communicable? So?

I went into the kitchen to fix myself a cup of coffee, and left the news on. Maybe they'd get to something important – like who was sleeping with whom. I couldn't wait to hear.

My name is Mick Maux. The last name is French, and it's pronounced like it's "Mouse." Occasionally, this causes trouble for me: people don't believe me when I tell them my name.

I'm a scientist. Rather, I'm retired. I studied hard, and math always came easily to me. So my professional work was always in science. I've lived and studied in Boston, in California, and in Texas. I've worked in private industry, I've taught at universities, and I've worked for the government. Once I'd made enough money to retire, which I did when I was relatively young, I came back to where I was from: Connecticut.

In Connecticut, we have the four seasons. In the spring, the daffodils come up, the grass turns an emerald green, and the forsythia turns a golden yellow. And in the fall, the leaves become a panoply of vivid colors before they fall from the trees. While the summer is hot, it's not nearly as hot as it is down South. And while the winter is cold, it's not nearly as cold as it is in the Midwest.

In the Northeast, we have our seasons, which cause me to cycle through my many perspectives of life. And the states here are small. It is an easy drive to New York City, and an easy drive to Boston. While the population density is high, the population is diverse. There are many wealthy people, and many poor ones. And they all make a living, somehow.

Along the way, I'd met Carol. We married several years back, and she accompanied me through my professional journeys to eventually come here to Connecticut. She's a lovely woman with beautiful hair and a statuesque presence. And she has what I don't: raw intelligence, and common sense.

While I was always an "outside the box" thinker, Carol has an unusual perspective: wisdom. And she has a real sense for how other people think. This is a perspective that's lacking in me, and sometimes, it's caused me to do embarrassing things. Although *I* was never embarrassed, Carol has occasionally told me that I should have been.

Since retiring, I've only taken on detective cases that I thought were unusual and challenging. I have a perspective (and some computer expertise) that the police lack, and I can be discrete. Together, Carol and I have what it takes to crack difficult cases. While our fees are high, we make them high just to make sure that our customers are genuinely interested in the results.

Carol came downstairs, and poured a cup of coffee. She was still in her bathrobe, and the news was still on. "Good morning," she said.

"Good morning," I replied, lifting my coffee cup as if making a toast.

She looked at the TV. "Any news this morning?" she asked.

"Nope," I said. "What's-'is-name is sleeping with what's-'er name. Other than that, nothing."

"That's the same as yesterday," she said.

"Well, there was a weird story about a bat-virus in China," I said. "But it only effects bats, and maybe the people that eat them. They said that there's nothing to worry about."

"So why did they waste time reporting on it?" Carol asked.

"Good question," I said. "You'd think that they'd report real news."

I was in the family-room, sitting on the sofa, reading. Our kitchen area opens up into a dining area, which opens up into the family-room. It's what might be called "open concept," although we do have a separate (formal) dining room, a living room, a foyer, and a pantry. These are not open-concept.

Carol came in and sat with me so that we could watch the news together.

As she sat, the story about the Chinese bat-virus came on again. They showed the very large open markets in China again, which looked very unsanitary. It showed merchants putting items down on the ground to hack them up. And it was all open-air, with no air-conditioning.

The same Chinese spokesman came on to again say that the virus did not come from their lab, and that it did not effect humans. There was nothing to worry about.

This time, a new character came on. His name was Dr. Grouchi, and he was introduced as the chief medical advisor to the President of the United States. He looked like a miniature, beady-eyed vampire.

Dr. Grouchi explained to us that the Chinese virus was called "RBG," that it might have come from rabid bats, and that it might have come from the Chinese labs. This was the opposite of what the Chinese spokesman had said, although we all know that (unlike our government) their government lies. Again, the name "RBG" stood for "Rabid-Bat Guano"; the presumed source of the disease.

Dr. Grouchi said that the virus was not dangerous to humans, and that even if it was, there was no need to do anything in particular. We should keep a "safe distance" from people that we didn't know, and not exchange saliva with them. And there was no need for wearing masks, since masks didn't work anyway.

Dr. Grouchi gave us a hungry-looking, ghoulish, vampire-smile, then he started steepling[1]. And finally, he signed off.

"It sounds like there's nothing to worry about," Carol said.

"Outside of Dr. Grouchi, there probably isn't," I replied.

"He looks like a vampire," Carol observed.

"A miniature, beady-eyed vampire," I added.

---

[1] "Steepling" is the act of pushing one's fingertips together while keeping the palms apart. Classes in body language will tell you that steepling is used to convey superior intelligence.

2. Chess, and Detective Danny

Chess is a lot like life. I had gone to Holy Moly, which is the coffee shop where I hang out when I don't know where else to go. I'd ordered a latte, grabbed a table by the window, and had started playing chess on my computer.

I found that while playing chess required me to focus part of my mind, it allowed other parts of my mind to drift – not consciously, but subconsciously. Allowing your mind to drift when there is no specific objective is very useful: it lets you see the world more clearly.

Yes, I was aware of people entering and leaving the shop, chatting with each other. And I was aware of the occasional ruffling newspaper. And yes, I was aware of cars circling around outside looking for places to park. But it wasn't a conscious awareness; it was all background noise. It's easy to lose the conscious mind in background noise.

I was also aware of the intensity of my concentration on the game of chess that I was playing. I was focusing on "the whole" of the board, and the pieces on it; contemplating various moves and likely countermoves, and my probable responses to those. That was my focus.

I was also vaguely aware of my mind contemplating other problems in my life and in the world. But my contemplation of those things wasn't conscious: I saw them, but I wasn't thinking about them. This is what allows us to be objective. It is the stuff of dreams.

"Chess," could have been another answer given by Oedipus to the Sphinx when he was asked: "What has four legs in the morning, two during the daytime, and three at night?" But chess didn't exist yet. The Sphinx had been alluding to "man," who crawls on all-fours as an infant, walks on two legs as an adult, and uses a cane when old.

Like man, a game of chess comprises three parts. It has four legs in its infancy, two in its adulthood, and three in its end.

The infancy of a game of chess is in its opening. The opening is what sets the scene for the battle ahead. It's relatively gentle. This is a lot like life. Yes, there are well known families of openings: the Sicilian Defense, the Ruy Lopez, and the Queen's Gambit. But there is no real bloodshed in opening games. In fact, moving pieces in significant ways is difficult because there are too many other pieces in the way. In the opening game, you're like an infant crawling on all-fours.

The object of the opening game is to develop the board in anticipation of the slaughter that's to come in the middle-game. Developing the board involves moving your pieces to (hopefully) control the center of the board. Why the center of the board? Because pieces in the center of the board have a larger "range" than those on the edges. That means that they pose threats to more of the board.

Once most of the powerful (non-pawn) pieces have been moved into places where they can act, and once the kings have been castled where they are safe, we are now on two legs, and the bloodshed starts. This is the middle game; this is adulthood; this is reality. After the bloodshed, and after most of the pieces are gone, comes the end-game. In the end-game, we are on three legs, and moving is cumbersome.

If few powerful pieces are left after the middle-game, it's difficult for either side to checkmate the other in the end-game. We now are walking with a cane. Quite often, the key to winning in the end game is to have one of your pawns make it all the way across the board to be converted into a queen.

Then, with a queen, you can sting. Without a queen, games are seldom won by either side. The game ends when a king is toppled. And what better way to topple a king than with a queen? Again, chess is a lot like life.

If Oedipus had answered "chess" to the Sphinx, I'm sure that the Sphinx would have been confused, and would have torn him apart. Chess was invented in India around the 6th century AD, and the Sphinx never would have heard of it.

While I was contemplating my position, someone interrupted my reverie. "Do you mind if I join you?" he asked.

I broke my focus and looked up. It was Police Detective Danny, standing there in mufti. Good. No one would think that I was being busted. At least not yet.

Danny and I have known each other for quite a while. We grew up together. He's one of the only cops that I trust. And he has been helpful on several of the cases that I've worked on with my wife, Carol. While I can break into most computer systems to get information, it's much easier if I can get the information from Danny. While he never breaks the law, he has given me useful information about several people when I've needed it.

A while back, I had introduced Danny to our neighbor across the street. Her name is Dottie. I had never seen any men over there until I introduced her to Danny. Now I usually see his car over at her house in the early mornings when I take my run.

"Hi Danny," I said. "Good to see you. Have a seat."

The table was a two-top, so he took a seat facing me. He had already bought his coffee.

"How are things?" he asked. "How's Carol?"

"Great," I said. "Except that Carol is talking about replacing some of our furniture. I don't mind spending the money if she wants new furniture, but I don't like having to go to furniture stores with her. All I do is stand around looking stupefied. I usually bring a book with me. How's Dottie?" I asked.

"Couldn't be better," he said. "I still owe you for having introduced us."

"It was my pleasure," I said.

When I'd introduced them, I'd never imagined that they would have become involved with each other the way that they had. Dottie had never dressed nicely before then, and had always seemed to be scowling. Since meeting Danny, she dresses nicely and she's always smiling. And most of her wrinkles have disappeared. Danny usually seems to be in a good mood too. Love changes people.

"What do you think of this RBG?" Danny asked.

"Ruth Bader Ginsberg?" I asked. "She was what's today an unusual combination: an originalist, yet also a liberal. She had a conscience."

"Who?" Danny asked.

"The second woman in the Supreme Court," I said.

"You mean she backed Diana Ross?" he asked.

"Yes," I said. "Basically."

"I wasn't talking about her," he said. "I meant the RBG."

"Oh, you mean the 'Red, Blue, and Green'?" I asked. "The colors used in cathode-ray tubes to make nearly any other color by mixing the three of these appropriately? It's based on what's called an 'additive color model,' which allows us to make nearly any other color by mixing these three. I think that the original concept is brilliant."

"No," Danny said, "I meant the RBG."

"Oh, you mean the national flag of the Republic of Azerbaijan?" I asked. "It has a red, a blue, and a green stripe. The red band is in the middle. It has a white crescent and an eight-pointed star centered within the red band. A very interesting design."

"No," Danny said. "I meant the RBG virus. I think it's called 'RBG.'"

"Oh, that," I said. "I forgot what they were calling it. 'The Vampire' was on TV, and he said that it's nothing to worry about," I said.

"The Vampire?" Danny asked. "Who's that?"

"Dr. Grouchi," I said. "I saw him on TV, and he said that it's nothing to worry about."

"You're right," Danny said. "He *does* look like a vampire. I'll bet that he throws a mean fastball."

"Why did you bring it up?" I asked. "Dr. Grouchi said to ignore it."

"Then why did the President shut down flights from China?" Danny asked.

"I hadn't heard that," I said. "When was that?"

"Last night," Danny said. "The President said that not enough is known about it, so he shut down flights from China because it might be dangerous if we allow people from China in. He said that in China, they've shut down travel from Wuhan to other parts of China, but not to the rest of the world. Why would China restrict domestic travel out of Wuhan if they didn't think it was dangerous?"

"Lots of reasons," I said. "In communist countries, and throughout much of history, dictators have made lots of stupid arbitrary rules that the people have to follow."

"Why do they do that?" Danny asked.

"First," I said, "because it makes them feel powerful. And second, if the rulers micro-manage the people, it changes the people. The people start to think that they're not smart enough to run their own lives, and that they *need* the rulers to tell them what to do. It *does* make the rulers more powerful. For example, a dictator could mandate something ridiculous, just to make the people know that he's the boss."

"Like what?" Danny asked.

"I don't know," I said. "Something arbitrary. Like, suppose he said that everyone had to wear a mask?"

"They could never do that in *this* country," Danny said. "We think for ourselves."

"That was the idea when this country was founded," I said. "But lots of things have changed, and other things are changing. We should never be too sure about 'the people' always doing the right thing. Money, avarice, laziness, drugs, and lots of other things can change people's priorities."

"Whatever," Danny said. "You think too hard."

"Only when I play chess," I said.

"The President probably knows lots of things that we don't," Danny said. "I'm sure that he shut down flights from China for a reason," he added.

"Probably," I said. "But in the meantime, Dr. Grouchi has said that we needn't do anything special, and that there's no evidence that the virus is harmful."

"I hope that he's right," Danny said.

"Do you have any interesting cases that you're working on?" I asked.

"Not much," Danny said. "And as you know, I'm not allowed to talk about them, except very generally. How about you?"

"Nothing," I said. "Carol and I have just been relaxing. Except that she's shopping for furniture. I already told you that."

"Well, good to see you Mick," he said, and got up to leave.

"Always a pleasure," I said. "We'll have you and Dottie over soon."

Mick left, and I got back into my game of chess. I was still in the opening game. There was no bloodshed yet. That would happen soon.

I thought about the bat virus.

3. Carol and I Talk About RBG

I was cooking tonight. Last night, Carol had cooked, and I did the dishes. Tonight, she'd do the dishes. I'd rather cook than do the dishes.

While I started my prep work, Carol came into the kitchen and sat at our center island so that we could talk while I worked. Our kitchen is large. The outer wall has lots of windows that overlook our back yard, which is surrounded by forest. A countertop runs along the outer wall. The counter is interrupted at its midpoint by the range and stove, and a hood above the range that vents fumes to the outside.

The center-island is opposite the stove. It contains the main sink, and has seating on the other side. There is ample room on either side of the sink to do prep-work. Carol was sitting at the island drinking a glass of wine. I'd poured myself a glass of wine too. She was drinking white, and I was drinking red. It was a nice time to chat.

Because I'd been thinking about all of that yummy food in the Wuhan markets, I'd decided to stick to American basics tonight. I was making a salad with a fresh vinaigrette, chicken piccata, and some baby zucchini. These are all simple. The most complicated part is the salad, since it requires lots of cleaning and chopping.

While chicken piccata was once considered Italian, it's become standard American fare. That's how our culture is. Maybe someday, we'll eat bats too.

I was washing some Boston lettuce, some bibb lettuce, some radicchio, and some arugula in the sink, which was nice because I was facing Carol. I put it all in a colander to drain, then dried my hands on a towel, and took a sip of my wine.

"What do you think about this virus?" I asked her.

"It sounds like there's not much to it," Carol said. "Dr. Grouchi said that it's nothing to worry about."

"Why do you think that China has isolated Wuhan?" I asked her.

"That's hard to say," she said. "China does lots of strange things for reasons that we don't know. My bet is that their President, Pi Hum-Ping, has isolated it for other reasons."

"But then why did our president ban flights from China?" I asked.

"He's probably just playing it safe," she said. "I guess we'll have to wait until we learn more about the RBG virus."

I took out the chicken cutlets, dredged them in flour, and sautéed them, putting them into a large rectangular baking dish when I was done. Then I added butter and capers to the pan, put in a small amount of stock, and adjusted the salt. I added some lemon juice, poured this over the cutlets, topped it with thin slices of lemon, and I put the baking dish in the oven on warm, just to hold it. I'd add chopped parsley before serving it.

I put the baby zucchini into a pan with some olive oil, and started a slow sauté over low heat, sprinkling a little bit on salt on them. Then I made the vinaigrette: a crushed clove of garlic, some good olive oil, a small dash of balsamic vinegar, a larger dash of cider vinegar, some mustard, salt, pepper, oregano, and some chopped fresh parsley. I shook it well, and then gave the zucchini a stir.

I started chopping the other vegetables for the salad: a tomato, half of a red onion, a bell pepper, and a cucumber. I'd add some olives, sunflower seeds, and gorgonzola before tossing it. This was all simple stuff: no cicadas or bats.

I let the zucchini continue to cook on low, and took another sip of my wine.

"I had a nice chat with Danny today," I said.

"Really?" Carol asked. "Where did you see him?"

"I was sitting in Holy Moly playing chess on my computer, and he came in," I said.

"What's new with him and Dottie?" she asked.

"He still looks like a man in love," I said. "So I think that everything's great."

"What else did you talk about?" she asked.

"This new virus," I said.

"It's strange how it supposedly isn't dangerous, yet it's creating so much discussion," Carol said. "Harmless or not, it's starting to occupy too much of our consciousness."

I thought about that, gave the zucchini another stir, put in a small amount of butter – just for flavor, and whisked them onto a small serving plate. I gave the salad dressing another shake, poured it over the salad, added the extras, and tossed it all. Then I took the chicken out of the oven, added the parsley, turned the oven off, and brought all three items into the dining room.

Our dining room is quite large, and we have a broad crystal chandelier that's suspended over the center of the table. Carol and I sat opposite each other, each of us on one side of the table with the chandelier above us. That way, we could talk at a moderate volume, and hear each other easily.

"What else is new?" she asked.

"I've been thinking about the environment lately, and studying carbon footprints," I said.

"Really?" she asked. "That sounds interesting," she added with a disinterested tone.

"Exactly," I said. "While carbon itself is straightforward, carbon footprints aren't. As we all learned in high school, carbon is an element in the periodic table," I said. "And it's a building-block used by much of what's real. It's essential element in any fuel."

"That sounds fascinating," she said, looking un-fascinated.

"I'm going to Ethan Allen tomorrow to look at some furniture," she said. "Would you like to come?"

"That sounds fascinating," I said, feeling un-fascinated. "But I'm pretty sure that I have work to do. I'm working on carbon," I added.

"That sounds fascinating," she said, looking un-fascinated.

"We haven't had any detective work in a while," I said, changing the subject.

"I guess that everyone's been behaving," she said.

"That can't last," I said. "I miss working with you. You always bring a certain amount of common sense to our cases. That's something that I don't seem to have."

We raised our glasses, and gave them a good "clink" across the table, toasting each other. This was another good reason not to sit at opposite ends of the dining table. I really did miss working with her. And I was glad that I wouldn't be doing the dishes.

4. The Carbon Footprint of Coffee

I was thinking about life, and about carbon. And about how much money Carol might spend at the furniture store – Ethan Allen. I was upstairs in my lab – the lab that I had built above our kitchen. I use the lab to do experiments – mostly computer things, although I do have some expensive electronic equipment in there too. I had done a lot of work for the government over the course of my career, and still had ties into their computer systems.

And I was drinking a cup of coffee.

While there are over 1,000 chemical compounds in a cup of coffee, I was thinking about the element carbon. Carbon is in many compounds. And it's in coffee. While this discussion of carbon will seem to be a digression in our story, please bear with me. Carbon becomes an essential element to its outcome.

Carbon is an element that has six electrons. Two of those are in its first shell, which can hold exactly two electrons, and four are in its second shell, which can hold as many as eight electrons. And since the second shell has room for eight electrons total, the second shell of carbon has room for four more electrons.

Carbon atoms bond to other things very easily so that they can share electrons. For example, they bond very easily to other carbon atoms.

Catenation is the ability of an atom to combine with other atoms of the same kind (e.g., carbon to carbon). And compounds made entirely of one element are called *allotropes*. While carbon has four different allotropes, until very recently, we only knew about two of them. These were graphite, and diamond. One is very soft, and conducts electricity, and the other is very hard, and does not.

In *graphite*, each carbon atom is bonded to just three (not four) other carbon atoms. This leaves one electron vacancy in each carbon atom, so it will easily take on another electron from whatever's touching it. All of those electron vacancies are what conduct electricity. Inexpensive resistors are made of graphite mixed with a few other compounds. The other compounds are there primarily to make the resistor hard and durable: graphite by itself is brittle. And graphite is a three-dimensional structure: its carbon atoms connect to each other in all three dimensions.

A more recently discovered allotrope of carbon is essentially two-dimensional graphite. It's called *graphene.*

Graphite makes good pencil lead. Since it's fairly soft and flaky, it's easy to write with. It also makes good cores for nuclear reactors. And because graphite has lots of electron vacancies, it's a very good electrical conductor.

Quite unlike carbon, *diamonds* have a tetrahedral structure in which each atom is connected to four other atoms. This makes a very hard and stable lattice. There are no electron vacancies in this structure. Diamonds have the hardest and most stable lattices that there are. Diamonds also have a very high refractive index, so they sparkle and glisten. What's not to love? And since diamonds have no free electrons or electron-vacancies, they don't conduct electricity.

While graphite and diamonds are found in nature, and it used to be believed that carbon only had these two allotropes, *graphene* was isolated and studied in 2004 at the University of Manchester. Until then, it had only been theoretical. Graphene is essentially a single layer of graphite comprising planar hexagonal lattices of carbon. It's ultra-light, pretty strong, and elastic. And like graphite, it's a very good electrical conductor.

And finally, a fourth allotrope that was called *buckminsterfullerene* was discovered in 1985 at the University of Sussex. It's denoted C_{60} since it contains sixty carbon atoms that are bonded into the shape of a soccer ball. Because it's shaped like a ball, and it's named after Buckminster Fuller, it's sometimes called a "buckeyball." The buckeyball comprises twenty hexagons and twelve pentagons, with each carbon atom connected to three other carbon atoms. It's now being sold as a food supplement that will cure all ails, and the government *has* classified it an antioxidant. It has another variant with seventy carbon atoms, and another with eighty atoms, all of them are very similar.

While the allotropes of carbon are all inorganic, life is based on carbon. That's why carbon is so important. The human body is about 60% water, but about 18% of a human's mass is carbon. And since there are nearly 8-billion people in the world, and the average weight of a person (including children) is 140 pounds, that's about 200-billion pounds of carbon contained in just the world's people. That's 100 MegaTons (MT), or 0.1 GigaTons (GT) of carbon.

But believe it or not, that's small.

To digress even further, let's consider how carbon is part of life.

If we consider the carbon in all living creatures (animals), the carbon in humans makes up only about 2.5% of it. By far, the largest category of animals is anthropods. These are invertebrates that have an exoskeleton, a segmented body, and paired, jointed appendages (arms and legs). This includes insects, spiders, myriapods, and crustaceans. All of the anthropods in the world contain about 1.7 GT of carbon. Compare that to the 0.1 GT of humans.

And next are the fish. All of the fish contain about 1.2 GT of carbon.

Next come the annelids, and the mollusks. Annelids are ringed worms and segmented worms. There are over 22,000 species of annelids, including ragworms, earthworms, and leeches. Mollusks include snails, octopuses, squid, clams, scallops, oysters, and chitons. It is estimated that there are about 200,000 species of mollusks. And each of these (annelids and mollusks) accounts for about 0.3 GT of carbon. The total is 0.7 GT. That's still seven times more carbon than there is in people.

Livestock accounts for 0.2 GT of carbon. And as we've said, humans account for 0.1 GT of carbon.

Next come nematodes, which are roundworms. These are the most abundant creatures on god's earth. They all contain about 0.03 GT of carbon, about a third of what all humans contain.

Finally, there are wild mammals (i.e., not farmed) and birds. Wild mammals account for 0.012 GT, and birds account for 0.003 GT.

If we add all of this of these things up, we get 3.8 GT of carbon. A big number? Not really. (And remember that humans make up only 2.5% of this.)

Why isn't it big? If we look at trees, plants, and grass, these have over 500 GT of carbon. And I haven't included the seaweed. Animal life is more than 100X smaller than this. It's the plants that matter.

True, we haven't considered single-cell microorganisms. And there are roughly 100 GT of carbon in these. There are about 75 GT of carbon in *bacteria*, and about 12 GT of carbon in *fungi*. Fungi includes mushrooms, molds, mildews, yeasts, and other things. There are about 8 GT of carbon in *archaea*, which is a group of microorganisms, and about 4 GT in *protists*. Protists include single-celled protozoans, algae, and slime-molds.

So we have about 500 GT of carbon in plants, 100 GT of carbon in microorganisms, and less than 4 GT of carbon in all living creatures. People account of 0.1 GT. That's small. It's *very* small.

Why do we care about carbon? Among other things, because we use it for fuel. Petroleum is about 87% carbon, and the world uses about 44 billion barrels a year. Current estimates are that there are 1.2 trillion barrels left to be mined, not counting oil sands (tar and things that are hard to process). These would yield another 2.5 trillion barrels.

Note that we don't actually use the carbon up. That is, the carbon itself remains after we've burned the fuel. But as the fuel is burned for energy, most of the carbon is emitted in the form of carbon dioxide, denoted CO_2.

At our current rate of using oil, we have about 27 years of oil left, excluding the oil sands. If we could use the oil sands, we'd have about 80 years left.

And what about the carbon-dioxide that we produce when we burn the oil? Carbon dioxide is the primary carbon source for the plants and trees, which as we've just seen, make up most of the life on earth. Plants, algae, and cyanobacteria use light to photosynthesize their life source using carbon dioxide and water. For plants, the waste product of photosynthesis is oxygen.

How much carbon dioxide is in the atmosphere? Not much. The earth's atmosphere contains 78% nitrogen, 21% oxygen, about 0.9% argon, and only about 0.04% carbon dioxide. There's also some hydrogen, which combines with the oxygen to make water. Air contains a variable amount of humidity. On average, the amount of water in the air is 1% at sea level, but it's variance is very large. It can go up to 4%.

This might all seem like a digression. But later, we'll see how carbon plays a crucial role in the solution to the events that follow.

One of the good things that water in the air does is that it insulates the earth thermally. While humidity makes us uncomfortable, it helps the earth hold its heat after the sun goes down. In fact, the main problem with climate in the deserts is that there's very little water in the air, so after the sun goes down, it can get very cold. Deserts are very hot during the day – especially if they're near the equator, and they can get very cold at night. The Sahara drops to about 25 degrees Fahrenheit – well below freezing – at night.

Carbon footprints? Life isn't that simple. If carbon was all diamonds, then diamonds would be cheap, and we'd all be dead.

I shut my computer down, turned the lights off, and went downstairs to get another cup of coffee. Current estimates are that a cup of coffee has a carbon footprint of about 60 grams. Whatever that means.

I wondered how Carol was making out at Ethan Allan. And how I could use carbon to deal with the new bat-virus.

5. A Call from Washington

I was sitting at our kitchen island drinking my coffee when the phone rang.

Not my cellphone, but our house-phone. Usually, I never answer our house-phone, since all of the calls that come to that are for Carol. And she was out furniture shopping.

But I looked at the phone, and it said "Number not Available," so I answered it. Sometimes I get a call from a government agency who wants me to do some work, and they hide their originating number. As long as it wasn't the IRS, I was OK with that.

"Hello?" I asked.

"Hello," a woman's voice said. "I'm trying to reach Dr. Maux."

"Who is this?" I asked.

"My name is Annie," she said.

"Hi Annie," I said. "I'm married."

There was a pause. I guessed that I'd confused her.

"Is this Dr. Maux?" she asked again.

"Who is this?" I asked.

"Annie," she said, again.

I thought for a minute.

"I give up," I said. "Annie reason for calling?"

"What?" she asked.

"Were you telling a 'knock-knock' joke?" I asked.

"No," she said.

"Then why is your name Annie?" I asked.

"What?" she asked. "My name is Annie."

"Annie reason that you called?" I asked again.

"I'm trying to reach Dr. Maux," she said.

"This is he," I said. "And who is this?"

"Annie," she said.

"Are you going start that again?" I asked.

"Start what?" she asked.

"Knock-knock jokes," I said. "I hate those."

"So do I," she said. "Is this Dr. Maux?"

"It still is," I said. "Who's this?"

"Annie," she said.

"Are you going to start that again?" I asked.

"I'm just trying to contact Dr. Maux," she said.

"Speaking," I answered. "Who's this?" I asked.

"I'm with the NIH," she said. "In Washington."

"NIH?" I asked. "What's that?" I asked. "The 'Not Invented Here'?"

"No," she said. "It's the National Institute of Health."

"Yes," I said. "I remember now. As long as you're not with the IRS."

"I calling on behalf of Dr. Grouchi," she said.

"Dr. Grouchi?" I asked. "Who's that?"

"The President has tasked him with leading the investigation into the new bat virus," she said.

"Is it anything like 'the old bat virus'?" I asked.

"What's the 'old bat virus'?" she asked.

"I don't know," I said. "You called this one 'the new bat virus.' So I assumed that there was an 'old bat virus.'"

"Not that I'm aware of," Annie said.

"I thought that this virus was harmless," I said. "Dr. Grouchi said so on TV."

"He hopes that it is," she said. "But whenever he makes a statement to the press, he has to be careful about what the statement actually says."

"You sound like you're from Washington," I said. "When you make a statement, you need to be careful about what the statement says?"

"Dr. Grouchi was tasked with determining whether this virus really *is* harmless," she explained.

"I see," I said. "You mean that we're not sure?"

"No," she said. "It's a new virus."

"I see," I said. "And why did you call me?"

"You're a well-known scientist, and have worked with the government's top computers," she said. "Dr. Grouchi thought that you'd be able to help with this effort."

"I see," I said. I explained my rates.

"That will be fine," she said. "Dr. Grouchi will be having a conference call soon. We'll be in touch."

"One more thing," I said. "Don't call me at this number. This phone is for top-secret calls to Carol. I don't have the authority to listen to those."

"Who's Carol?" she asked.

"My wife," I said. "Carol."

"Oh, I see," she said, clearly not seeing.

"Text me on my cell when a meeting is scheduled," I said, and I gave her my number.

I took my coffee back upstairs to the lab, got on my computer, infiltrated the government's network, and connected to the NIH site. I wanted to know what Dr. Grouchi knew that the rest of us didn't yet know.

I learned that Dr. Grouchi knew a lot that he wasn't telling us.

Wuhan is the capital of Hubei Province in China. It's the largest city in Hubei. With a population of over eleven million people, it's the most populous city in Central China. While Wuhan has been a manufacturing hub for many decades, today it's an important city that's focused on modern industrial innovation in China. It contains three national development zones, four scientific and technological development parks, over 350 research institutes, 1,656 high tech enterprises, numerous enterprise incubators and investments from 230 Fortune Global 500 firms, and several of China's top universities. Wuhan produced GDP of 224 billion dollars in 2018.

Although it was not being reported by the US news, China was afraid of the virus. While telling the outside world that there was no evidence that the virus was deadly, China had shut down travel between Wuhan and other parts of China, although they hadn't shut it down between Wuhan and other parts of the world.

The President had been right to close down travel from China.

It was thought that the virus had already spread to parts of Europe, and this was causing problems there. Mainly, it was disrupting many businesses.

RBG was thought to be more that an insignificant virus, and we needed to take some precautions against spreading it.

So far, Washington insiders didn't yet know how it was spread. But government insiders were saying that we needed to be "hygienically aware."

Apparently, this simply meant that we should wash our hands frequently, don't have physical contact with strangers, don't drink from the same vessels, and other obvious things.

But they didn't yet know how to stop the virus.

The word was that the president was on the verge of shutting down more travel, and there was some concern about what it would do to the economy if lots of people became sick. The supposition was that this would be like people getting the flu. It happens every year. While it isn't good, it isn't disastrous either.

Interesting. "The News" wasn't talking about this yet. They were still reporting on it like it was known to be harmless. Who knew what the actual truth was?

I finished my coffee, and shut my computer down.

6. Another Call from Washington

I was sitting in the living room reading when Carol got home. She was in a very good mood. I assumed that she'd bought something. Furniture?

Carol got a soft-drink from the fridge, and came into the living room to join me. I put my book down.

"You look like you're in a good mood," I said. "Did you find something?" I asked.

"Yes," she said. "I found a lovely couch that I think could replace the one that you're sitting on. That couch is getting old."

"You're right," I said. "We've had it for quite a while."

"And I found a fainting-divan that matches it perfectly," she said.

"Where would you put it?" I asked.

"We can put it in the corner of the room," she said. "We can use it for holding cushions. I think that it would set the couch off nicely."

"I can picture that," I said. "But it never would have occurred to me. What color is it?"

"Well, we'd need to paint the room first," she said.

I didn't want to ask any more questions. Each one was getting me in deeper.

The phone rang. Carol picked it up and said "Hello?"

After a few seconds, she looked confused.

"Let me put it on 'speaker,'" she said.

There was a moderately high-pitched wheezing voice on the other end.

"Mickey Mouse?" the voice asked.

"This is Mick," I said. "Who's this?"

"Your voice sounded higher when you said 'Hello' before," the wheezing voice said. "Did you put it on speaker or something?"

"Are you a detective?" I asked.

"Mickey Mouse?" the voice asked again.

"This is Mick," I said. "Who's this?"

"This is Dr. Grouchi," the voice said, wheezing.

"This is Dr. Maux," I said. I usually didn't like to use formal titles, but he started it. "Who did you say this was?"

"Dr. Grouchi," the voice wheezed, bovaristically.

"I think you have the wrong number," I said.

"Is this Mickey Mouse?" he wheezed.

"This is Dr. Maux," I replied. "Why are you calling?"

"I'm calling about the bat virus," he said.

"I already gave at the office," I responded.

"What?" he asked.

"I gave at the office," I said.

"I'm not calling about money," he said. "I'm with the NIH. You were recommended as a person that could help us with RBG."

"You mean the bat virus?" I asked.

"Yes," he said. "You were highly recommended. I guess that's because a bat is a lot like a mouse."

"What?" I asked, not understanding.

"It's a bat virus, and your name is 'Mouse,'" he said. "And a bat is a lot like a mouse. Except that it has wings."

"I'm not a mouse," I said. "My name is 'M-A-U-X.' It's actually pronounced 'moose,'" I lied. "A moose is more like a deer. Maybe you should call me when you have a deer virus."

After a confused pause, he replied. "Well that's OK. Mickey Moose. You can still help."

"How can I help?" I asked.

"Can you come to Washington?" he wheezed. "It would be better if we could work together down here."

"Of course," I said. "And it isn't merely I that would come. I'm part of a team."

"A team?" he asked.

"Yes," I said. "Carol is my better half. She sees obvious things that I don't see. And sometimes I say things that I shouldn't, and she hushes me up. I need her. We work as a team."

"OK," he said. "I have to warn you that we will have to research both of you so that we can issue you security clearances."

"That's fine," I said. "I'm also going to run one on you. Do you have any parking tickets that I should know about?"

Carol tried to hush me.

"Parking tickets?" he asked.

"Would you like some?" I asked in return.

"So you'll come to Washington?" he asked, sounding confused.

"Of course," I said. "Carol and I. We'll be there."

"Well, nice talking to you, Dr. Moose," he wheezed.

"You too Dr. Bat," I said, and hung up.

7. Carol and I go to Washington

In the morning, Carol and I each packed a suitcase, drove down to Stamford, and parked in long-term parking at the train station. We took the express Amtrak Acela, which makes it to Washington in just under four hours. It would be much quicker than that, except it makes a stop in Penn Station. It's a comfortable ride with big reclining seats.

We'd booked the Intercontinental at the Wharf on Sutton Square. It's a waterfront hotel on the Washington Channel which is in a tidal basin off the Potomac River. People dock their boats in the Washington Channel, but there's an easy view of the Pentagon and Arlington Cemetery across the way. Carol and I got a suite with a waterfront view and a small balcony. To the Northwest, we could see the Jefferson and Washington Monuments.

The Wharf has recently been built up. It's full of new restaurants, shops, and condos, and it's relaxing just to sit and watch the people walk by. At the North end of the Wharf is a huge fresh-seafood marketplace where many of the Washington restaurants buy their fish.

We took a stroll, and stopped for coffee at a Cuban coffee house. Cuban coffee is like espresso, but with a few distinctions. First, it's traditionally brewed in a moka-pot instead of by an espresso machine, although that's starting to change. And it always is done with a dark-roasted bean. The moka-pot produces the shot with less pressure, and more temperature. This makes the espresso bitter. And second, the first part of the espresso shot is beaten with lots of sugar to make a very thick, creamy foam (called "espuma") which is poured over the espresso. The espuma is necessary to cut the bitterness of the brew.

Leaving the coffee house, I felt slightly buzzed from the caffeine and all that sugar. While I don't use sugar in coffee, Cuban coffee is different.

The walkway along the Wharf is cobblestone, and it's wider than a two-lane road. It's closed to vehicular traffic. And it's full of people, all meandering. Some were strolling, and others were flouncing-about in groups. So I tried to sashay. While that's hard to do on cobblestone, it's neither strolling nor flouncing.

We went down to the seafood market on the North end, and got a dozen oysters on the half-shell, which they shelled to order. Carol and I found a nice place to sit, overlooking the channel, and ate the oysters. Then I called the NIH.

I'm not sure who answered, but after some back-and-forth, I got someone on the line who was connected to Dr. Grouchi's department. I said: "Tell Dr. Grouchi that 'The Moose' is in town, and that he should give me a call." I left it at that.

Carol and I spent the rest of the afternoon enjoying ourselves on the Wharf, and had an early dinner at Del Mar.

First, we ordered some of their specialty cocktails. I chose something called an *oscuro deseo*, which contained rum, mescal, tempus fugit crème de banane, orgeat, and lemon. Carol chose a cocktail called *mas fuerte*, which contained tequila, manzanilla sherry, green chartreuse, lemon, and pineapple. We tried each other's drinks, and both were delicious. Mine was strong, smoky, and tasted of bananas. Carol's was also strong, but it was sweet and fruity.

We ordered a swordfish carpaccio to share with our cocktails, and chose three tapas to share for our dinner.

I relaxed with my drink, sat back into my comfortable chair, and watched all the people walk by on the cobblestone walkway. It was cooling down.

"This is a very nice place," Carol said.

"You mean Del Mar?" I asked.

"We'll have to taste the food first," Carol said. "I meant the Wharf in general."

"It's new and lively," I said. "And it's hard to believe that it's only about half-a-mile to the National Mall. It's an easy walk. I thought that Dr. Grouchi might want to meet with us at the Capitol."

"But the Mall itself is over two miles long," Carol said. "The Capitol is much farther than a half a mile."

"We'll take an Uber," I said. "While we could walk it on a nice day, it's getting hot."

My phone rang, and I answered it.

"Mickey?" the voice wheezed. "Is this Mickey Moose?"

It was Dr. Grouchi, so I put it on speaker.

"It's pronounced 'mouse,'" I said.

"I thought it was 'moose,'" the voice said.

"No," I said. "It's pronounced like 'mouse.' Who is this?" I asked.

"This is Dr. Grouchi," he said. "Remember? We spoke yesterday."

"Of course," I said. "This is Mick, and I'm here with Carol. We came down today."

"I thought you'd like to know that your background checks came back clean," he said.

"Yes," I said. "I know that."

"What?" he asked. "How did you know that?"

"Because I looked at the government's computer system," I said. "And there's nothing on me or Carol. You, on the other hand…"

"You looked at the government's computer system?" he asked. "How did you do that? It's totally secure."

"I have friends over at the New York Times," I explained.

He paused, clearly confused. "Can we meet tomorrow morning?" he asked.

"Sure," I said. "We're staying on the Wharf, so we're close. What time should we come?"

"How's 10:00?" he asked. "Does that work for you?"

"Sure," I said. "We'll be there. How do we come in?"

"Go to the Russell Senate Office Building," he said. "It's across the street from the Capitol, on the North side of the Mall."

"OK, we'll see you then," I said.

"Goodnight Mr. Mouse," he said.

"It's 'Dr.,' not 'Mr.," I said. "And my last name is pronounced 'moose.'"

"Oh, sorry," he said. "Goodnight Dr. Moose."

"Goodnight," I said. "See you tomorrow."

The waiter brought our tapas. These were some crab-stuffed piquillo peppers with a sea-urchin sauce, two charred romaine hearts dressed with a rhubarb hibiscus compote with strawberries and Monte Enebro cheese, asparagus, and marcona almonds, and a Wagyu beef tartare with black truffle dressing and quail eggs.

Carol and I sat, had dinner, watched the boats come in and out, and all of the ambulators perambulating. I didn't sashay on the way back to the Intercontinental.

8. We Meet with Dr. Grouchi

In the morning, I woke up before Carol, so I took a run along the Wharf. I came back to find Carol dressed and reading her latest book. She looked lovely.

I took a shower and got dressed, and we went out for a simple breakfast on the Wharf. Then we called an Uber, and took it to the Russell Senate Office Building. The Uber went up to Independence Avenue, and then across to First Street. He took us North on First Street to the Russell building - passing the Capital - where groups of tourists were climbing the stairs to see the sights.

We checked in at the Russel entrance, and told the guards that we were there to see Dr. Grouchi.

Dr. Grouchi came out a few minutes later, and we all shook hands. I thought that he really did look like a vampire. A little vampire, but a vampire. His beady eyes glistened.

"Good morning Dr. Moose," he said, "and Carol."

"Good morning Dr. Grouchi," we both said.

"And by the way, my name is pronounced 'mouse,' not 'moose,'" I said.

"Oh, sorry," he said. "Are you staying in a comfortable hotel?" he asked.

"Yes," Carol said. "We're at the Intercontinental, and have a nice room with a balcony overlooking the Wharf."

"That's very nice," he said. "I hope it's comfortable."

"It is," Carol said.

"What floor are you on?" He asked.

I thought this to be an odd question. "Two and a half," I replied.

He looked puzzled.

"I have a conference room booked, and I've asked some people to join us. We'll go there, and we can fill you in on what we know. And of course, you understand that what we'll talk about is all confidential. You'll not share any of it with people outside of that room."

"Of course," I said. "We understand."

Carol and I walked to an elevator with Dr. Grouchi, and took it down to the basement. We went into a conference room, and he closed the door. There was a conference table inside with people seated around it. They all looked at us.

Dr. Grouchi introduced us. Most were people from the NIH that I didn't know or recognize. But there were two people there that we both recognized immediately: Senators Chuck Schlomo, and Elizabeth Warden.

"Drs. Carol and Mickey Mouse are experts who can trace the emergence of this virus for us, and who can generate statistics for us on its spread throughout the world," Grouchi said.

"My name is actually pronounced 'moose,'" I said.

There was an uncomfortable pause.

"But how will we know that they will generate the *right* statistics?" Senator **Schlomo** asked.

I looked at Schlomo, and I asked him: "When you see a 'V' formation of flying geese, why is the formation longer on one side than on the other?"

Schlomo looked puzzled. "I don't know," he finally said.

"It's because there are more geese on that side," I said. "You've got to know statistics."

Schlomo still looked puzzled.

"But hypothetically," Senator Warden asked, "what if the numbers that you generate aren't right? Then what?"

"Hypothetically, can you imagine a world with no hypothetical situations?" I asked her.

She looked puzzled too.

We all settled in, and Carol and I took seats. A man started projecting data and graphs on the screen at the front of the room.

"While this virus started in Wuhan, we know that it has spread to Italy," he said.

I raised my hand, and he asked whether I had a question.

"Since you've mentioned Italy, I was wondering whether in Rome, the nurses give sick people 'IV's. Or do they call them '4's?"

He wasn't sure what I was asking, so he simply said, "they haven't needed to use IVs yet."

"What have they needed to do when people get sick?" I asked.

"So far, there are no symptoms," the man said.

"Then how do you know that the disease is spreading?" I asked.

"Because we've measured it in people," he said. "We can test for the virus, and it's there."

"So there are no symptoms, but it's spreading?" Carol asked.

"Yes," the man said.

"If there are no symptoms, then why do you need to cure it?" Carol asked.

"There are no symptoms *so far*," the man explained. "But the Chinese are very clever. We think that symptoms may manifest soon."

"What kind of symptoms?" I asked.

"We don't know yet," the man explained.

"How do you tell the difference between infected people and uninfected people? Do you know that I once asked a mime and a pantomime what the difference between them was, and neither one would say? I was wondering whether this is the same thing."

"I'm not sure that I understand," he said.

"This sounds like it's a disease with no symptoms, and no one's sick, but the government is making a big deal out of it," I said.

"Exactly," Senator Schlomo said. "We need to protect the people. No matter what the cost."

"I see," I said, not seeing.

The speaker continued on, explaining that the Chinese government was saying that the virus came from the wet markets, and that it was carried by bats. But some people thought that the virus was made in the labs, and it got out. What was embarrassing about this was that Dr. Grouchi's organization was funding some of the research there.

"I see," I said, this time seeing, and understanding very well, so I asked a pointed question. The question itself wasn't pointed, but I raised it to make a point. "Why did Franz Kafka cross the road?" I asked.

"Who's he?" Senator Warden asked.

"And why did he cross the road?" Senator Schlomo asked.

"It seems that on the morning of his thirtieth birthday, Franz Kafka was unexpectedly arrested by two unidentified agents from an unspecified agency for an unspecified crime. While not imprisoned, and left 'free' for the time being, the agents told him to await instructions from the Committee of Affairs, which would be forthcoming shortly. A few days later, the Committee of Affairs sent him notice to appear at a certain address that coming Sunday for a trial in which he was to defend himself. No crime had yet been alleged. The address that he was given was across the road, which is why he needed to cross it, although he had a very hard time finding the address, since the buildings weren't marked. His summons didn't reveal either the time or the room for his hearing, but after crossing the road, and spending quite a bit of effort searching for the court, he found it upstairs in the attic of a certain building. Upon entry into the court, he was severely reproached for his tardiness. Then he aroused the assembly's hostility by giving a passionate plea about the absurdity of the trial and the emptiness of the accusation."

"I'm not sure that I understand," Dr. Grouchi said. "So why did he cross the road?"

"Exactly," I said. "You've understood perfectly." I thought that I'd made my point, although they both looked confused. Apparently, they didn't know who Franz Kafka was.

The rest of the meeting carried on like this, and neither Carol or I got much out of it. But afterwards, Dr. Grouchi gave me some homework to do. He wanted to know about certain people and their possible symptoms. Some of those people had been sitting in the room.

9. The Sturgeon Moon (August 3), A Disturbing Dream

That night, Carol and I took a leisurely walk along the Wharf after dinner, and we went to bed early. It had cooled down, so we left our balcony door open. I was tired. There was a full moon out. Maybe that's why.

I learned later that this full moon was called a "sturgeon moon." At the time, I had no particular interest in the different kinds of full moons, but took an interest in full moons probably because of what I think happened that evening. Before that night, a full moon was a full moon as far as I was concerned.

But this night in Washington, it was August 3, 2020. A full moon in August is called a sturgeon moon because huge numbers of sturgeon could once be caught in the lakes of North America in August when America was more of a wilderness, although summer fishing is still plentiful today.

Before electricity, people paid much more attention to the moon and its effects on the wildlife and the crops.

While I slept soundly that night, I had a lucid dream that was very strange.

A lucid dream is one that you have when you're aware that you're dreaming. You're aware that the events flashing through your mind aren't really happening, although they feel vivid and real. I'd been training myself to have lucid dreams, so I wasn't that surprised that I was having one, although the dream itself was very disturbing.

In the dream, I had just finished a lovely dinner on the Wharf with Carol, and we went back to the hotel, and went to bed. I felt tired because it had been a long day, and I knew that I was going to sleep very well. Before going to bed, I stepped out on the balcony to look at the beautiful full moon drifting across the sky. I gave Carol a kiss, she kissed me back, and we both went to sleep.

I was drifting in space in my sleep – floating horizontally above the bed. And the drapes on either side of our open balcony door were fluttering. The door was open, and the breeze was blowing through. It felt cool and refreshing. It was a beautiful night, and I admired the moon, which seemed to have grown bigger. It was lighting up our room.

Bach's Prelude and Fugue in E-flat Minor was playing in the background. The fugue isn't at all gloomy, but it's very slow. Its minor tone made me pensive. I was thinking about the virus that hadn't really manifested, but that Washington knew was real. It was hard for me to wrap my mind around it, but it was just a dream, so I didn't fight it. I just went with the flow.

People had the virus, but they didn't actually seem sick. People might have thought that they were sick, but they were just living in E-flat minor. They felt like I did: living in E-flat minor.

My body – which was floating, rotated forwards in the air. I wound up sitting on the ottoman at the foot of the bed. The drapes were blowing inwards, harder than they'd been blowing before. All at once, Dr. Grouchi appeared on our balcony. He seemed to materialize, and then he was just standing there. He was wearing a long black cape.

All I could do was to stare at Dr. Grouchi. He fixed my gaze with his beady little eyes, and drifted forwards into our room. He wasn't walking. It was more like he was floating in the air; gliding. Once he was in front of me, he floated and held my stare, beadily.

"There doesn't seem to be a virus," I remember saying to him, although I was starting to feel dizzy. "I don't think that the virus is real."

"There *is* a virus," he said. "You'll all see. The virus is *real.*"

He smiled, and I saw two small fangs, one on each side of his mouth. They were where his maxillary canines[2] should have been. You don't tend to notice people's canines, since they're not prominent in humans. This wasn't true of Dr. Grouchi - as I was seeing him in my dream. His canines were long and thin. You couldn't *not* notice them.

He put his hands on my shoulders, and effortlessly lifted me off of the ottoman into a standing position. Rather, he didn't actually lift me; it was more the case that I floated upwards, with his hands guiding me. Once I was upright – floating in the air with Dr. Grouchi, he wrapped his arms around me, and leaned his head into the crook of my neck. I didn't feel anything. He was weightless, and so was I. We floated. Grouchi was

---

[2] The maxillary teeth are those on the top. The canines have a single pointed cusp and a single root. They are on either side of the incisors.

sanguivorous. I was ataraxic. And while I couldn't feel it, I knew that he was feeding on my blood.

I disappeared into a void. While I couldn't feel any motion, I could see a rainbow of colors rocketing past me as if I was moving through space at the speed of light. This was quite a sensation with Bach's fugue playing in the background. The rainbow of colors never seemed to end. It was making me dizzy as I spun around rocketing through space in E-flat minor. It was a phantasmagoria the likes of which I'd never imagined.

When I came through the void, he was still there, holding onto me, and I was still weightless. He lifted his head from my neck and let me go. He drifted backwards, back onto the balcony.

"There *is* a virus," he repeated. "There *is* a virus."

His beady eyes got beadier, and he held my gaze. I could see his fangs retracting. I still felt dizzy.

I floated upwards, and rotated back into a horizontal position. Then I floated backwards, and down. I was lying in bed again. Dr. Grouchi drifted there in space, still holding my gaze. Then he lifted his arms. Each of his hands held its corresponding side of his long cape, so his cape billowed outwards, like giant wings.

Then Dr. Grouchi flew upwards into the sky. I could see his silhouette as he passed in front of the full moon, which now filled the sky. The last I remember of my dream is his silhouette. It looked like that of a giant bat. I instantly fell into a very deep sleep as the fugue ended.

Then darkness.

Carol woke me up the next morning. I had slept late, and we had to catch the Acela back to Connecticut. I felt well-rested, although tired.

We went down to the Wharf and got some strong coffee. I drank it, but I still felt tired. I had slept very well. I had been in a very deep sleep, so I would have expected to be wide awake and refreshed. But I didn't feel that way. Maybe I was catching something. I hoped not.

Carol and I packed, and we took an Uber to the train station. Because I was dragging myself through the morning, we caught the Acela with only a few minutes to spare.

I put our luggage up into the overhead rack. It seemed heavy. I sat, and leaned my seat back. By the time we left the station, I was fast asleep once more.

I got a couple of hours more sleep while Carol read her book. When I woke up, we were in New Jersey. I felt much better: a strange feeling for anyone who wakes up in New Jersey. I wondered whether I was OK. I mean, New Jersey. Seriously?

10. The Corn Moon (September 2), The Weeks Pass

The morning after we got home, I threw the clothes that I'd worn in Washington into the washer. I always go through my clothes while I'm putting them in the washer. I check the pockets to make sure that I've not left anything in them, and I look for spots that I might want to put stain-remover on.

I noticed a spot of black truffle dressing on the shirt that I'd worn to Del Mar. Luckily, I hadn't worn that shirt the next day when Carol and I went to meet Dr. Grouchi. A guard might have noticed it, and thought that the truffle sauce made me look "suspicious." After all, who eats truffles?

I sprayed some spot remover on the stain as I put it into the washer. I also noticed a small blood spot near the shoulder of the shirt that I'd worn on the train for the ride home. I thought that was curious. I hadn't cut myself. I hadn't even shaved that morning. I wondered where it had come from. I sprayed spot remover on that too. I was sure that both stains would wash out.

Over the next few days, I did my computer homework for Dr. Grouchi by tapping into the government's secure database, and I learned some interesting things about the people he had asked me about. I learned some interesting things about a few other people too. That included Dr. Grouchi.

Carol contacted Dr. Grouchi's office, and asked them to set up two meetings for us. We wanted to meet with Mayor deBozo in New York City, and with Governor Blowmo in Albany, to get their perspectives as to what damage the virus was causing in New York, if any.

She knew that Mayor deBozo and Governor Blowmo wouldn't meet with us if we called them directly. They had no idea who we were. But a call from Dr. Grouchi's office would ensure that the meetings would happen. New York was having problems, and both men were busy.

The president had sent a large Naval hospital ship named "Mercy" to New York City. It was docked at Pier 90. It was capable of holding over a thousand patients, should New York City need the space. The president had also sent in the military to set up the Javits Convention Center as an emergency hospital that would be capable of holding about twenty-five hundred more patients.

So far, Mayor deBozo and Governor Blowmo hadn't needed this added capacity. No one was sick. They didn't see the symptoms, so they sent (possibly) sick people back to live wherever they had lived. The disease was thought to possibly be dangerous for older people, but Governor Blowmo didn't think that this was true. He sent older people back to live in the senior facilities from which they'd come.

He explained all of this in a book that he wrote about his Herculean efforts regarding the disease. While he didn't actually write the book, nor did he make any Herculean efforts, he did give nightly press conferences. It's all in there. And he did insist that people wear masks. It's funny that this was the hypothetical example that I'd given to Detective Danny as to what a dictator might do.

While masks had been suggested by many when this virus was first known, Dr. Grouchi had said that they were unnecessary, and that they provided no protection. In March, Dr. Grouchi advocated against masks. But now he was insisting that people wear them. Again, I thought of Detective Danny, and my hypothetical example: wearing masks.

Why the change? And why masks now? Dr. Grouchi now believed that if people have the disease, they can infect others by breathing. Dr. Grouchi had determined that to prevent this, it was essential for people to wear masks. Or to not breathe.

Mayor deBozo decided that it was essential to shut down most businesses in New York City, so he did. Most restaurants were closed, Broadway plays and musicals were closed, Lincoln Center was closed, museums were closed, all sporting events were closed, and nearly anything a resident or a tourist might be interested in doing was closed. This caused most of the hotels to close too. This caused most small businesses to close and to go out of business. And the schools were closed. But this had no effect on the economy. Or so he said.

And Mayor deBozo kept the city safe! People were forced to wear masks, and to not congregate.

The exception was that people that wanted to express their feelings by congregating, looting stores, setting fires, and shooting at other people were allowed to do so, and didn't need to wear masks. He told the police to allow these people to express their feelings. It can be dangerous to not express your feelings.

Feelings are important, and riots are actually a good thing – especially when they're violent. By allowing riots, tourists who didn't know that everything was closed would be sure to stay away. It kept everyone safe.

And most of the police who were able to retire did so. This took them off the streets, and made the city even safer, since they were no longer there to spread the disease. Besides, they might have interfered with the riots, which would have facilitated the congregation of law-abiding citizens. This would have been dangerous.

I personally noticed that I had changed somewhat since coming back from Washington.

In addition to my new interest in full moons, I liked my steaks rarer than usual, and had a hankering for a certain cold-cut that I hadn't eaten in a long time: *zungenwurst* (also called "blood and tongue"). This is basically a head cheese made with pig's blood, suet, and oatmeal, with chunks of pickled beef-tongue added. While the tongue itself has a neutral flavor, it was the taste of the blood that I found compelling. I wasn't sure why.

We had another full moon on September 2. This is known as the "corn moon," and was so-named by native-Americans as marking the beginning of the corn-harvesting season. It's sometimes called a "barley moon" for similar reasons. And I had another lucid dream on the night of September 2 which involved another visit from Dr. Grouchi. This time his fangs were longer.

It started with the music of Beethoven's Moonlight Sonata. It's in C-sharp minor. Again, it's music that causes deep introspection.

I was sleeping on my back, and levitated horizontally out of our bed. I rotated forwards in the air, and then was standing – floating really – at the foot of our bed. Dr. Grouchi was floating in front of me, and the full moon was gleaming through our windows, lighting up our bedroom.

His beady eyes were focused intensely on mine, and I felt helpless. Like before, Dr. Grouchi was wearing a long cape. But what was new was that he had a mask on. It was a light-blue hospital mask. It didn't go with his black cape.

"Why are you wearing a mask?" I asked him.

"Masks are required," he told me.

"But that's a blue hospital mask. It doesn't go with your cape." I said what I thought.

He looked as if he was thinking about this, and it disturbed him. Then he lifted his mask, and I saw his fangs. They were longer than the fangs that he'd had a month ago.

"Is that why you're wearing it?" I asked. "Because it hides your fangs?"

"They've grown," he said. "I don't know why. You might not need one, but I do. What would you do if you had fangs?" he asked.

I didn't know. I thought about it, and then realized that it was just a dream.

"I'd get a mask that matched my cape," I said.

He wrapped his arms around me, and again, I disappeared into a void, with the feeling of weightlessness and acceleration, with the Moonlight Sonata playing in the background, as I rocketed through rainbows of colors. It was another phantasmagoria.

I wound up back in bed with Grouchi's silhouette flying across the moon as the sonata ended. And I fell into a deep sleep. Again, it was ataractic.

The next day I was tired for most of the day. Dream visits from Dr. Grouchi seemed to do this to me. So I scheduled a doctor's appointment for the following week just to make sure that I was OK. I was overdue for a physical.

Everything came back OK, except for the blood test. That showed that I was slightly anemic. So I started taking an iron supplement, and vitamin B12.

11. A Visit to Albany

One morning after returning from my run and making a cup of coffee, my phone rang. It was Governor Blowmo's office. I went into the living room where Carol was sitting with her coffee, reading a book, and I put my phone on speaker.

"Yes?" I said to the phone. "Did you say that this is the governor's office?"

"Yes," said the voice on the line. "Dr. Grouchi has asked Governor Blowmo to meet with you, Dr. Maux."

Carol stopped reading, put a marker in her book, and closed it. She looked at the phone and listened.

"There are two of us," I said. "I have the phone on speaker. She's here with me."

"Governor Blowmo would like to meet with both of you, Dr. and Dr. Maux," she said.

"How is his schedule tomorrow or the next day?" I asked.

"He has time tomorrow," she said. "When can you come?"

"Albany is about two hours from here," I said. "We could probably leave at 9:00, and be there a little after 11:00. Does that work?" I asked.

"He has a meeting at 11:00. Why don't you come for lunch?" she asked. "I'm sure that the Governor would like some company for lunch."

"That sounds like a good idea," I said. "What time?"

"Try to arrive at around noon," she said. "Do you like Italian?" she asked.

"Italian what?" I asked.

"Italian food," she said. "The Governor always eats Italian food."

"You mean a simple antipasto, some risotto, and something grilled? Something like that?" I asked.

"What's risotto?" she asked. "I meant something like spaghetti and meatballs."

"I see," I said. "You meant Italian-American food. Yes, that's fine. Should we bring anything with us?"

"What do you mean?" she asked. "Like what?"

"Cannoli?" I asked. "Does the Governor like cannoli?"

"Yes," she said. "But we're all set. Just bring yourselves."

"OK," I said. "No cannoli. We'll see you tomorrow."

I hung up.

"Imagine how that would have changed the entire movie," I said to Carol.

"What movie?" she asked.

"*The Godfather*," I said. "What if Peter Clemenza had said: *'Take the gun. Leave the cannoli.'?*"

"I don't understand," Carol said. "So what if he'd said that?"

"That would have reversed the entire meaning of the movie. It would have meant to bring the violence forward, and to leave the sweet things in the past."

"You thought that it meant that?" Carol asked. "I thought he was just reminding Rocco not to forget the cannoli."

"Maybe," I said. "But I like it better with all the meaning. Since the woman on the phone said that we shouldn't bring cannoli, do you thing she was really using code-speak to tell us to bring a gun?"

"Probably not," Carol said. "I don't think that we should bring either."

Wow," I said. "Governor Blowmo seems to be a real kill-joy, and I haven't even met him yet."

"A kill-joy?" Carol asked. "How's that?"

"What if instead, Clemenza had said: *'Leave the gun. **And** leave the cannoli.'*? Imagine if that had been the line in *'The Godfather'*," I said. "They could have ended the movie right there."

"I don't think that Governor Blowmo meant anything," Carol said. "He probably doesn't even know who we are or that we're coming tomorrow."

"I'm sure you're right," I said. "Maybe I should bring a gun just in case."

"Don't," Carol said.

In the morning, I took my run and thought about the cannoli: *"Take a run. And have a cannoli."*

He should have said: *"Take the gun. And take the cannoli."* It would have been the best of both worlds. They could have ended the movie there too. Or they could have continued it, like they did. It would have been like telling all of us in the theater: *The movie ends here. Or maybe it doesn't.* Maybe that's why Francis Ford Coppola was the director, and I wasn't.

We'd be going to see Governor Blowmo without cannoli and without a gun. I wondered what he was like in person. I'd only ever seen him on TV.

I went upstairs, took a shower, dressed, came back down, and poured myself a cup of coffee. The TV was on in the family room, so I went in to join Carol. And speak of the devil: Governor Blowmo was on TV. He was telling everyone that they needed to wear masks. We'd be visiting him in a few hours. I wondered whether he'd be wearing a mask.

"Are you looking forward to meeting the governor?" I asked Carol.

"We'll see what he knows," Carol said. "It never hurts to learn more."

"I'm going to have a very light breakfast," I said. "We'll be having spaghetti and meatballs for lunch."

"I've already had a light breakfast," Carol said. "Dr. Grouchi was on before. He also said that we should all wear masks."

I thought of him in my dream. He'd been wearing a mask.

"Do you know where the Executive Mansion is in Albany?" I asked.

"I looked it up," Carol said. "It's on Eagle Street."

"Where's Eagle Street?" I asked.

"It's about a mile off the Thruway," she said. "It's right past the Catholic High School."

"What time do you think we should leave?" I asked.

"Probably at about 9:30," she said. "Maybe a little later."

"Sounds good," I said.

I sat there drinking my coffee, and listening to the rest of the news. It was supposed to be a nice day. I was looking forward to the drive upstate.

Carol and I left at about 9:45. I took another cup of coffee with me to drink on the way up. We drove over to the Thruway, and headed toward Albany. Finding the Executive Mansion was easy. Parking wasn't.

I pulled up the main drive, parked in front of the mansion, and shut the car off. A guard came running out, and told me that I couldn't park there.

"Where's your mask?" I asked him.

He fumbled in his pockets, found his mask, and put it on.

"You can't park here," he said.

"I'm sorry," I said. "I can't understand you with that mask on. It muddles your voice."

"You can't park here," he repeated.

"I'm sorry," I said. "I can't understand you. Maybe you should take your mask off."

He pulled his mask down. "I said 'you can't park here.'"

"You need to cover your mouth with a mask," I said. "It's the law."

"You can't park here," he repeated, and then put his mask back in place.

"What do you mean?" I asked. "I just did."

He pulled his mask down. "Well you need to move it."

"We're here to meet with the governor," I said. "I don't know where to park." I pulled out a dollar. "Can you handle it?" I asked.

"Don't worry about it, sir," he said. "I'll handle it. And you can keep your dollar."

"Thanks," I said.

Carol and I got out, and he got in. He took our car, and drove away. I've no idea where he went.

We went up the front steps. There was another guard there.

"Can I help you?" he asked.

"You need to wear a mask," I said.

"Oh," he said. He fumbled in his pockets, found a mask, and put it on.

"Can I help you?" he asked again.

"I'm sorry," I said. "I can't understand you. Maybe you should take your mask off."

He pulled his mask down. "I said 'Can I help you?'"

"You need to cover your mouth with a mask," I said. "It's the law."

"Can I help you?" he asked again, and then put his mask back in place.

"We're here to see the governor," I said.

"And you are…?" he asked.

"Great! I'm great!" I responded. "Thanks for asking. How are you?"

"Great," he said. "What is your name?" he asked.

"I'm sorry," I said. "I can't understand you with that mask on."

He pulled his mask down again. "What is your name?"

"We're Mick and Carol Maux," I said. "What's your name?"

"I'm Sargent Southerland," he said.

"Nice to meet you," I said, and nodded toward him.

After a moment of silence, he said, "What I meant to ask was: 'Why you are here?'"

"Just to suffer?" I responded inquisitively.

"What do you mean by that?" he asked.

"I thought you were talking about that line from that video game. It became a catchphrase that's commonly used today to express frustration and hopelessness: *'Why are you here? Just to suffer?'*"

He looked confused. "No, I simply meant to ask you why you were here at the Governor's Mansion."

"Because we have a lunch appointment with the Governor," I said.

"Oh, I see," he said. "You should have said so."

"I just did," I said, confused.

"I'll announce you," he said.

He opened the front door, and we heard a loud scream, and some laughter. He went inside, and a minute later, he came back out.

"Please come in," he said.

We stepped into the foyer, and heard another scream. A pretty young woman went running past us, screaming. Governor Blowmo was running after her, laughing, and he was trying to grab her backside. He stopped when he saw us, and came over to say hello.

"Hi," he said. "I'm Governor Blowmo. Pleased to meet you."

"What happened?" I asked. "I thought we heard a scream."

"Oh that? Nothing," he said. "I was just grabbing that intern's butt, and she was pretending to not like it, but she really does like it, so the scream was all pretend."

"Why were you grabbing her butt?" Carol asked him.

"It's just an Italian thing," he said. "If I don't grab young women's butts, they might not think that they're attractive. An Italian thing is all it is," he said.

"I see," I said, not seeing. "I'm Mick Maux, and this is my wife, Carol."

He reached out, and gave Carol several kisses on each cheek.

He looked at me apologetically, and said, "It's an Italian thing." He shrugged his shoulders.

After a moment, he said: "I got a call from Dr. Grouchi's office asking me to give you whatever help I could investigating this virus. The 'RBG' is what it's called."

"Yes," I said. "We're trying to figure out its origin, whether it's dangerous, and how to stop it."

"Since there are no symptoms, I'm not sure what to say," Governor Blowmo volunteered.

After a moment, he said, "They told me that you were joining me for lunch today. Do you like lasagna?"

"Yes, I do," Carol said.

"They told us it was going to be spaghetti and meatballs," I said.

"No," he said. "Today is Wednesday. That's lasagna. Thursday is spaghetti and meatballs. And on Friday, I have to have some kind of fish – *pasta con sarde*, or something like that. Is lasagna OK?"

"Lasagna is great," I said.

"I'm happy to hear that," he said. "Let's go into the dining room," he said, gesturing.

We all went into the dining room, and sat. Governor Blowmo sat at the head of the table, and Carol and I sat opposite each other, one of us on each side of the governor.

There was a basket of Arthur Avenue bread between us all, and a bottle of olive oil. Governor Blowmo poured some oil into his bread dish, and took a piece of bread, which he started to eat.

A young woman came in with a bottle of wine, which she uncorked, and started pouring. She started by pouring for Carol, and then me, and then the governor. As she finished, the governor lightly slapped her backside, and she jumped. He laughed as she scampered from the room. She had left the bottle on the table.

"The girls like it when I do that," he said. "It makes them feel attractive."

"*Salute*[3]," he said, holding up his glass. We all clinked our glasses.

I tasted my wine. While I hadn't seen the label, I could taste that it was an Italian Chianti.

This time, a young man came out of the kitchen with a tray holding three medium-sized plates of salad. It was a simple salad: some bibb lettuce, arugula, red onion, tomato, and a sprinkling of gorgonzola. It had been tossed with a simple Italian dressing. He put each of our salads in front of us, then walked around the table with a pepper mill, grinding some for

---

[3] An informal Italian toast.

those who wanted it. Governor Blowmo didn't touch him. I was surprised. Maybe Blowmo thought that the man already felt attractive.

"What's your opinion of this virus?" Carol asked.

"Virus, shmirus," he said. "I haven't seen anyone who's actually sick."

"But didn't the president send lots of medical help?" she asked.

"Help, shmelp," he said. "The last thing that we need is help."

We finished our salads, and the young man came back out and cleared our plates. He returned to the kitchen, and came back with the lasagna. He brought it on a tray, with some locatelli and a grater. He made the rounds, giving each of us some grated cheese.

The governor picked up the wine and asked, "Do either of you want a little more?"

I had him pour me half a glass, and Carol declined. The Governor poured some more into his own glass. Then he raised it.

"Here's hoping that this virus isn't real," he said.

We all clinked our glasses again.

"Here, here!" I exclaimed. That seemed to confuse him.

"Have you spoken with Mayor deBozo about the virus?" Carol asked.

"I've tried, but he's too much of a *jadrool*[4]," Blowmo said. "He's letting the city fall apart."

"He said that the virus poses no danger," Carol said.

"But he's letting low-life people tear the city apart," Governor Blowmo said.

"What's he supposed to do?" Carol asked.

"As we'd say back in the old country: '*Spaccare il capo*[5], and they'll cutta the crappo,'" the Governor said.

"Are you talking about the mayor or the mobs?" I asked.

"Both," he said.

"Then what are your plans for the city and the state?" Carol asked.

"I really don't have any," he said. "But I'm giving a press conference every morning. And I'm having my staff write an autobiography."

"Who are they writing the autobiography about?" I asked. "Themselves?"

"No," he said. "Me."

---

[4] Italian-American slang for a loser.

[5] In Italian, this means "break the leader(s)."

"But they can't write an autobiography about you," I said.

"Really?" he asked. "Why not?"

"Because by definition, an 'autobiography' is a biography that's written by the person that it's about," I explained.

"Whatever," he said. "Then it's an autoshmiography. Is that better?"

"Much," I said. "Can I get a copy?"

"It's not done yet," he said. "We'll have to see how it ends."

"What do you mean by 'how it ends'?" I asked.

"Do I cure the disease, or not?" he asked. "That's what I need to find out. Maybe I can name a bridge after myself, or something like that."

"And technically," I added, "an autobiography should end with you writing the autobiography."

He gave me a blank stare. We had all finished eating.

"Espresso?" he asked. "Cannoli?"

"Yes, please," Carol said. "But I can't eat an entire cannoli[6]. I'm full from the lasagna."

"I'll take the espresso. And take the cannoli," I said, thinking about the movie, *The Godfather*. Maybe it shouldn't have been a gun. Maybe it should have been espresso. That would have changed the meaning of that scene entirely: *"Have an espresso. And have a cannoli."* I tried to imagine Peter Clemenza as a waiter, and I couldn't.

The young man came back out and cleared our plates. Governor Blowmo glanced his way, and made a circular motion with his index finger to indicate all three of us. The young man nodded.

He returned a few minutes later with a tray having three espressos and three cannoli on it, and placed one of each in front of each of us. Each espresso had a slice of lemon peel, and a demitasse spoon on its saucer. In Campania, a slice of lemon peel is thought to cut the bitterness of espresso.

If you're from Campania, be my guest. Modern espresso shouldn't be bitter.

The young man went over to the bar, grabbed the bottle of anisette, and placed it on the table in case anyone wanted to put some in their espresso.

The governor put a little anisette into his espresso; neither Carol or I did.

"What about Dr. Grouchi?" Carol asked.

---

[6] In Italy, the singular form of cannoli is cannolo. In America, "cannoli" is used to mean either plural or singular. And in America, sometimes people say "cannolis" to mean plural.

"What about him?" Governor Blowmo asked.

"He says that the virus is real, and that we should all wear masks," she said.

"He used to say that we shouldn't wear masks," Governor Blowmo observed. "He's a frikin' *gagootz*[7]."

"Does that mean that you're uncertain of his judgements?" she asked.

"He's a *mameluke*[8]," the governor said.

"Well, Dr. Grouchi is the one that suggested that you meet with us," she pointed out. "Does that mean that you're skeptical of us being able to do much?"

"I don't see what the problem is," Governor Blowmo said. "If there was a real disease, I'd take it seriously. But this is all bullshit."

We all sipped our espressos in silence for a minute. Governor Blowmo had put us into an uncomfortable position.

Quite right," I finally said, to break the uncomfortable pause. "I think we agree with you. Nonetheless, Dr. Grouchi is running this study so that we can all put it to bed."

Good," Governor Blowmo said.

He looked at his watch.

"Well I have some meetings that I need to prepare for," he said. "So if you'll excuse me, I'll say goodbye now. Stay and finish your espresso and cannolis. The guard will show you out when you're ready to go."

(*"Leave the espressos. And leave the cannolis."*) I tried to imagine this as the line in the movie. I wanted to say this, but I didn't.

"Well it was a pleasure meeting you," Carol said. "Thanks for your warm hospitality."

We all shook hands.

A guard went and fetched our car. As we were walking out the front door, we both heard a young woman shriek, and could hear the Governor laughing. A scampering sound came from upstairs.

---

[7] Italian-American term for a crazy person.

[8] Italian-American term for a person that does stupid things.

12. Cheesecake at Junior's

I'm surprised that it hadn't occurred to me before, but Governor Blowmo had left me with a conundrum that had puzzled me all the way home. I had a hard time falling asleep that night, because it continued to puzzle me.

The next morning, I was sitting in the family room with my coffee, and the news was on. I wasn't at all focused on the news. Instead, I was thinking about the problem that the governor had posed: the place setting at his dinner table. It had been disturbing.

In the canonical place-setting at a dinner table, demitasse spoons are not part of the setting. This is because not everyone will be having espresso. For example, children, and people with heart problems don't usually have espresso. Instead, demitasse spoons are brought out with the espresso itself – as was done at the Governor's Mansion.

At every place-setting in a canonical service, dessert utensils are placed horizontally above where the serving plate goes. Everyone has dessert, and the placement of these utensils will give dinner guests a hint as to what's for dessert: a fork for pie or cake, a spoon for ice cream or custard, and sometimes both.

In the case of cannoli, while some people simply pick it up and eat it, many start by using a small spoon – a demitasse spoon works best – to eat the mascarpone filling from each end prior to trying to eat the pastry itself.

The question is then: should a demitasse spoon be placed horizontally above the serving plate when you'll be serving cannoli *and* espresso? Since cannoli and espresso are typically served together, I'm sure that I'm not the first who has been puzzled by this.

Whoever had set Governor Blowmo's table had not put a demitasse spoon in the canonical place for dessert. Was this as it should have been? Or was this wrong? It was a puzzle indeed.

My cellphone broke my reverie, and I answered it: "Hello?"

"Hello?" said a female voice on the other end. "Who's this?"

"Who's this?" I asked. "Hello?"

"Hello?" she said again. "Who's this?"

"Who's this?" I asked again. "You first."

"This is Mayor deBozo's secretary," she said. "I'm trying to reach Dr. Maux."

"This is he," I said. "How can I help you?"

"I was asked to set up a meeting between the mayor, and you and your wife," she said.

"I see," I said. "Can you hold for a minute?"

I took my coffee and the phone into the living room, where Carol was reading.

"I've got Mayor deBozo's office on the phone," I told her. "They want to set up a meeting."

Carol stopped reading, and I put the phone on speaker.

"We can come down and meet with him whenever it's convenient," I said. "I assume that we'd meet in his office on Broadway across from City Hall." I said. "Is that right?"

"He's a very busy man," his secretary said. "It depends on what time of the day."

"OK," I said. "How's tomorrow? What time is good?"

"Well, the mayor starts the day at 7:30; earlier than most," she said.

"That's very impressive," I said. "That's too early for us."

"Well, he couldn't meet with you then," she said. "He needs to do a few things first," she explained.

"How's the rest of his morning?" I asked.

"His limo leaves Gracie Mansion every day at 7:30," she said. "That's when his day begins."

"It's probably about twenty minutes down to City Hall at that time in the morning," I said. "His office is across Broadway; right across from City Hall. Does that mean that he starts work at 8:00? We could probably meet him at 8:00 – or maybe 8:15."

"Well, he doesn't go to his office right away," she said. "First, they go over the Brooklyn Bridge. They take him to the Park Slope YMCA on 7th Avenue and 14th Street. First, he does his workout."

"So we'd be talking 9:30 or 10:00 by the time he got to his office, right?" I asked.

"No," she said. "He does a two-hour workout. You really have to admire that in a man his age."

"So he'd be at his office closer to 10:30?" I asked.

"Not quite," she said. "After his workout, his limo takes him up Prospect Park to Flatbush, and then they go up Flatbush with a final stop at DeKalb."

"Why do they stop at DeKalb?" I asked.

"He goes to *Junior's*," she said. "He's always at *Junior's* at 10:30."

"*Junior's?*" I asked.

"Yes," she said. "After his workout, he goes to *Junior's* for some cheesecake and some coffee."

"So he'll get to his office at around 11:15?" I asked. "We could come then. That time works nicely for us."

"No," she said. "At 11:15, he's just coming in. So he'll have to go through his email first. I help him with that. That usually takes an hour. Then he goes out to lunch."

"When does he get back?" I asked.

"It's hard to say," she said. "Lunch is always business. It depends on who he's meeting for lunch, and where they're going. It could be an hour, and it might be two hours."

"I guess we could come down after lunch," I said. "How's 2:00?"

"He likes to take a nap after lunch. He has a nice comfortable couch for that," she said.

"3:00?" I asked.

"That's when the masseuse gets here," she said. "He might have sore muscles from his workout, so he always gets a massage at 3:00."

"How's 4:00?" I asked.

"That's when he's busy doing city business," she said. "Responding to emails, making phone calls, and things like that."

"I guess that takes us to 5:00," I said.

"The mayor leaves at 5:00," she said. "It's a very long day for him. Remember that he starts his day at 7:30. By 5:00, he's tired: too tired to make important decisions. So he never works past 5:00."

"Wow," I said. "He sounds like a very busy man."

"Yes," she said. "He is. Busier than most people. People don't realize how hard their mayor works."

"Well," I suggested, "we could meet him at *Junior's*, and have a slice of cheesecake with him."

"That's an excellent idea!" she said. "I'll pencil that in."

"Just to confirm," I said, "tomorrow at 10:30 at *Junior's*."

"That's correct," she said. "He'll see you then."

Junior's is on Flatbush Avenue. It opened in 1950, and is famous for delicious, plain, American food. This includes Greek, Italian, Asian, and Jewish food. Like I said, "American food." It's especially famous for its cheesecake.

Like its menu, its outside appearance is deceptive. At a glance, its appearance is all "uniform." But if you look at the details, it's eclectic. The entrance is on the corner. It's a simple, clear glass door with red frames. Its floor-to-ceiling windows stretch down Flatbush, and down DeKalb. The middle thirds of the glass panels are clear, while the top and bottom thirds are red. Their business logo runs along the top of the first floor: between their first and second floors. It's made using a very large set of lighted words.

Their second-floor windows have awnings with brown and white vertical stripes. Each awning has the "*Junior's*" logo on it.

Their eclecticism comes across in their business logo – their set of lighted words on the front of the restaurant. The middle two words are "*Junior's* RESTAURANT," which are both in red. "*Junior's*" is in script. Except for the "*J*," it's in lower case. "RESTAURANT" is done in strict printing, and all of its letters are capitalized. To the left of "*Junior's* RESTAURANT" is the single word, "cocktails." It's gold, and it's all in lower-case printing. To the right of "*Junior's* RESTAURANT" is the single word "BAR," also in gold, and all in upper-case printing.

Eclectic? Someone chose those colors, fonts, and capital-versus-small letters. Why? That combination never would have occurred to me. Maybe the person who made the sign was dyslexic. We're lucky that they didn't scramble the letters too. It could have said: "ARREST *Junior's* AUNT."

We'd come over the Brooklyn Bridge, and found a parking spot on Flatbush Avenue near *Junior's*. Two spots ahead of us stood the mayor's limousine. There were two very large goons standing next to the limousine. They were both wearing long overcoats, despite the warm weather. I could tell from the various lumps and bumps in their overcoats that both of them were heavily armed. That's how I knew that it was the mayor's limousine.

Carol and I went into *Junior's*. Right inside the front door stood another pair of large, heavily-armed goons in long overcoats. They were standing so that they each had a clear view of the entire restaurant, and so that they could prevent people from entering and leaving.

As we stepped inside, one of them asked, "May I help you?"

"In fact, yes, you can," I said. "I've had a tough year, and I'm a little short on funds. I could certainly use a few thousand dollars."

He looked confused.

In his moment of confusion, I looked around *Junior's*, and saw Mayor deBozo sitting at a table with two more large goons in overcoats. The mayor was eating a large piece of cheesecake. I started walking towards him, and the second goon - who had been at the door - stepped in front of me.

"Excuse me," I said, and I attempted to walk around him.

He took another step to block me.

"Can I help you?" he asked.

"Yes," I said. "And I'm so glad that you asked. You see, I've had a tough year, and I'm short on funds. I could use a few thousand dollars. Can you spare that?"

He glared at me.

"Don't tell me that you're broke too - like your ugly friend here," I said, pointing to the other bodyguard.

The two bodyguards "surrounded" me. That is, one got on each side of me, but they were large enough to make me feel surrounded.

"I didn't hurt your feelings, did I?" I asked the bodyguard that I had called ugly. "If it's any consolation, your friend is even uglier than you are."

The two of them looked like they weren't sure what to do.

"Do you guys want to step outside?" I asked.

"Huh?" one of them asked.

"Do you want to step outside?" I asked.

"Are you serious?" he asked, looking down at me.

"Of course, I'm serious," I said. "If you guys stepped outside, the place would stink a little less. I'm supposed to be having a meeting with the mayor," I said. "And you guys are wasting my time."

"Why didn't you say so?" one of them asked.

"You asked me if I needed help," I said. "And I told you that I could use some money. You weren't at all helpful."

"Hey boss," the other one shouted to Mayor deBozo. Mayor deBozo looked up.

"This guy says that he and the lady are supposed to join you for cheesecake," he said. "Is that true?"

Mayor deBozo nodded. The two goons patted us down, and then got out of our way. Carol and I walked over to Mayor deBozo's table. The two other goons that had been sitting there got up and moved out of the way.

"Please," Mayor deBozo said. "Join me." He indicated the seat on either side of him – one on each side of the table – for me and Carol.

We sat.

"I'm Mick Maux," I said. "And this is my wife, Carol. We work together. Dr. Grouchi has commissioned us to investigate the bat virus."

"Pleased to meet you," he said, shaking hands with each of us. "Cheesecake?" he asked.

"Maybe we'll share one," Carol said.

"It's a great cheesecake," Mayor deBozo said. "I come here every morning after my workout."

The mayor waved to a waitress, and hollered to her: "Bring another cheesecake, and two forks."

"Coffee?" he asked. "I think that the city can pay for it."

"Yes," I said. "And I'd like some coffee."

"Me too," said Carol.

"And two cups of coffee," Mayor deBozo hollered to the waitress.

The waitress came back very quickly. She had a slice of cheesecake and two cups of coffee on her tray. She put the cheesecake down in the middle of the table so that both Carol and I could reach it, and set a cup of coffee down in front of each of us. She put two forks on the plate that had the cheesecake: one facing me, and the other facing Carol.

I put some milk in my coffee and stirred it. Carol took hers black. The cheesecake had a generous portion of whipped cream on top of it, so Carol took her fork, and pushed the whipped cream off. Neither of us eat whipped cream, except on rare occasions.

"Are you gonna eat that whipped cream?" Mayor deBozo asked.

"Probably not," Carol said.

"Can I have it?" he asked.

"Sure," I said. "Help yourself."

Mayor deBozo slid his plate of cheesecake forward so that it was touching ours, then he took his fork and spoon, and moved the whipped cream from our plate to his. "Thanks," he said, pulling his plate back to its original position. He started to eat the whipped cream.

"What's your opinion of the virus, RBG?" Carol asked him.

"The key is for people to get out on the town, and to go on with their lives," he said. "While China was slow to report this, it isn't anything that we can't handle. The exception is the Jews."

"What about the Jews?" I asked.

"I think that while most restaurants and social organizations can operate well above 50% capacity, religious organizations - and particularly the Jews - should operate below 25% capacity," he said.

"What's different about the Jews?" Carol asked.

"Well," he said "they're Jewish!"

"I see," I said, not seeing.

"I also think that we need to ban all guns," he said. "Then the police wouldn't need to do 'stop and frisk,' since there wouldn't be any guns."

"Excellent thinking," I said.

"People don't need guns," he said. "New York City is completely safe. I've *never* had anyone bother me," he said.

I thought of the six heavily-armed goons that we'd had to get past to talk to him, and I understood his perspective.

"The important thing is marijuana," he said. "If everyone smoked marijuana, we'd have world peace, and then we wouldn't need guns."

"And the city would get some nice revenue," Carol said.

"Exactly," he said. "Budgets are important. To keep the city vital, we need to increase spending at about three times the rate of inflation. We also need to cut costs."

"What can you cut?" I asked.

"Police," he said. "It's a peaceful city. We don't need them."

"Anything else?" Carol asked.

"Jails," he said. "We need to close them. I've already cut costs by eliminating bail for people that are arrested. That way, we don't need to hold them. It's very effective."

"But what if they don't show up for their trial?" Carol asked.

"Then they don't go to jail," he said. "It saves even more money."

After a minute, he asked, "I'm not delusional, am I?"

"No," I said. "You're not delusional; you just *think* that you are. Back to the virus. What do you think we should do?"

"Nothing," he said.

"But what about Dr. Grouchi?" I asked him.

"What do you expect?" he asked. "He's a Jew."

"No he's not," I said. "All of his grandparents came here from Italy."

"Really?" he asked. "I never would have guessed that."

"You know what else you'd never have guessed?" I asked.

"What?" he asked.

"He was actually the captain of his basketball team in high school," I said.

Mayor deBozo started laughing, hysterically.

"You're a really funny guy," he said, and looked at his watch.

"He can throw a mean baseball, too," I said.

"Look," he said, laughing even harder, "I need to go. I have a long day ahead of me."

"We understand," Carol said. "It was nice to meet you."

"Keep in touch," he said. ("Not.")

"You too," I said. ("Not.")

Mayor deBozo got up and left *Junior's* with his four heavily-armed goons. Carol and I sat, drank our coffee, and finished our cheesecake.

The cheesecake was outstanding.

13. The Harvest Moon (October 1)

The "harvest moon" is a full, bright moon that occurs near the beginning of autumn. This year, it was on October 1. The term "harvest moon" was used by people before there was electricity. In addition to being full, it's early: it begins illuminating the earth at sunset. Farmers depended on it to harvest crops late into the night.

And I had another lucid dream with Dr. Grouchi in it.

Since it was October, it was getting cool out, and I'd closed the bedroom windows. Dr. Grouchi got into the house downstairs somehow, and he floated up the staircase, and into our bedroom. He stood at the foot of the bed, and stared at me.

He was dressed as he had been in my previous dreams, except this time, he had *two* masks on. I opened my eyes and looked at him. His beady eyes stared back.

"*Two* masks?" I asked him.

"Yes," he said. "Two."

"First there was no mask, then there was one, and now there are two," I said. "Why two masks?"

"Because two are better than one," he said.

"Then wouldn't three be better than two?" I asked him.

This gave him pause. I could tell that he was thinking about it. "Three masks?" he asked.

"Yes," I said. "And what about four masks?"

"Please," he said. "Stop talking."

This time it was Chopin's Nocturne Opus 9 Number 2 in E-flat Major. Dr. Grouchi seemed to like the oldies. The music was very relaxing.

I levitated off the bed, and saw the room, all lit up by the harvest moon as I rotated forwards into a vertical position. Dr. Grouchi removed his two masks, and I could see his fangs again. They'd grown even longer.

As before, I rocketed upwards into space with Dr. Grouchi holding me, with rainbows of color shooting past. I focused on the nocturne. Like the previous pieces, it was slow, peaceful, and introspective.

Finally, the nocturne ended. But this time, I wasn't in bed. I was simply standing there. And Grouchi was standing opposite me, putting his masks back on.

"Why do you visit me?" I asked him.

"I'm a vampire," he said.

"How did you get to be one?" I asked. "And how come I'm not one? I think you've fed on my blood."

"I'm a Wuhan vampire," he said. "You get cursed with this if you eat the guano of a rabid horseshoe-bat from the Yunnan province. Actually, I'm what's called a 'wúdí-wáng' vampire."

"Wúdí-wáng?" I asked him. "What's that?"

"That's Mandarin for 'invincible-king,'" he said. "I'm an 'invincible-king' vampire because I ate the guano of a rabid Chinese bat. While you could become a vampire, you couldn't become a wúdí-wáng vampire unless you ate some rabid-bat guano."

"What kind of a vampire would I be?" I asked. "And does it really matter?"

"You'd just be a generic vampire," Grouchi said. "If another vampire drank too much of your blood, you'd die. But on full moons, you'd come awake, and fly the skies, looking to feed on others."

"How is a wúdí-wáng vampire different?" I asked.

"While a regular vampire is dead, and only comes awake when there's a full moon," Grouchi said, "a wúdí-wáng vampire is 'undead.' A wúdí-wáng vampire appears to be human. He functions every day during the day, and seems human to everyone that he interacts with. He might also fly the skies and feed on blood when the moon's only partially full. You can only become undead - a wúdí-wáng vampire – by eating rabid-bat guano. That's why we called it 'the RBG virus.' But that doesn't tell the whole story. It doesn't distinguish wúdí-wáng vampires from regular vampires."

"Why would you want to be a wúdí-wáng vampire?" I asked.

"Because you're undead," Dr. Grouchi said. "You've a vampire, but you're a human too."

"But why would anyone eat bat guano?" I asked.

"No one would eat it on purpose," he said. "But when you eat a bat that you purchased in the Wuhan markets, and the bat is rabid, and you don't clean it properly, its guano makes you a vampire. But it makes you a wúdí-wáng vampire. Being undead isn't all that bad. It makes me feel strong and indestructible."

"Are bats a Chinese specialty?" I asked him. "And why would you eat their guano?"

"Yes," he said. "The Chinese like bats. And most of them aren't rabid. But once in a while, there's a rabid one. You can't tell by looking at it once it's dead. The important thing is to clean it well. You don't want to eat their guano. While the Chinese eat lots of strange things, bat guano isn't one of them. My Chinese host hadn't cleaned the bat properly, so I became a vampire with the RBG virus."

"Does that make me a vampire too?" I asked him.

"No," he said. "You haven't eaten rabid-bat guano, and I haven't killed you."

"But doesn't contact with you make me infected?" I asked.

"Probably," he said. "If you had a blood test, they'd probably find the RBG virus. But you're relatively young, and strong. It won't change your life. You're just carrying the virus. You're not dead, and you're not a vampire. You're what we call a zombie."

"A zombie?" I asked. "What's that mean?"

"It means that you're a living human who has been fed on by a vampire," Grouchi said. "You've not died; you're a zombie. If you die, you become a vampire, but not a wúdí-wáng vampire."

"What about people who aren't young or strong?" I asked.

"They are more likely to die. Then, like everyone else, they become bats, and fly the skies during full moons," he said. "Other than that, they're dead. Their families bury them, and don't know that they emerge from their graves during full moons. Let me show you."

He floated over to the bedroom window, and motioned me to follow. "Look at the moon," he said. "Look carefully."

I stared out the window at the full moon, and made an effort to focus. Sure enough, I started to see lots of bat-shaped creatures flying through the sky.

"Those are almost all vampires and zombies," Grouchi said. "The vampires will fly around looking to feed. But the zombies won't bother anyone. The zombies aren't vampires; they simply have the virus. In the morning, they'll all wake up just like you do. And usually, they won't remember being bats flying through the sky."

"So all that the RBG virus does is that it might make you fly the skies during full moons?" I asked.

"For zombies, yes," he said. "And cruising through the sky with a large set of wings is safe, and it's good exercise. As a doctor, I could make the argument that it actually *helps* the old and the weak."

"But what about vampires?" I asked.

"Well, then you're dead," Dr. Grouchi said. "Unless you're a wúdí-wáng vampire."

"I like to cook," I said. "How was the bat guano?" I asked him.

"It tasted like crap," he said. "Good crap, but crap."

After a minute, he asked, "Did you meet with the mayor and the governor?"

"Yes," I said. "Carol and I visited both of them."

"What did you learn?" he asked.

"Governor Blowmo is a *gavone*[9]," I said. "But he serves a mean lasagna. And I'll bet that if he ever went to see a mind-reader, he'd get a discount."

"I've never had his lasagna," he said. "What about Mayor deBozo?"

"His pace is very deceptive," I said. "He's actually much slower than he seems. But he holds grand delusions of adequacy."

"How can we have two guys like that in such powerful positions?" he asked, rhetorically.

"Some people descended from the apes later than others," I said. "They're good examples."

He thought about that. Then he changed the topic.

"How do I get out of here?" he asked.

"What do you mean?" I asked. "Are you lost?"

"Your bedroom windows weren't open, so I came in downstairs. But I don't remember where I came in. It was a little confusing."

"That's because there are actually two staircases," I lied. "If you take the wrong one, you'll get lost."

"Which one should I take?" he asked.

"Which one did you take to come up here?" I asked him.

"I don't know," he said.

"Then I can't help you," I said.

"But I can't just stay here," he said.

9 Italian for an ill-mannered, unkempt pig.

"Why not?" I asked.

"Because I can't be here when the sun comes up," he said.

"Why not?" I asked.

"Sunlight will kill me," he said. "That's why I stay inside during the day. I only go out when there's a full moon. It's the moonlight that makes me thrive."

"But moonlight is sunlight," I said. "It's just sunlight reflected off the moon."

He looked stunned. He looked at the full moon and withdrew, hissing. He backed away, and seemed to wither. "Really?" he asked, shrinking down to minimize his exposure to the moonlight. He covered his eyes.

"Really," I said. "The sunlight bounces off the moon, and it comes back to the earth. Moonlight is really the same as sunlight."

He hissed again, and ran from the room.

I floated upwards, drifted over to my bed, and back down to where I was lying. Eventually, I went back to sleep.

What I hadn't told Dr. Grouchi is that sunlight and moonlight are actually different.

The color temperature of sunlight within our atmosphere is 5780 degrees Kelvin (about 9950 degrees Fahrenheit). The *color temperature* of a light source is the temperature of a black-body that radiates light that's the same color. In fact, the color temperature of the sun is 5900 degrees Kelvin (about 10,160 degrees Fahrenheit), but our atmosphere scatters some of that light.

The moon has no atmosphere, and has a much lower-color temperature. It's about 4000 degrees Kelvin (about 6740 degrees Fahrenheit). It has a warm white glow. And since the surface of the moon is mostly basaltic lava (now inert) and powdery soil, it doesn't reflect much light. It only reflects 3% to 12% of the sunlight that hits it.

I'm sure that Dr. Grouchi consulted some of the scientists who worked for him, and learned that the moonlight was probably safe. I could picture him smiling now, with his long fangs and his beady little eyes.

14. Coffee with Detective Danny

In the morning, I woke up late. I woke up because my cellphone was ringing on my nightstand. And I woke up late because the visit from Dr, Grouchi had worn me out.

I opened one eye, and looked at the phone. It continued to ring. Carol was already up, so I didn't worry about my phone waking her. But I felt dreary. I guess that zombies feel dreary sometimes.

I was lying face-down, but could see the phone on my nightstand by angling my head slightly. It kept ringing, so I reached for it.

"Hello?" I asked.

"Mick?" said the voice on the other end. "It's Danny."

"Hi, Danny," I said. He rarely called me, so I wondered what was up. "What's up?"

"It's a nice day," he said, "and I thought you might want to meet me for coffee."

I looked at the clock. 9:30. I never slept this late. And Danny never called me suggesting that we meet for coffee in the morning. I wondered what was up. Probably his romance.

"Sure," I said, feeling drowsy. I suggested the usual place: "Holy Moly?"

"Of course," he said.

"I slept late," I said. "Give me about forty-five minutes."

"OK," he said. "See you over there."

I felt like going back to bed, but I got up and stepped into the shower. Then I brushed my teeth and combed my hair. I figured that shaving could wait until later.

I went downstairs. Carol was sitting in the living room reading. I stuck my head in.

"Good morning," I said.

"You slept late," she observed.

"Yes," I said. "I feel like I have a hangover. I don't know why."

"Get some coffee," she suggested.

"Danny called me," I said. "He wants me to meet him for coffee. So I figured I'd go see what's up. He never calls me in the morning to suggest getting some coffee."

Carol smiled, knowingly. "Tell him I said 'hi.'"

"I will," I said.

I went downstairs, got in my car, and left for Holy Moly.

When I got there, I saw Danny's car parked outside, and I saw him sitting in front of one of the windows. I gave him a wave, walked in, and got in line to buy some coffee.

When I got my coffee, I went over to the service stand, poured in some milk, took a long stirrer and a few napkins, and went over to join Danny.

"Good morning," I said. "I slept late."

"I know," he said. "You told me that when I called. Are you OK? You look like crap."

"I don't feel well," I said. "I had a strange dream last night. I've had it twice before. And all three times, I've felt lousy the next day."

"What kind of dream?" he asked.

"I dreamt that I was visited by a vampire," I said.

He looked startled. "And you feel like crap the next day?"

"Yes," I said.

"Maybe you *were* visited by a vampire," he said. "But I think that vampires aren't real. They're just in the movies."

"Yeah, you're right," I said. "Maybe I should get a blood test, or something like that. It could be that I'm just anemic."

"You know, I just started taking this new vitamin," Danny said, "and I feel much healthier."

"A vitamin?" I asked. "What vitamin?"

"It's a new thing," he said. "It's called C60."

"You mean the new buckyball," I said.

"No," Danny said. "It's called C60."

"That's the same thing," I said. "When it was discovered, they named it after Buckminster Fuller. That's why they call it a 'buckyball.' Actually, that name is just for short – it's really called 'Buckminsterfullerene.'"

"Who's Buckminster Fuller? And what's he got to do with C60?" Danny asked.

"Buckminster Fuller was an American architect," I said. "While he didn't create geodesic domes, he popularized them."

"So I repeat: What's that got to do with C60?" he asked again.

"The structure of a C60 molecule makes it look like an empty soccer ball. The people who discovered C60 named it after Buckminster Fuller because they thought that the molecule looked like a geodesic dome," I said. "Clever?"

Buckminster Fuller
Geodesic dome

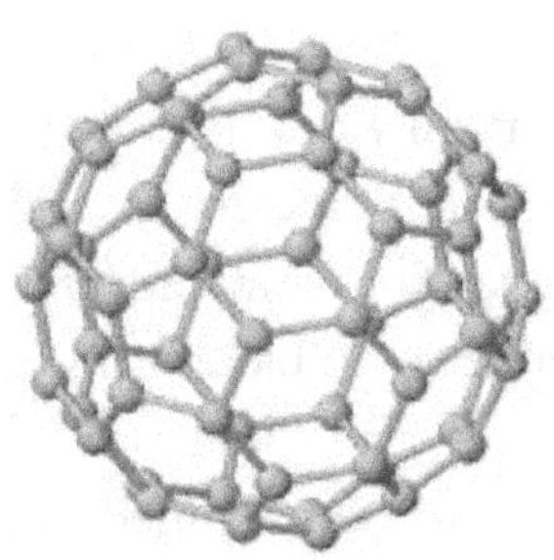

Buckminsterfullerene
C$_{60}$

"What's a geodesic dome?" he asked.

"Have you ever seen a building that looks like a sphere or a hemisphere with its surface made of regular polygons?" I asked.

"What's a regular polygon?" he asked.

"A polygon is a multisided shape having straight sides: triangles, rectangles, pentagons, and so on," I said. "A *regular* polygon is a polygon having all of its sides equal."

"So a geodesic dome is a sphere made of triangles or squares?" he asked.

"Triangles are an example," I said. "You can't do it with squares. I don't want to go off into left field here, but technically, geodesics should also lie on what are called 'Riemannian manifolds.' That's named after the mathematician Bernhard Riemann. Basically, what that means is that the sides of the polygons shouldn't be straight; they should curve like the surfaces that they're suggesting. So while architects call their buildings 'geodesics,' technically, most of them aren't."

"Whatever," Danny said. "Have you tried C60?" he asked.

"I haven't," I said.

"Well you should," he said. "I'll bet it would make your tired look disappear."

"I'm tired because of my strange dreams," I said.

"Maybe if you took C60, you wouldn't have strange dreams," he said.

"That's worth a shot," I allowed.

"What else is new?" he asked.

"Carol and I are now working with Dr. Grouchi's team to try to figure out this bat virus," I said.

"What do you mean by 'figure it out'?" he asked.

"I mean where it came from, and what its effects are," I said.

"I thought it came from the Chinese markets," he said. "They sell dead bats there. The Chinese eat them. And there are no effects, although it shows up as a 'virus' in blood tests – whatever that means."

"We don't really know whether there are any effects yet," I said. "But so far, China has claimed that there are none."

"I wouldn't trust anything that China says," Danny said. "There's a reason that they eat bats."

"Apparently, the virus doesn't come from healthy bats, and it doesn't come from the bats themselves," I said.

"I know," Danny said. "It just comes from rabid bats. But what do you mean when you say that 'it doesn't come from the bats themselves'?"

"It comes from their guano," I said.

"What the hell is guano?" Danny asked.

"Their excrement," I explained.

"So not only do the Chinese eat bats, but they eat bat shit? Is that a delicacy?" Danny asked, incredulously.

"They don't eat the guano on purpose," I explained. "That only happens when the bats aren't cleaned properly."

After a pause, I changed the subject. I had suspected that this was not what Danny really wanted to talk about. Why else would he call me and ask to meet for coffee in the morning?

"How's Dottie?" I asked. Dottie is Danny's girlfriend. She lives across the street from me and Carol. I usually see Danny's car over there when I get up early in the morning to run.

"Actually," he said, "that's why I asked you to meet me for coffee."

"Because of Dottie?" I asked. "I don't understand." This confirmed my suspicion.

"I've been thinking about getting married," he said.

"That's great to hear!" I said. "That's not what men usually think about unless they're really in love."

"But I've never been married," he said. "What's it like?"

"Your problems will be at an end," I said. But I didn't say which end.

"Really?" he asked. "That's what I thought."

"To get married," I said, "you need to be in love. Most people who get married are. But marriage is about much more than just being in love. Teenagers sometimes think that they're in love, but they don't know anything about life yet. Gazing into each-other's eyes and thinking about sex all the time isn't what life is about, and it's not really 'love.' Life is about going to work, paying the bills, maintaining your home, and lots of other things like that. None of these things have anything to do with being in love. When you marry, it's a partnership. The two of you will commit to working together on those things. And those things have nothing to do with being in love, although being in love helps you to do them."

"You make it sound so wonderful," Danny said, sarcastically. "How come no one told me this before?"

"Because being in love is something that you should enjoy. But 'being in love' and 'getting married' are very different in their scopes. You need the former to even think about the latter," I said, "but it doesn't suffice."

"You don't make it sound so great," he said.

"It *is* great," I said. "But some people – particularly young people – don't understand that marriage is a contract and a commitment. It's *more than* 'being in love.' In fact, it's much richer than being in love. And it comes with problems that you need to get through. Being in love helps you to do that, but it doesn't solve the problems for you."

"I think I understand," he said.

"You won't fully understand until you're married," I said. "Once you're married, Dottie will stop putting up with your crap."

"My crap?" he asked. "What crap? Or should I ask: 'What guano?'"

"That you sometimes leave your socks on the floor. That you leave the toilet seat up. That you don't put the twist-tie back on the loaf of bread correctly – you twist it the wrong way. That you turn the wrong lights on, and leave the wrong ones off. That you haven't yet painted the wall that she asked you to paint a month ago. That you don't re-wrap the cold-cuts correctly. That you park in the garage the wrong way. That you don't put the cap on the toothpaste correctly. That you wear the wrong combinations of shirts and slacks. That you put your beer cans in the wrong garbage can. That you drink too much. You know, things like that."

"But I don't do any of those things," he said. "And Dottie doesn't care when I do."

"That's because she's your girlfriend," I said. "If she were your wife, she'd fix all of your problems."

"But I don't have any problems," he said.

"Like I said, when you get married, your problems will be at an end," I said.

I paused for a minute, and thought of another thing. "Another good thing about being married is that she'll stand by you through all the troubles that you wouldn't have had if you were single," I added.

"But I don't have any troubles!" he said.

"Exactly," I responded. "Finally, I'll leave you with a Zen koan that should give you some insights."

"What's a Zen koan?" Danny asked.

"It's a paradoxical riddle, used to demonstrate the inadequacy of logical reasoning and to provoke enlightenment," I said. "Suppose that a man is alone in the woods, and that he utters an idle thought. And suppose that his wife isn't there to hear him. Is he still wrong?"

I could see Danny contorting his features to try to make sense of it. He's never been married.

15. Tumultuous Times

So far, it had been a year like none other.

Everyone was wearing masks. People were instructed to stand six-feet apart when waiting in lines. Bottles of alcohol were kept in most cars, and on tables at the entrances to most stores so that people could disinfect their hands. And most cities had destruction and riots, with the police being instructed to "stand down."

A new group that called themselves "BLM" had become very visible. I wasn't sure who they were. The first time I saw a BLM rally on TV, it showed lots of wealthy white people kneeling in a parking lot in Westchester making some kind of a pledge. I assumed that it was some kind of spiritual movement for wealthy white people. They used it to assuage their guilt over being wealthy white people.

"What do you think of BLM?" Danny asked me.

"Who are they?" I asked. At the time, I'd never heard of them.

"Haven't you seen them on TV?" he asked. "What do you think 'BLM' stands for?"

I thought of the footage I'd seen of all of the wealthy white people kneeling in a parking lot full of very expensive cars.

"Bogus Little Meltdowns?" I guessed.

"No," he said. "Not even close. Guess again."

I thought some more. "Blame Ludicrous Morons?"

"No, think harder," he said.

"Well the only rally that I saw showed a bunch of rich white guys kneeling in a parking lot in Westchester," I said.

"They're not all rich people. And lots of them are involved in the riots," Danny said.

"Bouquet Like Manure?" I guessed.

"No," he said. "That's not it either."

"Belch Like Men?" I guessed.

"That would be politically incorrect," Danny said.

Danny waited a minute, and finally said, "Black Lives Matter."

"Are you joking?" I asked. "Of course, black lives matter. All lives matter. I don't get it. I think 'Belch Like Men' is catchier."

"Sounds sexist," he said.

"Women are allowed to do it too," I said. "Maybe since Connecticut has decided to allow boys to compete in girls' track events, the girls should be allowed to belch like men."

"That sounds fair," he said.

Meanwhile, the cities burned and became more dangerous. The estimates of damages were as high as ten-billion dollars. The insurance claims were over two-billion dollars, and those are usually less than 20% of the actual damages. And that doesn't even count all of the businesses that went under. Over four hundred police were injured in the riots, and over twenty-five people were killed.

There was also a rampage in which historical monuments and statues were toppled, defaced, and removed. It was exactly like the Cultural Revolution in China in which the Red Guard destroyed historical relics and artifacts, and ransacked cultural and religious sites with the goal of erasing history so that they could repeat it. They also murdered about twenty-million people with this lofty goal in mind.

We learned that America was a terrible place that was founded for the purpose of spreading slavery throughout the world, and that all of the 1776 nonsense was merely that: nonsense that was made up to hide the true goal of America, which was to promote slavery. We learned that people in what was called "Education" were re-writing the textbooks to teach this.

Martin Luther King had dreamt that one day, we'd all be color-blind. That had happened. But groups like BLM were trying to bring it all back. Why? A very good question.

The president was working very hard to figure out the real ramifications of the RBG virus, and had put Dr. Grouchi in charge of that mission. The president had cut lots of the beaurocracy associated with the development and production of medicines, and had given lots of money to America's pharmaceutical companies with instructions to prioritize the development of an RBG vaccine.

At the same time, the president was preparing for the coming election, and his opponent was selected by the Democrats. While the primary vote was probably won by a candidate that they called "BS," because those were his initials, but the Democrats chose the other candidate, a man named Slow Hidin'. Slow Hidin' had spent most of the year in his basement, hiding. Whenever he appeared in public, he usually embarrassed someone if they couldn't put a gag on him.

Hidin' helped us see past the masks. In 2019, if I'd seen anyone walk into a 7-Eleven wearing a mask, I'd have thought that they were going to rob the place. Hidin' explained that if you were in a 7-Eleven, the clerk probably had an Indian accent. That helped a lot.

Slow Hidin' had spent his entire life in politics. While he had once been good friends with an Exalted Cyclops of the KKK, and had given the eulogy at his funeral, he was very charitable toward a black politician that he'd met a while ago. With amazement, he told us that despite being black, the man was both clean and articulate! He thought that this was unusual for a black person. And he'd been thinking of telling the clean and eloquent black person: "You ain't black!"[10] But he didn't. He saved that one for another time.

Hidin' told us that he had once worked as a lifeguard at a pool in a black neighborhood. People – and especially the girls – would swim up to him so that they could admire the curly blond hair on his legs. Hidin' liked to focus on girls' hair. That's probably why he assumed that the girls liked his hairy legs. Even a guy named Corn-Pop liked his hairy legs.

While Slow Hidin' was a great champion of black people, he had wanted to keep the public schools segregated. He felt that if black students were allowed into white schools, it would turn them into what he termed "jungles." This seemed like an unusual word to describe a school. After all, he'd said that "poor kids are just as bright as white kids."[11]

Slow Hidin' had been advised to hide instead of campaigning. And he did. He stayed in his basement. A very good place for him. Some called him "The Cellar Dweller."

I'd become very tired of the mask mandates, and had decided to work on a new invention: invisible masks. Boron-nitride was first made by General Electric in 1957. They gave it the trade name "borazon." It's harder than diamond, but like diamond, it can be transparent.

---

[10] A quote from a well-known person in politics during an interview with a black interviewer.
[11] Another quote from a well-known person in politics.

Boron-nitride has a crystaline structure. My concept was to do with boron-nitride what had been done with graphite to make graphene: make it two-dimensional. This would allow it to be flexible and stretchable. If I could pile up multiple independent layers of two-dimensional boron-nitride, we'd have flexible masks that filtered germs, and that were invisible. We could exchange our ugly masks for invisible ones!

That would allow us all to wear masks without the ugly spectacle that had been imposed on us by various political machines.

I succeeded in making such a mask in October, in time for our next meeting in Washington with Dr. Grouchi's group. I thought that Carol and I could wear these masks to the meeting. Dr. Grouchi would certainly be happy with this new innovation: an invisible mask.

16. The Blue Moon (October 31), Halloween

Dr. Grouchi held another meeting on Halloween, and he invited me and Carol. This year we had a full moon on Halloween. It was both a "hunter's moon," and a "blue moon."

The hunter's moon is also known as a "blood moon." It refers to a full moon that appears during the month of October, but it's the first full moon that follows the harvest moon. Again, the harvest moon is the full moon closest to the autumnal equinox. This year, the harvest moon had come on October 2. That's what made this year's hunter's moon a blue moon as well.

The term "blue moon" is a little more involved, and it can mean any of several things.

The original definition of a blue moon refers to the third full-moon in a quarter having four full moons. These are relatively rare: they happen roughly every thirty months. This was not that kind of a blue moon.

Its second meaning is that it's the second full moon in a month. Since there are exactly 29.5 days between full moons, they never happen in February. And since we'd had a full moon on October 2, this particular full-moon fit that definition – great for a Halloween night.

There *is* a third definition. The moon can actually appear blue if there are dust particles in the atmosphere that are about 900 nanometers in size. These particles will reflect red light, so the moon really appears to be blue. (Note that blue light has about half the wavelength of red light – between 450 and 495 nanometers.) This only happens after some rare and major geological or weather events.

Carol and I had come down to Washington on October 30th – the day before Halloween. We took a long stroll, had a nice dinner and a nightcap, and turned in early. We'd brought our new invisible masks with us.

On Halloween morning, we had a light breakfast, and took an Uber to the Russell Senate Office Building, and tried to enter. The guard stopped us.

"You need to wear masks," he said.

"We are wearing masks," I told him.

"What?" he asked. "Are they invisible, or something?" he asked.

"Exactly," I said. "You must have graduated near the top of your class."

"Sorry, but you need masks," he said.

"We're wearing them," I said. "And you said it yourself: they're invisible."

"Sorry, but I need to be able to see them," he said.

"Is that a new rule?" I asked. "I hadn't heard that 'being able to see them' was a rule."

"It's *my* rule," he said.

"Oh, I'm sorry," I said. "I didn't recognize you, Mr. President. Are you dressed for Halloween, or something like that?"

He scowled.

"OK," I said. "You need to see them. Just a minute."

I ruffled through my backpack, and produced the two Halloween masks that I'd brought. One was of Vladimir Putin, and the other was of Kim Jong-un. Carol and I put them on.

"There," I said. "We're here to see Dr. Grouchi," I said.

The guard looked like he wasn't sure what to do. After a minute, he picked up the phone and punched in some numbers. "Tell Dr. Grouchi that there are two people here to see him," he said into the phone.

He leaned forward, covering the phone. "What's your name?" he asked.

"Mouse and Moose," I said.

"Tell him that it's Mouse and Moose," he spoke into the phone. He hung up.

"Wait here," he said.

About ten minutes went by, and a staff person came up to the guard and told him that he was there to bring the two guests to see Dr. Grouchi. "Where are they?" he asked the guard.

The guard gestured toward us. The staff person looked unsure of what to do. He was flustered.

"Happy Halloween!" I said.

"This way," he said. He motioned with his hand, and started walking the way we had come the last time that we were here.

We went to the same elevator that we'd taken before, took it to the basement, and went into a different conference room. The meeting was already in progress. It stopped, and everyone turned to look at us: Vladimir Putin and Kim Jong-un.

"Carry on," I said.

Dr. Grouchi said, "Sorry, but we can't tell who you are with those masks on."

"We didn't want to wear them, but the guard made us," I explained. We pulled our costume-masks off, and put our invisible masks back on.

"It's Dr. and Dr. Moose," Grouchi said.

"Actually, it's pronounced like 'mouse,'" I said. "Nice to meet you all."

Carol and I took our seats. An aide handed us standard masks.

Dr. Grouchi said, "Drs. Mouse, do you mind putting your masks on?"

Carol and I had our invisible masks on.

"I've developed a new kind of mask that's invisible," I said. "We're both wearing them. And it's pronounced 'moose.'"

"Invisible?" he asked.

I looked around the table. As before, Senators Schlomo and Warden were there, and several other people that I didn't recognize. But this time there was also a member of the House. She was introduced as Alexis Often-a-Cabron[12].

Alexis Often-a-Cabron introduced herself, and explained that her role was to ensure that whatever solutions we found to deal with the virus were sufficiently diverse. I had no idea what she meant by that, so I smiled and nodded.

"What have you done?" she asked.

"I've developed invisible masks," I explained.

"What good are they?" she asked.

"If people wear these, we can still tell who's black and who's white," I explained.

She seemed satisfied with this answer.

"*Bueno*[13]" she said. "*Mi abuela*[14] would be happy with that."

I had seen Alexis Often-a-Cabron on TV several times. She didn't want to go by "Alexis," or even by "Cabron." She felt that using her *entire* moniker: "Alexis Often-a-Cabron," made her sound more "authentic,"

---

[12] *Cabron* is Spanish for dumbass.

[13] Spanish for "good."

[14] Spanish for "my grandmother."

although I'm not sure what her authenticity was. She'd grown up and gone to High School in a wealthy white Westchester suburb.

Maybe she just didn't want all of her wealthy white friends to recognize her. Maybe she'd taken some Spanish in college, so could now use words like "*bueno*" with confidence. Well, *bueno*.

"Excuse me," I said. "But is there something I can call you besides 'Alexis Often-a-Cabron'?" I asked. "It's rather long, and I'm not sure that I'm pronouncing it correctly."

"*Si*[15]," she said. "You can just call me 'AOC.'"

"I can't do that," I replied.

"*Por qué no?*[16]" she asked.

"Because if I say 'AOC,' people won't know whether I'm taing about 'Alexis Often-a-Cabron,' or about the '*Abuela* Of Cabron.' I don't want people to be confused," I explained. "Would AOC mean *you*? Or would it mean *your abuela*?"

She looked confused.

After a minute of AOC (or whomever she was) looking confused, Dr. Grouchi made a surprise announcement. "We're having two very special guests today. The fact that they'll be here is confidential. So please don't tell anyone that you saw them here."

He nodded to a guard who was standing by the door. The guard opened the door and beckoned to someone out in the hall. About a minute later, President Trompe[17] entered with two bodyguards, and then Slow Hidin' came in after him, also with two bodyguards.

Both the President Trompe and Slow Hidin' took seats at the front of the conference room.

"Thanks for having us," said the President. "I need to understand what you've all been working on, and where we stand with this virus. And I need to understand it bigly. Because I need to take this message to the people."

"And I need this to campaign with," Slow Hidin' said.

"Thanks for coming," Dr. Grouchi said. "What we've been able to learn is that this virus *did* come from rabid bats that were sold in the Wuhan markets. It *did not* come from their labs," he said.

---

[15] Spanish for "yes."

[16] Spanish for "Why not?"

[17] French for "deceived, fooled, or tricked."

"And how do you know this?" the President asked.

"Because they're our friends," Dr. Grouchi answered, "and they told me that."

"Is there a way to cure it?" the President asked. "I've given billions of dollars to the major US labs to create vaccines. They've all said that hydroxychloroquine will help most people that are infected. And zinc."

"We don't yet know how to cure it," Dr. Grouchi said. "But we're working on it. AOC also raised the issue of whether these vaccines will work on black people in the same way that they work on white people."

"When you say 'AOC,'" I asked, "are you referring to the congresswoman, or to her *abuela*?"

"I meant 'Congresswoman AOC,'" Dr. Grouchi said. "For those who don't know, '*abuela*' is what she calls her grandmother."

"Really?" Slow Hidin' asked. "Her grandma is a 'Beulah'[18]? I always loved that show."

There was an uncomfortable silence in the room. The younger lab people had never heard of "Beulah."

"Who's Beulah?" someone finally asked.

"If you don't know who Beulah is, then you ain't black![19]" Slow Hidin' proclaimed. "Beulah is the maid for the Hendersons."

After a moment of awkward silence, Dr. Grouchi said, "We expect to have vaccines within the next month; maybe two months."

"We have to take care of the cure that will make the problem worse no matter what, no matter what![20]" Slow Hidin' exclaimed.

Everyone looked confused.

"Well, keep up the good work," President Trompe said. "I'll need the latest data on infections, and where the disease has spread to. Please put this together, and get it over to the White House."

Slow Hidin' had been staring at AOC. "You know what I can tell just by looking at you?" he asked. "That you ain't black."

He'd found the perfect way to end the meeting.

---

[18] "Beulah" was an American sitcom series that ran on CBS radio from 1945 to 1954, and on ABC television from 1950 to 1953. "Beulah" was controversial for its caricatures of African Americans. The character Beulah was the Black housekeeper and cook for a white family.

[19] A partial quote from a well-known political figure in our government.

[20] An actual quote from a well-known political figure in our government.

"You have pretty hair though," he concluded. We could all see him curling and uncurling his fingers in synchrony with his breathing as he stared at Alexis Often-a-Cabron and contemplated her hair.

Carol and I went to Le Diplomat for dinner that evening. Le Diplomat is on 14th Street between Q and Corcoran in a lively part of town that's just West of Logan Circle. Its atmosphere is modest and unobtrusive – that of a brasserie. And like a brasserie, it's very busy.

Like a steakhouse, Le Diplomat has wooden-paneled walls. But unlike a steakhouse, the wood isn't dark; it's a light cedar color. And the wooden paneling doesn't go to the ceiling. It only goes to the height of the doors. Above the paneling, the walls and ceiling are an off-white. The ceiling has wide wooden beams that run across it in both dimensions, dividing it into several large, deeply-recessed areas. And each of those areas is further divided into squares that are set-off with carved joists. Lights hang from the centers of many of those squares. The atmosphere is somehow both casual and elegant, which is usually difficult to pull off.

The entire front of the restaurant is glass windows, so it never has the kind of darkness that's typical of a steakhouse. And the bar against the back wall provides some lighting as well. There are wooden floors and the traffic is brisk, so it has the all the sounds and busy bustle of a true brasserie. But the food is a cut above that of most brasseries.

Carol and I were seated at a table near the center of the restaurant, so we were right in the middle of its bustle. Professional waiters are quick, and when you're sitting in the middle of a busy place with wooden floors, it makes you appreciate just how quick they are. That can cause a ruckus unless the waiters move with professional grace.

Carol ordered a 2019 Vourvay from the Loire Valley, and I ordered a 2014 Bordeau, Château Le Boscq. Then the waiter handed us our menus. The menu at Le Diplomat is a standard French menu. It doesn't feature new abstract creations, so reading it isn't difficult – it doesn't require much imagination. Is this a good thing? While I like to imagine new creations, the basics can be the best.

"The invisible masks didn't seem to generate much discussion," Carol said.

"I thought that was strange," I said. "It's almost like they don't *want* the masks to be invisible."

Carol and I looked at our menus again, made our choices, and laid the menus down as a signal to our waiter, who came and took our order.

Carol ordered the foie gras parfait with a wine gelée for her first course, and pan roasted halibut with Hakurei turnips, baby fennel, fines herbs, and sauce *Bourride* for her entrée. Hakurei turnips are white, and sauce *Bourride* is a specialty of Provence and Languedoc. It's a sauce made from fish, shellfish, and vegetables. I ordered the steak tartare with capers and a raw quail egg sitting in the center of it for my first course, and duck l'orange with braised kohlrabi and sautéed spinach for my entrée. I realized that I'd probably need a different wine to go with my entrée.

"I think that the politicians are using masks – essentially mandating them – as a way to assert their imagined power," Carol said.

"My friend Danny told me that this would never happen in America," I said.

"I think that we've seen many new behaviors in the last year that most of us couldn't have imagined," she said.

"Like what?" I asked.

"Violence in the cities," she said. "Massive looting and vandalism. Businesses closing. And politicians mandating masks."

"You're right," I said. "A year ago, I never could have imagined much of this. Parts of Seattle and Minneapolis have been taken over by mobs. I didn't think that could happen."

We both thought about it, and sipped our wine until the waiter brought our first courses.

Carol's was a solid rectangle of goose livers that hadn't been pureed, but instead had been pressed into a block. It had a layer of wine gelée on the top of it, and was garnished with watercress and slices of black mushrooms. There were decorative symmetric swirls of sauce on her plate. Mine was a finely ground mound of red meat with an indentation in the center into which a raw quail egg had been placed. My plate had capers and chopped herbs surrounding the steak tartare.

While Carol had probably made the better choice for culinary flavor, I had been craving raw meat. I wondered whether this had anything to do with my imagined dreams with Grouchi in them. Since tonight would be a full moon, I couldn't help but wonder whether I'd see him again.

I tasted mine. It relieved some of those cravings. Then I broke the egg, folded it into the meat, added a few capers, and took another sip of my wine.

"What did you think of the special guests today?" I asked.

"That was a real surprise!" Carol said. "I'd love to be able to tell some of my friends about it."

"We were told that we're not allowed to tell anyone that they were there," I said.

"I wonder why not?" Carol asked. "Both of them came to a meeting about the virus. So what? I'd think that people would want to know that both of them were engaged."

"Like the masks, I don't understand that either," I said.

"Besides being in a meeting where the two of them dropped by, I didn't see the value of the meeting today," Carol said.

"Maybe there wasn't supposed to be any value," I said. "Maybe Dr. Grouchi just wanted lots of science-types in the room for those two so that they could see that Dr. Grouchi was working on the problem."

"Sometimes I think that Dr. Grouchi is part of the problem," she said.

I thought again about the visitations that I had from Dr. Grouchi in my dreams, and I took another bite of raw meat. It tasted really good!

We finished our first courses, and our wine, so the waiter asked if we'd like more. I asked to see the wine list again.

To go with my duck, I ordered a Brut Réserve, which is a Champagne. I thought that the bubbles would set off the orangey flavor nicely. Carol ordered another Vourvay. She said that it was very good, so she'd stick with it.

Our second glasses of wine were brought, and then our main courses. I took a sip of Champagne, and enjoyed the sensation of bubbles in my mouth before swallowing. It was very good, and very cold – as it should be.

My duck had a deep orange color. The skin had been roasted so that it was dark before the orange sauce had been added. It made the duck look almost like candy. And the dark green colors of the braised kohlrabi and sautéed spinach set off the orange color in a way that was almost startling. The duck had the sweet flavor of oranges. I was happy that I'd ordered the Champagne.

Carol's halibut was white, which made the yellowish color of the sauce *Bourride* look slightly orange. The Hakurei turnips, which are white, and the baby fennel, which is light green, gave her plate a light and healthy look. The chopped fines herbs showed up as a bright contrast atop these light colors.

We each tasted each-other's entrées. We usually do; that's one of those things that people who are married can get away with.

"Do you really think that this virus came from rabid bats?" Carol asked.

"That's what Dr. Grouchi said," I replied. "Why would he lie?"

"Many reasons," Carol answered. "Sometimes you're naïve. You always want to believe that people are telling the truth."

"You're right," I said. "But why would he lie?" I asked.

"Maybe the virus came from research that he was funding," Carol said.

I thought about that. "You mean that Dr. Grouchi is dirty? He's partly responsible for this virus?"

"I don't know," Carol said. "But that would be a reason for him to lie."

"You're right," I said, and I tried to picture Dr. Grouchi with his beady little eyes.

I drank some more Champagne, and ate my duck. I really enjoyed the greens that had come with it. We sat in silence for a few moments.

"What did you think of AOC?" Carol asked.

"Who?" I asked.

"The woman at the meeting who spoke Spanish," Carol said.

"Spoke Spanish?" I asked. "All she said were words like '*si*' and '*bueno*.' Everyone knows those words. She grew up in Westchester; in Yorktown Heights."

"Well I guess it's important to have someone in charge of diversity when it comes to viruses," Carol said.

"*Si*," I answered, and thought about it some more. "*Bueno*," I added, allowing her point.

We finished our entrées, and the bus-service cleared the table. The waiter re-emerged with dessert menus.

"Dessert, anyone?" he asked.

"Let's take a look," I said.

The waiter put the menus down and left. I picked mine up, and finished my Champagne. Carol picked her menu up and took another sip of wine. She still had a little bit to go. We each studied our dessert menu.

"What do you think about the apple-tart tatin?" Carol asked. "I don't think that I could eat an entire dessert by myself."

"That sounds good to me," I said. "I'll share one with you."

The waiter reappeared, and we ordered the apple tart. I also ordered a ramazzotti, which is an Italian liquor that has an almost syrupy consistency. Ramazzotti tastes a little like cola and bitter orange – it seemed like the right thing to follow my dinner of duck l'orange. Carol ordered an espresso – a decaf.

The waiter came back with our tart, two forks, and my ramazzotti. I took a sip of my liquor as Carol finished her wine. We waited until he returned with the espresso before starting to eat the apple tart, which came with some vanilla ice cream. It's good that we'd decided to share it.

"The election is this Tuesday," I said. "Have you decided who you're voting for?"

"Well, we got a first-hand look at the two candidates today," Carol said. "Which one impressed you the most?"

"They both impressed me," I said. "But in different ways."

"I just hope that we don't get a cure that will make the problem worse," Carol said. "No matter what!"

"No matter what!" I added.

We didn't know it at the time, but this was prescience at its very best.

We called an Uber, paid the bill, and left. Outside, there were Halloween revelers making their ways up and down 14th street, some in costume, and others not. The Uber came and took us back to the Intercontinental at the Wharf.

We were staying in a different room this time. It didn't have a balcony, and since it was now October, it was cool out. So we kept the windows closed. Maybe that's why I didn't have a dream about Dr. Grouchi this time, although I did notice the full moon before drifting off to sleep.

Although Dr. Grouchi wasn't in it, I did have another lucid dream.

In this one, I climbed out of bed, sprouted a set of wings, and flew through the wall of windows out into the cool evening, and clung to the outside of the window-frames. I could feel the breeze. It was refreshing. I looked back over my shoulder through the glass, and I could still see Carol. She was fast asleep.

I could hear the faint sound of the small waves in the harbor as they bounced off the seawalls, travelling downstream with the wind. While it was a mere pleasant breeze where I was, it was likely blowing harder out on the channel. I could still see the lights on at the Pentagon when I looked North.

Then I let go, and I flew! Soaring up into the sky, I looked at the spectacular blood moon in all of its glorious color. It lit up the harbor. And then I noticed others who were flying too.

I flew North and was soon at the National Mall. I circled the Washington Monument several times, and then flew to the Lincoln Monument, where I sat in Abe's lap, looking at the inscription of his second inaugural address on the North wall. Reading the second paragraph gave me pause:

> *"On the occasion corresponding to this four years ago all thoughts were anxiously directed to an impending civil war. All dreaded it, all sought to avert it. While the inaugural address was being delivered from this place, devoted altogether to saving the Union without war, insurgent agents were in the city seeking to destroy it without war—seeking to dissolve the Union and divide effects by negotiation. Both parties deprecated war, but one of them would make war rather than let the nation survive, and the other would accept war rather than let it perish. And the war came."*

He may as well have been talking about this coming Tuesday's election. I wondered who would win.

I awoke well-rested in the morning – not at all like the mornings following my dreams about Dr. Grouchi. I was eager for Carol to get ready quickly so that we could go get some coffee. Today I was full of energy! I felt like a new man.

17. The Presidential Election

While President Trompe had given special funding to six large pharmaceutical companies to develop a vaccine as quickly as possible, the first vaccine hadn't become available until December 11. The President had already had the virus, so he didn't get a vaccine until January. But Slow Hidin' was able to get one right before Christmas – on the winter solstice[21], which was December 21.

In fact, nothing like the progress on the vaccines had ever been seen before. Three of the vaccines had been developed in nine months, and were ready for deployment two months later.

But back to Tuesday's election. It was on November 3, about five weeks before the first vaccine became available. Because of the virus, many people hadn't come to the polls. Because of the virus, a record-low turnout was expected. But some people voted by other means. And some of them voted many times. And many new records were set.

Despite the virus, Slow Hidin' took more votes than any other candidate in the history of presidential elections: 81,268,924. While the incumbent president – Trompe – had also broken the national record by a wide margin, 74,216,154, Hidin' did *even better* than this. The two of them took first and second place in "most votes ever placed for a candidate in a presidential election." And this was despite the virus, which had kept many voters away from the polls.

This was especially impressive because Slow Hidin' didn't actually campaign. He had stayed in his cellar for most of the season.

But after having met Slow Hidin', Carol and I understood why he got so many votes. Slow was a delible[22] person: sharp as a spoon, with the quickness[23] of a fingernail. His vice-president was a new person in

---

[21] The shortest day of the year.

[22] While "delible" isn't an actual word, *indelible* means "making a mark or impression that can't be removed."

[23] While "quick" usually refers to speed, it also refers to the skin under your fingernail. That's its meaning in this case.

Washington called the Cackling Camel. While I'm not sure why they called her that, she never talked. Instead, she cackled in response to all questions.

Q: "Hi, Camel, how are you today?" A: "Caaacacacacackle!"

I could see how Cackling Camel had helped Slow. The main qualification that she had was that she was half black. Her father was Jamaican (not African-American), and her mother was Indian. Because of her Jamaican half, Slow would be unlikely to touch her hair. It would remind him too much of Corn-Pop's hair. That would scare him.

And she grew up in Canada, so she'd understand the African-American mindset. She was a great choice for capturing "American Blackness." At least she'd be safe around Slow, not that she minded "older men." Her early political career was facilitated by one of them whom she was – *(ahem)* – "friends" with. He opened many doors for her in return.

And on top of the cackling, she was very predictable in other ways. One of those was her attire.

There was a movie entitled "The Fly" that was about an eccentric scientist who builds a teleportation machine. He tries it on himself. He teleports himself from a chamber on one side of his lab to a chamber on the other side. Unbeknownst to him, when he does this, there's also a fly that's trapped in the chamber with him. And so on.

One of the scientist's eccentricities is that he wears the same outfit *every day*: black slacks with a black and gray tweed jacket. That way, he doesn't have to think about what to wear. In case you're not sure, the movie shows us his closet containing his entire wardrobe. It contains half-a-dozen pairs of black slacks, and half-a-dozen black and gray tweed jackets. He wears the same outfit *every day*.

But he's a weird and eccentric scientist. And he's a man. That almost makes it understandable. And always wearing the same outfit would make sense to lots of men.

Cackling Camel *also* wears the same outfit every day too: a navy-blue pantsuit with a white blouse. But she's a woman! Talk about *weird*. "Caaacacacacackle!" Eccentric? You bet. At least Slow doesn't touch her. Corn-Pop might give him what-for.

The election was on November 3, but the vaccine didn't come out until December 11. And Slow Hidin' wouldn't be sworn in until January. But since the vaccine came out a month after Slow Hidin' won the election with a record number of votes, Slow was able to claim credit for having developed the vaccine. And he was vaccinated on the solstice, before Christmas.

Slow Hidin' now came out of his cellar on rare occasions, but he always wore a mask. His handlers made him wear one so as to hide the gag that they'd put under it. Whenever they forgot his gag, Slow Hidin' had a knack for saying lots of things that embarrassed his supporters.

We now had a new president. It was an election that will go down in history.

While Carol and I had sat through a meeting with Slow Hidin' there in person, and had gotten a feeling for who he was, he seemed to go downhill after the election. I couldn't help but wonder whether the virus had anything to do with it.

Despite that, Slow Hidin' was one of the nicest old ladies that I'd ever met.

In this election, the incumbent president set the all-time record for the number of votes received. But Slow Hidin' beat that by almost 10%. And that was without campaigning.

The incumbent president – Trompe – had also carried four vital bellwether states: Ohio, Iowa, North Carolina and Florida. These states are reliable bellwethers because they contain strong bases of urban, suburban, rural, union, and ethnic minority voters. That is, they all have large diverse mixtures of people. In addition, these four states have all elected the same candidate thirteen times since 1896. Every single time, that candidate won the presidency.

"Bellwether" is a term applied to regions that overwhelmingly predict the election correctly.

In addition to bellwether states, there are nineteen bellwether counties that always go to the winner. The incumbent president – Trompe – won eighteen of these. The only one that he lost was Clallam County, Washington. It's truly amazing that eighteen of the nineteen counties that always pick the winner were wrong. Can you believe that?

Since 1892, *all* incumbent presidents who increased their total number of votes won re-election. Since then, only six presidents have lost re-election. All six of them had fewer total votes in their re-election campaigns than in their initial campaigns. But this year, the incumbent gained a record number of votes: eleven million. But he lost. If you can believe that.

The share of the votes received by an incumbent in the primary election has always been a reliable way to predict his chances for re-election. Primary elections weren't done before 1912. Since 1912, only four incumbents have lost re-election.

Of these four, only one of them, George H. W. Bush, got much more than half of the votes. He won 73% of the votes in the primary (which is lukewarm for an incumbent), and lost re-election. Herbert Hoover did miserably for an incumbent, getting 36% in his primary, and failing to be re-elected. Jimmy Carter got 51% in his primary, and Gerald Ford got 53% in his primary. Both lost re-election. That's understandable: if you can only pull half of your own base, you're not likely to win the general election.

Re-elections that were landslides were for Dwight Eisenhower (receiving 86% of the vote in his primary), Richard Nixon (receiving 87% of the vote in his primary), and Ronald Reagan (receiving 99% of the vote in his primary). As the incumbent, President Trompe won 94% of the vote in his primary. But he lost the election. If you can believe that.

Slow Hidin' lost the Democratic primaries in the three main Democrat bellwether states: Iowa, New Hampshire, and Nevada. His running mate, Camel, had dropped out of the election before the Democratic primary election because she wasn't viable: she failed to draw even 1% of the vote.

Florida bears special mention. For the last century, Florida's trajectory (increase or decrease in the direction of the votes) has matched Michigan's and Pennsylvania's. They all share (approximate) working-class demographics. If Florida became more Republican (with respect to the previous election), so did Michigan and Pennsylvania, and vice-versa. In 2020, President Trompe won Florida by a margin that was 2% higher than it was in 2016. For the first time in a century, Pennsylvania and Michigan followed the opposite trajectory.

So called "down-ballot voting" has always been a very strong indicator of election success. "Down-ballot voting" means that the electors choose the president, and *then* they vote for all of the other people in their chosen president's party. For example, when Obama won a strong victory in 2008, the Democrats also took 14 House seats from Republicans. And when Reagan was elected in 1980, the Republicans gained 34 seats. But in

2020, while Trompe allegedly lost, the Republicans replaced 13 incumbent Democrat seats without losing a single Republican seat. If you can believe that.

It only makes sense that if the Hidin' electoral landslide had been real, he would have taken at least a few House seats too. He didn't take *any*. Is that believable?

Another interesting fact is that candidates that sway the voting among minorities win. Trompe set historic records in swaying the minority vote towards Republicans (himself). He netted more than 25% of the minority vote in the 2020 election. And at the same time, the minority Democrat turnout was much lower than it had been when Obama was the candidate.

How was Slow Hidin' able to surpass Obama's popular vote record by 12 million votes with a low minority turnout?

18. Thanksgiving, and The Beaver Moon (November 30)

The full "beaver moon" came on November 30. The beaver moon is the moon during the entire month of November. This is when the beavers scavenge, and store food for the winter. After the full moon, they stay in their huts until the spring. This particular full moon also featured a penumbral eclipse. While the moon isn't actually eclipsed, and it can be in direct sun, the earth blocks some of the light that the moon would otherwise get.

It was Tuesday, less than a week after Thanksgiving. We'd had Thanksgiving leftovers for dinner, and I had another spectacular dream.

I actually prefer Thanksgiving leftovers to the Thanksgiving dinner itself. When you're eating leftovers, you really only take what you want. At a Thanksgiving dinner, you feel too compelled to try a little of everything – which can be a bad idea.

I made myself a turkey sandwich, and so did Carol. I prefer the dark meat because it's more flavorful. Carol prefers the white meat because she thinks it's healthier. I put mayo on my roll, layered on some dark turkey meat from the thighs, sprinkled on some salt and pepper, and topped it off with a handful of fresh mint leaves, and fresh corriander. I took a spoonful of cranberry sauce, which I put on the side. I make cranberry sauce using the whole berries, and some mandarin oranges. And I microwaved a serving of green-bean casserole.

Carol took some parsnips and some turnip greens, and heated up a small serving of mashed potatoes with gravy. It was a simple dinner for both of us. Simple dinners are among the best. And we didn't both have to have the same thing.

We ate our dinners in the family room, and watched the news. There was nothing new. The usual cities were on fire.

We cleaned up, watched a movie, and went to bed. And I had another lucid dream.

While asleep, I got out of bed, went downstairs, and somehow diffused through our bay doors, which put me on our back deck. Diffusing through the doors allowed me to leave the house without turning the alarm system off. This might have awakened Carol, as the buttons on the control panel beep when you push them. Diffusing through the doors was a better solution. That's how I knew that I was dreaming.

I looked up at the beautiful full beaver-moon. Despite it's being penumbral, it seemed to be as bright as it usually was. Sometimes it's hard to see the dimming effect of a penumbra. It depends a lot on the atmosphere. And the night was dry, which helped a lot.

As I looked up at the moon, I saw occasional winged people fly past with their wings spread wide. I spread my wings, and flew up into the sky. It felt wonderful! I remembered that Dr. Grouchi had told me that zombies could fly during full moons. But that might have been a dream. I still wasn't sure. Yet here I was, flying – or I seemed to be.

First, I flew around my block, seeing whose lights were still on. My bet was that most of them had had Thanksgiving leftovers for dinner too.

After circling the block, I flew straight up into the air, headed towards the moon. I looked down to see my tiny little neighborhood in the middle of a vast landscape – the way it looks on Google-maps. I could see lights on the few highways that crossed the landscape.

Finally, I flew back down to earth, landing on my deck. I stood and watched the beautiful moon for a few minutes with the occasional person flying past. And then I diffused back through our bay doors. I was standing in the kitchen which was lit by the single light that we'd leave on over the sink. The moon was still shining through the windows, and I could see my shadow against the far wall.

All that flying had made me very thirsty.

I got a glass from the cupboard, and poured myself some iced-water. I downed the water in a swallow. I thought about Google-maps again. The problem with the '*maps*' is that when you see them backwards, they're '*spam*.'

I left the glass on the counter, and went back upstairs; back to bed. It had been quite a dream. I slept soundly for the rest of the night, and I don't remember any more dreams.

When I got up the next morning, I felt great. I was fully refreshed by my night's sleep. While I knew that my dream about flying was just that

– a dream, it gave me pause when I went downstairs to get a cup of coffee, and saw the water glass that I'd dreamt that I'd used last night.

It was sitting on the counter – right where I'd left it in my dream. I wondered whether it had really been a dream.

19. A Letter to Santa

In preparation for Christmas, and as we do every year, we wrote and mailed a letter to Santa. Here's a copy of it:

Dear Santa,

I hope that all is well with you.

Carol and I don't really need anything, so whatever you were thinking of leaving us, please give it to a needy family instead. What we'd really like, if you can make it happen is world peace, although I know that's a tall order. If you can make it just a little more peaceful, that would be good.

What's new with me this year is that I was bitten by Dr. Grouchi, and now have some form of the Rabid-Bat Virus (RBG). If anything, it seems great: I'm as healthy as I've ever been. And on full moons, I can fly around in the sky. It's beautiful. I've gotten a small taste of what you must see when you fly your sleigh on Christmas Eve.

While the RBG seems almost like a blessing, my life's experience tells me that nothing is free. There must be a downside to having been infected. Can you let me know what the story is here?

Say "hello" to all of your elves for us. I know that they work very hard, and this makes lots of children very happy. And give Mrs. Claus a big hug from us.

While Carol and I don't need gifts, please stop by anyway. I'll bake some of your favorite cookies for you, and I'll leave a bag of carrots for the reindeer.

Best wishes, and Merry Christmas…
Carol and Mick

I proofread the letter, and mailed it to him at the North Pole. I hoped that he's get it on time.

20. Christmas Eve and Christmas Day

On Christmas Eve, the temperatures rose into the mid-forties, which melted one-to-three inches of the accumulated snow. In addition, we had another three inches of rainfall. It was a wet day. And we had high winds caused by low pressure in the West. The winds were as high as sixty-five miles per hour.

It wasn't to be a full moon. While part of me wanted a full moon – so that I could fly about, and perhaps see Santa – the other part of me wouldn't have wanted to fly through the sky in this weather. For the first time, I really knew how Santa must have felt.

Carol and I had put out tree up a week ago, and decorated it with some exotic ornaments that we keep in the attic. We've a set of large silver bells with ornate cloisonné carvings on their outsides, and with ivory insets on their insides, and another set of large copper bells that were made the same way. I always enjoy putting these up.

I'd put some Christmas music on to play in the background as Carol and I made dinner together. It was a mixture of Frank Sinatra, Bing Crosby, and Nat King Cole, all singing the standard Christmas songs.

We kept our dinner simple, but elegant: a medium-rare fillet mignon with half of a lobster tail atop each one, a twice-baked potato, using bacon, spring onions, cheddar, and blue cheese, and some steamed asparagus with hollandaise sauce. These are all very simple to prepare. The only thing that's a slight amount of work is the potato. I did the potato and the hollandaise sauce. Carol did everything else.

We sat in the dining room for dinner at about 7:30, and I changed the music. *Die Fledermaus* is an opera that's typically performed during the holidays, when everyone is merry. It's an opera by Johann Strauss II. In English, *Die Fledermaus* simply means "The Bat," although the opera is usually called "The Revenge of the Bat." I put on the last act.

Die Fledermaus is a comedy about a man named Eisenstein who skips his first mandatory night of jail (a penalty received for a minor infraction) to attend a fancy ball at which his wife, Rosalinde, appears masquerading as a semi-masked foreign countess. She comes with her maid, Adele, who's also dressed to kill. It's a very merry party, with lots of drinking and dancing. Eisenstein doesn't recognize his wife, and tries to seduce her, thinking that she's a foreign countess.

And all the while, he's being laughed at by Falke (the bat), and by the host of the party who is a Russian prince. The comedy of errors was created for the prince by Falke, a notary who was once humiliated by Eisenstein. A while back, when Falke had been very drunk and wearing a bat costume, Eisenstein had deliberately abandoned him in the town square to be discovered sleeping in his bat costume the next day.

Meanwhile, in the opera, Frosch, the jailer, goes to Eisenstein's house to pick him up. Frosch finds Alfred there. Alfred is Eisenstein's wife's boyfriend. But Frosh assumes that Alfred is Eisenstein, so he hauls him off to jail before going to the party – to which he'd also been invited.

At the party, he befriends the real Eisenstein. In the end, there's lots of merriment with everyone forgiving everyone else for their misbehaviors while dancing and pouring more wine. The grand finale is "The Champagne Song":

> *"I sing to the king fermented; bubbly ornamented. There's simply no describing the pleasures of imbibing. The curse of human dryness is banished by his highness. Champagne the first: The king by acclimation, the monarch of libation in bubbly coronation!"*[24]

Die Fledermaus is performed during the winter holidays because of all of its merriment and gaiety. This Christmas Eve, I thought *Die Fledermaus* was especially appropriate because of "the bat," who has a wonderful time getting his revenge in the middle of lots of merriment. I thought of Dr. Grouchi. Dr. Grouchi was "The Bat" – with his beady little eyes.

After cleaning up, I poured a brandy, and we went into the family room to watch "Miracle on 34th Street," a classic movie that came out in 1947. It's about Christmas. It was very "woke" for its time.

The location, 34th Street, is where the original Macy's still is: on Herald Square. In the movie, an old degenerate bearded man arrives in New York

---

[24] The character Orlovsky starts "The Champagne Song" from Die Fledermaus, by Johann Strauss II. English translation.

City. While he looks like most old degenerate bearded men in New York City, he wants to be the Santa Claus at Macy's. He is irate that the man that was hired to be Santa Claus in the Thanksgiving Day parade is a drunk, just like most of the Santa Clauses in New York City, as well as in most other cities.

So Macy's hires him. The problem is that he's senile: he thinks that he really *is* Santa Claus. The woman that organizes all of the Thanksgiving and Christmas events for Macy's is divorced. She has a young daughter, who's befriended by the new Santa Claus. She also has a pretty serious boyfriend.

Her boyfriend is a lawyer. He has his own apartment. Back then, men and women that weren't married didn't live together. In his bedroom, he has *two* single beds. Back then, movies never showed king-sized beds – even for married people. So the *two* single beds indicate some kind of a sexual relationship.

The lawyer boyfriend tells the old man that he's welcome to come sleep in his other bed (*wink, wink*). In other words, whether or not his girlfriend knows it, he swings both ways – even with an old bearded crazy guy that thinks that he's Santa Claus.

The bad guys (the guys who run "The Corporations") want Santa Claus removed because he's obviously crazy because he thinks that he's really Santa Claus. So (they argue), he's probably a danger to the children. And they don't even know about his sleeping arrangement with his lawyer! His boyfriend defends him, and he eventually wins.

The defining moment in court is when the Post Office delivers the mail that's addressed to Santa Claus – all of it. Everyone in the court was astounded by that: the Post Office delivering *all* of the mail! So the court decides that if he wants to think that he's Santa Claus, then even though he's not a drunk, fine. Something is funny when the Post Office delivers *all* of the mail: maybe the guy's really a union boss, they thought, so they let him slide. He could probably could have all of their heads busted if he wanted to.

Meanwhile, the little girl – the daughter of the lawyer's girlfriend – tells the old man that what she really wants for Christmas is a house in the 'burbs. The city was becoming too dangerous, and the mayor wasn't taking crime seriously. The mayor wanted to defund the police. But the problem was that the exodus from the city was driving suburban real-estate prices up. So the old man that thought that he was Santa Claus wasn't sure that he could actually help. But - he told the little girl, it was the thought that counted.

In the end, the lawyer proposes to the woman, they draw up some prenuptials, and they move to the 'burbs. They find the house that the little girl dreamed of. Everyone assumed that the interest rates would be going up, so they were in a hurry to close on the house before that happened. But the housing inspector found that the rear deck on the house had been built without a permit. This allows the lawyer to bid the price down quite a bit, and to close on time, although they had to bribe the building inspector.

When they move in, they find the old man's walking stick propped up against a wall. So now we realize that the old man had actually been the building inspector whom they'd bribed.

A very good movie, albeit with a pretty sleepy ending.

And speaking of sleepy, it was well after 11:00, so it was time for bed. Carol and I took our wrapped presents to each other out of their hiding places, and put them under the tree. We'd open them in the morning.

I put out a plate of cookies for Santa, and a bag of carrots for his reindeer, as I had promised. We went up to bed. I was going to miss Santa Claus, but I was too tired to stay up.

That night I had a strange dream. While I didn't have a visit from Dr. Grouchi, he was in it. He was *Die Fledermaus* – The Bat. The dream was a re-enactment of the opera.

Falke – "*Die Fledermaus*" himself – was played by Dr. Grouchi. He wore his bat costume throughout the opera. The president – Trompe - played the Russian prince. Dr. Grouchi ("The Bat") was always trying to amuse him, which never failed to amuse him, although to the audience, Dr. Grouchi became tiresome very quickly.

Slow Hidin' was Eisenstein. He didn't know who he was or where he was. He should have been in jail, but he skipped bail and went to a party with the Russians, who were paying him under the table. He forgot who his wife was, and he thought that his wife was his sister. But then he was smitten by the hair of a woman who was pretending to be a countess. She was played by the Camel. He lost interest in her when he found that her hair felt "Black" like Corn-Pop's.

The Camel never sang any words. She merely cackled her way through the entire opera: "Caaacacacacackle!" It was horrifying.

Cackling Camel brought her maid, Adele, with her. The Camel was wearing a navy-blue pantsuit and a white blouse. In this version, Adele went by her full name: Alexis Often-a-Cabron. And whenever she sang, she tried to sing in Spanish instead of in German. But she didn't seem to know many words besides "*si*," "*bueno*," and "*abuela*." That was about it. She could just as easily have sung "*ja*," "*gut*," and "*oma*" (those same words in German).

There were other people there too: Governor Blowmo, Mayor deBozo, and lots of people in white lab-coats. Governor Blowmo chased the women around and grabbed their butts ("an Italian thing"), and Mayor deBozo was wearing mirror shades, a Hawaiian shirt, and a Panama hat. The people in white lab-coats were there to keep the others safely medicated.

In the finale, everyone was chugging Champagne at The French Laundry in California ($350 a person, *prix fixe*), none of them wearing masks. It was a nightmare if I'd ever had one.

While *Die Fledermaus* (Dr. Grouchi) embarrassed Eisenstein (Slow Hidin') many times, Eisenstein never realized it – he was too senile to grasp what was happening. By the end of the performance, it became clear that while *Die Fledermaus* thought that Eisenstein was a fool, he was actually working for him.

And the Camel had the last laugh: "Caaacacacacackle!"

In the morning, we got up and had breakfast together before opening our presents. The cookies that I'd left out were gone, as was the bag of carrots. Santa had left a note on the plate where the cookies had been. I'd read it later.

For breakfast, we had bagels and lox. Who said that Christmas can't be a Jewish holiday?

Remember that Jesus was Jewish. In fact, when the Three Wise Men came to Bethlehem with their gifts to celebrate the birth of Christ, they appeared overly generous. They brought the baby Jesus some gold, some frankincense, and some myrrh. A lot of stuff! But then they reminded Mary and Joseph that while their gifts *were* generous, they were joint Christmas *and* Birthday presents, so they hadn't really gone that far overboard.

With our bagels and lox, I also opened a split of Champagne.

I'd gotten Carol two gifts: an Apple Watch, and a cardigan. Wrapping them had been difficult, since I always like to switch boxes just to keep Carol guessing. While the Apple Watch fit easily into the box made for the cardigan, I had to use some strength and pressure to get the cardigan to fit in the box made for the Apple Watch. I hoped that the cardigan would survive that ordeal.

Carol got me just what I wanted: a set of airpods, and a new Kindle. I like to use airpods to listen to music and classes when I'm out running in the morning. And the new Kindle has much better lighting, and is waterproof. And it has room for even more books.

At the time, I was re-reading "The Living Thoughts of Kierkegaard," the parts of which he wrote under different pen-names. It's the first book that adumbrates "existentialism," which puts the task of bringing a man to life squarely on his own shoulders through self-defining action and choice. What unites the entire work is his all-abiding concern with the meaning of "existence." This concept would sound foreign to many people today.

Many today think that this is the job of the government. That's a dangerous beginning.

21. A Letter from Santa

Carol and I each got another cup of coffee, then sat down to read the note that Santa had left.

Dear Carol and Mick,

You're right that world peace is a very tall order. I'll do what I can, but I can't promise much. Maybe your new president – Slow Hidin' – can bring it about.
The cookies were delicious, and the reindeer really appreciated the carrots. Thanks for those. I gave Mrs. Claus a hug from you both!
We – at the North Pole – tried to leave a toy for every child. And while you're right that flying through the sky is thrilling, having the RBG isn't a good thing. Flying through the sky is what I do. But I'm Santa Claus! Flying through the sky isn't for mortals.
My recommendation is that you find a cure for the RBG. While you think that flying through the sky is thrilling – and it is – it's like a drug: thrilling, but you shouldn't be doing it. It will slowly drain your life away.
Cure the RBG. Thousands – even millions – of people will benefit.
Again, stay good! And thanks again for the cookies and the carrots!

Merry Christmas,
Santa Claus

22. The Cold Moon (December 29)

The "cold moon" is the last full moon in December. This year, it came on December 29. It came between Christmas and New Year's Eve. Since it was only a week after the solstice, the night was very long, and the moon was very high in the sky.

The sky was crystal clear, and the temperature fell into the upper thirties. It was going to be a beautiful night for the long cold moon.

In the middle of the night, I arose from bed, went downstairs, and diffused through the bay doors out onto our deck. I looked up at the moon, and I saw occasional outlines of tiny winged persons, silhouetted, flying past the moon.

A pair of them flew down to my deck, where they landed lightly; one on each side of me. It was Dr. Grouchi and Slow Hidin'. Each of them was wearing three masks.

"Good evening, gentlemen," I said.

"Good evening Dr. Moose," Dr. Grouchi said.

"It's pronounced 'mouse,'" I said. "Good evening Dr. Grouchi."

"Do you know Slow Hidin'?" he asked, pointing to Hidin'.

Slow Hidin' looked confused.

"We were all in that meeting together," I said. "I met Slow there."

I shook hands with Slow Hidin'. He looked confused.

"I can tell you that I've known eight presidents," Slow Hidin' said. "And three of them intimately.[25]"

"Are you sure about that?" I asked.

"I'm not confident of anything. I'm just stating the facts," Slow said.

"I work for Slow now," Dr. Grouchi said. "Would you like to fly with us?"

"Yes," I said. "That sounds like lots of fun. How did you get all the way up here from Washington?" I asked.

"When you've got the virus, you can teleport," Dr. Grouchi said.

"Teleport?" I asked.

"Not exactly," Dr. Grouchi said. "But you can travel at nearly the speed of light!"

[25] An actual quote from someone who is very visible in politics today.

"How do you do that?" I asked. "From Washington D.C., you could get here in about 1.3 milliseconds."

"How long is a millisecond?" he asked.

"It's one one-thousandth of a second," I said. "It would take about 1.3 one-thousandths of a second to get from here to Washington."

"Well, just like how you diffuse through your door, you can travel at the speed of light," Dr. Grouchi said.

"But the physics of those things is very different," I said.

"Well, maybe it was the speed of sound," Dr. Grouchi said. "One of the technical guys told me, and I forgot."

"That would get you here in about twenty minutes," I said. "That I can believe."

"Twenty minutes?" Dr. Grouchi asked. "Yes, it was about that long," he said, looking at his watch. "Sometimes I get the things that the science guys tell me mixed up. I can never remember what a millisecond is."

"It's like watching a yo-yo," Slow Hidin' said. He paused, and gave us a glassy-eyed stare. "I shouldn't have said it that way."

"That's an interesting way to think about it," I said. "I'll tell you what. Let's all fly to Washington. You guys have to go back there anyway. And I can find my way home alone."

"OK," Dr. Grouchi said. "OK Slow?" he asked Slow Hidin'.

"OK," Slow Hidin' said.

"Let's go to the Jefferson Memorial," I said. "I want to show you something."

We all flew off of my deck, and took a trip to Washington. The moon was beautiful, and it lit our way. I could see Washington as we approached it. We went over the White House, slowed down, and landed in the middle of the Jefferson Memorial.

The Jefferson Memorial sits on the Tidal Basin off the Potomac River, across from the Washington Mall. Its architecture was based on the Roman Pantheon. The front of it is on the Tidal Basin, and comprises a rectangular portico having eight columns. The structure itself is circular, also supported by Roman columns. The ceiling is hemispherical, and there's a statue of Thomas Jefferson standing under the center of the hemisphere. The statue of Jefferson is done in bronze, and is nineteen feet tall. There are panels on the walls with inscriptions on them.

"Slow, I'd like you to read that to us," I said, pointing to the second panel.

Slow Hidin' looked up, squinted, and began:

> *"Almighty God hath created the mind free. All attempts to influence it by temporal punishments or burthens...are a departure from the plan of the Holy Author of our religion... No man shall be compelled to frequent or support any religious worship or ministry or shall otherwise suffer on account of his religious opinions or belief, but all men shall be free to profess and by argument to maintain, their opinions in matters of religion. I know but one code of morality for men whether acting singly or collectively."*

"I'm not sure that I understand what it says," Slow Hidin' said.

"It means that you can't make people wear masks," I said. "Got it?"

"Masks?" he asked. "Is that another three-letter word? Like 'jobs'?"

I looked at Dr. Grouchi, arching my eyes to ask for help.

Dr. Grouchi shrugged. "He's my boss," he said. He shrugged again.

23. A New Year's Eve Party

Dottie and Danny decided to throw a New Year's Eve party at her house. They invited us, and three other pairs of their friends. We hadn't met any of them before. One was a friend of Danny's from the police force.

Carol and I walked up our driveway to attend. Carol brought some Christmas cookies that she'd made, and I brought a fruitcake that we'd been gifting-around within my family for several years. I also brought a mediocre bottle of Champagne. I didn't want to waste an expensive bottle on this crowd; I thought that it would all taste the same to most of them. I'd also grilled some thick slices of halloumi[26] that I thought would make nice hors d'oeuvres.

There were three new cars in the driveway when we got there. We rang the bell, and Danny answered the door to let us in. We wished each other a happy New Year, Carol and Danny exchanged air kisses, and I shook his hand. We brought the cookies and fruitcake into the kitchen, and put the Champagne in the fridge. Dottie was at work in the kitchen. Air kisses all around. "Happy New Year!"

Danny came into the kitchen and asked whether we'd like beer. Carol asked for some white wine. I asked for some scotch on the rocks. Danny poured Carol a full glass of wine, and handed me a glass which he filled with ice.

"The bar is in the dining room," he said. "Help yourself." He looked at the halloumi, and asked "what's that?"

"It's halloumi," I said. "It's a very special kind of cheese that greets itself in the first person[27]."

I took my glass into the dining room. Dottie had a bottle of Glenfiddich on the bar, so I poured some. I went back into the kitchen to get Carol, who was helping Dottie.

---

[26] Halloumi is a semi-hard, unripened cheese made from a mixture of goat's and sheep's milk, and sometimes also cow's milk.

[27] As in: "Hello, me!"

"Let's go into the family room," I said. "I'd like to meet your other guests, and wish them all a Happy New Year."

We went into the family room with Danny, who introduced us to everyone. We met Bill and Melanie Roberts. Bill was a police officer who worked with Danny. Melanie was a nurse who worked at the local hospital. We met Sal and Monica Caciocavallo. Sal ran a car dealership, and Monica did the billing for the dealership. They worked together. And we met Gary and Lucy Chao. Both Gary and Lucy were x-ray technicians. All told, including Dottie, Danny, Carol, and me, that made five couples at the party.

After the introductions, Carol and I made the rounds again, and chatted with everyone. We enjoy meeting new people. We always learn new things when we do.

We started with Gary and Lucy Chao. "You're both x-ray technicians?" I asked.

"Yes," Gary said. "And what do you do?"

"Carol and I live across the street," I said. "I'm semi-retired, but we take on contract work. I was a computer guy. Carol and I work together. Sometimes we do government work."

"What did you do with computers?" Gary asked.

"I was a professor for a while, and I did some work for the government," I said. "That's what Carol and I still do. And sometimes we do detective work."

"That sounds interesting," Lucy said, clearly not interested.

"It can be interesting," I replied. "You're both x-ray technicians? When you met," I asked, "what did you first see in each other?"

This led to an awkward silence, so we moved on. We went to talk to Sal and Monica Caciocavallo. "You guys run a car dealership?" I asked.

"Yes," Sal said. "And what do you do?"

"Not much," I said. "I live across the street. I was a scientist, and still take some jobs. Carol and I work together. Sometimes we do private detective work. That's one of the reasons that I keep in touch with Danny."

"You were a scientist?" Sal asked. "What kind?"

"Computers, and things like that," I said. "What kinds of cars does your dealership sell?" I asked.

"It's the Ford dealership down by the highway," he said.

"The Ford dealership?" I asked. "I pass that all the time. It looks nice. But I heard that there's a problem with the Mercury," I said.

"Really?" he asked. "I hadn't heard that. What's wrong with the Mercury?" he asked.

"They found traces of tuna in some of them," I said.

He wasn't sure what to say. We all nodded, and Carol and I moved on.

Finally, we talked to Danny's police friend, Bill Roberts, and his wife, Melanie. It's funny that Danny had never mentioned him before.

"Hi," I said. "I've been friends with Danny for a long time, and sometimes he talks about you."

"Really?" Bill asked. "What's your name again?"

"I'm Mick Maux," I said. "Me and my wife Carol live across the street."

"Danny and I have worked some very interesting cases together," he said.

"Yes," I replied. "He told me. I thought that one of the most interesting cases that he told me about was the one with that paranoid dyslexic guy."

"The paranoid dyslexic guy?" he asked, trying to remember something that never happened.

"Yes," I said. "He told me that the guy always thought that he was following someone."

"He was always following someone?" he asked.

"Yes," I said. "But he was paranoid. And dyslexic."

"What's 'dyslexic' mean?" he asked. "I forget."

"It means that you can mix up the orders of things," I said. "Do you know that I once went to a toga party dressed as a goat?"

There was a loud clapping of hands at the end of the room. That broke the conversation.

"Everyone!" Dottie exclaimed. Then Danny clapped his hands again. "Everyone!" Dottie exclaimed again. Danny and Dottie had come into the room and disrupted the conversations to get everyone's attention.

The room was quiet, and we were all looking at our hostess, Dottie.

"I'd like to try something different," Dottie said. "I thought it would be fun if we held a séance! I've set up the dining room for it. Please refresh your drinks if you'd like, and then let's all go in there and sit."

Carol went into the kitchen to get more wine, and I went into the dining room, poured myself a little more Glenfiddich, and found a seat. I saved the one next to me for Carol. Eventually, everyone was seated around the dining-room table, most of us with refreshed drinks. There was a Ouija board in the middle of the table.

"I thought that we'd start with the Ouija board, just to set the mood," Dottie said. "Then we'll get to the real séance."

Not all of us could reach the Ouija board. Dottie got up and dimmed the lights, and then sat down again.

"Those who can touch the planchette on the Ouija board, please put the fingertips of one hand on it," she said. "Don't put any pressure on the board. Touch it lightly. I want everyone to focus and to be quiet. We'll ask it some questions, and see if it has answers."

Those of us who were within range put our fingertips on the planchette. Carol and I were in the center of the table, so we were both able to put our fingertips on the planchette. Dottie was sitting opposite Carol, so she was able to touch the planchette too. And Sal Caciocavallo was sitting opposite me. Dottie was to his left.

"Now," she said. "Who has a question?"

There was a long pause, and Dottie finally decided to break the silence. "If you could talk to anyone," she started to ask. "Anyone, living or dead, who would it be?"

I couldn't resist, so I pushed the planchette ever so slightly. I made it spell out: "The live one."

I could tell that the people weren't impressed. So I asked another question: "Why is the alphabet in the order shown on the board? Why is it 'A, B, C, …'? Why not a different order?"

I pushed the planchette again: "Because of the song," I made it spell.

The people weren't sure about that one either. Various other people asked other questions, and we got various answers. Finally, Dottie stopped the back-and-forth.

"That's enough of the Ouija board for now," she said. "Let's move on to the actual séance."

She lit a candle, which she put in the center of the table. Then she got up and turned the lights off. Dottie was sitting next to Danny, who was at the long-end of the table across from us. Dottie was directly across the table from Carol.

The only light in the room was from the candle. Dottie returned to her seat across from Carol. To the right of Carol was Gary Chao. He was at the end of our side of the table. His wife, Lucy was sitting at the end of the table; the end that was nearest the doorway.

"We need to all hold hands," Dottie said.

Everyone reached out to hold the hand of the person to their right, and to their left. I was holding hands with Carol on my right, and Melanie Roberts on my left. Melanie had been sitting next to her husband, Bill, the police detective. Bill was sitting at the other head of the table – the end of the table away from the door.

Carol was holding hands with Gary Chao, on her right, at the end of our side of the table, and Gary was holding the hand of his wife Lucy, who was at the end of the table nearest the door. Lucy Chao was holding hands with Danny.

"Now close your eyes, and let's all concentrate," Dottie said.

After a moment, she said: "Now open your eyes, and stare into the candle. What is the thing that we all need to know? Any ideas?"

"The bat virus," I suggested. "Where did it actually come from? How many people will it kill?"

"Let's focus!" Dottie said. "Stare into the candle! What do we know about the bat virus?"

We all sat there staring, and we thought about the virus. All at once, the candle went out, and there was a woman's scream. I think it was Monica Caciocavallo, but I'm not sure. It came from across the table, and I didn't think that it was Dottie.

After a few seconds, the lights came on. Danny had stood, and turned them on. He was familiar with the house, and knew where the switch was.

We were all sitting as we had been. Except for Bill Roberts. He was still sitting at the head of the table. But he was dead.

24. Who Killed Bill Roberts?

Bill Roberts was a police detective, and so was Danny. Danny knew the procedures, so he called downtown immediately. An ambulance and two police cars showed up in about twenty minutes – roughly the same amount of time that it would take to fly to Washington at the speed of sound.

Detective Danny had told everyone to stay so that they could provide statements for the police record, and he told us not to touch anything.

I didn't follow that particular rule: I picked up my drink and went into the living room. Most of us did. Danny stayed with Bill's body, as did Bill's wife, Melanie. She was crying, and Dottie brought her a box of Kleenex.

Two of the police officers were taking depositions. The others were taking photos. One of the police officers took my deposition, and I told him what I could remember:

> *"I'd been holding hands with my wife Carol, on my right, and with Melanie, on my left. Melanie had been holding hands with her husband, Bill, who was at the head of the table. I couldn't remember who was on the other side of Bill. We were all staring at the candle, and it went out. Then a woman on the other side of the table screamed — it sounded like a woman, and a couple of seconds later, the electric lights came on. Detective Danny was standing in front of the light switch when the lights came on. Since Danny was Dottie's boyfriend, and it was her house, he knew where the light switch was, and had no problem finding it in the dark. I didn't know who it was that had screamed, or why. And when the lights came on, Bill Roberts was slumped over in his chair. That's all that I remembered. Except for the people that I'd mentioned, I wasn't sure who had been sitting where."*

"Someone told us that Dottie had everyone use the Ouija board first, but that not everyone could reach it," the officer said. "Do you know whether Detective Roberts had his hand on the thingy?"

"What's 'the thingy'?" I asked.

"You know," he said. "That thingy that moves around on the board to spell things."

"You mean the planchette?" I asked.

"Is that what it's called?" he asked.

"Is that what what's called?" I asked.

"The thingy," he said.

"It depends who you're talking to," I said. "If you're talking to most humans, it's called a 'planchette,'" I said. "But for small children, and people who are mentally challenged, we call it 'a thingy.'"

"Did he have his hand on it?" the officer asked again.

"Did who have his hand on what?" I asked.

"Did Detective Roberts have his hand on the thingy?" he asked.

"I don't know," I said.

"We'll take some prints," he said.

"From the thingy?" I asked.

"Yes," he said. "We think that the Ouija board might give us a valuable clue."

"Why is that?" I asked.

"One person said that an interesting question was asked of the Ouija board," he said. "Someone asked: 'If you could talk to anyone, living or dead, who would it be?' And the Ouija board said 'a live person.' And then Detective Roberts died."

"I see," I said. "Are you a detective too?" I asked.

"No," he said. "But I'm studying. I'm hoping to take the test next year."

"I think you'd make a great detective," I said. "The way you tied the Ouija board into this, and all."

He smiled. "Well, thanks for your deposition," he said.

While I'd been giving my deposition, the paramedics had carried Detective Roberts' body out.

Carol told me that she'd been interviewed by the other police officer. She'd told him the same basic story that I had. We didn't know whether

Detective Roberts had simply died of a heart attack, or something like that, or whether it was a murder. Or whether he'd touched the thingy.

If it had been a murder, neither Carol nor I could imagine how it could have been done. We were sitting in a quiet room, all holding hands, and all looking at a candle. The candle went out, there was a scream from across the table, then the lights came on. And there Detective Roberts was – dead.

And if he was murdered, who did it? We didn't know him, and didn't know whether he had enemies.

Detective Danny? He was good friends with Detective Roberts. That's why he'd invited him to the party.

Detective Roberts' wife, Melanie? Maybe they were having marital problems. But why would she kill him at a party full of people that she didn't know? It was too likely that she'd be caught. If she had wanted to kill him, there were lots of better times and places. A séance on New Year's Eve? Not likely.

Was there someone else at the party who knew Detective Roberts, and that would have a motive to kill him?

And who was it that had screamed on the other side of the table? And why?

25. Assault on the Capital

On Wednesday, January 6, 2021, the president gave a speech on the Ellipse in Washington, which is the public commons that's behind the White House. He challenged the results of the election. At the same time, congress was meeting at the Capital to debate those results. They had lots of questions too.

The president's speech went from 11:58 AM until 1:12 PM. He asked the crowd to march to the Capital, and to protest the election results which had raised many questions. That's why congress was meeting. They were questioning those results too.

The president importuned the crowd: "I know that everyone here will soon be marching over to the Capitol building to peacefully and patriotically make your voices heard." It was truly the rallying cry of a madman.

While demonstrations at the Capital aren't unusual, the Capital is a little more than a mile and a half from the Ellipse. At a brisk walking speed of three miles per hour, this is a thirty-minute walk. That would have put people who had stayed for the president's speech at the Capital at about 1:40.

A peaceful crowd of about three-hundred had gathered outside the Capital at about 12:30, and the crowd gained mass as time went on. The crowd first went through the barriers onto the grounds of the Capital at 12:53, about twenty minutes before the president had finished his speech on the Ellipse, and about forty-five minutes before people who had attended the president's speech would have arrived at the Capital.

Apparently, entry into the Capital by the protestors was "unlawful," although among the very few videos released to the public, guards can be seen moving the barriers aside and waving the people in. I'm sure that had I been there, I wouldn't have known that I wasn't supposed to enter.

We saw lots of footage of people peacefully walking around in the Capital, looking lost.

We did see two windows being broken. Other than that, there was no footage of actual vandalism or theft. One man lifted a lectern in the Senate chamber, and put it back. Another was dressed funny, for which he was arrested. Apparently, he's a QAnon shaman. And no one who entered was armed. That makes it very hard to understand why Slow Hidin' called it "the worst attack on Democracy since the Civil War."

And someone needs to tell Slow Hidin' that the Civil War was actually an attack on slavery. I can understand why he was ag'in' it – given his long history of racist remarks.

We did see an unarmed woman being shot to death by a member of the staff at a distance of about three feet. While we do know that the woman was a patriotic veteran who had served in the Air Force for fourteen years, the government would not divulge the identity of the staff member that murdered her. She was petite. He probably felt threatened by that.

There was also a Capitol Police Officer who died of a stroke (his second one) the day after the "*insurrection.*" Slow Hidin' would later claim that "the protestors killed him." Maybe it was taxes. Or the election: the man still couldn't believe it.

Half of Washington immediately labelled this an "*insurrection,*" which by definition is an attempt to overthrow the government. This was a strange word to use, given that no one tried to overthrow the government.

Despite the fact that there was no real "insurrection," and despite the fact that none of the "insurrectionists" were armed, and despite the fact that many of the "insurrectionists" had been waived into the Capital by the guards, and despite the fact that the only person killed was an unarmed protestor who was shot to death by a Capital guard, and despite the fact that the "insurrectionists" entered the Capital about twenty minutes before the president had finished his speech on the Ellipse – which is a thirty-minute walk away from the Capital – the president was impeached again for having "incited an insurrection."

After all, Slow Hidin', the new president, was to be sworn in in about two weeks, and he wanted to "bring everyone together." What better way to do that than to impeach the outgoing president?

At the time we didn't know it, but first, the newly elected Slow Hidin' was going to try to round up everyone who had been at the Capital, and incarcerate them. He treated them like prisoners at Gitmo. The shaman is still in prison despite not having been charged with anything. I guess he just looks funny.

But in fairness, many of the protestors weren't wearing masks.

To demonstrate their new spirit of bipartisanship, congress impeached the president a week later, on January 13, for "having incited an insurrection." This was only a week before the new president, Slow Hidin', was to be sworn in on January 20th. It was of critical importance for them to do this. After all, how else could they bring everyone together?

26. America's #1 Problem

Slow Hidin' identified America's top problem, and our top threat to democracy as "white supremists." You could have knocked me over with a fender.

The last white supremacist that I ever saw had been the Senate Majority Leader and the Senate Minority Leader, and the leader of the Democrat party for twelve years. He was also an Exhaulted Cyclops of the Ku Klux Clan. Slow Hidin' had read the eulogy at his funeral in 2010. I guess they were good buds – shared ideologies, and all that. He lamented the direction that the country was going in (color blind) when in an interview in 2010, he actually said: "There are *white niggers*. I've seen a lot of *white niggers* in my time."[28]

We also saw the medical school yearbook of the Governor of Virginia. He was standing with a friend of his. One of them was wearing a KKK costume; the other wearing a gaudy outfit with blackface. Which one was the Governor? It was hard to tell: the Klansman's hood completely covered his face, and the blackface on the other was so black that you couldn't see his facial features. But does it really matter?

While I've never met a white supremist, I know that they existed a long time ago. The Ku Klux Klan sprang from the Democrat Party in the 1860's following the Civil War. *They* were white-supremists.

Abraham Lincoln was the first Republican president, and he built his legacy on the abolition of slavery. Many Southern Democrats didn't like this idea, since they needed slaves to run their businesses. So they formed the KKK. They wore hoods and lynched people.

After the Civil War, the Republicans controlled the federal government until the Great Depression (1929-1940), when Franklin Roosevelt formed the "New Deal" coalition. This had the effect of prolonging the Great Depression until World War II, which pulled us out of it. Rather, World War II left the rest of the world so enormously devastated that America began to prosper again, at least in proportion to the rest of the world.

---

[28] Robert Byrd, Senator Majority Leader at the time of this quote.

In 1963, Martin Luther King gave his "I Have a Dream" speech from the steps of the Lincoln Memorial, and some big changes happened. The Civil Rights Act was passed in 1964, and the Voting Rights Act was passed in 1965. The Southern states became reliably Republican, and the Northeast became reliably Democrat – at least in presidential politics. It's been that way ever since.

Before 1964, many places in some states – including schools – were segregated. That ended with the Civil Rights Act. Within a few decades, Americans became color-blind. By the time of the new millennium, interracial marriage had become commonplace. In America, no one payed attention to your last name, where your parents were from, or what color your skin was. In America, the rule for personal interaction became very simple: money talks, and bullshit walks.

And during that period of our nation's evolution (and in many cases, earlier), the ten largest cities in the United States have become (practically) one-party cities. They're all run by Democrats. These are New York, Los Angeles, Chicago, Houston, Phoenix, Philadelphia, San Antonio, San Diego, Dallas, and San Jose. Some have been run exclusively by Democrats for more than sixty years. All of these cities are financially under water, and all have big crime problems. While bankrupt, most of them are going to increase their spending while cutting their police forces. Smart? It doesn't sound like they care about black people that much. Or budgets.

Some think that the way to deal with budgets is to simply raise taxes on "the rich." The problem with this is that after a few cycles of it, raising taxes drives "the rich" (and businesses) out, and tax revenues fall. Remember that businesses employ people who pay taxes. Many companies (and people) have left once-prosperous cities because of taxes. This doesn't help "the poor" at all. But it helps the political machines that runs the cities.

Since the 1960's, blacks became prosperous businessmen, doctors, lawyers, engineers, and politicians. Before then, the only prosperous blacks had been in sports and entertainment. The only real disadvantage that some people have today is that people who grow up in areas with strong union control of schools can grow up with very inferior schooling. This is true of people who grow up in our largest cities who don't have enough money for private schooling. But blacks who have made some money have moved out of those cities, which put their children on an equal footing with everyone else's children. And all of their children grew up color-blind.

Finally, in 2008, a black man was elected President of the United States. That wouldn't have been possible if most Americans hadn't become color blind. The man was a talented orator. Unfortunately, he had very little experience doing anything else. The only skill that he had boasted of was that of being a "community organizer." When he told the people that – that he was a "community organizer," no one was sure what that meant. Then they all learned.

"Community organization" is a skill learned from the school of socialism. It's the art of dividing people over trivial things. If you can split the people into small groups, and get them to hate each other, they will spend their energy blaming the other groups for all of their problems. That way, they will never coerce into a large enough body to blame the leaders of their country for any of the real problems. This has been done many times under socialist and communist regimes.

The great irony in the case of America is that most Americans are middle-class, so it's hard to divide people based on class. In America, "middle class" means that you can live in a decent house or apartment with heat and electricity and running potable water, own a car, put food on the table, and buy other things that you like – gifts, vacations, and other material goods – without too much difficulty. The fact that we have a very large and predominant middle-class made it hard for this black president to divide people based on class, as had been done throughout history by many other governments.

So what did he do? Amazingly, he used *race*! He started telling black people that our society had been evolved by white people for the purpose of keeping black people at the bottom. While welfare (as a lifestyle) will keep people at the bottom of the ladder, it doesn't have to be a lifestyle. But if people are kept there, they represent a powerful voting-block. And he told white people that they were greedy, and should set their aspirations lower to "make up for" slavery.

Keep in mind that very few "white people" had ancestors that were slave owners. Most have grandparents and great-grandparents that immigrated here within the last century. And of those who can trace their roots back to the Civil War, few were wealthy slave owners. Many fought and died in that war – the principle purpose of which was to end slavery.

At least 620,000 died in the Civil War, and it could have been as many as 850,000 – the records weren't clear back then. And the number of Americans killed in all other wars put together was about 644,000. The Civil War was *very* important to Americans. It was the bloodiest war that America was ever in. And it accomplished a great thing, although it took time for all aspects of its main goals – equality – to really come to fruition.

But the first black president, elected in 2008, pushed the idea that people shouldn't set their aspirations in accordance with their abilities, or how hard they were willing to work. Instead, the government should set people's aspirations for them according to the colors of their skin. *Amazing*!

And this from a black man.

Was he an African-American black man? No. His father wasn't African-American; he was Kenyan. And in his infancy, his mother remarried, and moved to Indonesia, where he grew up. While he went to High School in Hawaii, Hawaii is not the place to get any idea of what it is to be an African-American. Hawaii is unlike the rest of America: it's a small tropical paradise in the middle of the Pacific that grew from its own unique (*Aloha*) culture.

This **new** "racial-division" has manifested as "critical race theory." Many are trying to rewrite history and to teach children lies: that America was created for the purpose of promoting slavery. This "teaching" has nothing to do with history. It's pure Marxist.

But if they can get the poor-class to believe this, many will never climb out of it. And they'll vote for Democrats, which is the real point. Young people today never saw real discrimination or bigotry. It existed in the 1960s. It's gone today.

But many have been taught that we are all very racist. We're not. Everyone's money is good in this game. The key is to not live so that you are exclusively dependent on the government.

We've seen what happens to civilizations in which most people depend on the government. And we've seen it many times. It always results in massive poverty with a dictatorship government. And as we've said, money talks, and bullshit walks.

Money can be an evil drug. People shouldn't take "free money" to stay poor. Money is *never* "free."

In addition to all of the nonsense about race, we now have fifty-four genders. Huh? That's a full deck plus a couple of jokers! "Gendering" is another game of division. And it's slowly destroying women's sports, which as a nation, we worked very hard to build up.

White supremists? Since the man that Slow Hidin' eulogized at his funeral, I've not seen any. Maybe this is why Slow Hidin' thinks that "it's a big problem." And the guy that Slow Hidin' eulogized died in 2010.

One more thing. What's *"The Black Community"*? Many news channels and commentators use the term a lot. Is there something called *"The White Community"* too? Or are white people individuals who think and act independently, and black people an autonomous entity: a "mindless Community." An ignorant notion, indeed.

What about calling people what they are: *individuals*?

27. Bill Roberts' Autopsy

Detective Danny and I were both present for Detective Roberts' autopsy in the basement of the hospital. He'd died during a séance with nine other people sitting around a dining-room table holding hands, with the lights off. How?

The purpose of the autopsy was to try to determine that.

The autopsy began with an external inspection of the body. The pathologist started by weighing Detective Roberts, and then he measured what would have been his height had he been standing. He entered this data into his log along with Roberts' hair color, eye color, and ethnicity. We knew his age, so he wrote that in too.

He removed Roberts' clothes, and searched through the pockets. He found Roberts' wallet and cellphone, and a small notebook. He put those into a bin. They'd be given to his wife Melanie later.

He examined the body looking for gunpowder residue. There wasn't any. Danny and I had been there when he died, and no one had shot anyone. Had there been any residue, it could only have come from Roberts practicing at the police pistol range. The pathologist didn't find any.

He looked for paint and stain residues, and any other deposits. He found none. He noted a scar that Roberts had on his torso from an old surgery. He had a single tattoo on one of his arms: a heart with "Melanie" printed in the center of it. He didn't take X-rays, but took a hair sample and a fingernail sample. He put each in a small vial. Roberts had two small puncture wounds on the right side of his neck. But they were very small, and had healed. The examiner didn't think that they were important.

That was the easy part. Then came the internal examination.

This starts with a Y-shaped incision. The two arms of the Y begin where the arms begin: at each shoulder socket. The arms of the Y run to the sternum. The lower, straight-line portion of the Y is a straight cut from the sternum to the pubic region. These cuts allow the pathologist to open up the body and examine the organs in-place prior to extracting them. That's the reason for the Y-shaped incision: it allows the pathologist to remove the rib cage without disturbing anything else. The pathologist needs to examine the organs in-situ before removing them.

Since the heart is no longer beating, there's no blood pressure, so there's very little blood that comes out of anywhere from these cuts.

Next, the pathologist uses a saw to remove the ribs entirely from the body. He simply cuts through the ribs, and lifts the ribcage off. Then he frees the intestines by cutting along their attachment tissue with a scalpel. Then he lifts those out.

I was glad that I was wearing a mask.

He extracted each of the other organs in a similar way, then weighed and took tissue samples from each. Each was put into a fixative fluid in its own container. The fixative fluid preserves the organ. The organs can them be put back into the body or not. Frequently, they're not – especially if the pathologist decides to do more tests.

Next, the pathologist emptied the stomach, and those contents were tested for traces of poison.

The pathologist also took fluids: urine, blood, vitreous gel from the eyes, and bile from the gallbladder. These samples are used to test for drugs, infections, unusual chemicals, and whatever genetic factors might be relevant. These are lab tests that would be done later.

Danny and I didn't stay for the second part of the show: putting the body back together. I was happy to get out of the room. If you can stand the gore, being a coroner has to be the easiest job in the world. It's surgery on dead people. What's the worst that could happen? If you screw it up, maybe you'll get a pulse.

"It doesn't look like the examiner found much," I said.

"He didn't do the lab tests yet," Danny said.

"Do you think that Bill was on drugs, or something like that?" I asked.

"I don't think he was, but these days you never know," Danny said.

"What else?" I asked.

"Poison?" Danny suggested.

"How did he get along with his wife?" I asked.

"As far as I know, they were very happily married," Danny said. "I've known Melanie for a few years now, and I can't imagine her wanting to kill Bill."

"What about other people at the party?" I asked.

"I don't think he knew any of them," Danny said. "I guess it's possible that he might have given one of them a ticket, or something like that. But no one kills anyone over that."

"I'm interested in seeing the blood results," I said.

"Why?" Danny asked.

"I'm wondering whether a vampire has been feeding on him," I said.

"A vampire?" he asked. "That's just in the movies."

"Did you hear someone scream when this happened at the séance?" I asked.

"Yes," Danny said. "That was Monica Caciocavallo," he said.

"How do you know that?" I asked.

"She was on the same side of the table that I was on, but at the other end of the room," Danny said.

"She was sitting adjacent to Detective Roberts," I said. "He could have touched her."

But why would she scream if he had touched her?" Danny asked. "He was her husband.

"I think that we'll need to talk to her," Danny concluded.

28. We Interview Monica Caciocavallo

Danny called the Ford dealership and asked to speak with Monica Caciocavallo. After a minute or two, she picked up.

"Hello?" she said.

"Is this Monica?" he asked.

"Yes," she said. "Who's this, and how can I help you?"

"I'm Danny," he said. "We met at my girlfriend's house on New Year's Eve."

"Oh yes," she said. "I remember you."

"I don't know whether I'd told you, but I'm a police detective," he said. "I was wondering whether I could come and talk to you about exactly what happened that night."

"Is there a reason why you want to talk to me in particular?" she asked.

"No," he lied. "I'll be talking to everyone. Detective Roberts is the one who died. He and I worked together. I'm trying to figure out what happened to him. His wife is devastated."

"OK," she said. "I'd be happy to help if I can. But I don't really remember anything more than what I told the officer that took my deposition."

"I'd just like to go through it again," Danny said. "It's a mystery, and I'd like to figure it out."

"Of course," she said.

"When is good for you?" he asked. "I can come by the dealership tomorrow if that's easiest."

"That's a good idea," she said. "We can go in my office and close the door. Can you come at about 10:00?"

"Sure," Danny said. "That works. I'll see you then."

In the morning, Danny drove down my driveway to pick me up. He'd spent the night across the street at Dottie's. I went out to meet him. I was dressed, and holding a cup of coffee. He wasn't wearing his police uniform.

"Have you had your coffee yet?" I asked him.

"Yes," he said. "I'm fine. We can go down to the dealership from here. I'll drive you home afterwards."

"Sounds good," I said, and I got into his car holding my coffee. "Drive slowly," I said. "I don't want to spill this."

We drove down to the Ford dealership, parked in the front, and walked in. I was still carrying my coffee.

"Can I help you?" asked the young woman at the front desk. She was very nicely dressed.

"Yes," Danny said. "We're here to see Monica."

"Of course," she said. "Just a minute."

She walked through a door into the office-space in the back, and a minute later, she emerged with Monica.

"Good morning," Danny said, smiling.

"Good morning," Monica said, smiling back.

"You remember Mick Maux, don't you?" he asked, deferring to me.

"My pleasure," I said. "We met at the New Year's Eve party. I was there with my wife, Carol."

"Of course," she said. "Are you a policeman too?" she asked.

"Not exactly," I said. "Sometimes I work for the government. I do detective work when there are unusual cases. And whatever happened to Detective Roberts was unusual. Danny and I have known each other for quite a while, and sometimes I help him."

"I see," she said. "Well let's go back to my office where we can all sit down."

"Good idea," Danny said.

We all walked through the door that she had emerged from, and went down the hallway. Her office was about halfway down. It was very neat. She had several filing cabinets, and everything on her desk was in its proper place. I could see why she did the books.

I opened the meeting. "I thought that the séance was very interesting until the candle went out," I said.

"Do you know how he died?" Monica asked.

"No," I said. "Everyone was fine. We were all focusing on the candle: thinking about the bat virus."

"And then the candle went out," she said. "Do you think that the bat did it?"

"What bat?" Danny asked.

"The one that touched me," she said.

"A bat touched you?" I asked.

"Yes," she said.

"Did you tell the officer who took your deposition?" Danny asked.

"No," she said. She thought for a moment. "I didn't want him to think that I was crazy."

"Had you had a lot to drink?" Danny asked.

"No," she said. "I was on my second cocktail. But I was aware and alert."

"Were you using any drugs?" Danny asked.

"Are you asking that as a cop?" she asked.

"No," he said. "It will be off the record. I just want to make sure that you actually saw a bat."

"I *felt* the bat," she said. "And I knew that it was one. It landed on my neck. So I screamed."

Danny and I looked at each other.

"How did you know it was a bat?" I asked.

"I just knew," she said.

I thought that was curious. It hadn't even been a full moon. On the other hand, in my dream with Dr. Grouchi, he had told me that wúdí-wáng vampires can come out when the moon was *nearly* full, as it had been on New Year's Eve.

"Well, that's a big help," I said. "I had heard someone scream, but I didn't know who."

"It was me," she said. "And it was because of the bat." She shuddered.

We sat there in uncomfortable silence.

After a minute she said, "that was the weirdest New Year's Eve party that I've ever been to."

"I've never been to one where someone died before," I allowed.

"And I learned some things," she said.

"Like what?" I asked.

"Like I never knew why the alphabet is in the order that it's in," she said. "And the Ouija board told us that it was because of the song."

Danny and I left, and Danny gave me a ride home.

"A bat?" he asked.

"*Die Fledermaus*," I answered.

"What's that?" Danny asked.

"The revenge of the bat," I said. "It's an opera. It's in German."

29. What the Coroner Thought

Abat?" Danny asked me again. We were back in his car. "Do you have a few minutes?"

"Sure," I said. "What do you have in mind?"

"I'd like to stop by and talk to the coroner again," he said. "We'll ask him whether he has any new opinions."

"That's a good idea," I said.

Danny drove us to the hospital, where the coroner did his work. We checked in at the desk, and the receptionist called the coroner.

"I have two gentlemen here from the police department that would like to review your findings on the autopsy that you did for a William Roberts last week," she said into the phone.

After a moment, she said, "He can talk to you now. Do you know where the office is?" she asked.

"Yes ma'am," Danny said. "Thank you."

We walked down several hallways, then took an elevator to the basement. We took another hallway, and walked into the coroner's office, where we'd been last week.

"Gentlemen," said the coroner by way of greeting when we entered.

"Good morning," I said. "You probably remember that we were here when you did the autopsy on William Roberts last week."

"Of course," he said. "I thought you were going to barf."

"So did I," allowed. "I've never witnessed an autopsy before."

"After you've been a coroner for a while, the bodies don't seem like they belonged to real people," he said. "You learn to detach yourself from the procedure while cutting a body up."

"I'm amazed that you can stitch it all back together so that the family can have a credible open-casket wake," I said.

"The cuts are all under the clothes," he said. "Usually, we don't put the organs back in. We just stuff the body cavity with filler."

"What's in the stuffing?" Danny asked.

"Some bread, some onions, celery, a little butter," he said. "Things like that."

"I'd think you'd only do that if the guy was a turkey," Danny said.

"Most people that wind up in here are turkeys," he said. "Can I help you gentlemen with something?"

"Yes," I said. "We'd like to know if you've determined a cause of death."

"Sometimes that's hard to do," the coroner said.

"Did you find anything unusual in the various samples that you took?" I asked.

"Not really," he said.

"What about the blood?" I asked.

"What about it?" he asked.

"Was he anemic?" I asked. "Or something like that?"

"It's funny that you mention it," he said. "He was a little anemic. Why did you guess that?"

"If I told you, you wouldn't believe me," I said.

"Try me," he responded. "I've seen it all."

"We think that he might have been bitten by a vampire," I said.

The coroner stopped what he was doing, and he stared at me. Then he burst into laughter. "You guys are really something!" he said. "A vampire!" he laughed some more.

"Do you remember the two small puncture wounds on the right side of his neck?" I asked.

"No," he said. "Let me check my notes." He got the autopsy report out and read the first part. "There's nothing in here about puncture wounds."

"You mean you didn't write that in there?" I asked.

"I guess not," he said. "And again, I don't remember puncture wounds."

"Can we examine the body again?" Detective Danny asked.

"It's been cremated," the coroner said. "His wife wanted it done right away."

"Well what do you think killed him?" I asked.

"Honestly?" he asked. "I think he had a heart attack."

"Wouldn't that have been obvious when you did the autopsy?" Danny asked.

"Not necessarily," he said. "Some people die of heart attacks, and their cadaver looks fine."

"How did you report it?" I asked.

"As a heart attack," he said. "Like I said, some people die of heart attacks, and their cadaver looks fine. That's what happened in this case."

30. The Coronation of Slow Hidin'

The newly-elected president had his *coronation* on Wednesday, January 20. Since there had been an "*insurrection*," and since the person responsible for the safety of the Capital building is supposed to be the Speaker of the House, she had a seven-foot fence erected around the Capital building. It was topped off with razor-wire.

The Capital was now off-limits to the public. This really made it really look like a representative republic. Not.

While the swearing-in of a new president is supposed to be open to the public, the *coronation* of this newly-elected president was not. Attendance was limited to members of the House of Representatives (425 people) and to Senators (100 people). Each was allowed to bring one guest. So unlike the previous president, this president only had about a thousand people witness his *coronation*.

To ensure the safety and security of the 525 congresspersons, the Speaker of the House also had 26,000 National Guard troops brought into Washington, despite the fact that the *coronation* wasn't open to the public. That's ten times as many troops as we had in Afghanistan.

This is a really scary number. To put it into perspective, the National Mall is about 0.3 miles wide (North to South), and 2.25 miles long (East to West) going from the Lincoln Memorial to the Capital building. With 26,000 troops, you could put a heavily-armed soldier in every twenty-foot by twenty-foot square on the National Mall. Imagine that kind of firepower!

Why did we need that many troops? Why did we need to close the Capital, and put a seven-foot fence around it with razor wire? That's obvious. It was to make a statement. There was a new sheriff in town. The Speaker wanted to send the message that "the people" are not on a par with those in Washington. "The people" were no longer welcome in town. They weren't welcome at the Capital.

The new president stuttered his way through a wonderfully written speech about a new era of "bipartisanship." While short, his lengthy periods of lost focus, and his stammering transformed it into an impressive peroration.

"*... Democracy is fragile. And at this hour, my friends, democracy has prevailed... So now, on this hallowed ground where just days ago violence sought to shake this Capitol's very foundation... And here we stand, just days after a riotous mob thought they could use violence to silence the will of the people, to stop the work of our democracy, and to drive us from this sacred ground...*[29]"

Violence? The only violence that occurred at the Capital was the murder of an unarmed protestor by one of the guards – a guard that remains nameless – a guard that shot a petite woman who had both of her empty hands visible at a range of about three feet. "The people" don't have a right to know this.

Slow Hidin' continued on like this. And he referenced others: *"All men and women are created, by the, you know, you know, the thing.*[30]"

The speech was an inspiration. Had I been allowed to attend, I would have stood at the end, applauded heartily, and yelled: "Author! Author!" It's been my rule to never voice disparaging remarks about politicians. And despite what he said and his delivery, his speech was not going to make me break my habit of a lifetime. Certainly not for him, the big asshole.

Cackling Camel was also sworn in. She wore a navy-blue pantsuit with a white blouse to the ceremony. When they asked if she solemnly swore, she replied: ""Caaacacacacackle!"

It's been my rule to never voice disparaging remarks about politicians. Assholes.

---

[29] An actual quote from the swearing-in ceremony.
[30] An actual quote by someone who is highly visible in politics today.

31. The Wolf Moon (January 28)

The first full moon in January is called the "wolf moon" because it was when Native Americans heard wolves howling the most. It was the coldest part of the winter, and the wolves were hungry. The wolf moon has also been called the "freeze moon," the "frost-exploding moon," and the "cold moon." It's January, and it's cold out.

Before going to bed, I'd been working in my lab. I was listening to Bela Bartók's String Quartet Number 4. While it's nearly ninety years old, it sounds contemporary in many ways. He'd meant for it to have four movements, which was standard in those days, but it became five movements because of how he played with symmetry. While the rhythm isn't complex, its syncopation makes his Hungarian background obvious.

He had become interested in mathematics, so the fifth movement is a reflection of the first movement, and the fourth movement is a reflection of the second movement. He inserted a third movement in between these to experiment with what he called "night music" (an abstract sound, for its day). The first and fifth movements, and the second and fourth movements make heavy use of *sforzandi*[31] to tie them together.

His composition departed from the (then) traditional use of keys, and instead focused on the (arguably simpler) chromatic scale, trying to weight each note equally, using tonal centers, with motifs around those centers that are based on what he called "axes of symmetry." Again, he was interested in mathematics. And in his third movement, he used what he liked to call his "night music" style. The idea was to emulate the sounds of nature.

After listening to Bartók, I went to bed. Although it was January 28, I'd forgotten that it was a full moon. And it was a great night for some "night music."

I dreamt that I got out of bed, and was wearing a black cape with wings. The beautiful wolf moon was shining through our bedroom windows. So,

---

[31] Rhythmically accented chords or tones.

I spread my wings, and flew through the wall into the moonlight. I was vaguely aware of others flying about as well, but none of them were close.

The winter cold made the night crystal clear. I didn't feel the cold, but I saw the vapor of my breath. I flew up into the sky and headed south, toward Manhattan, which was all lit up. I flew down the Hudson River, headed toward the lights. Then I flew between the suspension towers of the George Washington Bridge. It was wonderful view. I could look down and see the hundreds of cars crossing the bridge at any moment.

What had I learned about the bat virus? Not much.

Not much, except that when there was a full moon out, you could take a wonderful flight, and awaken re-invigorated in the morning. Someone should have invented this virus sooner! I felt blessed that I had been given this virus.

Then a sobering thought went through my mind: this is how a drug addict feels when he's high. Was it really a bad thing? I didn't know.

I flew some more and watched the moon above. Eventually I went home and stood on the deck for a moment, looking at the moon.

"Hello!" I heard.

I looked behind me. To my alarm, Bill Roberts was standing there.

"Bill?" I asked. "Bill Roberts?"

"The one and only," he said. "How are you?"

I was still quite surprised. "I'm fine. What are you doing here?" I asked.

"It's a full moon, and I found myself flying around town," he said. "I didn't know where to go, so I flew over to Dottie's. I see that Danny's car is in the driveway! I remembered that they'd said that you lived across the street, so I flew down your driveway, and here I am!"

"But you can't," I said.

"Why?" he asked. "I'm a cop."

"But you're dead," I said. "And you don't have a body. You were cremated."

"That doesn't matter when there's a full moon," he explained. "I come back to life – fully embodied. And I can fly like everyone else."

I was still shocked. "Well it was nice to see you, Bill," I said.

"You too," he replied.

"I'll tell Danny that you said 'hi,'" I said.

"Yes, please do," he said. And he flew up into the sky.

I went in – diffusing through the wall, and I wound up back in bed where I slept soundly through the rest of the night.

In the morning, I woke up refreshed. I felt great. Or did I? Maybe I was coming off of a high. I remembered my encounter with Bill Roberts, and wondered whether it had really happened, or whether it had been part of a dream.

I went downstairs, wished a "good morning" to Carol, who was sitting in the living room reading a book, and I poured myself a cup of coffee.

Had I been living on a "high"? And if so, what were its root causes? Were the root causes the virus itself, or were they deeper than that? And what were the root causes of many of the problems that we were having as a nation?

America was having lots of problems. There were nightly riots in most big cities with billions of dollars in damages, many injured police, and lots of dead people. Slow Hidin' had opened our Southern border and had stopped construction of the wall. The number of undocumented immigrants crossing the border went from about 6,000 per week to over 200,000 per month. Murder rates more than doubled in many cities. So did rapes and other kinds of violent crimes – many of those motivated by race.

But Camel put her finger on it when she told us that the objective shouldn't be to stop those things. It should instead be to understand the "root causes" of those things. Apparently, we needed to "re-imagine" them.

True, Mayor deBozo had eliminated bail for violent felons, and released them back onto the streets within a day of being arrested. But what were the "root causes"? And true, all charges of theft and vandalism that were filed during the numerous riots in New York City were dropped, but what were the "root causes" of those crimes? It was going to take some "re-imagining."

And while it's true that the flood of illegal immigrants across the Southern border started when Slow Hidin' publicly stopped work on the wall, the important thing was to understand the "root causes" of people flooding the border. Why do people want to illegally cross the border? And why are they more inclined to do it when there isn't a wall there? What were the "root causes"? We needed to "re-imagine" reality.

Cackling Camel explained to us that it's myopic to simply observe reality. The key objective should be to *understand* reality by looking at its "root causes." So when we open the border and people flood across it, the point is not that they're flooding across it. The point is their "root causes." What would be the "root cause" for aliens to illegally cross the border? Maybe it's because they want to come to America. But what are their "root causes" for wanting to?

We can't close the border until we understand the "root causes" for making people want to come here. Could it be that America is a much better place than where they're coming from? Could that be the main "root cause"? That, and the fact that Slow Hidin' has made it much easier for them to cross the border? But again, what's the "root cause"? The key is to "re-imagine" it.

There are two ways to fix the "root cause" for people wanting to come to a better place.

First, we can make America worse than where the people are coming from. Slow Hidin' is trying to do this — except for the very rich, like himself. There are lots of ways to do this. Keeping the border open is only one of them. Raising taxes, raising gas prices (by importing it instead of producing our own), paying people to not work (so that small businesses can't operate), and many other things are other ways to make the country worse.

And the second way to fix the "root causes" is to make other people's countries better. How would we do that? We can't make other countries better unless we take them over. Is this what he means? That we should invade other countries and run them?

Alternatively, we can finish construction of the wall. "But this doesn't address the 'root causes'!" Camel will say. While she's right, we *can't* fix the "root causes." We can't fix the "root causes" of most things without becoming the "root causes" of other things. Did you know that we (Americans) were the "root cause" for all of the brutality in Cuba? We've learned this recently from AOC. All it takes is some "re-imagining."

We can never fix the "root causes" of crime. Throughout history, and in every culture, there has always been crime. Some cultures have reduced crime by a lot by having dictators that routinely execute people – and their families – over trivialities. In some countries, they will cut your hands off for stealing. While this doesn't fix the "root cause," it makes it very hard for you to steal again.

I don't think that's what we want. While it would be nice to figure out how to peacefully make people not want to commit crimes, that's fantasy. The purpose of putting violent people into jail is not to enlighten them. The purpose of putting them in jail is to protect the overwhelming majority of citizens who obey the laws.

Pondering "root causes" is pure metaphysics; it isn't governing. And even if we knew the "root causes" (and in many cases, we do), the government should fix the problems, not their "root causes." That would be what's called "governing." Fixing "root causes" takes a dictator, and the willingness to murder lots of people.

And speaking of metaphysics, where would it end? Once we know the "root causes" (e.g., people want to come to America because it's better, and criminals want to rob stores because there is no punishment), why not ask what the "root cause" of the "root cause" is? For that matter, what are the "root causes" of the "root causes" of the "root causes"? Where does this line of thinking end?

Instead of "root causes," I think that the Cackling Camel should instead focus on accessorizing, so that she doesn't seem to be like the man in "The Fly." How many things can you wear with a navy-blue pantsuit anyway? What are the "root causes" for her to wear the same outfit every day? Can't she "re-imagine" a new outfit?

Cackling Camel did explain the "root causes" for "minorities" (black people) not being able to produce picture-IDs to vote. Apparently, the "root cause" is that "minorities" (black people) don't live in neighborhoods that have a Kinko's or an OfficeMax nearby. This makes it impossible to make photocopies of your ID to prove that you are who you say you are. True, everyone has a cellphone that can take a picture of it, but we're talking about "root causes" here.

To quote Cackling Camel, "Of course, people have to prove who they are, but not in a way that makes it almost impossible for them to prove who they are." Huh? Of course, this makes the concept of a "voter ID" racist. How? You have to look at the "root cause." Whatever that means.

And then there's the root cause: just "re-imagine" it.

"I had another dream last night," I said to Carol.

"I think that we've figured out that these aren't 'dreams.'" Carol said. "Dr. Grouchi infected you. We need to figure out how to undo that. Where did you go last night?"

"I went down the Hudson River to the George Washington Bridge, and I had a wonderful view of the city," I said. "Then I came home, where I met up with Bill Roberts. Despite the fact that he'd been cremated, he says that he comes to life when there's a full moon. You're right," I added. "Like Santa Claus said, I have to beat this thing."

"You can't simply fly around during full moons," she said. "It's lunacy."

"You're right," I said. "Literally. That hit me hard this morning," I added. "Especially after meeting Bill Roberts."

"How did you meet Bill Roberts?" Carol asked. "He's dead and was cremated."

"Flying in the sky during a full moon is elating," I said. "But it isn't 'real' in the sense that a human can't really do that. It's like a drug. I've been enjoying my flights. But I have to accept that people can't really fly. Doing it every month must eventually cause one's demise. That's what Santa Claus said."

"I'm glad you're seeing it the way that I do," Carol said. "We have to figure out how to beat this."

"But how?" I asked, rhetorically. "How?"

32. Slow Hidin' Explains

In the morning I went for a run, came back and showered, got a cup of coffee, and joined Carol in the family room. She had the news on. Slow Hidin' was explaining the latest thoughts on RBG. His presentation, like his thought process, was gormless, and hard to follow. He would occasionally pause for no apparent reason, and look stupefied. I couldn't help but wonder how much of his blood Dr. Grouchi had been taking.

Slow Hidin' was wearing a mask. Why? There was no one near him, and he'd been vaccinated back in December. It made him harder to understand. Maybe that's why his people had made him wear a mask.

"There have been outrageous allegations made by Trompe," he said. "An entire RBG conspiracy about hydroxychloroquine being a cure," he said. "Trompe said that RBG originated in a Wuhan lab!" he exclaimed. "And he said that schools are safe to open!" he exclaimed. "Has he thought about all of the teachers who might not want to get a vaccine!?!"

He went on like this, occasionally raging, and then becoming glazed from time-to-time. "And the Republicans!" he exclaimed. "These are the people that want to suck the blood out of kids! All I want is to smell their hair."

He announced a new policy. "As your elected leader, I have decided that everyone *must* get a vaccine."

This was setting a very dangerous precedent, and I thought that it was unconstitutional.

I've always thought that most conflicts between "the right" and "the left" boiled down to the interpretation of a simple concept. While "the right" thinks of rights as pertaining to *the individual*, "the left" views people as (simply) elements of "groups." To the left, the way to affirm equality is to guarantee the results of those groups. At the time of America's founding, the (entirely new) concept of "America" was based on the rights of the individual. But in the 1960s, people in the USA started focusing on "collective identities," or the rights of "groups." This wasn't a new concept in the world, but it was new for America.

In fact, as it is used in The Constitution, "rights" are things that you have because you are human; they're not things that you have because the government decides to give them to you. When The Constitution and The Bill of Rights were written, it was understood that the people in the government were just that: people. As people, they're subject to the same moral weaknesses and temptations as anyone else. These documents, and our system of government were architected to try to ensure equity and fairness for all. That's *why* we have three independent branches of government.

The rights of each individual are what draws people to America from all over the world. People can become successful (or not) based almost entirely on what they choose to put into their own efforts to do so. In America, it doesn't matter what your last name is, what part of the world you're from, or what your skin color is. If you work, you'll improve your lot. If you don't, you won't. To most Americans, this is obvious. In many parts of the world, it's not true.

And *yes*, it helps a lot if you're born into a wealthy family. There's nothing particularly "American" about this. A prime example was one of Slow's sons, who's not an artist, but who "sells" his "paintings" to wealthy individuals for huge amounts. It's obvious that the buyers are buying more than (simply) the paintings.

In his continuing monologue, Slow Hidin' announced that soon, he would have groups from the government go "door to door" to make sure that everyone had been vaccinated.

"What do you think of that?" I asked Carol. "People from the government will be going door-to-door wanting to see that our papers are 'in order.' This sounds like something from an old movie: Storm Troopers checking people on a moving train, asking ***'Vere ist your papers!?'***"

"That sounds unconstitutional," Carol said. "Congress should stop it."

"Congress doesn't seem to be doing much of anything," I said.

"They just want to add trillions of dollars to the debt," Carol said. "With no specific reason to need those trillions."

"That will certainly drive inflation," I said. "If they print more money, the money will be worth less."

"Why would they do that?" Carol mused.

"If they can make the poor even poorer, they'll have even more people that depend on 'the government,'" I said. "Also, it drives the DOW up, because dollars will be worth less. This helps the wealthy, and it creates the illusion that the government has created an environment in which industry is thriving. But that's all smoke and mirrors. It's not 'real' in any sense of the word. It's like the way I fly during full moons."

"It ensures the government's power-base," Carol said.

Carol is a lot more pragmatic and cunning than I.

"That's also the reason that they've opened the Mexican border," Carol said.

"Why is that?" I asked.

"They'll import millions more people who are uneducated and who don't understand the concept of America," Carol said.

"But how will they live?" I asked her.

"They will give the immigrants small amounts of money to live at the poverty level and to not become educated," Carol said.

"Why will they do that?" I asked.

"So that they'll vote for Democrats," Carol said. "After all, it would be Democrats who would be giving them the people's money to live at poverty level. The mean Republicans would want them to stop taking a pittance to live in poverty, and to instead become educated, and to make money."

"That's actually quite clever," I said.

"But it exploits people," Carol said. "It encourages poverty; not success. That's *not* the idea of America."

"America is changing," I said.

On TV, Slow Hidin's eyes started to glaze over. It was obvious that it was time for his nap. Again, I wondered how much blood Dr. Grouchi had been taking from him.

Hidin' concluded his remarks. *"And the question is whether or not we should be in a position where you are — why can't the experts say we know that this virus is, in fact — is, is, is going to be — or, excuse me — we, we, we know why all the drugs approved are not temporarily approved, but permanently approved.*[32]*"*

("Well said!") I thought. "Shit," I said.

---

[32] A direct quote.

33. What's Blood?

Determined to beat the virus that I had, I spent several days researching blood, and trying to figure out what was different about mine. Could I beat this thing?

As we all know, blood appears to be a liquid. In fact, it's a liquid that contains the stuff of life. The liquid itself is called "plasma." Blood plasma contains a mixture of water, sugar, fat, protein, and various salts. The function of plasma is to transport the (non-plasma) blood cells throughout the body to provide nourishment, and to eliminate waste products. In addition to the (non-plasma) blood cells, it's used to transport nutrients, antibodies, various proteins, and hormones. Together, this maintains the body's fluid balance.

Blood plasma transports the living cells in blood throughout the body as well. These are the red and white blood cells, and the blood platelets.

Platelets, also called *thrombocytes*, are actually cell fragments. They allow the blood to clot – thereby healing wounds - by gathering at the site of an injury, and causing blood coagulation. This is called a *fibrin* clot: it covers the wound and prevents additional bleeding. Too many platelets in the blood can cause unnecessary clotting, which can cause strokes and heart attacks. Too few platelets will enable excessive bleeding. That's not good either.

Red blood cells, also called *erythrocytes*, are the most abundant type of cell in the blood. They account for 40-45% of its volume. A cell is shaped as a biconcave disk: a round, donut-like structure with no hole. Production of red blood cells is controlled by *erythropoietin*, a hormone produced by the kidneys. Red blood cells have no actual nucleus. This allows them to be physically flexible, but it also limits the life of the cell.

Red cells contain hemoglobin, which carries oxygen from the lungs to the rest of the body and then return carbon dioxide to the lungs, where it's exhaled. Hemoglobin is what gives these cells their red color.

White blood cells, also called *leukocytes*, protect the body from infection. They only account for about 1% of the blood. The most common type of leukocyte is called the *neutrophil*, which accounts for about 2/3 of the total white blood cell count. Neutrophils are constantly produced by bone marrow, since each cell lives for less than a day. Neutrophils protect against infection.

The other major type of white blood cells are *lymphocytes*. There are two primary kinds of lymphocytes. T-lymphocytes control the immune system, and attack tumors and other infected cells. And B-lymphocytes make antibodies. Antibodies are proteins that attack bacteria, viruses, and any other foreign material.

My bet was on the B-lymphocytes. I thought that if I could identify how my blood differed from "normal" blood, it would something to do with the B-lymphocytes. Either that, or perhaps I could find a way to augment my body's lymphocytes so as to attack and kill whatever it was that was making me fly during full moons. Perhaps this would have to do with the T-lymphocytes as well.

Over the course of a few days, I took my own blood samples, and tried to compare them to "normal" blood. To do this, I ran several tubes of my blood in the centrifuge in my lab. This causes the red cells to be deposited at the bottom of the test tube. The blood plasma becomes suspended above the red cells, with the white cells and platelets suspended in it. I found some papers on isolating the lymphocytes, and did what was advocated.

Were my lymphocytes different than normal?

I discovered that my lymphocytes were mostly dormant. While they did eventually attack disease and other foreign substances, they worked much more slowly than they should have. Carol was right: the bat virus was dangerous.

I spent most of the next week working on accelerating the reaction of my lymphocytes. This required taking more blood samples, and doing lots of lab tests. I eventually figured out that the way to accelerate my lymphocytes was with a very basic element: carbon! And carbon had been my focus when all of this had started.

I immediately started supplementing my diet with "buckyballs," the new supplement that I'd thought was worthless, C_{60}. Maybe the entire purpose of the buckyball was to overcome viruses that attacked blood itself.

I'd find out. But I didn't know how long it would take to work, assuming that it worked at all. It's seldom that anyone finds a solution on their first try. My hunch was that it wouldn't be quite that simple.

One day that week when I was working in the lab, the front doorbell rang. I ignored it. And it rang again. I ignored it again. And it rang again. Resignedly, I went downstairs to see who was ringing the doorbell.

I opened the door. "Yes?" I asked.

There were three federal agents in uniform on my doorstep.

"Good afternoon sir," the one in the front said.

"Good afternoon," I replied.

After a long pause during which they looked uncomfortable, I asked them again: "Yes?"

"We are checking your neighborhood," he said. "We are checking to see whether everyone has had their shots."

"How would I know that?" I asked.

He looked uncomfortable. "Well, have you, here, had your shots?" he asked.

"I'm sorry," I said. "But no one's home."

He looked confused. "Have you had your shots?" he asked again.

"I'm sorry," I said. "But no one's home," I repeated.

"Well, what about you?" he asked.

"You'll have to come back when the people are here," I said.

"But what about you?" he asked.

"Like I told you, no one's home," I repeated.

I closed the door on them, and they stood there looking confused for a minute or two. Then they decided to leave.

34. Another Trip to Washington

In February, Carol and I took another trip to Washington for a meeting called by Dr. Grouchi. As before, there were lots of people in the room that I didn't recognize. The purpose of the meeting seemed to be to summarize our current understanding of the virus.

We went through security as before, and a staff person was sent up to the lobby to get us.

This time, we were in the room and seated before the meeting began. Dr. Grouchi wanted to take us through the latest data. He put up a graph showing the number of known cases of the virus by week in the country. It showed a dramatic rise through January, and since then, it was falling pretty quickly.

"That's the exact opposite of the average temperature," I said. "Do you think it's causal?"

Dr. Grouchi looked flustered. "I don't see how the temperature can drive the rate of infection," he said.

"Do you think it's the other way around?" I asked.

"What do you mean?" Dr. Grouchi asked.

"That the rate of infection is driving the temperature," I said. "In other words, do you think that the rabid-bat virus is causing global warming?"

"I hadn't considered that," Dr. Grouchi said. "Maybe we need to convene a task-force to study the question."

"We know that global warming is effecting crop yields," I said. "So why not the bat virus?"

"We can fix crop yields somewhat by genetically altering them," Dr. Grouchi said. "But some people worry about the possible side effects of genetically altered food."

"There's no proof of anything bad that comes from genetically-altered crops," I said.

"But how can you know that?" Dr. Grouchi asked.

"I know it because a cauliflower told me so," I said.

Dr. Grouchi thought about that. "But it doesn't seem normal to genetically modify food," he said.

"Why not?" I asked. "It can make some food better."

"I find that hard to imagine," Dr. Grouchi said.

"Why just last week, Carol and I made a really delicious leg of swordfish," I said.

"I can't imagine that," Dr. Grouchi said, flinching.

"Well I wasn't speaking for anyone else," I said. "Just for Carol and me. Genetically modified food might not be for everyone. But we think it's the way of the future."

Dr. Grouchi suggested that we get back to the topic. I agreed.

This time Dr. Grouchi put up a chart showing the number of cases by state or region in the United States, with the numbers shown by month.

Governor Blowmo was sitting there, and he pointed to the New York numbers. "Compared to all other governors, I did the best job of reducing the numbers over time."

"That's because you did the best job of making the numbers huge in the first place," I pointed out. "You had infected seniors discharged from hospitals, and sent back to senior centers where they infected many others."

"The important thing is to look at the *end* of the curve, not the beginning," Governor Blowmo said. "Who do you think made the curve come down?" Governor Blowmo asked. "I did!"

"Do you know how annoying it is when people answer their own questions like you just did?" I asked him. "It's very annoying!" I exclaimed, answering my question, as Governor Blowmo had just done.

"But I think that the New York numbers were exaggerated," Governor Blowmo said.

"And as we all know, exaggeration is a billion times worse than understatement," I said.

Some guards entered the room, and had a look at everyone, and then waved to someone out in the hall. President Hidin' entered, and sat in a chair in the middle of the room. He had a staff person with him who stood behind him.

"Please explain the latest findings to the president," the staff person said to Dr. Grouchi.

"Hello Mr. President, and welcome," Dr. Grouchi said. "The good news is that the rate of RBG is declining."

"What's RBG?" Slow Hidin' asked.

"That's the virus," Dr. Grouchi answered.

"I knew that," Slow Hidin' said. "Is there bad news?"

"We think that it might be causing global warming," Dr. Grouchi said.

Slow Hidin' went through a series of pendiculations, and then said, "C'mon man."

"It's an existential threat," I said.

"What is?" Slow Hidin' asked.

"Global warming," I said.

"I think that we can fix that by raising taxes," Slow Hidin' said. "What I wanted to know was about the RBG."

"It's an existential threat," I said again.

"Then we should be able to fix it by raising taxes," Slow Hidin' said.

"That's brilliant!" I declared.

Slow Hidin' contorted his face. I think he was smiling. Then he fell asleep.

"C'mon man!" I exclaimed.

Slow Hidin' jerked himself awake. "My butt's been wiped[33]," he said.

The president's staff person leaned over and said, "Mr. President, I think it's time for us to go."

"That's right," Slow Hidin' said. "It's time for my nap."

Two of the guards helped him to stand, and he said: "Keep up the good work, everyone."

"Goodbye Mr. President," we all said.

The guards led him out of the room.

"What do we need to do now?" Dr. Grouchi asked.

"I think that we need to find a cure for the RBG," I said.

"We all know that," Dr. Grouchi said. "Do you have any ideas?"

"In fact, I do," I said. "I've discovered that the RBG makes a person's lymphocytes mostly dormant. We need to find a way to accelerate the lymphocytes."

"And ideas how to do that?" Dr. Grouchi asked.

"Yes," I said. "They need carbon. I'm exploring buckyballs," I said.

"What are buckyballs?" someone asked.

"They're C_{60} molecules," I said. "They provide tons of carbon."

---

[33] A recent actual quote from a well-known political figure.

I didn't explain that I'd become infected, and was using C_{60} on myself, so far to no avail. I thought that I'd need another kind of vitamin or compound to work with it. I also didn't tell them that the one who'd infected me was Dr. Grouchi.

"Please keep us appraised of your work," Dr. Grouchi said.

"Yes sir, I will," I said.

Dr. Grouchi looked around the table. "Anything else?" he asked.

No one replied.

"I guess we're done," he said. "Then *adios* for today."

I leaned in to give him some advice, and I gave it to him softly. "Don't use foreign words in an attempt to sound intelligent. That will just backfire, and make you look like an idiot," I said.

"Comprende?" I asked.

That night, Carol and I went to Ristorante Filomena for dinner. It's on Wisconsin Avenue, just south of M Street. It has *very* hearty Italian-American fare. So we didn't order anything fancy; we just stuck to their very hearty Italian-American fare.

The interior is elegant for Washington. It's done in dark-wood paneling, and the wait-staff wears formal attire. This impresses the eyes, but it's just a little comical when you see (on the menu) that they are doing their best to emulate restaurants on Arthur Avenue in the Bronx. Those have primitive furnishings (like your grandma's kitchen) and the attire is casual. It makes you wonder whether they've ever been to the Bronx.

We ordered a bottle of Barbera D'Alba to share. It's a dark red wine from the Piedmont region that has an intense flavor and a very deep color. The tannins are low, but the acid content is relatively high – it's very good as a casual wine to have with pasta.

We ordered the *insalata di polpo* to share for an appetizer, and *"La Familia,"* also to share for our entrée. The portions at Ristorante Filomena are enormous, so sharing both dishes would be plenty for us.

The wine steward brought out our Barbera D'Alba, opened it, and poured me a taste. I sniffed it and nodded, so he poured Carol a glass, and then filled mine.

Carol and I both raised our glasses and said "Cheers!" We gave each-other's glasses a light "clink," then each took a swallow.

"What did you think of the meeting this morning?" I asked Carol.

"A waste of time," she said. "All of these meetings seem to be wastes of time."

"We got to see the president – again," Carol said.

"Yes," I said. "That was scary."

"There was one good thing about it though," she said.

"What?" I asked.

"It forced Dr. Grouchi to sanction your work on a cure," she said.

"Once we got it into the same category as global warming, that was a piece of cake," I said.

The waiter brought our *insalata di polpo*. It comprised octopus tentacle portions, which were braised and sliced, and then tossed with a basil-pesto sauce. It was served over mesclun greens.

I took a portion which I moved to my bread dish, and I gave Carol the rest. I took another sip of my wine. The *polpo* was nice and tender. The pesto flavored it nicely. While a pesto would have overpowered *calamari* (squid), it worked just fine with *polpo* (octopus). The mesclun basically made it look nice, but it didn't actually "go with" the octopus in any other way.

"What's next?" Carol asked.

"Finding a cure," I said.

"Didn't you say that you're taking C_{60} as a supplement now?" she asked.

"I am," I said. "But that hasn't cured anything yet. I'm sure that it will take time," I added.

"How long?" Carol asked.

"I don't know," I said. "I also don't think that C_{60} is sufficient. I think that I need to study the problem harder, and add something."

"Like what?" Carol asked.

"That's what I need to figure out," I said.

A runner came out and cleared our plates. We sipped our wine.

The waiter came over and asked: "How is everything so far?"

"Wonderful," I said. "It reminds me of Arthur Avenue."

He chuckled knowingly (indicating that he didn't know Arthur Avenue), picked up our Barbera, and refilled our glasses.

Another runner emerged with our pasta which they call "*La Familia.*" It's a large bowl of pasta. The pasta itself is made in house. It's covered with what's called a "Sunday sauce," which is a tomato sauce with ribs, sausage, and meatballs cooked in it to give it flavor. In addition to the pasta, the sausage is also home-made at Ristorante Filomena. The sausages are large. "*La Familia*" comes with two sausages, two ribs, and two large meatballs.

It was more than ample for our dinner. Delicious too! Dividing up the meat was simple, since there were two of each type. We shared the pasta as best we could – it was more than we could eat anyway.

"When is the next full moon?" Carol asked.

"February 27th," I said. "That's next week."

"Do you think you'll change again?" she asked.

"I don't know," I said. "I have some work to do. We'll see."

35. The Snow Moon (February 27)

The full moon in February was called the "snow moon" by the Native American tribes of the Northeast because the snowfall is usually the heaviest in February. While the temperature is colder in January, there's more snow in February. This year, the snow moon came fairly late.

It came on the 27th. It had been a rainy day, with temperatures near freezing, so there were some icy spots on the roads. Besides going for a run in the morning, Carol and I stayed in.

We made a simple dinner: salad and a quiche. Then we watched a movie about vampires on Netflix, and went to bed early.

A little after midnight, I arose. I was still infected. The C$_{60}$ that I'd been taking didn't seem to be doing much of anything. I had work to do. I floated downstairs, went into the kitchen, and diffused through the bay doors, out onto our back deck. I was alarmed: there was a crowd of bat-people waiting for me. Bill Roberts was standing in the front of the crowd.

"Hi Mick," Bill said. "We thought you might like to go flying with us."

I didn't recognize any of the other bat people. Some had wounds and other physical damage. I wondered what had happened to them.

"Who are your friends?" I asked.

"These are people like me," Bill said.

"What do you mean by 'like me'?" I asked.

"They were killed by vampires," he said. "So now they're vampires too."

"Vampires?" I asked. "I thought that this was merely a 'virus,' and that it wasn't deadly."

"People that are killed by vampires become vampires too," Bill said.

I thought about how Dr. Grouchi had fed on me. "But most vampires don't kill anyone," I said.

"They don't if they don't take too much blood," he said. "But after multiple feedings, or if they take too much blood in a single feeding, the person that they fed on can die."

"And what if that happens?" I asked.

"Then they will be vampires too, and will fly the skies during every full moon," he said.

"Even though they're dead?" I asked.

"Of course," he said. "You might recall that I was cremated. And I still fly the skies."

"Doesn't that mean that as time goes on, say a hundred years from now, the sky will be completely full of bat-people? It will be full of vampires?"

"Yes," Bill said. "Won't that be great?" he asked.

I thought about it. And I didn't think so. "How did you die that night?" I asked.

"A vampire got into the house, and bit me during the séance," Bill said.

"But it wasn't even a full moon that night," I said.

"No," he said. "The full moon was on December 29th. This was New Year's Eve. The moon was *nearly* full."

"You mean that the moon doesn't have to be *fully* full?" I asked.

"It depends on how long someone has been a vampire," Bill said.

"What do you mean?" I asked.

"For new vampires, the moon has to be full," he said. "But after someone's been a vampire for a while, moons that are simply 'bright' will suffice."

This was a little different than what Dr. Grouchi had told me. He had said that only wúdí-wáng vampires would fly the skies when the moon wasn't totally full. It might be the case that other vampires would start doing it too.

"You mean that a hundred years from now, vampires will be flying around whenever the moon's out *at all*?" I asked.

"Probably sooner than that," he said. "Probably in ten years. Isn't that great?"

I thought about what I'd just learned. "That sounds horrible," I said.

"It sounds horrible to you because you're alive," Bill said. "But what about me, and what about these people here?" he said, gesturing to the bat-people that surrounded him. "We're all dead. We don't exist anymore. But during full moons, we get to be alive again – to fly around the skies and have fun! Won't it be great when we can also fly when the moon's not totally full?"

"Yeah! Yeah!" many in the crowd said.

"Well eventually everyone will become a vampire," I said. "And *no-one* will walk the earth during daylight. And when there's a full moon, everyone that ever lived will come out, fly, and walk the planet. 'The Earth' will only exist at night."

"Isn't that great?" Bill said. "There will be no more carbon emissions. And no global warming. People will be able to live safely again."

"What do you mean?" I asked. "Everyone will be dead."

"That will end pollution," Bill said. "And it will end crime. The earth will become the way that God wanted it to be: a paradise."

"You're bringing an interesting point of view to light here," I said. "I'll have to think about it."

"Come fly with us," he said.

"I don't feel well tonight," I lied. "I'm going to go back upstairs to lie down," I said.

"OK then," Bill said. "Let's go bats!"

They all alit, and flew off up into the moonlight. I went back inside, drank a glass of water, and went back to bed. I lay there and sweated for the rest of the night. I couldn't sleep. I had to quit this thing, whatever it was.

Tonight, I sweated. It was cold-turkey:

> *"I declaim! While taken with delirium,*
> *I do not know what I am saying,*
> *or what I am doing!*
> *Yet it is necessary, I must force myself!*
> *Bah! Are you not a man?*
> *Thou art Pagliacci!"*[34]

---

[34] From *"Vesti la Giubba,"* the aria concluding Act 1 of Pagliacci, by Ruggiero Leoncavallo (English translation).

36. The Buckyball

I'd been taking C_{60} as a supplement, hoping that it would help my condition in some way. So far, I'd not seen any changes. I continued my study of carbon, and in particular, of C_{60}.

The structure of C_{60} is the same as that of a soccer ball. It contains pentagons and hexagons. C_{60} is round too – just like a soccer ball. But if you take a cut-set through the middle of the ball, you'll cut exactly ten bonds. This allows us to extend the C_{60} molecule with exactly ten more carbon atoms, making C_{70}, which is oblong rather than spherical. Similarly, you can make C_{80}, C_{90}, and so on.

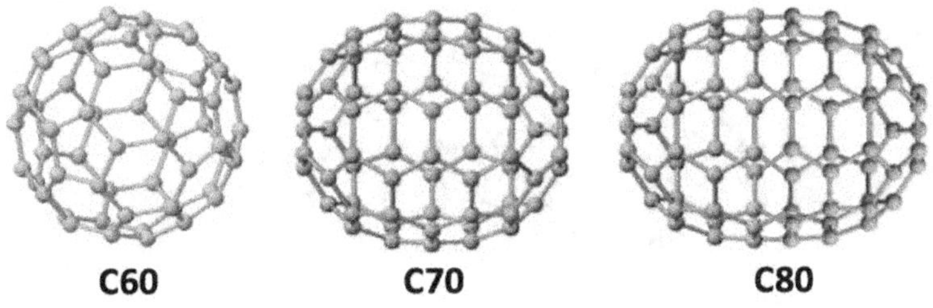

Note that the surface of a soccer ball (and C_{60}) comprises pentagons surrounded by hexagons, but not vice-versa. That is, while the hexagons touch each other, the pentagons don't. This figure cannot be constructed on a planar surface. Geometrically, that's what makes it a sphere.

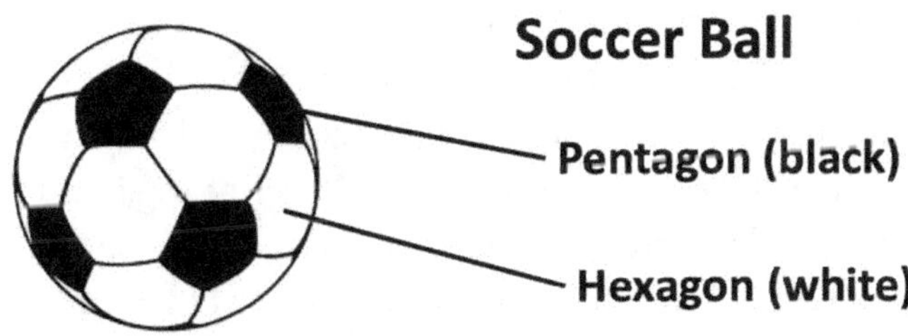

Now let's consider the planar structure, graphene. Graphene contains hexagons, exclusively, which is why it's planar, although the plane is flexible.

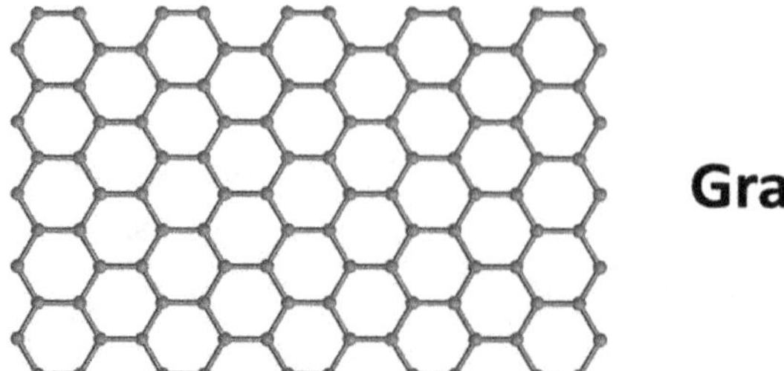

Note that each carbon atom has three bonds to its neighbors, leaving room for a valence electron. So it makes a good conductor. Since it's flexible, a fairly recent innovation is the carbon nanotube. This is simply graphene – a conductor – rolled into a cylinder.

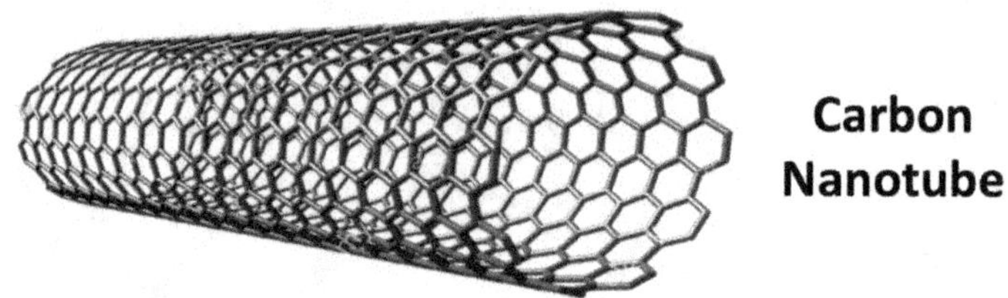

While not conductors, C_{70}, C_{80}, C_{90}, and so on become progressively more cylindrical (elongated) as layers are added. In fact, they start to look like carbon nanotubes with their ends closed off. The most significant difference is the fact that their surfaces contain pentagons – this is what makes them less conductive than a nanotube.

The question that occurred to me was whether I could open the end of a buckeyball, and splice something else onto it besides carbon.

After studying this for quite some time, it hit me that hydroxychloroquine would work quite nicely, since it contains a nice ring of six carbon atoms at its end, so it would bond easily. The compound would be a nutritional supplement as well as a medication. Maybe this would be the magic that I needed.

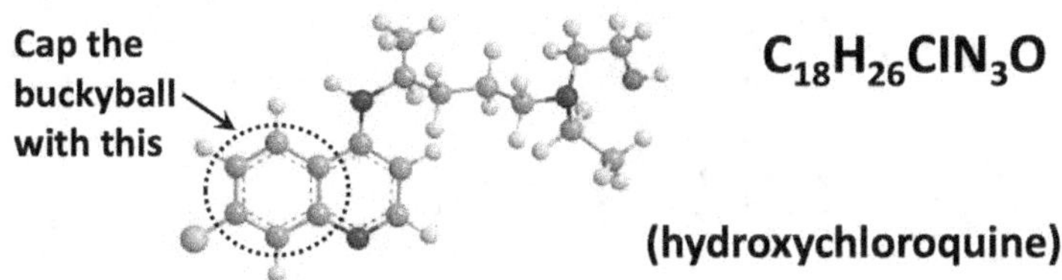

I was able to make some of this in my lab, and thought that I'd try it on myself for a few weeks to see whether it helped. I called it "Bucky-hydroxychloroquine."

If it worked at curing me, this was only the smaller of the problems. The larger problem would be to eliminate the existing vampires so that the scene that was brought to life by Bill Roberts would not ensue. This would take some more thought – and probably some more chemicals.

37. A Visit from the Goon Squad

I was upstairs, working in my lab, and Carol was in the living room, reading. I heard the doorbell ring. Just in case it was the goon-squad again, I didn't want Carol to get it, so I ran downstairs to answer the door.

I opened it. "Yes?" I inquired.

There were two men and a woman on our front doorstep, all wearing official-looking uniforms. The woman was holding a clipboard.

"We are going through the neighborhood to check and see whether everyone has had a vaccination," the more senior of the men said.

"How would I know?" I asked.

"Well, have *you* had it?" he asked.

"But I don't live here," I said.

"Can we speak with someone who does?" he asked.

"Sure, just a minute," I said.

I closed the door, waited a minute, put an eye-patch on, and re-opened it. They looked surprised to see me again, although this time I was wearing an eye-patch.

"Yes?" I inquired.

"We are going through the neighborhood to check and see whether everyone has had a vaccination," the more senior of the men said.

"How would I know?" I asked.

"Well, have *you* had it?" he asked.

"I only discuss things like that with my doctor," I said.

"We are doing a 'community outreach' on behalf of the government," the man said. "The president wants to make sure that everyone has had the vaccine," he explained. "So we are going door-to-door to educate people."

"Since we're talking about education, let's start with the president," I said. "'The Government' has no business asking me whether I've been vaccinated."

"I don't think you're understanding the big picture," the man said.

"Is that a threat?" I asked him. "The last time someone asked me that, it was a goon that was going to break my legs for not cooperating with his boss."

"It's not a threat," he said. "But the government has to step in to defeat this virus. And that starts with everyone getting vaccinated."

"Why?" I asked.

"We can't have those who chose not to get vaccinated threatening the well-beings of those who've complied," the man explained.

"Do you mean that if someone gets vaccinated, they become protected from the virus?" I asked.

"Yes, exactly," said the man.

"But they can still catch it from those that have not been vaccinated?" I asked.

"Yes, exactly," he said again.

"So while being immune, people can catch the virus from those who aren't immune?" I asked.

"You understand perfectly," the man said.

"That makes no sense," I said.

"May we come in?" the woman asked. "Perhaps we can sit and educate you."

"I'm sorry, but I can't let you in," I replied.

"Why not?" she asked.

"This isn't my house," I said.

"But your brother told us that you lived here," she said.

"I do," I said. "But it's not my house."

"Who's house is it?" she asked.

"It's my brother's," I said.

"You mean it's his house, but you're the one that lives here?" she asked.

"Yes, exactly," I said. "Would you like me to get him?"

"Please," she said.

I closed the door, waited a minute, took off the eye-patch, and then re-opened it. This time they didn't look surprised.

"Yes?" I asked.

"May we come in?" the lady said.

"But I don't live here," I said.

"I know," the lady said. "But your brother said that it was your house."

"But he's the one that lives here," I said. "So I'm not sure that I have the authority to let you enter. It's kind of like my being the landlord. Can I grant permission to someone to enter my property for the purpose of engaging my tenant? Legally, I can't."

"Well maybe he can let us in then," she suggested.

"Wait a minute," I said. "I'll get him."

I closed the door, waited a minute, put the eye-patch back on, and then re-opened it.

"Yes?" I asked.

The woman said, "we'd like to come in to talk to you. We spoke with your brother, and he said that he doesn't have the authority to let us in."

"Well he's the owner," I said. "So if he didn't let you in, I don't know what to tell you."

"You could let us in," she said.

"But it's not my house," I said.

The three of them stood there looking confused.

"Have a nice day!" I said, and I closed the door on them.

I took the eye-patch off, and went back to my lab.

38. Coffee with Danny

In the morning, I went for my run. I saw Danny's car over at Dottie's house again, so when I got home, I called him.

"Hello?" he said. "Mick?"

"Yes," I said. "Do you feel like meeting for coffee? I have a few things that I'd like to discuss."

"Sure," he said. "I was just getting up, and I'd like to shower first. How's about forty-five minutes from now?"

"Sounds good," I said, and hung up.

I went upstairs, showered, and got dressed. I poured a small cup of coffee to have before I left; I'd be way too early if I left now.

I went into the family room where Carol was watching the news. They were talking to various dress-makers. Since Slow Hidin' had taken office, "the news" never had news on anymore. Every day, instead of news it was a public interest story. Frankly, it was boring.

"Good morning," I said as I sat down.

"Good morning," Carol said. "Where are you off to? You usually don't get dressed this early unless you're going somewhere."

"I'm going to meet Danny for coffee," I said.

"Why doesn't he just come over here?" she asked. "Isn't he across the street?"

"Yes, he is," I said. "But I guess that a coffee shop is much more neutral territory."

"Did he call you?" she asked. "Why doesn't he just go through with it?"

"Go through with what?" I asked.

"Getting married," she said.

"I'm sure that he will," I said. "But I'm the one that called him," I reminded her. "I wanted to tell him what we've learned about vampires. And about my visits from Bill Roberts."

"What do you think he can help you with?" Carol asked.

"I don't know," I said. "I just thought that if I talked to him, maybe some ideas would come to me."

"How are your experiments with that medicine coming along?" Carol asked.

"I don't know," I said. "I'm working on a new one that I'll start taking when I'm done."

"And?" Carol asked.

"I don't think it will kill me," I said. "But you were the one that got me to see that I had to beat the virus with *something*, or *that* would kill me."

I finished my coffee and got up.

"Say 'hello' to Danny for me," Carol said.

I put my cup in the dishwasher, got my computer, and left. I drove to Holy Moly, went in, got a large cup of coffee, and took a seat by the window.

I opened my computer, and started to read the news. Apparently, the rate of infection by the new bat virus was down. At the same time, global warming was going up. I told them! I wondered whether Dr. Grouchi had a task-force studying this yet.

Danny came in, got a cup of coffee, and joined me.

"What do you think of this global warming?" he asked.

"What global warming?" I asked in return.

"Dr. Grouchi was on TV. He said that he had figured out that the rate of bat-virus infections was going in the opposite direction to the rate of global warming. Can you believe that?" he asked.

"So that means that if we can increase the rate of RBG infections, we can bring the climate under control?" I asked.

"Yes," he said. "I guess that's what he said."

"*God does not play dice with the universe*," I said.

"What's that mean?" Danny asked.

"Actually, it's a quote. Albert Einstein said it. He was expressing skepticism over the main idea of quantum mechanics," I said.

"What's quantum mechanics?" Danny asked.

"It's a bunch of theory as to how physics works at the sub-atomic level," I said. "Don't worry about it."

We each took a sip of coffee.

"Are you and Dottie still taking about marriage?" I asked.

"Yes," he said.

"Remember that if you get married, you'll have to pick up all of your crap," I said. "And you can't lie in bed in the morning anymore. There are always things in a house that need to be fixed."

"What's that mean?" Danny asked.

"Maybe I should switch back to quantum mechanics," I said. "It's much easier to understand."

We each took another sip of coffee.

"You'll never believe who I bumped into," I said. "And that's caused me to start working on some new things."

"Who?" Danny asked. "And what?"

"Bill Roberts," I said, and I watched his expression.

His face showed alarm, which he quickly smoothed over.

"Who?" he asked again.

"Bill Roberts," I said again.

"He's dead," Danny said.

"I know," I said. "We were both at the autopsy."

"And he was cremated," Bill said. "He's ashes."

"He's a vampire," I said. "He comes back to life when there's a full moon."

Danny stared at me, looking slightly horrified. Then he burst out laughing.

"You're really a piece of work, Mick," he said.

"Danny, I'm not kidding," I said. "You know how I do 'science' things?" I asked.

"Yeah," he said. "So?"

"Dr. Grouchi asked me and Carol to help them understand this virus," I said. "We've had several trips to Washington to attend some very classified meetings about this virus. While I can't discuss the specifics of those meetings, I *can* tell you about my personal exposure to the RBG virus."

Danny was looking at me like he wasn't sure whether I was joking.

So I continued. "The first time that we went to Washington for a meeting, there was a full moon that night, and I was visited by a vampire who fed on my blood. At the time, I thought it was just a dream. I felt weak the next day, but other than that, I was fine."

"Does that mean that *you're* a vampire?" Danny asked.

"No," I said. "It doesn't work that way. The people who are vampires are those who've actually been killed by vampires, and those who've eaten rabid-bat guano. They all crave blood when there's a full moon. And they feed on the blood of others – me in this case."

"So what happens to you?" he asked.

"Amazingly, when there's a full moon, I sprout wings, and I can fly," I said.

Danny stared at me, then started laughing again. "You're *really* good," he said.

"I'm serious," I said. "While I'm not a vampire, I transform into a human with wings, and I can fly when there's a full moon. Either I'm flying, or I'm imagining it within an enormously vivid context. And what's the difference?"

"That actually sounds pretty cool," Danny said. "What's the problem with that?"

"I didn't think that there was one," I said. "Until I met Bill Roberts. And that was after he was dead, and had been cremated."

"Did he come back to life?" Danny asked.

"I'm not sure what you call it," I said. "But he told me that when there's a full moon, he's reincarnated, and flies the skies with everyone else."

"What's the problem with that?" Danny asked.

"Bill was killed by a vampire," I explained. "It doesn't have to be a full moon for vampires to fly around and drink blood. It just needs to be fairly full, and bright out. New Year's Eve was a very clear night, and the full moon had only been two nights earlier, on December 29th. Bill told me that somehow, a vampire had gotten into our séance, and killed him. I guess that Monica Caciocavallo isn't crazy: a bat *did* land on her. She must have slapped it off, so it fed on Bill Roberts, and killed him."

"We can't have vampires killing people," Danny said.

"And think of the long-term implications," I said. "What happens, years from now, when everyone has been killed by vampires? The only people walking the streets will be vampires. And on full moons, billions of billions of dead souls will emerge to fly the skies. The earth will cease to exist as we know it. The only 'living people' will be vampires."

"That's a very gloomy picture that you're painting," Danny said.

"And it's real," I said. "I need to find a way to stop it."

"But how?" Danny asked.

"First, I'm working on an antidote," I said. "I need to stop whatever has infected me so that I won't fly the skies during full moons."

"And then?"

"And then I need to find a way to end the RBG virus. I need to eliminate all vampires," I said.

"Eliminate?" Danny asked. "As in *'murder them'*?"

"Think of it more as a *cure*." I said. "I'm trying to save the human race."

We had a long pause as we considered that. It was a weighty concept. We either solved this, or the world as we knew it would change.

"Let's go back to the New Year's Eve party," Danny said.

"What about it?" I asked.

"Let's go through all of the people that were there," he said.

"It didn't have to be anyone that was there," I said. "The vampire could have entered the house while we were sitting around the table."

"It was cold out," Danny said. "Dottie had all of the windows in the house closed. And so were the doors."

"Vampires can diffuse through walls," I said.

"What's that mean?" Danny asked. "Diffuse?"

"When I awaken during a full moon, I can simply pass through walls like they're not there," I said. "So the vampire could have come into the house from outside. He saw several cars, knew there was a party, so he knew that there would be plenty of people to feed on."

"But why would he?" Danny asked. "Why would he go into a house full of people who are all awake, and all together? They'd all see him."

"But we were having a séance," I said. "The only light was a candle."

"How would he know that from outside the house?" Danny asked. "If he was a vampire looking for a victim, there were plenty of other houses that he could have gone to; houses with all the lights off; houses in which the people had all gone to bed. Remember that it was probably after midnight."

"What are you saying?" I asked.

"I'm saying that the vampire might have been a guest at our party," Danny said.

"Who?" I asked.

"Well I know that it wasn't me," Danny said. "And while you can't be sure of that, I'm the one that's raising this as the likely scenario. If it were me, why would I do that?"

"You wouldn't," I said.

"Maybe it's you," he said.

"But if it was me, why would I have just spent the last half-hour explaining vampires to you?" I said. "I'm sure that you took the coroner's word for it: that Bill Roberts had a heart attack. If I had killed him, why would I tell you that he'd visited me after he was dead?"

"You wouldn't," he said. "But you're a vampire."

"But I'm *not* a vampire," I said. "I was bitten by a vampire. During full moons, I fly in the sky. I don't drain people's blood."

"Whatever," Danny said. "We interviewed Monica Caciocavallo. She told us that a bat had landed on her. If she was a vampire, she wouldn't have told us anything about a bat. Also, she screamed. She wouldn't have screamed if she was the person that was going to feed on Bill Roberts. Similarly, her husband probably isn't a vampire either. He wouldn't have landed on *her* if he was."

"So that eliminates me and Carol, you and Dottie, and Monica, and her husband Sal," I said. "Who else was there?"

"There was Bill Roberts and his wife, Melanie," Danny said. "It wasn't them."

"How do you know?" I asked.

"The vampire killed Bill," Danny said.

"Oh, right," I said. "So who does that leave?"

"That leaves the Chaos," Danny said.

"Gary and Lucy, isn't it?" I asked.

"Yes, I think so," Danny said. "I don't know them that well. They're friends of Dottie's."

"How does Dottie know them?" I asked.

"Dottie went to NYU," Danny said. "She shared an apartment with a few other girls, and Lucy was one of them. The two of them became friends. And then Lucy got married."

"To Gary, I assume?" I asked.

"Yes," Danny said. "That's his American name. I forget what his Chinese name is."

"He's from China?" I asked.

"Both of them are," Danny said.

"I wonder whether they've been back to visit lately," I said.

"I can probably find out," Danny said. "Do you think that either of them is a vampire?"

"Maybe," I said. "Maybe both of them are."

"Let me sketch the room as I remember it," I said.

I took a napkin, and drew a diagram of Dottie's dining room as I remembered it. I put people's names at each place, and put a skull in front of Bill Roberts so that it was clear where the murdered man had been sitting. Danny had been at the end of the table nearest the doorway, and he'd been the one that got up to turn the lights on when we heard the scream.

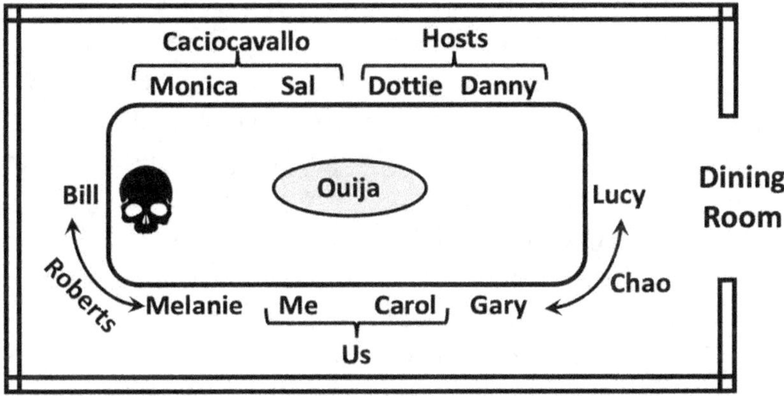

"This is how I remember it," I said. "Do you remember anything different?"

Danny studied my sketch for a minute, then said, "no, you've got it right. I was sitting nearest the door at the end of the table. That's what made it easy for me to get to the light switch. Lucy Chao had been at the head of the table, and her husband Gary was opposite me. Dottie was next to me – on my right. And Bill was at the opposite head of the table – the end that was furthest from the door. I remember that the Caciocavallos were next to Dottie, and we'd been sitting boy-girl-boy-girl, so Sal must have been next to Dottie, and Monica was next to him."

"If one of the Chaos is a vampire, why would they go all the way across the table to choose a victim?" I asked.

"And why would they do it at a party?" Danny asked.

"If it's one of the Chaos that's a vampire, it must be that the craving for blood became overwhelming, and they couldn't resist," I said. "I've told you that I'm not a vampire – I'm merely a victim. I wasn't killed by the person that turned me into what I am now, but since that happened, I crave rare meat, and things with blood in them. It could be that for real vampires, the craving for blood becomes like a drug-addict's craving for drugs."

"But why did they kill him at the party?" Danny asked. "I thought you said that the vampire that fed on you merely took some of your blood, but left you alive. Why would one of the Chaos bleed Bill Roberts dry?"

"I don't have an answer to that," I said.

"And why would they cross the table completely?" Danny asked. "Gary Chao was sitting next to Carol. He could have simply fed on her. And Lucy Chao was sitting next to me. She could have fed on me. Didn't you say that when the vampire feeds, you kind of go into a trance, and it doesn't seem real? Neither of us would have screamed, and we probably wouldn't have remembered it – or we'd have thought that we'd dozed-off, and it had been a weird dream."

"That's a good question," I said.

"Why would the vampire fly across the table and startle Monica Caciocavallo to make her scream?" Danny asked.

"I don't know," I allowed. "He wouldn't."

"And why would the vampire feed on Bill Roberts, kill him, and then take the trouble to startle Monica?" Danny asked.

"I think that we're raising more questions than we're answering," I said. "And they're all good questions."

"I think that you and I need to talk to Gary and Lucy Chao, and tell them that we're just 'following up' as part of the investigation," Danny said.

"Is there an investigation?" I asked.

"No," Danny said. "As far as the police are concerned, Bill Roberts died of a heart attack."

"Let's leave it that way," I said. "If we tell people that he was killed by a vampire, his life insurance company will probably tell his poor wife – Melanie - that being bitten by vampires isn't covered."

39. Carol and Dottie go for a Drink

When I got home, Carol was in the living room reading a book. I stuck my head in: "Hi Carol. Let me know when you're at a good point to take a break."

She looked up. "OK," she said.

I blew her a kiss, and she chuckled. I went into the kitchen and sat at the island. I took my computer out, and started playing with chemical formulations. After about ten minutes, Carol came in.

"What's up?" she asked.

"Danny and I went for coffee, and we had a very interesting discussion," I said.

"About marrying Dottie?" she asked.

"Well that was most of it," I lied. "But then I told him the truth about my condition."

"What did he think?" she asked.

"He didn't believe me at first," I said. "He laughed a few times. He thought that I was joking, but I finally got through to him."

"And again, what did he think?" she asked again.

"I could tell that the entire concept of 'vampires' was new to him," I said. "But he's very quick and very clever when it comes down to asking good questions. That's probably why he's a police detective."

"So what did he think?" she asked a third time.

"I explained to him that I was bitten by a vampire," I said. "I told him that this didn't make me a vampire, but that when there's a full moon, I'm compelled to fly the skies. I told him that I knew that Bill Roberts was killed by a vampire, and that I knew this because Bill visits me when there's a full moon."

"And?" she asked.

"Bill was killed by a vampire at Dottie's party," I continued. "So Bill didn't do it. Danny knows that he didn't do it. I told him that I didn't do it, because I was the one that was explaining all of this to him, and I wouldn't do that if I'd killed Bill. And we were pretty sure that neither of the Caciocavallos did it either, since Monica screamed during the séance, and told us that she'd been 'surprised' by a bat. So the only people that we weren't sure about were the Chaos. The Chaos are the only people that Danny doesn't really know. They're friends of Dottie's."

"Do you suspect them?" she asked.

"I don't know," I said. "But we've ruled everyone else out."

"Is it possible that the vampire came from outside the house?" Carol asked.

"Yes, but highly unlikely," I said. "Danny and I discussed this. I won't bore you with the details."

"So what are you going to do?" Carol asked.

"Danny is going to ask a friend of mine at the station to look on certain databases to see whether the Chaos have been to China recently," I said.

"What if they have?" Carol asked.

"It doesn't prove anything, but it gives us one more piece of information," I said.

"What can I do?" Carol asked.

"I was hoping that you'd get together with Dottie, and pick her brain about the Chaos," I said. "Danny said that Lucy Chao shared an apartment with Dottie when they were both students at NYU. Then Lucy married Gary. That was all that Danny knew."

"OK," Carol said. "Let me see what I can find out."

It was almost 4:00, so Carol called Dottie.

"Hello?" Dottie said.

"Dottie? This is Carol," she said.

"Hi Carol," Dottie said. "What's up?"

"Mick has been talking to Danny lately, and he told me that the two of you are talking about making your situation permanent," Carol said.

"He told you that?" Dottie asked.

"Yes," Carol said. "But I want to hear the real story. It's almost time for happy hour. I was going to go into town to get a glass of wine. Would you care to join me? I'd love to talk about what's been going on."

"Sure," Dottie said. "That sounds like fun. Should we meet somewhere?"

"I'm leaving now," Carol said. "I'll pick you up on my way out. We'll go downtown together."

"How soon?" Dottie asked.

"Ten minutes," Carol said.

"Make it fifteen," Dottie said. "I just want to change my shoes and brush my hair."

"OK," Carol said. "I'll be up there in about ten minutes."

"Bye," Dottie said, and hung up.

Carol drove over to Dottie's house. Dottie came right out, and got in the car.

"Hi Carol, good to see you!" she said. "This was a good idea – you and I getting together just to chat."

"Yeah," Carol said. She turned the car around and left Dottie's.

"I haven't seen you since New Year's Eve," Carol said. "Mick caught up with Danny this morning over at Holy Moly, so I figured that you and I should get together too. And happy hour is much better than morning coffee."

Dottie chuckled. "Did Mick tell you what they talked about?" she asked.

"I got the impression that it was mostly you," Carol said.

"Really!?" Dottie asked.

"That's what he told me," Carol said.

"Where are we going?" Dottie asked.

"A new place called 'Three Sheets,'" Carol said.

"Have you been there before?" Dottie asked.

"No," Carol said. "But I wanted to see it."

They arrived at Three Sheets, parked, and went in. The front wall of Three Sheets was all floor-to-ceiling windows that had been tinted. You could see in, and you could see out. It had light wood floors, and dark wood paneling. This would have made it look like a "man's bar," but one wall was floor-to-ceiling mirrors. This opened up the space a lot, and made it lighter. The mirrors also allowed you to watch people without them knowing that you were watching them. There were brass wall sconces, and three large brass chandeliers that went down the center of the space. The bar itself was long; it ran along the wall opposite the mirrors. People could sit at the bar, or they could grab a tall round table in the middle of the open space. The small tables had high bar chairs that went with them.

They grabbed a small table, and looked at the drink menu. A young handsome waiter stopped by.

"What can I get you?" he asked.

"What's the vieux carré like?" Carol asked.

"It's heavy with whisky and brandy," the waiter said. "If you like those, you'll love the vieux carré."

"I'm not really a whiskey person," Carol said. "I'll have a white Russian instead."

"I'll take a Chardonnay," Dottie said.

"Would you like six or nine ounces?" he asked.

"Better make it nine," Dottie said.

The waiter nodded and walked off.

"So have you guys set a date yet?" Carol asked.

"No," Dottie said. "Frankly, we're still both getting used to the whole idea."

"Well the two of you seem inseparable," Carol said.

"I'm very comfortable with Danny," Dottie said. "While sometimes he comes across as a little rough, he's a very caring person."

The waiter came back, and set their drinks down. They each took a sip.

"Then let me get to the really tough question," Carol said.

"What's that?" Dottie asked.

"If you get married, what kind of dress are you going to wear?" Carol asked.

Both of them laughed.

"While that sounds silly, is actually is a tough question," Dottie said. "There are lots of styles. But to choose a beautiful dress requires a big dose of reality."

"What do you mean?" Carol asked.

"Well, I'm not twenty anymore," Dottie said.

"But you've managed to stay slim," Carol said. "I think that most dresses would fit you very nicely."

"And then there are all of the styles," Dottie said.

"That's complicated," Carol said. "And the styles keep changing. For a while, shoulderless gowns were the style. But many of the new wedding gowns have brought the shoulders back. And floral motifs are starting to show up."

"Floral motifs?" Dottie asked.

"Yes," Carol explained. "The gowns are still pure-while, but floral patterns have are woven into the fabric and into the lace."

"That's a great idea," Dottie said. "I'm going to check those out."

They each took a sip of their drinks, and there was a pause in the conversation.

"Have you spoken to Danny since he talked to Mick?" Carol asked.

"No," Dottie said. "Why?"

"There are another set of facts regarding Mick and Bill Roberts that you need to be aware of," Carol said.

"Bill died of a heart attack," Dottie said. "I feel sorry for poor Melanie. We should invite her out some time. And what about Mick?"

Carol looked around the room to see whether anyone looked like they were focused on them. Satisfied that it didn't look this way, she started telling Dottie what was happening with the virus. She lowered her voice a little. "As you might know, Mick does some consulting for the government. They bring him in when they need his specific expertise."

"And?" Dottie asked.

"Mick and I have been going to Washington to attend some of the meetings held by Dr. Grouchi," Carol explained. "They're trying to get to the bottom of the RBG virus."

Carol took a sip of her drink, and continued. "What they're not telling people are some of the (frankly) gruesome facts about the bat virus. When we went to Washington the first time, Mick was bitten by a vampire. That changed him."

"A vampire?" Dottie asked. "Are you joking? How has Mick changed? He looked normal to me at our New Year's party."

"When there's a full moon," Carol said, "Mick awakens. He can pass through walls and other solid objects. And he spends the night of the full moon flying through the skies."

Dottie looked at Carol carefully to see whether she was serious. "He passes through objects? How?"

"He just diffuses through," Carol said. "He can pass through our walls without opening the doors. He goes out when there's a full moon, and he flies."

"Is he a vampire?" Dottie asked.

"No," Carol said. "He was fed on by a vampire. This just causes him to awaken and fly during full moons. Mick is what's a called a 'zombie.'

He doesn't feed on people's blood, and he's still alive. Vampires feed on people. They drink their blood. And most vampires are dead."

"*Most* vampires?" Dottie asked. "Aren't they all dead?"

"No," Carol said. "The ones that became vampires by ingesting rabid-bat guano are alive. They function the same way that we all do. But they fly the skies during full moons, and they feed on other people."

"I'm confused. How does someone become a vampire?" Dottie asked.

"There are two ways," Carol said. "One way is to eat rabid-bat guano in a certain part of China. The other is to be killed by a vampire by having your blood drained. Vampires feed on the blood of the living."

"I see," Dottie said. "So it must primarily be people from China who become vampires."

"No," Carol said. "That may or may not be true in China. Here, most people become vampires by having their blood drained by other vampires. And you can see how the number of vampires in increasing because more and more people are becoming victims to vampires. But there's another disturbing fact that I need to tell you, and then I've an uncomfortable question."

"What's the fact?" Dottie asked.

"Mick has met Bill Roberts during the last two full moons," Carol said.

"But Bill is dead," Dottie said. "He had a heart attack at our séance."

"Still, he comes back when there's a full moon," Carol said.

"But he was cremated," Dottie said. "He doesn't have a body."

"He told Mick that when you're killed by a vampire, you come back to earth when there are full moons – even if you've been cremated," Carol said.

"But a vampire didn't get Bill Roberts," Dottie said. "He had a heart attack."

"No he didn't," Carol explained. "He told Mick that a vampire killed him at your party."

"A vampire?" Dottie asked. "But how? Oh! You said that they can pass through walls."

"Mick and Danny talked about that," Carol said. "While that's true, they didn't think that the vampire came from outside. They think that the vampire was someone that was at your party – someone that was sitting at the table during the séance."

"But who?" Dottie asked.

"It wasn't Bill," Carol said. "Bill was the victim. And I'm sure that it wasn't Mick or Danny. They also – more or less – ruled out the Caciocavallos. You might remember that Monica let out a scream. She said that a bat had landed on her."

"She said that?" Dottie asked.

"Yes," Carol said. "So that leaves the Chaos. Danny told Mick that he doesn't really know the Chaos. He said that they are old friends of yours."

"Yes," Dottie said. "Lucy and I shared an apartment when we were in college. Then she met Gary, and they got married."

"They're both from China, aren't they?" Carol asked.

"Yes," Dottie said.

"Do you know if they've visited China recently?" Carol asked.

"No, I don't," Dottie said.

"Mick and Danny will be talking to them soon to see if they can find that out," Carol said. "I thought it was important to let you know."

"Yes," Dottie said. "Well I appreciate that."

"It's possible that one of the Chaos is a vampire," Carol said. "It's possible that they killed Bill Roberts."

Carol and Dottie each took another sip of their drinks. Carol looked at all of the people reflected on the wall of mirrors to see whether any of them looked like they'd been listening.

40. Danny and I talk to the Chaos

Danny called me in the morning after I'd finished my run.

"Hello?" he asked. "Mick?"

"Yes, it's me," I said. "Have you found out anything about the Chaos?" I asked.

"Yes," he said. "They visited China for two weeks last Summer. Which proves nothing."

"You're right," I said. "It also disproves nothing. Why don't you arrange an interview with them?" I asked. "As we'd discussed."

"I'll call them now," he said, and hung up.

He dialed the number that he had for Gary Chao.

"Hello?" said a man's voice.

"Hello?" Danny said. "Is this Gary?"

"Yes," Gary said. "Who's this?"

"This is Danny. You remember, Dottie's boyfriend. We had the party on New Year's Eve."

"Of course," Gary said. "How are you? And how's Dottie?" he asked.

"We're doing good," Danny said. "But we're still pretty shaken by my friend's heart attack at the party."

"Yes," Gary said. "That was horrible. Lucy and I felt really bad about that. How's his wife doing? What was her name again?"

"Melanie," Danny said. "She's still upset. A heart attack! There was nothing about his health to warn them that he might have one."

"I'm sorry to hear that," Gary said. "Is there anything that I can do…?"

"In fact, as you probably know, I'm a police detective," Danny said. "I'm doing routine follow-up interviews with everyone that was there, and I'd like to come by to talk to you and Lucy."

There was a long pause.

"But he died of a heart attack," Gary said. "Why are you doing interviews?"

"It's standard procedure," Danny said. "I'm just reconfirming everyone's recollections."

"Well, sure," Gary said.

"When is a good time to come by?" Danny asked. "We'd like to talk to you and Lucy together."

"Who is 'we'?" Gary asked. "I thought that it was just you."

"Do you remember Mick?" Danny asked. "He was also at the party with his wife, Carol."

"Yes," Gary asked. "We met them. What's he got to do with this?"

"Not much," Danny said. "But he is very clever, and he helps me on certain occasions."

"For investigating heart attacks?" Gary asked.

"Sometimes he has unique insights," Danny explained.

"Well, OK," Gary said.

"When's good?" Danny asked.

"We both finish at 4:00 today," Gary said. "Why don't you come by our house at about 5:00?"

"OK, we'll see you then," Danny said, and hung up.

Danny called Mick back.

"Hello?" Mick said.

"Hi Mick," Danny said. "I talked to Gary, and he said that we should come to their house at about 5:00 this afternoon."

"Do you know where they live?" Mick asked.

"I'll find out," Danny said. "I'll pick you up at your house at about 4:30."

"See you then," Mick said, and hung up.

At about 4:30, Danny drove down our driveway, and I went out to meet him. All I brought was my computer so that I could jot down any notes as they occurred to me. I got in the car.

"Did you find out where they live?" I asked.

"Of course," Danny said. "They're not that far from here. They're just a neighborhood over."

"We'll be there well before 5:00," I said.

"Gary didn't make it sound like it mattered that much," Mick said. "He'll probably be happy to see us early. That means that we'll leave early too."

"Good point," I said.

I relaxed as Danny drove. I knew the roads well, and recognized the house when we pulled up into the driveway. We got out, went to the door, and rang the bell.

Gary answered the door. "Hello," he said. "I'm happy that you got here a little early. Lucy just got home a few minutes ago. She's upstairs changing. Let's go in."

He waved us in. "It's probably most comfortable if we sit in the living room," Gary said, and he led the way. "Choose a seat," he added. "Can I get anyone something to drink?" he asked.

"Thanks, but I'm fine," Danny said.

"Me too," I added.

We all sat, and we heard Lucy coming down the stairs. She entered the living room, and Danny and I stood.

"Hi, Lucy," I said. "Danny and I have come by to update the police records on Bill Roberts so that we can close them out."

"Of course," she said. "Please sit."

We sat, and Lucy joined us.

Danny started. "We were all there when Bill died. While the pathologist is fairly certain that Bill had a heart attack, his wife was very surprised. So was I."

"Why is that?" Gary Chao asked.

"He was fairly young, and he was in good shape," Danny said. "He exercised regularly."

"That doesn't necessarily prevent heart attacks," Lucy said. "While exercise and diet help the heart, it's still heavily driven by genetics."

"You're right," I said. "But we'd like to rule out everything else."

"Of course," Lucy said. "How was his health, if you don't mind my asking?"

"I didn't discuss it with his doctor, since that's privileged information," Danny said. "But there are no 'red-flags' on his police records, and his wife was very surprised."

"I see," Gary said. "Well we don't know what to say."

"Do you remember where people were sitting?" I asked.

"What do you mean by 'where they were sitting'?" Gary asked.

"During the séance," I clarified.

"Bill Roberts was at the head of the table on the opposite side of the room from the door," Gary said. "I remember that because it almost looked like a bad piece of theater when we turned the lights on."

I thought that was an unusual way to describe it, but he was right. Maybe it *was* a bad piece of theater. Maybe that's why the vampire chose Bill.

"I was at the other head of the table," Lucy said. "I was at the end of the table by the door. I was facing Bill Stewart. I remember that like a bad dream. And you were on my right," Lucy said, indicating Danny. And Dottie was next to you."

"You and Dottie were good friends in college?" I asked.

"Yes," Lucy said. "We shared an apartment until I met Gary, and married him."

"You and Gary are both from China, aren't you?" I asked.

"Yes," Lucy said. "Our parents introduced us."

"Where do your parents live in China?" I asked.

"Wuhan," she said.

"Do you ever go back to visit?" I asked.

"Yes," she said. "We went back last summer. We spent a week with my family, and then a week with Gary's family."

Danny and I looked at each other.

Gary Chao interrupted. "Your wife – Carol – was sitting next to me, and you were sitting next to her."

"Yes," I said. "That's how we remember it too. Bill's wife was next to me, and Bill was at the head of the table – as we've already said. The Caciocavallos were between Bill and Dottie."

Gary thought about it. "Yes, that must have been where everyone was sitting."

"Danny and I had placed it this way, and I just wanted to see if you remember the same thing," I said. "I'm satisfied with that."

"Is there anything else?" Gary asked.

"Yes, there's one more thing," I said. "It's just a funny little detail. Monica Caciocavallo screamed when the lights were out. She told me that a bat had landed on her."

Gary and Lucy looked at each other.

"A bat?" Gary Chao asked. "Does Dottie have bats in her house?"

"No," Danny said.

"But sometimes bats fly down chimneys if you don't screen them properly," I added.

"That's probably what happened," Lucy said.

"But what happened to the bat?" I asked.

"What do you mean by 'What happened to it?'," Lucy asked.

"When Danny turned the lights on," I said, "it was gone. Where did it go?"

"Maybe when Monica screamed, she scared it, and it flew back up the chimney?" Lucy suggested.

Danny and I looked at each other.

"You're probably right," I said. "By the way, I heard that they actually eat bats in China."

"Yes they do," Gary said, a little too quickly. He was obviously eager to change the subject.

"Did you eat any bats when you were in China?" I asked.

"No," Gary said, again quickly, and he motioned to Lucy with his eyes for her to stay silent. She had just started saying "Ye..," but she cut it off. She turned red.

"I'd like to try a bat sometime," I said.

After an uncomfortable minute, Danny said, "well, I guess that just about wraps it up."

"Thank you both," I said.

Danny and I both noticed Gary staring at us – like he was wondering what we were *really* thinking. I had I hunch that I would hear from the Chaos about this pretty soon.

41. The Worm Moon (March 28)

Tonight would be the "worm moon." The worm moon is the last full-moon in March, so-called because beetle larvae start to emerge from the bark of trees and other places as the earth thaws. It's usually the last full-moon of the winter.

While I'd been looking forward to the spring, I wasn't looking forward to this particular full moon. I'd been working on my Bucky-hydroxychloroquine, and had figured out how to get the two molecules to bond. I'd also added another secret ingredient, and wondered whether I'd see its effects tonight.

Getting that secret ingredient to bond with the others had been very tricky. It's quite volatile. I'd been taking my self-made medication for about a week, and I didn't really know its effects.

Carol and I had had a late dinner. I hadn't told her what I was expecting to happen later tonight. She has more common sense than I do, and probably would have talked me out of it. I was expecting a number of visitors. It would be a lively party if things went the way that I was expecting. And I didn't want Carol to be in the middle of it. So I slipped a sleeping-pill into the drink she was having after dinner.

Carol slept soundly. I didn't.

The sun went down, and the moon came out. I hadn't been able to sleep, which was good.

I was lying there with my eyes closed, and felt someone touch on my face. I opened my eyes, and saw my visitors. I wasn't sure that they'd come, but I'd been hoping that they would. It was the Chaos. They were both standing over me.

I put a finger to my lips, and gave them a quiet: "Shhh!" I pointed to Carol, who was sleeping soundly, and I said, "don't wake her." Then, "I'm not too surprised to see you," I said.

They looked surprised that I'd said this. I got out of bed.

"Let's go downstairs where we won't disturb Carol," I said, and I led the way. They followed. As I walked, I wasn't completely gliding the way I had before. While I was still slightly elevated above the floor, I had to walk down the stairs. The medicine that I'd developed was having some effects.

When we got to the kitchen, I turned, and said: "You both ate bats when you visited Wuhan, didn't you? And you're both vampires now, aren't you?"

They looked surprised.

"Let's go out on the deck where you can bask in the moonlight," I said. "If you've come to take me, I'd rather go in the beautiful moonlight."

Gary said, "We didn't want to take you, but you know too much, so you've left us no choice."

"Then let's go outside," I said. "I want to see the moon, and so do you."

I pushed on the door to see whether I could pass through it. I no longer could. I hadn't set the alarms tonight because I thought that I might have to open the door, and I didn't want to wake Carol. I opened the door, and walked out onto the deck. The beautiful full-moon lit up the night sky.

"You killed Bill Roberts, didn't you?" I asked. "Why did you kill him?"

"You're very smart," Lucy said. "We didn't mean to kill him. We'd picked Bill and Monica to feed on. Feeding on them wouldn't have killed either of them. But I landed on Monica, and she screamed, so I chose the person next to her – Bill. I didn't know that Gary had already fed on him. There were two of us, and eight of you. There was only a one-eighth chance that I'd pick the same person that Gary did."

"Technically, it was a one-seventh chance, since you'd already picked Monica, and you didn't feed on her," I pointed out. "And you weren't going to feed on each other."

"You're right," she said. "A one-seventh chance – almost like rolling a die, but even less than that. It was just bad luck."

"Your *really*-bad luck was that I was at the party," I said.

"Why is that 'really-bad luck'?" Gary asked.

"Because I've got some friends…" I said, and I left it at that.

Bill Roberts stepped out of the shadows with about ten of his friends. I'd been out on the deck earlier this evening. I was waiting for Bill, hoping that he'd come. He came, and I explained my plan to him. He'd brought back some friends, and waited for me to bring the Chaos out. We had both hoped that they'd show up. And they did. They'd been hiding behind our chimney.

"Hi," Bill said. "Remember me?" he asked, and he took a swing at Gary Chao.

Gary ducked, and took a *renoji-dachi*[35] stance. "I have a black belt," he said. "I'll *kick* all of your asses if you don't back off."

"You're gonna *kiss* all of our whats?" Bill said, sounding like a cop. "You bastards killed me. You owe my wife big-time."

Bill advanced, and landed a punch on Gary. Gary staggered back, and then threw a kick at Bill. The kick knocked Bill into his friends, who caught him, and held him up. Bill and all of his friends swarmed Gary. They encircled him, and searched for an "in" to hit him, or grab him. Gary went through other stances, and threw occasional kicks at those who got too close.

"Get him!" I yelled.

They all swarmed in from all directions at once. Gary couldn't ward all of them off, so he shot straight up into the sky. Bill and all of his friends followed. I could see them all flying across the center of the beautiful orange moon in the sky. The moonlight lit them up. They flew with Gary in the front. Those in the mob would occasionally catch up to him, and hit him, which would cause him to veer.

Now it was just Lucy and I on our deck.

"I guess Gary has left you all for me," she said. "At least until he gets back."

She changed into a bat, and flew at me, landing on my neck. I didn't fight her. I wanted to see whether my innovations had worked. I felt her teeth sinking into my neck, and heard her drink some blood.

All at once, she released her hold on me, changed back into her human form, gasped, and fell on the deck.

"Ahhh!" she screamed. "What did you do?" she asked. "What did you do?"

"That's just a touch of my secret sauce," I said.

She writhed there for a minute, then burst into flames, and exploded. There was nothing left of her.

I'd been able to bond some sodium hydride onto my new medication. Sodium hydride is wicked stuff. It will combust. Apparently it didn't agree with vampires. When bonded to Bucky-hydroxychloroquine, it was inert. Normal people would simply pass it through. But not vampires. Apparently, vampires would burst into flames. And explode.

I had a solution. But I needed to improve the bond, or the compound would be too volatile to distribute.

---

[35] A martial-arts fighting stance.

42. A Meeting with Melanie Roberts

In the morning, I filled Carol in on what had happened. We were in the kitchen. Carol was having breakfast at the center island, and I was cooking mine. Today I didn't crave blood.

"Gee," she said. "And I slept through that? It sounds like it was a real racket."

"Yeah," I said. "I don't know how you managed to stay asleep. You must have been very tired."

"I was," Carol said. "I don't know why."

"I think that we should talk to Melanie Roberts and tell her what's happening," I said.

"What do you mean by 'what's happening'?" Carol asked.

"That her husband Bill didn't die of a heart attack," I said. "And that he comes back on full moons."

"That sounds like a lot for her to absorb," Carol said.

"But she should know," I said.

"Who would tell her?" Carol asked.

"I think that Danny should," I said. "He was good friends with Bill. At least, Danny should suggest that we all get together. I'll tell her."

"Should we have them all over here?" she asked.

"Yes," I said. "I think that would work best."

I had finished making my breakfast, and sat diagonally opposite Carol to eat. And I called Danny.

"Hello, Mick?" he asked. "What's up?"

"I had an interesting encounter last night," I said.

"What happened last night?" he asked.

"It was a full moon," I said.

"So?" he asked.

"That's when I awaken," I said. "And it's when the vampires come out. Guess who visited me?"

"I give up," he said. "Who?"

"The Chaos," I said.

"Is one of them a vampire?" he asked.

"Both of them are," I said.

"And what happened?" Danny asked.

"Bill Roberts was there with some friends," I said. "They chased Gary Chao up into the sky. I think they got him."

"Really?" he asked. "What about his wife?"

"Lucy?" I asked.

"Yes," he said, "Lucy."

"I killed her," I said.

"That's murder," he said. "As a police officer, I need to warn you that you have the right to remain silent. Anything you say can and will be used against you in a court of law..."

I cut him off. "Uuugh! Ouch. Ow! Please don't hit me again officer! I confess!!!"

"Stop it, Mick," he said.

"You too," I said. "She tried to kill me by drinking my blood. I've been taking a certain compound that I fabricated here in my home, and it didn't agree with her."

"I see," Mick said. "Where's her body?"

"She exploded and disintegrated," I said. "Her body is no more."

"What about her husband?" Danny asked.

"Some vampire victims chased him off into the sky," I said. "I didn't see the end of that, but I've a hunch that we won't be seeing him again either."

"I see," Danny said. "And you called to tell me this?"

"Not entirely," I said. "Although I needed to tell you that so that you'd understand what I'm going to ask you."

"What's that?" Danny asked.

"I'd like for us all to meet with Bill's widow," I said.

"With Melanie?" he asked. "Why?"

"First, because you and Dottie should keep her in your circle of friends," I said. "And second, I'd like to explain to her how Bill died."

"That he was bitten by vampires?" Danny asked. "Do you think that will comfort her?"

"There's something very special that I'd like to explain to her," I said.

"I see," Danny said. "What?"

"For now, I'll keep that under my belt," I said. "Can you call her and invite her to a meeting?"

"Who's gonna be there?" he asked. "And where?"

"Just me and Carol, and you and Dottie," I said. "We can meet here. At my house."

"What will be my premise?" Danny asked. "Why are we having this meeting?"

"Tell her that we'll be hosting for drinks and hors d'oeuvres. Tell her that it's purely social," I said. "I'm sure that she'd like to talk to some people. She's probably lonely."

"Whore's what?" Danny asked. "What's that got to do with anything?"

"What are you talking about?" I asked him.

"You said whore's something-or-other," he said.

"That's 'hors d'oeuvres,'" I said. "Another word for snacks. Little hotdogs, cheese, and stuff like that. See if she can come at about 5:00."

"OK," he said. "I'll call her."

We both hung up, and I finished my breakfast. My phone rang. It was Danny. I answered.

"Hello?" I said. "What'd she say?"

"She said that she can come today," Danny said.

"Good," I said. "We'll look forward to seeing all of you." I hung up.

A little before 5:00, an SUV came down our driveway. I assumed that it was Melanie. She parked, got out, came to the front door, and rang the bell. Carol answered the door.

"Melanie!" Carol said. "Welcome. I'm glad that you could make it. Come on in."

Carol brought Melanie into the living room, where I was sitting. I stood. "I'm glad that you came, Melanie. Danny and I have been good friends for many years, and he often spoke about Bill. I thought it would be nice for us all to get together. Danny and Dottie should be here in a few minutes. Can I get you a drink?"

"Do you know how to make a whisky sour?" she asked.

"Of course," I said. "Sit wherever you'd like, and I'll be back in a minute."

I went into the dining room where our bar is, and I mixed Melanie a whiskey sour. I made myself a dry martini. I thought that I'd need it. I brought the drinks back into the living room, and handed the whiskey sour to Melanie. She was sitting in one of our large stuffed chairs, and looked very comfortable. I got her a coaster, and sat at the end of the couch that was next to Melanie's chair.

The doorbell rang again, and Carol answered it again. It was Dottie and Danny. Carol showed them into the living room. Melanie stood, and they all exchanged "air-kisses."

"Can I get anyone a drink?" I asked.

"Beer?" Danny asked.

"What's Melanie having?" Dottie asked.

"A whiskey sour," I said.

"I'll have one of those too," she said.

I went back into the dining room, mixed another whisky sour, and brought it back into the living room for Dottie. Carol came in with a glass of white wine for herself, and a cold bottle of beer for Danny.

"How have you been holding up?" Danny asked Melanie.

"It's tough sometimes," she said. "But I'm getting by. I really miss Bill," she said. "Sometimes I wish that I could talk to him again. Even if it was just one more time."

Carol and I looked at each other, but didn't say anything.

"Not to change the subject," I said, "but have you been following the news about the bat virus?"

"You mean that new virus from China?" Melanie asked.

"Yes," I said.

We paused, and all sipped our drinks.

"We didn't have a chance to talk much at the New Year's party, but I sometimes do consulting for the government," I said. "I've been meeting with a group run by Dr. Grouchi to better understand what's happening."

Melanie looked confused. "So why are you bringing this up?" she asked.

"There's no easy way to say this," I said. "Bill didn't die of a heart attack," I said. "He was bitten by two vampires at the New Year's Eve party when the lights were out."

"What???" she asked. "Is this some kind of a tasteless joke?"

"No," I said. "I know that this is hard to understand, and hard to take. I was bitten by a vampire myself," I said. "This is all new. I'm a scientist, and I've been working to understand this *new* problem that we – the world – faces. It's vampires."

"Why didn't it kill you?" she asked.

"I was only bitten by *one* vampire," I said. "Bill was bitten by *two*."

"Where did they come from?" Melanie asked.

"They were at the party," I said. "The Chaos. They had been to China last Summer. They were infected. Both are vampires."

"Why did b*oth* of them bite Bill?" she asked.

"It was a mistake," I said. "Just bad luck."

"So why are you telling me this?" she asked.

"First, because you should know," I said. "And second," I added, "because you can still make contact with Bill."

Her eyes widened. "What??? Is this another bad joke?"

We all took sips of our drinks.

"No," I said. "Because I was bitten by a vampire, I awaken whenever there's a full moon, and I fly the skies. There are many others flying the skies with me."

"Are you a vampire?" she asked.

"No," I said. "I wasn't exposed to the RBG directly. So I don't bite people. But I do sprout wings, and fly the skies when the moon is full."

"Why are you telling me this?" she asked.

"Because Bill does too," I said. "He comes alive and flies the skies during full moons."

She looked shocked. "But I had him cremated," she said.

"That doesn't matter," I said. "When the moon is full, he comes back to life, and he flies the skies. I've talked to him several times. He helped me to eliminate the Chaos."

"Really?" she asked. "This is very hard to believe."

"I know it is," I said. "The RBG is an entirely new virus. I've been working in my lab on ways to cure it. But the first thing that's needed is a full understanding of its manifestations. I think that I know them. And Bill comes back when the moon is full."

"Really?" she asked again.

There was a long pause. I took a good swallow of my martini.

"Does that mean that I can get to see Bill?" she asked.

"Yes," I said. "At least I think so. He seems to drop by here to say 'hello' when there's a full moon. Maybe you'd like to spend the night here next time?" I suggested.

"Yes," Melanie said. "I'd love to if you think that I might see Bill."

Carol brought out some hors d'oeuvres, and we changed the subject. Melanie looked both tired, and hopeful. I took another swallow of my martini. Danny had finished his beer, so I brought him another one.

43. Slow Hidin' Explains

In the morning, we were having our coffee and watching the news. (This time, the lead story was about "street artists.") There was a special announcement that Slow Hidin' would speak to us on TV "at about 3:00." He was going to explain the latest thinking about RBG.

We each went about our business, and reconvened in the family room a little before 3:00. The press secretary came on and said that Slow Hidin' had "been delayed," and was expected at 4:00. Carol and I came back at 4:00, and the press secretary said that it would now be "at about 5:00." Slow Hidin' must have been taking a long nap today.

At 5:00, the press secretary told us that Slow Hidin' would be with us "at any minute." Slow stumbled into the room at about 5:15. He was wearing his mask, and he looked confused. He walked up to the podium, and displayed a graph showing the latest rates of infection. It didn't look good.

He leaned into the microphone, and with his eyes bulging out of his head, he whispered: *No more malarkey!* It was hard for him to punctuate his proclamation with an exclamation point while speaking in a whisper, but he managed. Very clever of him!

After a pause, he stood back up straight, and asked in a normal voice: "Should you get the vaccination?"

It was a pointed question. Many questioned the safety of the vaccine, since it had been developed under President Trompe, and Slow Hidin' had said that it wasn't safe because of this.

Slow Hidin' continued. *"Or, you know — or, or, or, or, or the mom and dad, or, or, or, or the neighbor or when you go to church or when you're — now, I, I, I, I really mean it. There are trusted interlocutors. Think of the people, if, if your kid wanted to find out whether or not there were — there's a man on the moon or whatever, you know, something, or, you know, whether those aliens are here or not, you know, who are the people they talk to beyond the kids who love talking about it?*[36]*"*

I thought that he'd put it quite eloquently. At least for Slow Hidin'.

[36] An actual quote from a certain president.

"The good thing is that as the rate of infection goes up, global warming diminishes," he said, pointing to the graph that showed that the rate of infection was on the rise, and that the local temperature had dropped.

I now regretted saying this as a joke in Dr. Grouchi's last meeting. I couldn't believe that they bought that BS.

He continued. "But what we need in these perilous times is a financial life *lime* for middle class folks.[37]"

He concluded his remarks with the following: "What I'm suggesting is that I know what has to be done and that in the following is that faster is better than slower.[38]"

I thought that summed it up nicely. At least it was almost a sentence. And it was true: faster is better than slower. That's why we need people like Slow Hidin' in that position.

The press secretary came on and said that we would now be treated to the latest information on the virus from Dr. Grouchi. I couldn't wait.

Dr. Grouchi came to the podium wearing two masks. I was glad to see that he was cutting back. He told us that the key to solving the problem was getting vaccinated.

"About 75 million Americans are eligible for vaccinations but have not yet gotten the shots," Dr. Grouchi said. "That's the key to ending this. I mean, that would be the key," he said. He called those who have decided against getting the vaccine a "recalcitrant group."

He continued. "People, because of their political bent feel that they don't want to be told to mask up, and they don't want to be told to get vaccinated. It's *inexplicable* ... to have people, because of the divisiveness in society, not wanting to contribute to the solution, and by doing that they become part of the problem. But that is, again, the way it is, unfortunately.[39]"

Dr. Grouchi took some questions.

"What's this about global warming?" a well-known journalist asked.

"We have a group of scientist studying this problem, and we noticed that as the rate of infection went up, the temperature went down," he said. "So we think that this virus could be a solution to global warming."

---

[37] A direct quote from a very important person in Washington.

[38] A direct quote from a very important person in Washington.

[39] A direct quote from a chief medical advisor in Washington.

"Did this virus come from China?" another journalist asked.

"That's not been substantiated," Dr. Grouchi said. "So implying it at this point is racist."

"Amen! Amen!" some in the press corps shouted. "Racist!"

"Do we know whether this virus affects some races more than others? That is, is the virus racist?" another person asked.

"We don't know this for certain," Dr. Grouchi said. "But some races don't want to take the vaccine."

"Why not?" someone asked.

"Because of the Tuskegee Airmen,[40]" Dr. Grouchi said.

"Amen! Amen!" some in the press corps shouted. "Racist!"

"I heard a rumor that some people that are infected become vampires," someone asked. "Is that true?"

Dr. Grouchi feigned laughter. It's good that he was wearing a mask. That way, his pointed teeth didn't show. "Vampires?" he asked. "Where did you hear that?"

"I have some friends in China," the same person said. "That's what they told me."

"But this virus isn't *from* China," Dr. Grouchi said.

"Where's it from?" someone asked.

"Italy,[41]" Dr. Grouchi said.

"When will we have a cure?" someone asked.

"The important thing is to get vaccinated," Dr. Grouchi said.

"I have a question for the president," a journalist said.

The press secretary came to the podium. "I'm sorry, but he can't take any questions now," she said. Slow Hidin' was slumped in a chair against the wall, fast asleep.

"Thank you!" Dr. Grouchi said, and everyone on the podium started to leave.

Two bodyguards picked Slow Hidin' up and carried him out.

---

[40] One of the theories expressed about the COVID vaccine.
[41] This had been the rumor about COVID for a while.

44. Another Trip to Washington

Dr. Grouchi called another meeting, so Carol and I took the Acela down again. The meeting was in the afternoon, so we were able to leave in the morning, have a nice lunch in Washington, and be on-time for the meeting. We recognized many of the same faces in the room, and managed to sit near the front again.

Dr. Grouchi started the meeting. He started by projecting the latest statistics on the virus by geographical location as a function of time.

"This is the usual data," I said. "What about other effects?"

"What do you mean?" Grouchi asked.

"Someone asked during the press conference the other day," I said. "Vampires."

There was a pause, and Grouchi stared at me, knowingly.

"What do you mean by 'vampires'?" he asked.

"Some have heard that those who have been directly exposed to the rabid-bat guano develop an insatiable taste for human blood," I said. "They fly the skies during full moons, and feed on people."

"That's ridiculous," Dr. Grouchi said. "It sounds like something out of a bad monster-movie."

"It does, doesn't it?" I asked him, staring him down.

"But if that were true, there would be lots of dead people the mornings after full-moons. People who'd had their blood drained," Dr. Grouchi said. "And I've not been aware of that."

"There was one in my neighborhood," I said. "It was at a New Year's Eve party."

"But that wasn't a full moon," Dr. Grouchi said. "And did the coroner say that the person was killed by a vampire?"

"I think that the moon doesn't need to be completely full," I said. "New Year's Eve was two nights after the full moon. But it looked full. It might as well have been. By the way, how did you know that New Year's Eve wasn't a full moon?" I asked. "Do you pay attention to when the full moons are?"

After a pause, Dr. Grouchi said, "…no, I don't. But it was New Year's Eve, and I noticed the moon, so I looked at the calendar. Like you said, the full moon was actually two nights earlier. What makes you think that this person was killed by a vampire?"

"Because I was there," I said.

"And the coroner agreed?" Dr. Grouchi asked.

"No," I said.

"What did the coroner say?" Dr. Grouchi asked.

"That it was a heart attack," I said. "The coroner doesn't believe in vampires. Why would he? I think that part of our mission needs to be to educate the public."

"Why are you talking about vampires?" one of the other scientists asked. "That's nonsense."

"That's what most people think," I said. "It's nonsense. But to beat this thing, we really need to understand it. I think that it's important to add this dimension to the information that we give people."

"But vampires?" the man asked. "Have you ever seen one?"

"Yes," I said. "One fed on me," I related, and I nonchalantly glanced at Dr. Grouchi, who was looking more uncomfortable.

"Does that mean that you're a vampire now?" the man asked.

"No," I explained. "It doesn't work that way. Becoming a vampire requires exposure to rabid-bat guano. And once you've been bitten by one, you fly the skies during full moons, but you don't feed on others. It's only the vampires that do that."

"While that's unusual – assuming that I believe you – who cares?" another scientist asked. "You fly the skies during the full moons? So what."

"What I think happens is that people who are infected will fly the skies during full moons even after they're dead," I said.

"Again, so what?" the man asked.

"There are about eight billion people in the world," I said. "If this disease spreads, the skies will soon have hundreds of billions of people flying the skies during full moons. We can't let this happen."

"Why not?" Dr. Grouchi asked.

"I don't yet know if there are other ways to become a vampire – besides direct exposure to RBG," I said. "The man that was killed on New Year's Eve was bitten by *two* vampires. They didn't mean to kill him, but they made a mistake. If some of the people who die become vampires, soon, many of those flying the skies on full moons will also be vampires – and they'll kill more people."

"And?" Dr. Grouchi asked.

"What happens if everyone on earth becomes a vampire?" I asked. "And what happens when all of the vampires, and everyone that ever lived flies the skies during full moons? The earth will become a place of nightmares. Maybe the only people that populate the earth will become vampires. They won't need to work. All they need is blood. They can probably get that from animals."

"If that's true, then we need to find a solution to it," said another scientist. "Any ideas?"

"I'm working on one," I responded, thinking of the medication that I had developed. I didn't explain this yet, because I wasn't sure that I trusted Dr. Grouchi. In fact, I was pretty sure that I didn't.

Just then, the door to the conference room opened, and two secret-service men came in.

"Is this a good time?" one of them asked.

"Of course," Dr. Grouchi said.

Slow Hidin' came in with a few more guards. He took a seat at the front of the room.

"What have you found out?" he asked Dr. Grouchi.

Dr. Grouchi addressed me. "Well, Mick, what have you found?"

"What, specifically do you mean?" I asked him.

"What's the correlation between the virus and global warming?" Slow Hidin' asked.

"It's strong," I said. While I'd never told Dr. Grouchi that I was going to try to correlate them, I'd done so, and had a graph on my computer. I connected my computer to the projector, and showed the graph. There was a strong anti-correlation.

"It looks conclusive," Dr. Grouchi said.

"Excellent work!" Slow Hidin' said.

I didn't want to try to explain to him that a correlation didn't imply a causal relationship. Two things that have nothing to do with each other might correlate: this is just statistics. While Slow Hidin' claimed to have finished at the top of his class, I didn't want to bore him with the meaning of "correlation."

"This is just the statistics," I said, and I left it at that.

"The thing about statistics," Slow Hidin' said, "is that when advertisers use mixed-race couples, it's because they're selling soap.[42]"

"We can find correlations between lots of things," I said.

"What I said was — let's get this straight — what I said was what will change the behavior is the rest of the world to them and diminishes their standing in the world,[43]" Slow Hidin' said. "I'm not confident of anything. I'm just stating the fact."

"I couldn't have put it any better," I said. "I think that this is why we need to study the problem that I'd mentioned before," I concluded.

"You need to show it for La-Teanecks too," he said.

"What are La-Teanecks?" I asked him.

"Mexicans from New Jersey,[44]" he said.

Dr. Grouchi glared at me. The meeting was over.

After Slow Hidin' left, I told Dr. Grouchi that I hadn't meant for him to take my anti-correlation analysis as proof of causality. In fact, I'd done it as a joke. It was metaphorical. And false.

"But higher-ups love stuff like this," Dr. Grouchi said.

"Sometimes, people who confuse the metaphorical with the factual literally make my head explode," I told him.

Dr. Grouchi replied. "Well, sometimes life throws you a curveball, and you just don't know enough about baseball to finish the metaphor."

---

[42] A quote from a well-known person in politics today.

[43] A quote from a well-known person in politics today.

[44] Teaneck is a town in New Jersey.

45. The Press and our Woke Culture

The media has a new hobby. They like to fawn over Slow Hidin' eating ice cream. "What flavor is it?" they'll ask him. That's hard-hitting.

And all the while, he's out there saying things like: "I love those barrettes in your hair![45]" And: "Man I'll tell you what; look at her: she looks like she's nineteen years old sitting there like a little lady with her legs crossed![46]"

The last president – President Trompe – had had nightly "grill" sessions, usually lasting for more than an hour. He was bothering to educate us on the government's progress with respect to the bat virus. All the while, the press would undermine him, and ask impudent questions purely for the sake of trying to trip him up, which they never seemed to do.

But Slow Hidin' doesn't bother with press conferences. And the media is fine with that. On rare occasions, Slow Hidin' will read prepared comments from a manuscript projected on his teleprompter. But he won't take any questions. He might get the wrong answer.

Our culture has changed in a few short years. And it's done it in ways that have been used in other cultures of the world throughout human history.

First, elements within our culture have subtly changed the definitions of words through repeated misuse. This makes people afraid to use these words, lest they be misunderstood. This has caused much of the population to simply stop engaging in entire sectors of thought. Without thought, our culture (and its popular beliefs) become more like a religion.

Things are "true" because the government says so.

If you disagree, you are "an *insurgent*." We saw peaceful "insurgents" walking around the Capital on January 6th. Many of them have been accused of "treason," and the Speaker of the House has told us that this was the worst thing that happened in our country since The Civil War – and certainly since the war of 1812.

Changing the definitions of words is always dangerous. It's been responsible for various governments murdering millions of people "to ensure peace."

---

[45] An actual quote from an important person in Washington.

[46] An actual quote from an important person in Washington.

In addition to this, the "woke" culture has co-opted language in general. If you say, "I'm not a racist," by definition, that makes you a racist. While this sounds like a clever invention of George Orwell's, it's both insidious, and evil. It creates a moral vacuum.

This is exactly what was done in the Salem witch trials: if you say that you're not a witch, it proves that you are one. We've created a new culture in which certain ideas are not allowed to be aired, certain cultural beliefs are deemed absolute truths, and it's heresy to express much thought.

One of the greatest ironies of this is that it's now more true on college campuses than anywhere else. College campuses used to be places where diverse ideas were aired and debated. That's how learning occurs. Now, many universities ban speakers having certain ideologies. They are no longer places of free thought. They've become "indoctrination centers." That shouldn't be why people go to college. People who go to college should learn to think and to argue. They should be places where students can learn to organize their thoughts.

The Press no longer asks tough questions of politicians, even when it's obvious that they're lying. They all simply jot down whatever's said, and echo it in their "news coverage." *This* is what's causing our system to become corrupt and incompetent.

Of course, if we all become vampires, this won't matter much. But if we don't, delivering straightforward news should re-emerge as essential to the American culture. And not bending the definitions of words is essential to imparting correct information. The witch-trials need to stop. We should aspire to be a nation of ideas and solutions; not division. We are not all vampires. At least not yet.

It was my goal to beat this disease, and then to beat the vampires. I saw the beating of both as essential to sustaining our world and our culture, as rotten as it was becoming. Perhaps this disease would awaken peoples' sense of humanity, and cause them to re-prioritize their thinking. Every gray cloud should have a silver lining.

Later this year, the White House Press Secretary would actually brag that the White House Administration was working together with Facebook to flag certain posts as being "misinformation," at least, according to them.

At the same time, Facebook banned the former president (Trompe) from making any posts – they terminated his Facebook account. In the ensuing lawsuit against Facebook, they argued that Trompe's demand for free speech on their platform violated *their* First Amendment rights, since they were a private company, and not an arm of the federal government. But that's a tough argument to make when the White House was working with them. It sounds a lot like China; not like America.

Clearly, there is a major problem with the White House assisting a private company to decide what "truth" is.

Therefore, in addition to reversing the Chinese virus that was turning people into vampires, I had higher goals in mind. I was hoping that a cultural consciousness about the dangers that we were facing would result in people becoming more aware of where our culture was headed.

46. A Meeting with President Hidin'

As Carol and I were leaving Dr. Grouchi's meeting, a White House staff person approached Carol and me. He had been in the meeting, sitting next to Slow Hidin'.

"Hello," he said.

"Hello," we said back. "Nice day, isn't it?" I added.

"Yes," he said.

We stood there awkwardly, staring at each other. Finally, he broke the silence.

"President Hidin' was very impressed with your statistical analysis," he said. "He'd like to meet with just the two of you, without Dr. Grouchi there. He thought that that way, the discussion could be more frank."

"That would be an honor," Carol said. "When would he like to see us?"

"Does tomorrow morning at 10:00 work?" he asked.

"Certainly," Carol said. "Where should we go?"

"Go to the main entrance of the White House, and tell them that President Hidin' is expecting you," he said.

"OK," I said. "We'll see him tomorrow."

In the morning, Carol and I had a nice breakfast, and then took an Uber to the main entrance of the White House on Pennsylvania Avenue. Of course, the Uber was unable to drive to the entrance, so he let us off on Executive Avenue. We walked into the grounds making our way to the entrance, showed our IDs when asked, and subjected ourselves to a search.

When we got to the main entrance, I told the guards that we were there to see the president, and that he had invited us. One of them made a phone call, and we were permitted inside. Another guard took us to a service elevator, and we went up a few floors. He walked us down a few busy hallways, taking a tortuous path, knocked on a large double-door, and opened it.

It was the Oval Office – just like it looked in the pictures, except bigger. Slow Hidin' was sitting on one of the couches, asleep.

"Sir!" the guard said loudly. "Sir!" He turned around and knocked loudly on the door again.

Slow Hidin' stirred, awoke, stood, and walked over to us. He extended his hand.

"Welcome," he said.

We all shook hands.

"Thanks for coming," he said.

"It's our honor," Carol said. "We've never seen the Oval Office before. It's very impressive."

"Comfortable too," Slow said.

"It's a pleasure to see you again," I said. "Last time you and I met, Dr. Grouchi was with us. It was a full moon."

After a moment, he continued. "You might wonder why I wanted to talk to you in private – without Dr. Grouchi. I don't trust him."

"Why not?" I asked.

"Because he's fed on my blood," Slow Hidin' said. "He's a vampire."

"I know," I said. "He's fed on my blood too."

"You know the way that I frequently look sleepy?" he asked. "Dr. Grouchi did that. By drinking my blood."

"I was sleepy in the months in which Dr. Grouchi was feeding on me," I said. "I thought that I was just anemic, but that wasn't the case. When he stopped feeding on me, I felt much more energized than I've ever been."

"I haven't gotten to that point yet," Slow Hidin' said. "I think that he still feeds on me."

That explained – to a large extent – why Slow Hidin' seemed slow.

"How did you get him to stop feeding on you?" Slow asked.

"I don't live around here," I said. "My guess is that that's most of the reason."

"Are there vampires where you live?" he asked.

"Yes," I said. "Carol and I caught two of them. They'd been to Wuhan to visit their families, and they killed a man at a party we attended on New Year's Eve."

"What happened to them?" Slow asked.

"A bunch of vampire victims – who are now vampires too, chased the husband down and killed him," I said. "I got the wife to take part of a potion that I'm working on, and she disintegrated."

"You're working on a potion?" Slow asked.

"Yes," I said. "We need a medication that can do two things. First, we need to cure people who have come under the spell of a vampire. These people are zombies, like you and I: not dead, but being fed upon. We're just people who have been bitten by vampires. And second, we need to eliminate the vampires."

"Will you and I become vampires?" Slow asked.

"Maybe," I said. "It depends on whether vampires bleed us dry. Right now, we're merely zombies. We're still alive. And I'm working on a cure for that. Vampires feed on people like us. While people like you and I can fly during full moons, we don't drink other people's blood. At least not yet we don't."

"Is that harmful?" Slow asked. "Becoming a vampire?"

"Yes," I said. "People who are dead come out and fly during full moons. In several generations, the skies will be full of dead people."

"I can see why that's a problem," Slow Hidin' said. "Especially if it happens during an election." Hidin' thought for a minute. "Do you have all of the resources that you need to solve this problem?" he asked.

"I have a small lab in my house," I said. "I could use some more equipment to nail this down."

"I will instruct my staff to allocate some funds to you," Slow Hidin' said. "You should write up a proposal, and suggest a dollar amount to do the work. I will see to it that it's handled."

"I think that we can beat this thing," I said. "But it won't be easy. Especially with Dr. Grouchi running things. He's a vampire."

"I know," Slow Hidin' said.

Carol, who's quicker than I, seized on this as an opportunity. "Perhaps we should maintain contact – just you and us – without Dr. Grouchi in the loop," she suggested.

"That's an excellent idea," Slow Hidin' said. "How can we do that?"

"Easy," Carol said. "First, you can call us anytime. I assume that Dr. Grouchi doesn't have your phone bugged."

"That's a great idea," Slow Hidin' said. "What about if we see each other in person?" he asked. "And what if there are lots of other people standing around? There always are. How will we know if it's OK to talk freely?"

"That's an excellent question," Carol said. "Mick and I won't know who's safe to talk around, and who isn't. Why not give us the TikTok 'distress' hand-signal?" Carol suggested.

What's that?" Slow asked.

"Simple," Carol said, and she showed him. "It consists of two hand gestures." She did them.

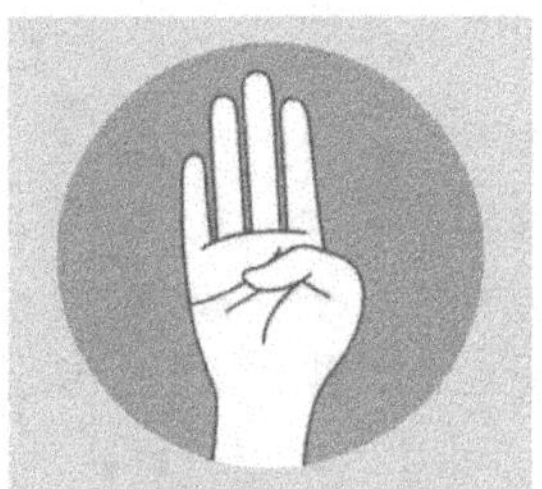

FIRST

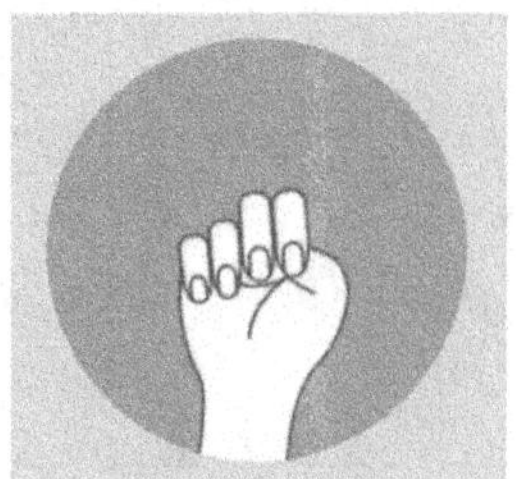

SECOND

"First, you extend all four fingers, and put your thumb across your palm. And then, you close your fingers over your thumb. Then you can repeat it," she said.

"And what does it mean if I do that?" Hidin' asked.

"It means that it's not safe to talk – that people are within earshot who shouldn't hear what we're going to say," Carol said.

"What if you miss the first gesture?" Hidin' asked.

"A good question," Carol said. "Keep repeating the gestures: first, then second, then first, then second, and so on."

"What if it *is* safe to talk?" he asked.

"Then do the second gesture first, and then the first gesture," I suggested.

"But what if you miss the second gesture?" he asked.

"Then keep repeating it, the way you would if it wasn't safe to talk," I said.

"OK," Slow said. "I think I've got it. First and then second if it's OK to talk. Second and then first if it's not. And keep repeating the sequence in case you missed the first signal."

"You've got it!," I said.

"The three of us should be friends, and should try to solve this thing together," I said.

"Yes," Slow Hidin' said. "I'll see to it that you get top security clearances."

"If you need anything, just call us," I said.

Carol and I shook hands with Slow Hidin' again, and we left the Oval Office.

47. The Pink Moon (April 27)

The name "pink moon" has nothing to do with the color of the moon. It is so-called because it occurs (roughly) when the early springtime blooms of a wildflower called *creeping phlox* or *moss phlox* are in bloom. These are native to Eastern North America, and they have pink flowers.

This particular pink moon was also a super-moon. A super-moon occurs when the moon comes the closest to the earth (it has an elliptical orbit) during a full moon. The technical name for this is a perigree syzygy. A full moon at perigree looks about 14% larger than a full-moon at apogee, which is when the moon looks the smallest.

Tonight, Melanie Roberts would be staying with us. Melanie arrived while I was cooking our dinner.

I was making *ropa vieja* (translates as "old clothes") using a flank steak, peppers of all colors, onions, tomatoes, broth, and a bunch of different seasonings, cooked-down until the flank steak starts to fall apart.

As it cooked down, I joined Melanie and Carol in our family room. Each had poured a glass of wine, so I poured myself one too. I'd be having coffee after dinner, so I wasn't worried about staying awake.

"How are you?" Carol asked.

"Again, I miss Bill," Melanie said. "I don't know if I'll ever get used to it."

"I can't imagine" Carol replied.

We made polite conversation as our dinner cooked. I went back to the kitchen to check on the flank steak a few times. When it was nearly done, I pulled it apart with two forks, to give it a "shredded" texture, then I added pimientos, green olives, capers, and some fresh parsley. I served it with seasoned black beans and some white rice.

We took our dinner in the dining room. We had Melanie sit at the head of the table so that Carol and I could sit on either side of her. This way, none of us would get lost in the conversation.

Since we hadn't known Bill or Melanie, it was only slightly awkward, but we always found things to talk about. I think that had we known them before Bill was killed, they would have made good friends of ours.

When we were done eating, Carol took the dishes into the kitchen. I had cooked, so she would do the cleanup.

"Would you like a cordial, or some coffee?" I asked Melanie. "I'm having an espresso."

We have an espresso machine on our bar in the dining room, and I got up and started making one.

"Just a coffee would be good," she said. "With some milk."

I went into the kitchen and got her a cup of coffee with some milk, and brought it back with a sugar bowl and a teaspoon. I finished pulling my espresso shot, and sat down. She didn't take any sugar.

"I didn't know Bill, but I've been friends with Danny since we were in High School together," I said.

"The two of you went to High School together?" she asked.

"Yes," I said. "We were best friends."

"And what about Dottie?" she asked.

"I didn't really know her," I said. "All that I knew was that she lived across the street."

"Did you become friends with her because of Danny?" she asked.

"In a way," I replied. "I knew Danny very well. On a case a while back, I took him across the street and introduced them. I could tell that Danny liked her right away. That was one of my successes," I said.

Melanie laughed. After a minute of silence, she spoke more quietly.

"Are you sure that Bill will come to your house tonight?" she asked.

"He has dropped by the last few months," I said. "I'd bet anything that he comes tonight."

"What time do you think he'll come?" she asked.

"Usually a little after midnight," I said.

"I'm very excited," she said. "And a little bit scared."

"Scared?" I asked. "Why?"

"Well," she said, "he's dead."

"Yes, but on full moons, he comes back to life," I said. "And I'm sure that he'll be excited to see you."

"I'm still a little nervous," she said. "Maybe I'll take you up on an after-dinner drink."

"Anything in particular?" I asked.

"Choose something that you think is good," she said.

I went to the bar and poured her a Courvoisier XO cognac. I thought that if she sipped it, it would be perfect for her – especially since our dinner had been slightly spicy. I poured myself one too, and brought both drinks back to the table.

Carol had finished cleaning up, and came back in. I asked her, "can I get you a coffee or an espresso?"

"No thanks," she said. "I'm not staying up tonight. But maybe I'll pour myself a cordial."

She went over to the bar, poured an anisette, and then joined us at the dining-room table.

"We were talking about what Melanie should expect tonight," I said.

"Yes," Melanie said. "I'm nervous."

"You won't know that Bill has changed in any way," I said. "And I'm sure he'll be surprised."

"Why didn't he come to our house to visit me?" Melanie asked.

"He probably did," I said. "And you were probably sleeping. He didn't want to wake you up and scare you."

Melanie nodded, understanding my point, took another taste of her cognac, and coughed.

"This is strong stuff!" she said.

"Yes," I said. "Just sip it. Don't try to 'drink' it."

She nodded.

We went back into the family room to sit more comfortably, and finally, Carol went to bed.

"It's late enough for me," Carol said. "I'm turning in."

"Goodnight," Melanie and I both said.

Carol went upstairs, and left Melanie Roberts and me to wait for the arrival of her husband, Bill.

Melanie and I sat in the family room continuing to make small talk. I learned some interesting things about my good friend, Danny, who was likely across the street at Dottie's again.

Eventually, Melanie dozed off. I wasn't at all tired. While the experiments that I'd done now prevented me from passing through walls, full-moons still drew me. Maybe they always would, from now on. So I was wide-awake, and waiting.

At about midnight, I decided to go out and sit on our deck. I hoped that Bill would show up. It was cool outside, so I put on a jacket. I also took a cup of coffee with me, which I balanced on our deck railing. I let Melanie sleep. I sat, looked at the super-moon, and enjoyed my coffee. I could no longer pass through walls, so I'd had to use the door.

As I was finishing my coffee and enjoying the moon, some people alit on the deck. One of them was Bill.

"Good evening," I wished them all.

"Hi, Danny," Bill said. Most of the others nodded.

"I have a surprise for you tonight," I said to Bill.

"What's that?" he asked.

"Inside," I said. "You'll have to come inside to see."

"OK," he said. "Should we all come?" he asked.

"It's better if you came in alone," I said.

I opened the door, and walked through.

"Can't you walk through doors?" Bill asked.

"The spell is fading for me," I said. "I can no longer walk through doors."

"Whatever," he said.

I held the door for him, and he followed me in. We were in the family room, although I had dimmed the lights, and he didn't see who my guest was.

"Melanie?" I said in a loud voice. And I turned the lights up.

Bill saw her, and nearly melted. Melanie opened her eyes and saw Bill, and she started crying.

"I thought I'd never see you again!" Melanie said, sobbing.

I got her a box of Kleenex. Bill went and sat down on the couch next to her, and they exchanged a long and passionate kiss.

"I think I'll go outside and talk to your friends," I said, and I went out the door.

They both ignored me. Both of them were crying, and hugging each other. It broke my heart to realize that if I was able to find a cure for this disease, Bill Roberts would probably cease to exist in any form.

Bill's friends asked, "What do you have in there that you wanted to show Bill?"

"His wife came to visit," I said. "She misses him dearly, and I told her that she should stay over."

"I miss my wife too," said one of the men.

"If you tell me who she is, I can try to unite you," I said. "I think that Bill will spend the rest of his evening here. You shouldn't wait for him."

The man who'd spoke of his wife wrote her name and number on a piece of paper that I gave him. He handed it back. The paper said "Aaron & Wanda Stevens," and there was a phone number. I assumed that he was Aaron.

I pocketed the paper, and then all of them flew up into the sky. It made me miss flying. I stood and gazed at the beautiful moon. I could see their silhouettes as they crossed it.

48. The Morning After

In the morning, I called my friend Danny, and asked him if he'd like to meet me for coffee.

"Holy Moly?" he asked.

"Where else?" I replied.

"When?" he asked.

"I'll be there in half an hour. Come when you can."

"See you," he said, and hung up.

I went to Holy Moly, and got a large cup of coffee and a window-seat. I took out my computer, and started going through the news. It was the usual nonsense: conflicting stories about the virus, and tabloid garbage about various singers and actors. Danny showed up, got himself a cup of coffee, and joined me.

"What's up?" he asked.

"I had a very interesting night last night," I told him.

"How so?" he asked.

"It was a full moon," I said. "Melanie Roberts came to stay with us."

"Why?" he asked.

"Because in the last few full moons, I had visits from her husband, Bill," I said. "I thought that she'd like to see him."

Danny stared at me. "How did it go?" he asked.

"Great," I said. "Bill showed up, and almost melted when he saw her. I left the two of them to talk in our family room, and I waited out on our deck."

"What did you do out on the deck?" he asked.

"I stared at the moon," I said. "It was beautiful. It was a super-moon at perigree syzygy."

"What's that mean?" he asked.

"The orbit of the moon isn't circular," I explained. "It's actually elliptical. That's because the earth is moving. A super-moon happens when the moon is closest to the earth. It makes the moon look larger than usual."

"I didn't know that," Danny said. "What else happened?"

"Not much," I said. "Rather, I left them in private. Bill had come with some friends who were waiting for him out on our deck. I explained that Bill was re-uniting with his wife, and that they shouldn't wait for him. They understood, and left."

"And that's it?" Danny asked.

"Almost," I said. "But one of the men gave me his wife's name and number, and asked me if I could do the same thing for him."

"And?" Danny asked.

"I didn't know him, and I don't know her," I said. "If I call her up and try to explain, she'll think that I'm a crazy person."

"And?" Danny asked.

"Well, I'd like to arrange a reunion for them," I said. "But I'm not sure how to do it. She'd have to come to my house to spend the night. Why would she do that?"

"She wouldn't," Danny said. "Maybe you should go to her house," he suggested.

"Why would she let me in?" I asked.

"She wouldn't," Danny said.

"So what should I do?" I asked.

"I don't think that you can help her husband," Danny said. "My advice is to let it go."

Unfortunately, Danny was right.

Since starting my work on a medication that would cure the virus, I could feel that I was getting better in some ways. Unfortunately, staying awake all night wasn't one of them, so I was still tired from last night. Nonetheless, I went home to my lab, and worked on stabilizing compounds containing sodium hydride. Its chemical symbol is NaH.

While I'd been able to bond NaH to the compound that I'd already made, it wasn't stable. It could explode, or maybe start a fire. I was trying to fix that. It wouldn't be safe to distribute it the way it was. While I'd been taking it, it was too dangerous to give to people that weren't careful with it. I was always very careful.

As I worked, I could hear the doorbell ringing. I looked on my phone to see who it was, and I saw three people in uniform; one holding a clipboard. I ignored them for a few minutes, but they kept ringing the bell. I wondered what I'd do this time.

I finally went downstairs and answered the door. "Yes?" I asked.

"Hi," the one with the clipboard said. "We are canvasing your neighborhood to make sure that everyone's been vaccinated," she said.

"I couldn't tell you," I said. "I don't know everyone."

"We didn't expect that you'd know *everyone*; that's why we're going house-to-house," she said.

"I see," I said.

After a long pause, she asked, "what about your house? Has everyone here been vaccinated?"

"I don't know," I said.

"Well, how many people live here?" she asked.

"Two," I said.

"And have you both been vaccinated?" she asked.

"I don't know," I said.

"How about you?" she asked. "Have *you* been vaccinated?"

"No," I said. "But I'm not a person."

"What do you mean: 'you're not a person'?" she asked. "You look like a person."

"My creator made me to look like a person," I said. "I'm really a cyborg."

"A cyborg?" she asked.

"Yes," I said. "They used to call us robots."

"What do you do here?" she asked.

"I cook and clean, and do security," I said. "Like when no one's home, I answer the door, and things like that."

"Well what about your wife?" she asked.

"I don't have a wife," I said. "I'm a cyborg."

The three of them looked very puzzled.

"I'll have to ask you to leave now," I said. "I've vacuuming to do."

"Vacuuming?" she asked.

"Yes," I said. "That's one of my jobs. I'll have to ask you to leave now. Bye," I said, and I closed the door.

I could see them on our security monitor. They stood there looking confused, and finally, they left. I went back to my lab to do some more work. I thought I was on the verge of making the compound safe and stable.

49. Aspirations of the Woke

Many in the United States find the idea of totalitarianism compelling. That's because they've never lived under it, although it's basically the entire concept of being "woke" today. During the Cultural Revolution in China, the *directives* of Mao Zedong were distributed to the people daily. These directives were the communications of his thoughts to his devoted followers. They served to enhance his authority. It made the people more "woke."

Becoming authoritarian requires an authoritarian state: it requires that the "free press" not be free at all. It requires that the "free press" and others in the entire politic unconditionally back their ruler instead of keeping him in check. While this didn't happen under President Trompe, Slow Hidin' has this going for him. That hurts our country.

The Cultural Revolution in China (1966-1976) had the goal of purging capitalism from their system, and imposing Maoism on the people. To do this, Mao charged that bourgeois elements had infiltrated the government to try to restore capitalism. While this did lead to protests, Mao deployed the People's Liberation Army to "restore order." It is estimated that they slaughtered over twenty-million people restoring order, and millions more were imprisoned in labor camps.

Authoritarianism is the control of the people by an elite ruling class. Unfortunately, in our country today, we have a president, and many people in congress who act as if they are elite. They think that they are above the "little people." They seem to believe that they are smarter than the people that work for a living. Inherent to this view is the (faulty) idea that "all people are the same." It's the idea that the "little people" all want the same things. They do not.

One of the greatest concepts behind the founding of this country was the idea that people are *different*; they're *individuals*. While money can improve anyone's life, some people really enjoy sacrificing their personal freedoms (time and leisure) for it, and others don't. There are lots of people who are happy being middle-income with a more leisurely lifestyle.

Further, the income-levels of individuals aren't static. Most people start their lives at a fairly low income level, and grow into higher levels as they gain professional experience.

The Cultural Revolution damaged China's economy and traditional culture. One of the many things done by Mao was the systematic destruction of art, and other mementos from China's culture. He wanted people to "forget" the old culture. Does that sound familiar? Mobs of people tearing statues down in America so that we could "forget" our past?

At the same time as many of our statues were torn down, we learned about the 1619 Project. On the one hand, we were eradicating our history by tearing down statues, and on the other hand, many wanted to teach children historical falsehoods: that somehow, the entire "concept" of America was rooted in slavery. While slavery was disgusting, and we fought a great Civil War to try to eliminate it (with as many people killed as in all other wars put together), the practice of slavery didn't start here. Slavery has been practiced throughout history, and throughout the world. And it's still practiced today. There is nothing uniquely "American" about it. America eliminated it here.

A major crime today is that adults are trying to teach children the concept of "racism"; they're trying to bring it back. Children today are born into a raceless society. It doesn't occur to (most of) them to wonder why some of the other children look different than they do (skin, hair, eyes, etc.). They were born that way. Fifty years after Martin Luther King, people had finally become color-blind. But Obama used it as a political tool, and brought some of it back. That was the true crime: it can be used to divide people, which helps some win elections.

Part of "wokeness" is to stultify speech. Today, people are severely ostracized for not being (perfectly) politically correct. They've been made to repeatedly offer profuse apologies when they've made the grave error of thinking that there are only two genders, and other things like that. You need "education" when you don't use the "right" language. And if you need real proof of how we're becoming more authoritarian, consider the new concept of "micro-aggressions." A micro-aggression is something that anyone can accuse you of having committed despite your not having done – or even said – *anything*. It's entirely in the eye of the beholder. Again, anyone can be accused of having committed micro-aggressions.

And sometimes, you don't even need to transgress, or to commit micro-aggressions. All you need to have done is to have been born to parents of a certain race. This is, de facto, a crime. Its entire concept is also racist.

Distributing "*directives*" (as was done by Mao) portrays the supreme arrogance of a ruler. While Mao was the chairman of the Chinese Communist Party, hence was a dictator, this goes against the entire concept of how our government was meant to work in America. While our president can wield power, he does *not* have the right to make up laws. He is our chief executive. He is supposed to be subject to the same Constitution as the rest of us. And our senators are certainly not above the rest of us: they exist to represent the peoples' interests in Washington.

So when senators speak with arrogance, it is a supreme affront to our system. At the time of our founding, the idea was that a senator should come from the private sector (so that they understood business), and shouldn't serve more than two terms. It's become a lifetime career for many of them. It's ridiculous to see senators who have never worked in the private sector announcing legislation that's (ultimately) damaging to jobs and to our economy. Many of them don't understand money, or how it works. They think that if the government simply prints more of it, then we have more of it.

While the number of dollars can be increased by printing more of them, they become less valuable when we do that. It's (basically) a zero-sum game. This hurts people's buying power, and it hurts people's savings.

Many seem to think that the answer to all of our problems is to tax "The Corporations" more than we do. What they forget is that "The Corporations" are not autonomous entities. "The Corporations" employ about half of all Americans today. When the government raises taxes on "The Corporations," three things happen. First, the cost of goods increases, since "The Corporations" produce those goods. That reduces peoples' buying power. Second, "The Corporations" stop increasing their employee's salaries, and wages become stagnant for about half of Americans. And third, many corporations move. Sometimes they move to other countries. That kills jobs in America, and it decreases the overall tax revenues.

Taxes are used disingenuously to score political points. Many seem to think that the purpose of taxes is to punish people. It's not, and never has been. The *purpose* of taxes is to pay our expenses. And our expenses should be (primarily) the ones for which a government exists: our military and our infrastructure (including roads and things that support transportation, basic education, and some healthcare). It should not have grown to include the numerous kinds of pork that it currently supports.

Who should be taxed? Everyone! Rather, everyone that is entitled to having a "vote" on how to spend our tax revenues. If someone isn't paying any taxes, why should they be entitled to a say as to how the taxes are spent? Currently, 50% of our population pays over 97% of the taxes. The bottom 40% pays nothing. If that 40% became 50%, couldn't they simply vote to take even *more* from the top 50%, and redistribute it to... themselves? Whether or not you like this idea, it's certainly not "fair," in any sense of the word.

While Carol and I had developed a working relationship with Slow Hidin', the fact was that he was a cockwomble[47] in the best sense of the word. He'd never worked in the private sector, and had a limited understanding of the pragmatics of money and business. He had the mistaken idea that people had made him the president because he was smarter than everyone else.

Unfortunately, many in the government think that they've attained their positions because they're smarter than everyone else. While being a politician requires a special kind of talent, it doesn't require raw intelligence. Many politicians were not star students. Many do not understand basic math or science or even the Constitution.

For example, Slow Hidin' admitted that he had been in the bottom two-thirds of his class in law school. He subsequently claimed that this was false: that he had been in the top half of his class. These are not mutually exclusive. He could have been both. (And both are false: he finished 76 out of 85 – in the bottom 10% of his class.)

Sometimes, Slow Hidin' barks orders like he's The King. Other times, he meekly asks for instructions as if he doesn't know what to do. Slow Hidin' seems to be schizophrenic. And so does Slow Hidin'. And schizophrenics are the two kinds of people that I don't entirely trust.

---

[47] Cockwomble: (Scottish) A person prone to making outrageously stupid statements while maintaining a very high opinion of their wisdom and importance.

It was clear that Slow Hidin' needed help. He clearly didn't know how to run the country. Carol and I were going to try to help him – at least when it came to this virus. I still wasn't sure of the side effects of the medicine that I was working on, although I was taking it.

50. A Call to Wanda Stevens

Despite Danny's advice, I decided to try to contact Wanda Stevens on behalf of her husband, Aaron. I called the number on the paper that Aaron had written when he'd visited me during the last full moon.

"Hello?" said a woman's voice on the other end.

"Hello," I said. "This is going to be an unusual call. Please hear me out before hanging up."

"I want to hang up already," she said. "Who's this?"

"My name is Mick Maux," I said.

"A call from Mickey Mouse," she said. "Are you a pervert?"

"That's really my name, but it's not why I'm calling," I said.

"Why are you calling?" she asked.

"It's about your husband, Aaron," I said.

There was silence at the other end.

"As you know, we have a new deadly virus that came from China," I said. "While I live up here with my wife, part of what we both do is to work with Washington to try to understand what this virus is, and how to defeat it. I met your husband within that context."

"What's that mean?" she asked. *"Within that context?"*

"I was infected by the same disease that took Aaron," I said.

"He died because he became severely anemic," she said.

"Not exactly," I said. "He was taken by the virus."

"But he wasn't sick," she said.

"We don't know exactly how the virus works," I said. "But we do know a few things; some are hard to believe."

"Like what?" she asked.

"Do you know who Dr. Grouchi is? The guy who's always on TV?" I asked.

"You mean that creepy guy with the beady eyes who looks like a vampire?" she asked. "What about him?"

"He really *is* a vampire," I said.

There was a long silence.

"A vampire?" she asked. "Are you crazy?"

"Sometimes," I said. "But not this time. As I said, my wife and I are working with Washington to better understand this disease. Dr. Grouchi is a vampire. Unfortunately, he ate something in China that he shouldn't have. That's what made him a vampire."

"And what happens when you're a vampire?" she asked.

"When there's a full moon, you crave blood," I said. "You can turn into a bat, fly the skies in the moonlight, and search for prey to drink blood from."

There was another long pause.

"Are you joking?" she finally said.

"No," I answered. "Dr. Grouchi fed on me."

"Does that mean that *you're* a vampire?" she asked.

"No," I said. "It doesn't work that way."

"So, how does it work?" she asked. I thought I detected sarcasm in her voice.

"There are bats in China that have rabies," I started. "If you happen to eat their guano, you become a vampire."

"What's guano?" she asked.

"In the vernacular," I answered, "shit."

"Why would anyone eat bat shit?"

"No one does it on purpose," I said. "In Wuhan, they eat bats. If they happen to have rabies, and they're not properly cleaned, it can make anyone that eats them a vampire. Vampires feed on people's blood when there's a full moon. I had a vampire who fed on me."

"Did that make you a vampire?" she asked.

"No," I said. "But it weakened me; like I was anemic. Fortunately, they didn't take enough of my blood to kill me. But apparently, they killed Aaron."

There was a long silence.

"That never even occurred to me," she said. "I thought it was anemia."

"In a strange way, it was," I said. "But anemia doesn't work that fast. It was a vampire that took his blood."

Wanda started crying. I could hear her.

"I have a very strange suggestion," I said. "And you might not believe it. If you don't, that's fine. All I ask is that you think it over."

"What's that?" she finally asked.

"Believe it or not, people that were killed by vampires come back to life when there's a full moon," I said.

"People can't come back to life," she said.

"Then I'm not sure what to call it," I said. "But people that were killed by vampires re-materialize when there's a full moon, and they fly the skies with others like themselves."

"How do you know that?" she asked.

"Because it happened to a friend of mine who was killed by vampires, and who came and visited me at my house during the last full moon," I said.

"Really?" she asked.

"Really," I said. "And Aaron was with him. Aaron is the one that gave me your phone number. He wants to meet you during the next full moon."

"But why didn't he just come to our house?" she asked.

"I'll bet he did," I said. "But you were probably sleeping, and he couldn't wake you up. He said that he'd come to my house again during the next full moon. If you were here, you could talk to him."

"…well, I don't know…" she said.

"It will be me and my wife Carol," I said.

After a moment of silence, I continued.

"Let me give you the phone number of a woman that stayed with us during the last full moon, and met up with her husband," I said.

"Who is she?" Wanda asked.

"Her name is Melanie Roberts," I said.

"Melanie Roberts?" she asked. "We are friends from a long time ago. I can simply call her up and ask her."

"We'll re-invite Melanie too," I said. "I'm sure that she'd like to see her husband again."

"Let me talk to Melanie first," she said.

"Sure," I said. "Save my number, and give me a call either way."

We both hung up.

51. The Flower Super-Moon (May 26)

The full moon in May is known as the "flower moon" because of the abundance of blooming plants and flowers in the early spring. It has also been called the "hare moon," the "corn planting moon," and the "milk moon"; all for obvious reasons. Like the pink moon of April 27, this year's flower moon was also a super-moon.

Wanda had spoken to Melanie, and both came to our house for the full moon. We had some cocktails, and dinner, and then I made a large pot of coffee. We had decided that we'd all stay up to greet the zombies that came to our house. I was sure that Bill Roberts and Aaron Stevens would be among them.

Today had been the hottest day of the month – reaching into the 90s. Because of the heat, I'd made some jerk chicken and grilled vegetables, both of which I cooked out on the grill, and coleslaw.

It was still quite warm in the evening, so we all sat out on the deck to await the arrival of the zombies. Because of the heat, I'd turned the coffee off after dinner so that it would cool down. I brought everyone an iced coffee. We sat and talked in the evening warmth.

The moon was beautiful: another super-moon, like it had been last month. They'd predicted thunderstorms, but those didn't materialize. Our landscaper had mown the lawn that afternoon, and we could smell the fresh and inimitable scent of freshly cut grass. It was a lovely evening; the perfect evening for Wanda and Melanie to see their husbands. Even if they were zombies.

Midnight rolled in, and I refilled everyone's coffee. Then we all saw it: a small flock of zombies flying across the illuminated backdrop of the full moon. They landed on our deck. There were eight of them, including Bill, and Aaron. I stood.

"Gentlemen," I said. "Good evening."

"Hi Mick," a few of them said. Most of them knew who I was by then.

"Tonight we have company," I said. "This is my wife, Carol," I said, gesturing towards her.

"Hi Carol," they all said.

"Aaron!" exclaimed Wanda.

And "Bill!" exclaimed Melanie.

Both women stood. Aaron and Bill both stepped forward and hugged their wives.

"Honey, it's so good to see you!" Aaron said. "I thought I'd never see you again!" Wanda and Aaron both started tearing up.

"If you two couples would like to go inside, you'll have some privacy to discuss personal things," Carol said. "Bill and Melanie, why don't you go into the living room. And Aaron and Wanda, why don't you go in the family room."

"OK," the four of them said: Bill, Melanie, Aaron, and Wanda.

One of the zombies whom I didn't recognize asked: "Go inside? I'm missing something. Why are they going inside when the rest of us are staying out here?"

"Those two, Bill and Aaron, had us contact their wives. Their wives are still living," I explained. "I invited their wives over for the full moon so that they could get together. I thought that since they were married couples, they might have private things that they'd like to discuss. The rest of us don't, so we can stay out here. If you'd like to have a seat, please make yourself comfortable. There are enough seats for everyone."

The zombie who had asked this then asked, "you knew Bill and Aaron, and their wives?"

"No," I said. "We met Bill and his wife at a New Year's party the night that the vampires took Bill, but we'd never met them before. Bill came two moons ago, and asked if I could contact Melanie for him. We invited her over during the last moon, and she was able to talk to Bill. We'd never met Aaron or his wife, but during the last moon, Aaron came with Bill, saw that we'd connected Bill with Melanie, and asked if we could contact his wife too. We did, and she came tonight."

"Really?" he asked.

"Really," I said.

"I really miss my wife," he said. "My name is Steve Flanders. If I give you my wife's phone number, can you contact her for me, and maybe bring her here during the next full moon?"

He wrote his name, his wife's name, and her phone number on the pad that I had lying on the table.

"Well, I don't know," I said. "I was reluctant to try to contact Wanda, since she doesn't know me. She thought that her husband had died of anemia. She was very reluctant to talk to me. But it so happened that she knew Melanie fairly well. The reason that she came here is that she talked to Melanie – who explained vampires to her."

"But can't you at least give my wife a call, and see what she says?" he asked.

"I don't think I can," I said. "She probably doesn't know about vampires and zombies. And I'll just be a strange man on the phone. I doubt that she'll believe me."

"I can contact her," Carol. "I'm a woman, so she probably won't think that I'm some nut," she added.

"Oh, thank you very much," Steve Flanders said. "I'll come for the next moon. Hopefully, you'll be able to convince her to be here."

"I'll try," Carol said.

Another zombie asked: "You think you can get his wife to come here too? What about my wife?"

He picked up the pad of paper and wrote his name, his wife's name, and her phone number on it.

"Why don't you give her a call and try to get her to come here for the next moon?" he asked.

"And what about my wife?" another zombie asked. He picked up the pad, and wrote his information on it.

Next, a woman said, "I'd like to see my husband. Can you call him?" She added her information to the pad.

There was another man, and another woman among the zombies. They both added their spouses names and numbers to the list.

"I'll call the four wives," Carol said. "And you can call the two husbands."

I wasn't sure that I wanted to do that, but said, "Yeah, sure. Would anyone like some coffee?" I asked.

"I don't drink coffee," Steve Flanders said. "It keeps me up at night."

I took another swallow of mine. This virus was getting us in deeper and deeper. I would have to find a cure. I worked extra hard on it for the next few days. We'd been invited to join the president for lunch on Memorial Day, which was only five days away.

I hoped that I'd have something safe for this virus by then. I wanted a potion that was safe to carry, that would eliminate vampires, and that would cure the people that were under their spells.

After all of the zombies had left, I expressed my concern to Carol. "That was very nice of you to promise that we'd try to contact all of their spouses. But that's not sustainable."

"Not sustainable?" she asked. "What do you mean?"

"At the next full moon, there won't be eight of them," I said. "There'll be thirty. And at the one after that, there'll be a hundred. We can't contact everyone's spouse."

"We can try," Carol said.

"I think that it would be much better if I found a cure for this disease," I said. "Tonight's implications make me want to work at it extra hard."

I worked extra hard. By Memorial Day, I thought that I had a cure.

52. Memorial Day at Le Diplomat

Slow Hidin' had invited Carol and me to come down for Memorial Day, and to join him and The Cackler for lunch at Le Diplomat. Dr. Grouchi would be there too. It sounded like a great opportunity, so we said that we'd be there. We didn't really know The Cackler, so this would be a great opportunity to meet her. Carol and I had recently dined at Le Diplomat, so we both were familiar with the menu there.

We took the Acela down the day before – which was May 30, and we spent a pleasant afternoon in Washington. The cherry blossoms had started blooming, so Carol and I spent some time on the National Mall, wandering around the tidal basin. It was a lovely afternoon. If we'd just come down for this, it would have been worth it.

That night, Carol and I had dinner at Al Volo Osteria. It's in the Adams Morgan neighborhood. From the outside, it's the kind of place you might pass without noticing it. Similarly, the inside is very plain – not ostentatious in any way. But the food! The pasta is freshly made, and the sauces are thick, each with a distinctive flavor. The sauces are rich without being unctuous. I had the pappardelle with lamb, and Carol had the ravioli with a sauce made with short ribs.

After dinner, we went to the Echostage for a couple of drinks. It's an impressive night-spot: about 30,000 square feet with two 60-foot bars, and live music. We didn't stay too long because it's hard to have a conversation in there, although we did cut a few steps.

In the morning, we took a short walk and got some coffee and bagels. We went back to the Mall to enjoy the cherry blossoms some more. A little after noon, we caught an Uber, which we took up to Le Diplomat. Carol and I went in, and went to the front desk to be seated.

"Can I help you?" said the man at the desk.

"Yes," I said. "We're here to enjoy your fare on Memorial Day."

"That's good to hear," he said. "We are totally booked up. Do you have a reservation?" he asked.

"I'm sure that we do," I said.

"What name is it under?" he asked.

"I'm not sure," I said.

"You'll need a name, or I can't seat you," he said.

"Do you have anything under the name 'Hidin'"?" I asked.

"I've no time for jokes," he said. "We're very busy. If you don't have a reservation, we can't seat you."

"Look under 'Slow Hidin','" I said.

He ignored me, and gestured to the people in line behind me. "Can I help you?" he asked them.

"Excuse me," I said. "I'm here to have lunch with the president."

He ignored me, and continued helping the people behind us. As we stood there, some Secret Service people came in. They were all wearing the same kind of suit, and each had sunglasses on. They did a quick scan of the restaurant, walked through it, and then the one that seemed to be "in charge" gestured toward the door. Another agent opened the door, and Slow Hidin' came in with The Cackler and their spouses.

"Hi Mick and Carol," Slow Hidin' said. "Good to see you. Have you been here long?"

"Not at all," I said. "This gentleman was just about to seat us," I said, gesturing toward the man at the front desk.

The man looked shaken. The maitre d' came running over, and said, "welcome sir, welcome. We have your table ready, sir. Please follow me." He took us to a back corner of the restaurant to a round table with eight seats.

Slow Hidin' sat with his back to the restaurant. His wife sat on his right side, and Carol sat on his left side. I sat next to Carol, and to the left of me was The Cackler. Slow introduced us to The Cackler, and she said: "Caaacacacacackle!"

We already knew Dr. Grouchi, and he introduced us to his wife. Slow Hidin' introduced us to the First Lady. And we introduced ourselves to The Cackler's husband: she was cackling too much, and had been unable to do this herself.

We all ordered drinks, and several of us took some bread. Le Diplomat has excellent bread.

I looked at President Hidin' and asked: "How is the work coming with the virus?"

Dr. Grouchi was busy talking to The Cackler, and didn't hear us. President Hidin' looked at me, and then did a dramatic shift of his eyes toward Dr. Grouchi, looked back, and gave me the TikTok "distress" signal.

"What?" I asked him. "I said, 'How's the work coming with the virus?'," playing dumb.

President Hidin' looked more panicked. He shifted his eyes (and head this time) toward Dr. Grouchi, and gave me the TikTok "distress" signal again.

"What?" I said again, looking confused. "Oooohhhh!..." I said. "I got it."

Then I gave the TikTok signal, and asked: "Did you mean this?..." And then I did it backwards, "or this?..."

President Hidin' gave the TikTok signal again.

"I got it," I said. "How's everything else going?" I asked, trying to change the subject. I gave him the TikTok signal, and pointedly shifted my eyes towards Dr. Grouchi, and then back again.

"Great," he said. "Everything's great."

"That's great," I said.

The head waiter came over and said, "Ladies and Gentlemen, I can simply handle the menu for you if you'd like. I will choose the dishes. If you have anything in particular that you do or don't like, please let me know. Would that be OK?"

We all nodded, and he went off to the kitchen.

We sat back, and I exchanged some pleasant talk with the First Lady as Carol spoke to the president for a few minutes.

The sommelier came out with a Champagne, which he poured out for everyone, and then a few servers came back with the restaurant's "Grand Plateau," which comprised chilled lobsters, salmon, littleneck clams, shrimp, and scallop crudo, which was made with lemons. The waiters portioned out the "Grand Plateau," and we started dining. The Champagne was a relatively robust one. While I didn't get a chance to see the label, it went nicely with the "Grand Plateau."

After we'd finished the "Grand Plateau," the servers brought modest salads for us. Each salad plate contained three tomato slices at its base: one red, one yellow, and one purple. There was a moderate pile of mesclun atop those. Then a few slices of cucumber and a modest pile of radish spirals.

The idea was clearly to refresh the palate; not to fill us up. The salads were dressed with a simple vinaigrette, and three servers came with pepper mills to give pepper to whomever wanted it.

The salad plates were cleared, and the sommelier re-emerged, this time with a white wine. I did get to see the label this time. It was a Grüner Veltliner. That made me wonder what the coming course would be.

The waiters came out with fairly small servings of freshly grilled branzino. Each was accompanied by roasted peppers and gigante beans. Now I understood the Grüner Veltliner; it was a nice choice.

Slow had been talking to Carol. I tried to get his attention by raising my hand, and giving the TikTok signal. A waiter came running over, and asked me whether there was a problem. I thanked him, and assured him that there wasn't. But Slow looked over to see why the waiter had come to talk to me, so I waived him down with a TikTok.

"Slow," I said. "I wanted to tell you that I think that I've made lots of progress with the medication that I've been working on."

"Really?" he asked. "What do you have?"

"It's a potion that's based on hydroxychloroquine, with a bucky-ball, and a secret ingredient that I've added," I said.

"And it cures the virus?" he asked.

"I think it does," I said. "I think that it's curing mine. I also think that it cures vampires in a sudden way."

"Sudden?" he asked. "What's that mean?"

"Maybe we'll see when they serve dessert," I said.

We went back to eating, and I tried to chat with The Cackler. The problem was that she never conversed. Every time I said something, she just cackled.

We'd finished our branzino, so the servers cleared our plates.

This time, the sommelier came out with a Beaujolais, which caused me to guess that we'd be served duck – I'd remembered the menu from last time. The waiters came out with small servings of duck confit, which had been plated with lentils and braised root vegetables. Again, it was a very nice pairing.

As I dined, I addressed Dr. Grouchi, across the table from me.

"How are the studies coming along?" I asked him.

"Progressing," he said.

"Did I tell you that I think I've found a cure?" I asked.

"A cure?" he asked in return.

"Yes," I said. "A cure. I was just telling the president."

"Last we spoke, you'd been working with hydroxychloroquine. Is it based on that?" he asked.

"Yes," I said. "But I've added a Buckyball to it," I said.

"A Buckyball?" he asked. "Anything else?"

"A little magic. Other than that, NaH," I said, so that "NaH" sounded like "no." I didn't tell him that I was talking about sodium hydride. Again, its chemical symbol is "NaH," so Dr. Grouchi probably understood it to just be "nah."

"When are you going to show us?" he asked.

"Maybe I can show you when we're having dessert," I said.

We were all finished with our duck, so our plates were cleared. The waiters distributed dessert menus. While the head waiter had proscribed the first four courses, we could each choose our dessert of preference. I ordered the *millefeuille* and an espresso.

The head waiter brought over a bottle of their top brandy, and put glasses in front of each of us. "Would anyone like something other than brandy? A cordial, perhaps?"

Slow, Dr. Grouchi, and I all motioned toward our glasses, and the waiter poured brandy for us. Carol and the First Lady took a pass. The Cackler ordered a cordial.

They brought our desserts, and a cordial. We started on our desserts.

"Now," Dr. Grouchi said. "You said that you'd show us your cure when we were having dessert."

"Are you sure you want to see it now?" I asked.

"Yes," Dr. Grouchi said. "You've made a big claim, and I'd like to see it."

"OK," I said. "We know that you, the president, and I have all been infected with this disease."

I took out a small bottle with an eyedropper in it.

"I'll put a dose of this medicine in each brandy, and you'll see," I said. "It has no taste, so all you need to do is to drink your brandy."

I put a couple of drops in mine, then in Slow's and then in Dr. Grouchi's. I had to reach across the table to put it in Slow's, and in Dr. Grouchi's.

"You first," Dr. Grouchi said.

I took a nice swallow of my brandy. It tasted very good.

"I've been taking this for a while now," I said. "And most of my symptoms are going away."

President Hidin' took a good swallow of his. While he coughed – because of the strength of the brandy, he seemed fine.

Now it was Dr. Grouchi's turn. He took a good swallow of his, sucked in his breath, and exploded in a cloud of smoke, which evaporated almost instantly. He'd simply disappeared! Slow Hidin' was surprised by this, and started laughing. He couldn't help it.

"That's how my 'cure' cures vampires," I said. "Poof!" I exclaimed, making an exploding motion with my hands.

The president eructed, laughing again. "Where did he go?" he asked.

"Poof!" I exclaimed again, waving my hands, by way of answer.

The president eructed again with more laughter. Dr. Grouchi's wife sat there looking confused.

"Anthony!?" she exclaimed. "Anthony!? Where did you go?"

53. How to Administer the Cure

President Hidin' called a special meeting for the morning after Memorial Day. The topic was announced to be "Administering the Cure."

We had what seemed to be "a cure." But it had not been evaluated in government labs, and was not known to be safe. It *seemed* to be curing me. But was it really working for good? And would it cure everyone? An even bigger question had to do with the vampires: if they knew that they would explode when they took the vaccine, why would they take it?

The second question had a natural answer. It seemed that if a vampire drank the blood of someone who was taking the cure, it would destroy them. This had happened when Lucy Chao had tried to feed on me. The key here was to get enough of the population vaccinated – or drinking my potion – so that if vampires tried to prey on them, the vampires would be destroyed.

Carol and I arrived at President Hidin''s meeting a little bit early. It was in a conference room that was adjacent to the Oval Office. We took seats near the front of the room. Other people arrived: military people wearing lots of stars, and medical people – some of whom I recognized from earlier meetings. President Hidin' came in last, followed by his staff.

He was drooling. One of his staff people whispered something in his ear, and handed him a handkerchief. He wiped the drool off, and stood at the podium. He read from notes.

"People of America," he started. "I beat Donald Trompe fair and square. But then he worked with his friends in China to develop this virus to threaten mankind. What we know is that if you eat contaminated bat-shit, you become a vampire. Here, people don't eat bat-shit, but in China, they do. Dr. Grouchi said so. Too bad he couldn't be here today. Vampires come out during full moons, and they feed on the blood of innocent people – many of whom voted for me. Those people become zombies – like me."

"What happens to zombies?" a general asked.

"Nothing," President Hidin' said. "They just become kinda slow. If vampires drink too much of their blood, it will kill them. But if they don't, it just makes the zombies kinda' slow – like me."

After a pause, he continued. "Today, I've asked the Drs. Maux to join us." He indicated us. "The Maux's think that they have developed an antidote to the disease – and hopefully, a way to destroy the vampires. Mick, can you take it from here?"

"Sure, Mr. President," I said.

Slow Hidin' took a seat, and immediately fell asleep.

"As you can see," I said, looking at the president, "if you become a zombie, it reduces your energy-levels. If too much of your blood is drained before it can regenerate, you'll die. Most people that are bitten by vampires are bitten by a single vampire, which doesn't kill them. If that vampire feeds on them once a month, they probably won't die. But they'll become lethargic and slow. They will exist in a state that's stupefied," I said, looking over at the dozing president.

"What happens if there is more than one vampire, or if one vampire takes too much blood?" a general asked.

"Then the person that was the prey probably dies," I said.

"Do they then become a vampire too?" he asked.

"Yes," I said. "At least I think they do. They *do* fly the skies when there's a full moon."

"They fly the skies?" one of the doctors asked. "Why?"

"I don't know," I said. "They just do. When there's a full-moon out, they awaken, and they fly the skies. They sometimes search for blood, and they fly the skies."

"Is that a bad thing?" a senator asked.

"Yes," I said. "The problem is that they will fly the skies forever, and they'll prey on people."

"Why is that a problem?" the senator asked.

"Because if we let this go, the skies will become full with everyone who ever dies," I said. "We will have trillions of people flying the skies. Everyone will become a vampire."

"I'm confused," another doctor interjected. "Who flies the skies? Is it the vampires, or their victims?"

"They all do," I said. "Vampires fly the skies. I've seen that not only do vampires fly the skies when there's a full moon, but they sometimes fly the skies when the moon is not quite full. This gives them a several-day 'window' to feed on people. People who have been bitten by vampires, but who are still alive, fly the skies during full moons too. But they don't prey on people. While these people are lethargic for most of the month, when there's a full moon, they come alive, and fly the skies. I call people like this 'zombies.' So that covers vampires, and zombies. But worse, people who are killed by vampires will become vampires too. They're the flying dead."

"How can you tell them all apart?" someone in the back of the room asked.

"You can't," I said. "Wúdí-wáng vampires, and people who are zombies haven't died yet. They're alive. During the day, and for most of the month, they are exactly as they were before they became vampires and zombies. But the zombies are lethargic." I glanced at Slow Hidin'. "People who are killed by vampires become vampires too. But they're not wúdí-wáng vampires. They're dead. They only emerge when there's a full moon."

"You mean they come out of the ground?" a presidential aide asked.

"I don't know where they come from," I said. "I know one who was cremated, but who materializes during full moons. Where does he come from? I couldn't tell you."

"And you've developed an antidote?" one of the doctors asked.

"I'm not sure what to call it," I said. "It's curing me."

"What do you mean by that?" a staff person asked.

"I was bitten," I said. "I was bitten by a certain vampire for a few months in a row. I was becoming a zombie. I developed a compound that turned that around. I no longer exhibit the traits of a zombie, and I feel healthy again."

"If it works for you," a medical person asked, "how do we know that it will work for everyone?"

"We don't," I said. "That's where we'll need government labs."

"But what stops the vampires from feeding on them again?" a military person asked.

"Nothing," I said. "But if a vampire is exposed to this medication – or to the blood of anyone who is taking the medication – it will kill them. They will cease to exist."

"That means that they can simply feed on the blood of those who aren't taking the medicine," a staff person said.

"But how will they know?" I asked.

"How will they know what?" the staff person asked.

"How will they know who is taking the medication, and who isn't?" I asked. "If they simply choose a victim to feed on, the person's blood could kill them."

"The solution is obviously to mandate that all citizens get vaccinated," the staff person said.

"Isn't that unconstitutional?" I asked.

"But this is an emergency," the staff person said. "We can override the Constitution when there are emergencies."

"How is this an emergency?" I asked.

"It's an emergency because if you don't get vaccinated, you can be bitten by a vampire," they said.

"So?" I asked. "If that makes someone a zombie, we can cure them."

"But what if they refuse to take the medicine?" they asked.

"Then they can live as a zombie," I said. "There's no law against that. Also, if they become a zombie and they want to be cured, we can cure them."

"You said that the medicine, and that includes the blood of anyone who is taking the medicine, will kill vampires," another staff person said. "Is that legal?"

"It won't kill them unless they voluntarily take the medicine," I said. "No one would be killing them if we give them ample warnings."

"But what about vampires that die by trying to feed on someone who is taking the medicine?" they asked.

"Do you mean vampires that commit assault on citizens who don't resist, and they wind up dead?" I asked. "Again, I'm not sure what the crime is."

"How do you know that a citizen won't resist?" they asked.

"Vampires have a way of hypnotizing people before feeding on them," I explained. "The citizen won't resist. The only 'crime' is that a vampire tried to feed on someone. Besides, who will bring the criminal complaint?"

"The vampire," the staff person said.

"But they'll be dead," I said. "They won't bring a complaint."

"Well what about their dead body?" they asked. "Won't someone need to explain the dead body?"

"No," I said. "I forgot to tell you: when the vampire ingests blood with this medication in it, they cease to exist. There's no body."

"How can they 'cease to exist,'?" a doctor asked.

"They explode," I said. "Their body ceases to exist."

"Isn't that dangerous?" a senator asked. "Couldn't that injure bystanders?"

"I used the wrong word," I said. "They *implode.* Then they cease to exist."

The chief medical person said, "We need to get your prototype and study it. Then we need several industrial research facilities to study it, make sure that it's safe, and come up with a way to produce it on a large scale."

"I'll give you some samples, and make my notes available to you," I said.

"Excellent," he responded.

"It's essential that we beat this thing," I said. "And I think that we can."

54. Lunch with the President

Our meeting finished at about noon. A staff person roused the president, and helped him to stand. He whispered something to the staffer. Carol and I got up to leave, and as we were exchanging contact information with the chief medical person who had asked whether we would share our findings, the president's staff person came over to us. When we were done talking to the chief medical person – his name was Dr. Sanders, the staff person asked us whether we'd stay for lunch.

"Stay for lunch?" Carol asked. "Where?"

"Here," he said. "In the White House. The president said that he'd like to discuss this with you over lunch."

"We'd be delighted," Carol said.

We were accompanied by some staff people to a small, private dining room. Carol and I sat. The president had taken a detour; one of the staffers told us that he'd had to change his bib. So we waited for him. He entered about ten minutes later. He'd been all cleaned up.

"I'm glad that you could join me for lunch," he said.

"That's our pleasure," Carol said. "If we can beat this virus by working together, we should."

A waiter came in, and looked at the president. "The usual?" he asked. Slow Hidin' nodded. Then the waiter looked at us. "We have poached salmon with a salad. Is that OK with both of you?"

"Yes," we both said.

The waiter disappeared, and the president continued. "Do you really have a cure for this thing?" he asked.

"Honestly, I don't know," I said. "It's curing me. I think it will cure you too if you keep taking it. You had a dose at Le Diplomat. Do you feel any different?"

"Not much," he said. "By the way, what happened to Dr. Grouchi? That was a neat trick you played."

"It wasn't a trick," I said. "He imploded. The medicine that I've developed causes vampires to implode."

"You mean he's gone?" Slow Hidin' asked.

"Yes," I said.

"For good?" he asked. "You mean he didn't go to China?"

"No, I think he's gone for good," I said. "I don't think he's coming back."

"Really?" he asked. "I'm going to miss him, although he was a creepy-looking little vampire. Well, what do the two of you need to do to fix the vampire problem?" Slow Hidin' asked.

"We need to visit government-approved labs, and show their technical teams what we have so far," I said. "We talked to Dr. Sanders as the meeting broke up this morning, and he's going to have that arranged."

The waiter returned. He had plates of salad with poached salmon for Carol and me. As he served them, a security person came in and fastened a bib around the president's neck. It was one of those bibs with a big plastic pocket at the bottom of it – to catch whatever fell. Another waiter brought the president a bowl of Maypo. Another man emerged with a Riesling, which he poured for Carol and me.

Predident Hidin' took a spoonful of Maypo. "Mmmmm, my favorite!" he said. "Can you bring me some butter and maple syrup?" he asked.

"Certainly," the waiter said. He disappeared, and re-emerged with butter and syrup.

"Mmmmm!" the president said again. He put a big lump of butter on top of his Maypo, and then he poured syrup all over it.

Carol and I tasted our salads and our salmon. The salads had been dressed with a simple vinaigrette, and the salmon had been poached with some fresh dill. While very simple and elemental, it was a very nice lunch.

"Who did you say you talked to?" Slow Hidin' asked.

"Dr. Sanders," Carol said.

"I can't picture him," Slow Hidin' said. "Isn't he a negro? Colonel Sanders?"

"What's a negro?" I asked.

Slow Hidin's eyes went blank, and he got a glazed look on his face.

"Dr. Sanders will arrange for us to visit Pfizer, Moderna, and Johnson & Johnson, and to show them what we have developed," I said. "No doubt, people there will think of improvements that can be made."

His eyes were still glazed over.

"The important thing is to develop a vaccine that can be distributed to large numbers of people," I said. "The original attempts that I'd made had stability problems."

Slow Hidin' focused again. "Did you say *senility* problems?" he asked, looking like he was about to become upset.

"No. I said *stability* problems. The original formula could explode," I said. "We fixed that."

"But you said that it causes vampires to explode," Slow Hidin' said.

"Actually, they implode," I said.

"What's the difference?" Hidin' asked.

"In an explosion, the parts of an object move outwards," I said. "In an implosion, they move inwards. That's important because explosions can injure bystanders. Implosions can't."

"I see," Slow Hidin' said. "Dessert anyone?"

He pushed a buzzer, and a waiter appeared with a busboy. The busboy cleared the plates.

"I'd like the fruit cup," he said to the waiter.

"Anything for you?" he asked us. "Crèmes brûlée maybe?"

"That sounds good," both Carol and I said.

"Coffee?" he asked.

"Please," I said.

The waiter left, and returned with a fruit cup, two crèmes brûlée, and some coffee. He served all of us.

"What are the next steps?" President Hidin' asked.

"Carol and I need to meet with the technical teams at Pfizer, Moderna, and Johnson & Johnson," I said.

"In the meantime, I think that I need to impose some new laws," President Hidin' said.

"New laws?" Carol asked. "Like what?"

"Everyone must wear a mask," President Hidin' said. "And everyone must stand six feet apart."

"What do those things have to do with the bat virus?" I asked.

"I don't know," President Hidin' said. "But we need some laws. I want *everyone* vaccinated," he continued. "It should be *mandatory*."

"Mandatory?" I asked. "Why?"

"Because if you're bitten, it makes you a zombie," he said.

"And then you can take the medicine, and it cures you," I said.

"Well I still think that we need some new laws," President Hidin' said.

A staff person came in, and said: "Sir, it's time for your nap."

"Oh, yes," President Hidin' said. "Well, nice talking to you. I think that we need to meet again." He stood.

"I'll let you know when we've made progress with the vaccine," I said.

He nodded. "Well, goodnight," he said.

The staff person removed his bib, and led him out of the room. Carol and I looked at each other and shrugged.

55. Visits to the Corporate Headquarters

President Hidin"s staff arranged visits for us to the corporate headquarters of Johnson & Johnson, Pfiser, and Moderna.

Johnson & Johnson headquarters is on the Raritan River in New Brunswick, New Jersey, in the middle of the Rutgers campus. Pfiser headquarters is on East 42nd Street and 2nd Avenue in New York City. And Moderna headquarters is in Cambridge, Massachusetts, on the MIT campus.

We'd arranged to visit Johnson & Johnson on the Rutgers campus the following Tuesday morning, stopping in New York City to visit Pfiser that same afternoon. And then on Thursday, we'd go to Moderna.

On Tuesday, we left our house at a little after 7:00 AM, drove down to the city, and then took Interstate 95 (a.k.a., The New Jersey Turnpike) to New Brunswick, arriving at a little after 9:00. Since it was a college campus, lots of the lower-level people weren't in yet, but the senior executives certainly were, and their top medical people had been there for a while — drinking their coffee at a table in a large conference room.

Carol and I went through security, then were ushered into the conference room, where we were introduced. There were a couple of airpots of coffee with some Styrofoam cups on a table in the back of the room, and a tray with some Danish pastries on it.

"Please help yourselves to some coffee and Danish," our host said. "And then we'll get started."

Carol and I each got a cup of coffee, and I took a bagel with a pack of cream cheese. The senior executive started the meeting as I connected my computer to the overhead projector so that I could show visuals.

"Dr. Maux and Dr. Maux have been working on an antidote to the virus," he said. "There are lots of things about this virus that you might not know. While they think that they have an antidote, their sample size is insufficient to draw real conclusions from it. Its side-effects are unknown. And so far, there's no way to mass-produce it. That's where we need your expertise. Is it safe? How do we manufacture and distribute it? And are there long-term side-effects?"

I stood, and said "Thank you. Like all of you, we'd first heard about this virus on the news. Carol and I didn't think much about it, but then it became personal. I became infected."

A person near the front asked: "What does that mean? Infected? What are the manifestations of being infected? How did you become infected?"

"I'm sure that you've heard that the infection comes from the guano of rabid bats," I said. "What happens when you are exposed to this? Believe it or not, you become a vampire."

"A vampire?" another man asked. "Are you joking?"

"No," I said.

"In what way do you become a vampire?" he asked.

"You crave blood," I said. "When there's a full moon, you fly the skies looking for people to feed on."

"And if you're fed upon, does that make you a vampire?" he asked.

"No," I said. "But it makes you a zombie. And if feeding on you results in your death, you become a vampire too."

There was laughter.

"Are you joking?" he asked. "What does a zombie do?"

"A zombie flies the skies during full moons," I said. "But he doesn't feed on people. He's not a vampire – yet."

"You said that you were exposed to it," another man asked. "How?"

"I was bitten by a vampire," I said. "That's why I started working on a cure."

"Finally we'll get to the technical stuff," a senior scientist said.

"Yes," I said. "Well, Carol and I worked on a cure for zombies. I wanted to end my dependence on the moon. As a zombie, I also craved food with blood in it. That gets tiresome, although I wasn't feeding on other people. I first tried taking C_{60}. That didn't seem to do anything, although it made me feel healthier."

"Then what?" someone asked.

"Then I bonded C_{60} to hydroxychloroquine," I said. I showed the picture.

"And?" someone else asked.

"That didn't work either," I said. "What I did after that was to add sodium hydride to this compound." I showed the picture.

"Did that work?" someone asked.

"In my case, it seemed to work," I said. "But there's a problem with it," I added.

"What?" the senior executive asked.

"It's not stable," I said. "It can explode. We'd have a hard time distributing it," I said.

"Then what?" someone finally asked.

"I added olive oil," I said.

"Olive oil?" someone asked.

"Yes," I said. "Not only does it stabilize it, but it makes the compound taste good."

"Does that mean that it shouldn't be injected?" another scientist asked.

"I wouldn't," I said. "The olive oil is too thick. I just swallow it. It's stable, and it tastes good."

I pulled a small jar out with the compound in it, and some droppers. "Would anyone like a taste?" I asked.

A few people tasted it.

"How did it occur to you to combine your compound with olive oil?" someone asked.

"I was thinking about Chanukah, and that's when it occurred to me," I said.

"Chanukah?" someone asked. "What's Chanukah have to do with the bat virus?"

"Nothing," I said. "But back in those days, in what was then Persia, olive oil was the fuel that was used for lighting. They used lamps that were based on what we call 'wicking.' They submerged a string – a 'wick' – into the oil, and had the string emerge from the end of the lamp. By igniting the wick, they'd get a flame that was continuously fed by the olive oil."

"And?" a man asked.

"It took about twenty olives to produce enough oil to provide flame for an hour," I said. "Olives were a very large and essential commodity back then. One of the things that Chanukah celebrates was the burning of a lamp for eight nights using the only oil that they had. They only had enough oil for one night, yet it burned for eight nights. How did they burn it for eight nights?"

"The menorah is a lamp used to celebrate Chanuka. It has eight candles – which represent the eight nights – and a ninth candle, called a *shamash* which symbolically differentiates the eight holy flames from other light sources. It's also used to light the other eight candles."

"So what's that have to do with the bat virus?" the same man asked.

"Olive oil has a structure like this," I said, projecting a diagram.

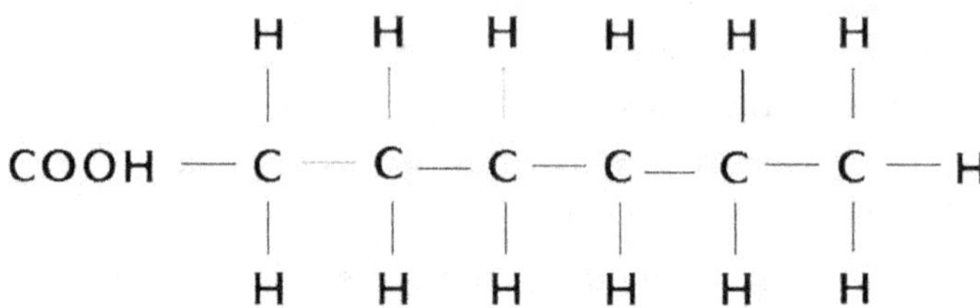

"This shows the saturated form. Of course, there's a monounsaturated portion in most oils in which some of the hydrogen atoms are missing, and there are double-bonds between the corresponding adjacent carbon atoms. And the actual carbon chain is much longer in both. The COOH is just carboxylic acid."

"What the Israelis did – perhaps unknowingly – was to oxidize the olive oil. You wouldn't want to cook with it, but that eliminated the oxygen atoms, which basically converted their olive oil into something like a kerosene.[48] While again, you wouldn't want to cook with it, its burning efficiency was far superior to that of olive oil."

"So you've bonded kerosene into your mix," a man asked. "I would think that this would make it even more dangerous."

"Like I said, at first it was explosive," I said. "But we've been able to make it stable," I added.

I picked up the bottle that I'd passed around, and I shook it to demonstrate.

"See?" I asked. "No explosion. But we could certainly use your help in perhaps improving the basic formula, and figuring out how to produce and distribute it in high volumes."

"I'm still a little concerned about the possible volatility of this compound," a senior technical person said.

---

[48] This isn't true.

"It's interesting that you mention volatility," I said. "Another effect of this compound is that it destroys vampires."

"Do you mean that it kills them?" someone asked.

"Yes," I said.

"How?" he asked.

"It makes them implode," I said. "Then they cease to exist."

"They implode?" someone asked. "Then why would the take it?"

"They probably wouldn't," I said. "But if they drank the blood of someone who was taking the medication, they'd implode."

"Then why would they try to feed on someone who is medicated?" the same man asked.

"How would they know?" I asked.

There was a long silence. The senior executive finally said: "Well I think we're done for today. Perhaps if you all exchanged email addresses, you can all keep in touch, and advance this thing. We also need to establish that this is safe for everyone."

We all got up, exchanged contact information, and went to lunch in the company cafeteria where Carol and I sat with the same group of people and made small-talk.

After lunch, Carol and I drove up to New York City where we had a similar meeting with Pfiser, and on Thursday, we drove up to Moderna in Cambridge, and did it again.

I thought it interesting that my solution to this potion had to do with Chanukah. I can never think of Chanukah without thinking about 2013. This was the first time that the first day of Chanukah fell on Thanksgiving. Thanksgiving tends to be too early for Chanukah.

The first year that Thanksgiving was celebrated was 1621 (a mere two years after slavery was first invented - in 1619, according to "woke" doctrine). That seems to be a long time – nearly four-hundred years – before Chanukah fell on Thanksgiving. But believe it or not, the first day of Chanukah won't fall on Thanksgiving again until 79811 – not quite 78,000 years from now.

I'd bet that in 78,000 years, we won't be celebrating Thanksgiving or Chanukah anymore. And I couldn't help but to notice that 79811 happens to be a prime number too.

56. The Strawberry Moon (June 24)

The first full moon of summer is called the "strawberry moon," since strawberries are ripe enough for harvesting. The strawberry moon has also been called the "mead moon," the "honey moon," the "flower moon," the "hot moon," the "hoe moon," and the "planting moon." It had been a hot day, with the temperature in the mid-90s.

Carol and I had contacted the six spouses of the vampires that had left us with their numbers during the last full moon, and all of them had confirmed that they'd be coming to our house tonight. I wasn't looking forward to it since I was nearly back to normal, and staying up after midnight wasn't my thing. While I was sure that the re-uniting of the six sets of spouses would bring a level of happiness to all of them, I still wasn't looking forward to it. I was also concerned that the midnight visitors were vampires, and might feed on their spouses.

With Melanie Roberts, Wanda Stevens, Carol and me, and the six other spouses that we'd now be hosting, there would be ten of us for dinner. We'd fit comfortably into our dining room, but we didn't feel like cooking for ten, so we told everyone that it was a "pot-luck." I was anxious to see what people would bring, although it didn't turn out to be as bad as I had imagined.

I made a roast turkey with some gravy to make sure that there would be meat for everyone. While turkey isn't exactly a summer thing, everyone seemed to appreciate it. Several of the people brought bottles (or cartons) of wine, so there was plenty of that. And I'd pre-made lots of coffee, which I had iced. Since the temperature was very hot, I was sure that most people would want iced coffee instead of hot coffee.

One person brought potato salad, and another brought coleslaw. I put some pickles out with those. A third person brought a tray of grilled vegetables: zucchini, onions, peppers, and brussel sprouts. Another person brought a large casserole of Italian meatballs cooked in tomato sauce, and another made a large salad to share. Finally, there were baked beans, and two deserts.

We had a nice dinner, drank some wine, and poured some coffee. The six new people stayed in the dining room to chat, and Carol and I went out on the deck with Melanie and Wanda.

"This was so nice of the two of you to do this," Melanie said.

"It was our pleasure," Carol said. "This will grow, though."

"Grow?" Melanie asked.

"Yes," I said. "I'm sure that the six spouses who are vampires will come tonight. And they'll each bring some friends. Those friends will want us to contact their spouses too. This will grow."

"Is that bad?" Wanda asked.

"No," Carol said. "But we won't have the space to accommodate all of the people. If we do it again next month, the following month it will be even bigger."

"Maybe we should arrange to use a church, or one of the schools," Melanie said.

"That's a great idea," I said. "Would you like to help us?"

"Sure," Melanie said.

"Me too," Wanda added.

We sat and drank our iced coffee. Eventually, the six who had stayed in the dining room came out and joined us. It got very late, and the moon rose high in the sky. We could see the silhouettes of flying vampires against the backdrop of the bright moon. All at once, about twenty vampires landed on our deck. I could feel the deck sway slightly.

Our eight guests stood up and greeted their spouses. Our six new guests looked amazed. They hugged their vampire spouses.

"Hello," I said to the group. "I see that we have some newcomers. Welcome."

One of them stepped forward. "Thanks," he said. "Bill told us that if we gave you our spouse's names and phone numbers, you'd contact them, and invite them here for the next full moon."

"Of course," Carol said. Carol and I looked at each other.

Our eight live guests each went off in private with their vampire spouses so that they could have some privacy. The remaining vampires hung out with me and Carol on our deck. I knew that I needed to fix this.

The new vampires in the group all gave me and Carol contact information for their spouses. There were fifteen new names. This was going to be lots of work. If we could work with the industrial labs to speed things up, perhaps we wouldn't need to do it. Our deck couldn't hold more people and vampires.

I was tired, and so was Carol. We weren't used to staying up this late.

57. The Buck Moon (July 24)

We had spent the latter part of June, and all of July working with the three industrial labs. This involved several telephone conferences, and numerous other one-on-one phone calls. Modifications were made to my formula by all three labs, and people figured out how to bottle and distribute the results.

The vaccine rolled out in the second week of July. The major problem with it was educating people about the virus and what the risks actually were. Distributing the vaccine happened rather quickly. Taking the vaccine was easy. All that people needed to do was to pick up a bottle of it, and use the eye-dropper to administer daily does to themselves.

We didn't think that there were any harmful effects, except for on vampires. Basically, it was a well-formulated supplement – C_{60}, together with hydroxychloroquine, and a sodium-hydride molecule that had been rendered inert by some olive oil. What could go wrong?

Slow Hidin' went on television several times, urging people to take the vaccine. In fact he *mandated* that they take it – which was being challenged by many civil libertarians. Several cities started *requiring* that people take the vaccine. Mayor deBozo made it a law that people could not enter privately-owned businesses (e.g., restaurants) unless they were taking the vaccine.

The 4th of July came and went, and Mayor deBozo cancelled most of the festivities, believing that the bat virus made it dangerous for people to congregate.

I again tried to explain to many in the government that if you didn't take the vaccine, you posed no risk to anyone else. The vaccine was merely a cure for those who were being fed upon. And it killed vampires.

So, who were the vampires, and who did they feed upon? As before, we had no way of knowing who was a vampire. But if they fed upon someone who was taking the medication, they would implode. Therefore, while more vampires were appearing through feedings that killed their victims, more of them were also imploding. It was hard to know what the actual number was. What I did know was that for the vampires, it was a losing game.

Carol and I called the spouses of the fifteen additional vampires who'd given us their phone numbers. This was difficult. All of the spouses were still grieving. And most didn't understand about zombies and vampires, and thought that we were making crank calls.

We also agreed to host an additional vampire evening at our house. This time we were to serve dinner for as many as thirty-three guests. We suggested that people come to our house at about 6:30. We had a large and eclectic mixture of food that people brought. Some of it was very good, and some of it wasn't. But it was a very nice social event. I met lots of interesting people that I never would have met otherwise, and had a number of lively discussions.

This month, the full moon was on July 24, but we didn't know how many of the vampires would actually be there. Some would have been eliminated by the new vaccine. (Remember that vampires are able to feed on people when the moon is nearly full, so it was possible that some would be eliminated on July 22nd and 23rd.)

The "buck moon" finally arrived. It's called the buck moon because the antlers of male deer (bucks) have reached their full size by this time. Bucks shed and regrow their antlers each year. And each year, they produce a larger and more impressive set of antlers than the year before. They use their impressive antlers to spar with other males over the right to mate with does.

During this full moon, there were about fifty vampires that came. But only about ten of those were vampires from the last moon, with spouses that were our guests. The others were new vampires who had come just to ask that we contact their spouses, and ask them to come to our house for the next full moon.

While I felt sorry for our living guests whose vampire-spouses didn't make it, it meant that the formula was working! Most of the vampires that were the spouses of our guests, but who didn't make it, had likely fed on someone that had been taking my formula. They imploded, and didn't exist anymore.

Carol and I tried our best to pack up the leftovers, and urged the guests that had brought food to take their leftovers home with them. It was not all going to fit into our refrigerators, and we would have had to throw most of it away.

Gradually, people left, and vampires alit and flew into the sky, leaving our party. When it was just me and Carol, we took most of the garbage down, and went to bed. We were both very tired.

To my surprise, in the morning I got up at the usual time. I knew that Carol would likely sleep in late, so I decided to go to Holy Moly for coffee. I would take my computer and play chess. I took a shower and got dressed, grabbed my computer, went downstairs, and started my car. But when I opened the garage door, there was a surprise waiting for me.

Another car was parked right behind my garage so that I couldn't get out. I wondered who's car it was, why they'd parked it there, and why they'd left it. Maybe they'd had too much to drink, and caught a ride home with someone else. But leaving their car there had been inconsiderate.

I got out and took a look at their car. Perhaps they'd left a message under a windshield wiper, explaining the situation. There was no message. Frustrated, I took out my phone, jotted down their plate number, closed the garage, and walked up our driveway. Maybe Danny was still at Dottie's and maybe he could help me figure out who's car it was.

When I got to the top of our driveway, I saw Danny's car, so I was in luck. I walked over to Dottie's house and rang the bell. She answered.

"Hi Mick," she said. "That looked like quite a party you had last night. What brings you here?"

"I would have invited you, but it was for reuniting people with their dead spouses. It was for vampires. I think you would have found it a little creepy," I said.

She made a face. "Yes, I would have. I'm glad that we weren't there."

"Is Danny here?" I asked.

"Yes," she said. She turned towards her kitchen. "Danny!" she shouted.

"Yes, dear," he shouted back.

Danny walked out into the foyer, finishing a donut that he'd been eating. "Hi Mick," he said. "What's up?"

"I was just telling Dottie that we had a vampire-reunion party last night," I said. "You wouldn't have enjoyed it."

"You're right," he said.

"But this morning I found a car parked behind my garage, and I can't get out," I explained.

"Who would do that?" he asked.

"It might have been someone who had too much to drink, and who got a ride home with someone else," I said.

"Yeah," Danny said, "but don't you think that they'd have left you with their keys?"

"Yes," I said. "So I'm rather annoyed about it."

"Let's get their plates, and maybe I can figure out who's car it is," Danny suggested.

"I've got their plates," I said. I showed him on my phone.

Danny looked at the number and called the police station. He was transferred twice, but eventually, someone gave him a name and a phone number. He hung up.

"I know who owns the car," he said, looking at me. "I'll call them now."

He dialed the number. It rang, and an answering machine picked up. He left a message. "This is the police. We've found your car behind the garage at the Maux's house, and they can't get out. Can you come move it?"

He called the same number twice more to give a human a chance to pick up. That didn't happen.

Finally, he said, "I have a hunch. Let's go back to your house."

We left Dottie's and walked down my driveway. We went into my house, and Danny said, "let's search it. Nothing fancy; let's just have a look around."

We went through the family room looking everywhere. We looked behind the couches and behind the drapes. We went through the dining room and into the pantry, opening all of the closets. We went through the living room, through the foyer, and through the kitchen. Then we went upstairs. We started looking in each of the bedrooms, and we found her. She was on the bed in the second bedroom. She was dead.

Her purse was lying on the dresser, and a set of keys was attached to her purse.

"Don't touch anything," Danny said. "I'll have to call this in."

"What are you going to tell them?" I asked. "That her dead husband, who's now a vampire, got her into a bedroom at a party at my house, and drank her blood?"

"Well that's what happened, isn't it?" Danny asked.

"Yes," I said. "But how did he get here?" I asked. "He's a vampire."

"It was a full moon, and you had a party for all of the vampires," Danny said.

"And you think that they'll simply write it that way on the police report?" I asked.

"No," he said. "I think you'll be the primary suspect. Don't go anywhere without talking to an attorney."

"Why would I want to talk to an attorney?" I asked.

"Because you'll probably need one," he said.

"But what if they suck all of the blood out of me?" I asked. "That's the last time I'll have a party here," I added.

"I have to have the police in so that they can do a report," Danny said.

"OK," I said. "Let's go downstairs to get some coffee, and you can call them."

"Sounds like a good idea," Danny said.

Danny and I went downstairs, and I made some coffee for both of us while he called the police station and explained the situation. We sat catty-corner at the island in our kitchen waiting for the police to arrive. In the meantime, Carol came down.

"Good morning," she said, pouring herself a cup of coffee.

"Good morning," Danny and I both said.

"Good to see you, Danny. What brings you here?" she asked.

"It's not all good," I said. "Someone parked their car behind my garage, so I couldn't get out this morning," I explained.

"And that's why Danny came over?" Carol asked.

"Well," I said, "I went up to Dottie's to see if Danny had any suggestions, or to see whether he could find out whose car it was. He suggested that we come back here and look around."

"And?" Carol asked.

"We found the owner of the car," I said. "At least I assume that she's the owner."

"Where?" Carol asked.

"Upstairs," I said. "She's dead. She's lying on the bed in one of the spare bedrooms."

"Well that was just a matter of time," Carol said.

"The police are on their way here," I said. "They're going to want to file a report. I'm not sure how to explain that we hold vampire parties whenever there's a full moon. They're not going to like that. They'll think that we're crazy, and that maybe we had something to do with killing her."

"I assume that now she'll be a vampire too," Carol said.

"Probably so," I concluded.

The police showed up. It was two policemen and a medical examiner. They all knew Danny. We showed them where the body was. The examiner examined the dead woman and concluded that her heart had stopped. (Duh.) One of the policemen dusted for prints on her handbag (I assume that he found hers), and on the end-tables (I assume that he found mine).

The examiner had come in an SUV, and the two policemen got a stretcher out, and moved the body from the bed to the SUV.

Danny explained what had happened.

"And you witnessed this?" one policemen asked.

"No," he said. "Mr. Maux came up his driveway and got me. I was staying across the road at my girlfriend's house. Mr. Maux knows me well, and came up to look for me when he found the dead woman's car behind his garage. He couldn't get out."

"And?" the policeman asked.

"And we looked around his house, and found the dead woman," Danny said. "I assumed that the car behind his garage was hers."

"So you didn't actually see the murder, and Mr. Maux brought you in here and explained what had happened?" the policeman asked.

"No," Danny said. "Mick came up asking for help. I came down here and found the body, and called you guys."

"Is it possible that Mick murdered the woman, and created this scene as an illusion?" the policeman asked.

"No," Danny said.

"Why isn't that possible?" the cop asked.

"Because he's not that stupid," Danny said. "Why would he quietly murder someone, and then go out of his way to bring the cops into it?"

The cop had no answer.

"This was done by a vampire," I said.

The cops looked at me like I was crazy. They finished their notes, and the examiner left with the body. Danny had taken her car keys so that we could move her car. He'd given her purse to the other cops.

58. A Hot, Woke Month

It was a hot, woke month.

We found out that the dead woman was named Patricia Gordon. Her husband had died a few months back, and the coroner had though that it was a loss of blood that had killed him. The coroner couldn't explain how he had lost the blood. The same thing had killed Patricia. The police picked up her car, and notified her estate that they would need to sort things out.

I was invited to the police station to – again – give my account of what had happened. They didn't believe me, but wrote down what I said, shaking their heads. *A vampire party? Really?*

There was a congressional hearing about the people that had wandered into the Capital building on January 6. The people running the hearing – and the press – kept calling it an "*insurrection*," which is defined as "a revolt against a civil authority." None of the people had come armed, they seemed completely disorganized, and many of the Capital guards were seen on film directing them into the building. Aside from a couple of broken windows, there was no real damage. But nonetheless, it was an "*insurrection*."

The exception to the violence was that a young, petite, unarmed woman was shot to death by a guard at an extremely close distance of about three feet. The guard had given her no warning; he just murdered her. The Woke News had been hailing him as "a hero."

Congress had a hearing about the "*insurrection*" on July 27. They had arranged for a nice lineup of people that were to testify. Representative Kingfinger took the stand, and cried throughout his testimony. It was almost as good as watching several professional actors crying in court lately, but they are professional actors. Kingfinger isn't. His crying bordered on the comical.

Then there were four "military people" who were brought in to testify. While all of them were wearing uniforms, all of them cried too. It was humorous to watch: four uniformed girlie-men crying! Hot! One slammed the table with his fist. A violent one. And he did it while crying. Hot!

While slamming the table with his fist was an attempt to convey macho outrage, no doubt, after studying how some professional actors cried, he couldn't cry nearly as well as Jessie Wallet, nor did he come across nearly as macho as Jesse Wallet. But was he woke? Quite.

We also had action in the sports world. The Cleveland Indians decided that their name might be offensive to one or two native Americans. So they changed their name to "The Woke Warriors." It has a much better ring to it, but their fan's hats needed to be made wider: "WW" instead of just "C." But their hats make them look much more "woke." And from the air, looking down at the hats from above, the Cleveland stadium looked like it was full of M&Ms.

On August 10, Governor Blowmo resigned as the Governor of New York. "The News" claimed that it had been his pattern of harassing women that had finally caught up with him. But no reasonable people were fooled by this. He'd been sexually harassing women for nearly fifty years, and no one had complained about it before. People are still wondering why Governor Blowmo was really pushed out. Sexually harassing women?

"Women like it when you do stuff like that," Blowmo explained. "I don't know why I was pushed out," he continued. "I probably stepped on the wrong person's toes. That's usually not a problem if I step on their toes hard enough. I'll have to be more careful next time. This isn't in my autobiography." (How would he know? Has he read it?)

After Governor Blowmo resigned, his brother was pushed out of his very cushy news-anchor job. Now that he wasn't the brother of the governor, he didn't have any useful, confidential tidbits that he could bring to the news channel.

Medication for the RBG virus was now being distributed nationally by all three pharmaceutical companies, and most people were now safe from the virus. And my hunch was that the vampire population would be thinning out very quickly.

Carol and I took two more trips to Washington to meet with the staff people that were managing the medications, and to meet with Slow Hidin'. Like me, Dr. Grouchi hadn't taken Slow Hidin' over to the other side yet. I guess Dr. Grouchi realized that Slow couldn't be the president if he was actually dead. And we hadn't heard from Dr. Grouchi since I'd given him my medication at Le Diplomat.

I had the feeling that Slow Hidin' missed Dr. Grouchi in a strange way. When his eyes would glaze over, sometimes I had the feeling that he was remembering Dr. Grouchi. While Dr. Grouchi was no longer feeding on him, he... still... seemed... a... little... slow.

250

59. The Sturgeon Moon (August 3), A Disturbing Dream

It had been a year ago when Carol and I had become aware of – and involved with – the RBG virus. Since then, we'd learned a lot, and many things had changed. We'd developed an antidote to the virus, and the person who had pulled us into it – Dr. Grouchi – was gone. He'd fed on me, so I didn't regret him leaving us.

Tonight would be another full moon. Carol and I had agreed to hold another party, but we'd made the upstairs in our house off-limits to guests. We didn't want any more deaths here. While the police hadn't pushed me too hard on the first one, I didn't think they'd tolerate another. We also didn't want any of our guests "ruffling the covers" in the spare bedrooms.

I was skeptical that we'd get many vampire guests. My hunch was that many of them had been destroyed by feeding on people that had taken the vaccine. It was likely to be more of a social get-together among the living than gloomy visits from vampires, so we invited Danny and Dottie over.

It had been several months since I'd craved blood or flown the skies. I was healed. My biggest problem tonight would be staying up late.

This was the thirteenth full moon since Dr. Grouchi had made me a zombie. It was a little over a year ago. There are 29.5 days between full moons. Note that while it's 29.5 days, we don't usually see the moon during the day, although we sometimes do. Tonight was a full moon, and it was August 22. I'd first met Dr. Grouchi, and had become a zombie on August 3, 2020. That was 384 nights ago. That was when I'd first started noticing – or more precisely, "paying attention to" – the moon.

The year 2020 had been a leap year. Remember that leap years occur every four years, unless the year is divisible by 100, unless the year is divisible by 400. So 2020 was a leap year. That's how I knew how many full-moons there had been. "But what about kamo'oalewa?" you might ask. We'll get to that later.

During the last full moon – the buck moon – we'd had about thirty human guests, and about fifty vampires. Those vampires had given me and Carol their names, and contact information for their loved ones. We'd tried to contact most of them. I was worried about the human crowd we'd get tonight, which was one of the reasons that I'd invited Danny. If the cops showed up, he could talk to them.

I was worried that we might get as many as eighty people tonight: the thirty-plus that had come during the last full moon, plus most of the fifty that we'd contacted since. Vampires? If none had fed on medicated people, it would certainly be 150-200. The question was: how many drank blood containing my medicine, and wouldn't be returning on full moons anymore?

It was this last question that had me nervous. If we saw lots of vampires, then my medicine wasn't working, or people weren't taking it yet. But if the number of vampires was less that last time, there would be a great cause for optimism.

As it had been during the last full moon, dinner was to be a "pot-luck." I wondered what kind of eclecticisms I'd be savoring. It made me shudder.

Carol had been straightening out the living room, the dining room, and the family room so that our house would look "nice" (or at least neat). While that was a good idea, I assumed that most people would socialize outside, just because there would be too many of them to fit in our house.

People started arriving at about 6:30. They brought food, and various kinds of beverages. Carol and I both started making the rounds, introducing ourselves, and talking to people.

Danny and Dottie showed up, and I went over to welcome them. Dottie had brought the fruitcake that we'd given them on New Year's Eve. She probably didn't remember where it had come from.

Pretty soon, our living room, dining room, family room, deck, and patio around our pool were all full of people waiting the arrivals of their vampire loved ones. If we got a hundred vampires, I didn't know where they'd all fit.

Finally, the police showed up. They had walked down the driveway, and started questioning people. Enough people had figured out that I was the host, so the police eventually found me.

"Good evening, sir," one of them said.

"Good evening," I replied.

"Can I ask what's going on here?" he asked.

"Of course," I said.

"Of course, what?" he asked.

"Of course you can ask," I replied.

"Well, what's going on here?" he asked.

"We're having a party," I said.

"A party?" he asked.

"Yes," I said. "A party. That's why they call it 'a party.'"

"What's the purpose of the party?" he asked.

"The purpose?" I asked. "I hadn't thought about that. Would you gentlemen like something to eat?" I asked.

"No, thank you," he said.

"Is there some kind of a problem?" I asked.

"No," he said.

"I'm glad to hear that," I said. "You gentlemen are welcome to stay. But if we're done here, I'd like to go talk to some of my other guests."

"I see," he said.

"Can I take down your name and badge number?" I asked. "Just in case we *do* have a problem?"

"Of course," he said.

I wrote those down. The police stood there for a few minutes, and then they left.

At close to midnight, a group of vampires crossed the moon, and then landed on my deck. There were only about fifteen of them. About ten had come to reunite with their loved ones, and five more came to see if we could get them connected for the next full moon. Carol took their names, and their contact information.

Of the nearly eighty people that had come tonight – I was unable to actually count them – about seventy were very disappointed. Several actually accused me of running "a scam." I'm not sure what they thought I had scammed them out of, but I gave them the police officer's name and badge number, and told them to contact him. I hadn't told him about the vampires that would be coming to the party. I thought that they could do that – and then complain to him that their vampires hadn't shown up.

By about 2:00 AM, all of the vampires and most of the people had left. Carol and I started straightening up, and the remaining people took the hint, and left too. I checked our driveway to make sure that there were no remaining cars parked in it. And then I checked all of the rooms upstairs to make sure that there were no dead people.

Tonight's party had been a success. My bet was that there wouldn't be any vampires left in another month. But God had a surprise for me.

60. The Harvest Moon (September 20) and Kamo'oalewa

The "harvest moon" came and went. This year, it was on September 20. And the equinox[49] was two nights later. We didn't have a party for the harvest moon, but I stayed up late and sat out on our deck. No vampires came calling. I took this as a sign that my medicinal formula – or whatever the three labs had done with it - had worked. As I was about to learn, this wasn't quite true.

It was true that what we call "the moon" had stopped awakening vampires. But unknown to many, the earth has a second moon, called *kamo'oalewa*[50]. It was discovered by Pan-STARRS at Haleakala Observatory in Hawaii in April of 2016. Its period in orbiting the sun is about 366 days – slightly longer than the earth's period, although its period is slowing down very slightly. The earth will eventually pass it. And it orbits the earth in a quasi-elliptical manner, at a distance ranging from forty-times to one-hundred-times the distance of what we know as the distance to "the moon" that we all know and love.

---

[49] Equinox is when the night and the day have equal durations (12 hours). This happens twice per year.
[50] In Hawaiian, this refers to a single floating item.

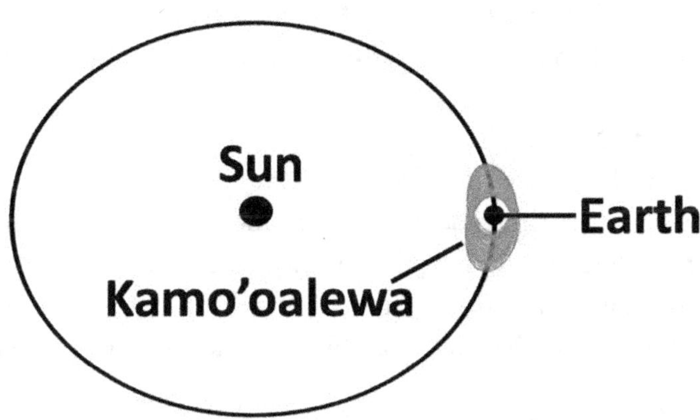

While the earth is about 91,500,000 miles from the sun, the moon is about 240,000 miles from the earth. So the sun is about 340 times as far away as the moon is. Kamo'oalewa is quasi-elliptical, so its distance from the earth varies between 9,600,000 and 24,000,000 miles. It's much farther away than the moon that we all know. It's also far enough from the earth so that it gets a substantial amount of its energy from its gravitational attraction to the sun. That's what makes its orbit "quasi-elliptical." The accompanying diagram shows its quasi-elliptical orbit. Notice how flattened its orbit appears. Again, this is because of the sun.

Kamo'oalewa is also quite tiny, which has an unexpected effect that we'll get to. While the moon that we know and love is 2,160 miles in diameter, kamo'oalewa is only about 100 meters in diameter – maybe twice that size. And I wondered: just because vampires are no longer awakened by what we think of as "the moon," what about kamo'oalewa? This was never considered in any of the older literature about vampires. But when that literature was written, they didn't know about kamo'oalewa. Now we know about earth's second little moon.

Long after the harvest moon, and long since I'd seen a vampire, I was working late one night in my lab. It was a new project that I was excited about, so I was having difficulty sleeping, although I eventually became weary, and my vision started to fade. I put my reading glasses up on my forehead and rubbed my eyes.

There was a slight motion on the corner of my desk, so I straightened up, and dropped my reading glasses down so that I was looking through them again. There, on the corner of my desk was Dr. Grouchi. But he was less than an inch tall. At first, I thought he was an optical illusion. But that's what I thought the first time that I'd seen him in my hotel in Washington DC.

"Hello Dr. Mouse," he said.

He spoke, I thought. *Maybe he's not an illusion*, I thought. It was a wheezing voice, but this time it was a very high-pitched wheezing voice. I picked up my large round magnifying glass, and used it to bring him into focus. Sure enough, it was Dr. Grouchi.

"My name is Dr. *Moose*," I told him. "Hello Dr. Grouchi. How have you been?"

"Fine," he said. "And how are you?"

"I'm great," I said. "I'm very surprised to see you. Why are you less than an inch tall?"

I started wondering whether I was hallucinating. I rubbed my eyes, and focused on Dr. Grouchi again, just to make sure that he was really there. I looked through the magnifying glass again. He really was there.

"That formula that you concocted prevents the moon that we all know from turning people like me into vampires," he said. "But when kamo'oalewa is full, people like me re-emerge. The problem is that we're tiny – less than an inch tall."

"Why are you tiny?" I asked.

"Because kamo'oalewa is tiny," he said. "I used to be a wúdí-wáng' vampire. But now I'm a kamo'oalewa vampire. We are now the world's tiniest bats."

"But now you're too tiny to feed on people," I said.

"Yes, we are," Dr. Grouchi answered.

"So what do you feed on?" I asked.

"Small creatures," he said. "Mice, lizards, and sometimes even insects. But most insects don't have blood. Mosquitos do. But they tend to burst. Feeding on mosquitos is disgusting. And you can't take a chance with mosquitos, since you don't know who they've fed on. They might contain blood with *your* medication in it. And the problem with lizards is that they are cold-blooded. They're actually pretty terrible to feed on too."

"Do they become vampires?" I asked.

"Who?" he asked. "Do you mean the mice and the lizards?"

"Yes," I said.

"Yes," he said, "but they're kamo'oalewa vampires like I am. They become much tinier versions of mice and lizards. They shrink down to such a tiny size that you probably couldn't even see them as 'dots' without your magnifying glass."

"So what do *they* eat?" I asked. "Especially when they're that tiny?"

"I don't know," he said. "Probably plankton and other organisms."

"So you mean that our eco-system is becoming vampire-ridden?" I asked.

"What do you mean?" he asked.

"If I eat organisms that came from that ecosystem, what happens to me?" I asked.

"I don't know, Mick," he said. "I guess that we'll wait and see."

"What's it like, feeding on mice and lizards?" I asked.

"I've already told you that I don't like the flavor at all," he said. "But I'm in the minority."

"Minority?" I asked. "What do you mean?"

"I was one of the few wúdí-wáng' vampires that grew up in America, with American-food tastes," Grouchi said. "Most of the wúdí-wáng' vampires are Chinese. They liked things like mice and lizards when they were growing up. Remember that this all started because they eat bats. In fact, it's the flavor of *people* that the Chinese aren't used to. I think that many of them are happier as kamo'oalewa vampires. They think that the food's better."

"With what had been happening in Wuhan, China must now have millions of kamo'oalewa vampires," I said. "Wouldn't it be easier for you to live over there?"

"No," Grouchi said. "In fact, because of our size, the bats in Wuhan now feed on us."

"That's quite the irony," I observed. "People became wúdí-wáng' vampires by feeding on bats. Then the wúdí-wáng' vampires became kamo'oalewa vampires, and now the bats are feeding on *them*. It's poetic justice. Don't take it personally."

"In Wuhan, the people that are now kamo'oalewa vampires spend most of their time hiding," Grouchi said. "When they go out in public, the bats get them."

The Hubei Province in China had over a hundred species of bats. In fact, the current academic literature puts the number at 147. Now there's a new one: the kamo'oalewa vampire. But the kamo'oalewa vampire is the tiniest of them all.[51] And because they usually take the form of tiny people, the other bats feed on them. Grouchi was right. Today, it was very dangerous to be a kamo'oalewa vampire in Wuhan. He was much better off living here.

"How's Slow Hidin'?" I asked him. I hadn't seen Slow since the vampire problem had been solved. But seeing Dr. Grouchi again made me think that perhaps it hadn't been solved.

"I try to visit him, but he doesn't seem to see me," Grouchi said. "Or at least he never acknowledges me. He looks much worse than he did before. He must be contemplating a re-election campaign."

"Good," I said. "I think he'd make a great president."

"And he's re-instituted mask-mandates," Grouchi said.

"We can't be *too* safe," I pointed out.

---

[51] Today, the world's tiniest bats are called bumblebee bats. They live in Thailand and Myanmar, and are between 1.1 and 1.3 inches long.

61. The Truth About Life

We can't make everyone happy.

For many, their greatest fear is their fear of mortality. And we all have it: mortality, that is. The most important things that we have are our values and principles; not our mortality.

In fact, Dr. Grouchi may have beaten mortality. We'll see. But he lacked values and principles. While still alive, he now lives on the blood of lizards and mice. Do you call that living?

If we try to make everyone happy, we'll lose. Not only can't we make everyone happy, but we'll lose ourselves trying to. Politicians do this all the time. That's why most of us who aren't politicians have values and principles. Most of us call these principles "ethics."

And we all need to make the best use of the time that we have on this planet. Ethics help us to do this. Again, we can't make everyone happy. But what are ethics? Ethics are morality. And morality trumps mortality. That's what many in this world don't seem to understand.

In fact, many people sacrifice their morality to try to achieve a life that's "greater" in some way: they try to beat mortality. It never works. Here was Dr. Grouchi, the world's tiniest bat. He comes out when kamo'oalewa comes out. He lives on the blood of mice and lizards. And a real bat might eat him if they find him. Has Dr. Grouchi beaten the system? I don't think so.

"But masks?" Dr. Grouchi continued. "Why does President Hidin' think that people still need masks?"

"So that people don't bite each other?" I ventured a guess.

"But people already don't bite each other," Dr. Grouchi observed.

"See?" I said. "It works."

"But it works without the masks!" Dr. Grouchi said.

"We can't be too safe," I said again. "Believe it or not, I have a good friend who's a police detective. When RBG first emerged, he and I were having a discussion. I'd said that dictators – like in China, for example – sometimes make arbitrary rules. I made up an example. I said that a dictator might mandate that everyone had to wear masks. He told me that that could never happen in *this* country because here, we think for ourselves."

"Our government is changing," Dr. Grouchi said.

"That's because many of the people are changing," I said. "Many believe that socialism sounds like a great idea. And part of the socialist doctrine is that the government makes all of your decisions for you. The government takes care of everything, and tells you what to do, and how to think. In exchange, all you have to do is to *not* think, and to lose your aspirations. Your personal aspirations are a cog in the wheel of a smooth-running socialist society."

"Many people find thinking hard," Dr. Grouchi said. "Many find it easier if someone does the thinking for them."

"Yes," I said. "It *is* easier. It's easier if you've no aspirations. The entire concept of 'America' is color-blindness. Anyone can aspire to be anything. It doesn't matter where you're from, or who your parents are. Achievement comes to those who are willing to work. That *requires* individuality. People have different talents, different tastes, and different aspirations. In socialist societies, 'the people' are a conglomerate. Here, they're individuals. This also seems to be a fundamental disagreement between 'the right' and 'the left.' Conservatives tend see people as individuals. Liberals tend see them as members of groups."

"I'm not sure that I understand," Dr. Grouchi said. "What difference does that make?"

"When you view people as members of groups, it's those aspects that are common to the people within the group that become very important. When you view them as individuals, they are just that: individuals. You don't see them in terms of their presumed – and sometimes arbitrary and superficial – aspects. Thus to the left, things like a person's skin color are very important. To the right, they're irrelevant," I explained.

"Could *I* be a 'group'?" Dr. Grouchi asked.

"In mathematics, yes. But in real life, I don't see how," I said. "There's only one of you. Maybe if you were schizophrenic, you could be. But if you *are* schizophrenic, don't worry: you're not alone."

"What if all of the kamo'oalewa vampires got together? Then could *we* be a group?" Dr. Grouchi asked.

"Certainly," I said. "But how would you contact all of the other vampires? How would you become 'a group'?"

"I haven't figured that out yet," Dr. Grouchi said.

"What would you do as 'a group'?" I asked. "Why is that important to you?"

"Maybe we could form a voting block," Dr. Grouchi said. "We could lobby."

"You're always thinking about politics," I said. "Instead, ask yourself a question. If a man that can't count finds a four-leaf clover, is still he entitled to happiness?"

After thinking for a minute, Dr. Grouchi said, "I don't know."

After a longer pause, I responded: "exactly."

Finally, Dr. Grouchi asked, "do you believe in coincidences?"

"That's funny," I replied. "I was just about to ask you the same question."

"Do you find it odd that Slow Hidin' doesn't seem to be getting any better?" Dr. Grouchi asked. "I thought that he was acting tired and slow because I'd been feeding on him. No one has fed on him in a long time. My guess is that his overall torpor had nothing to do with me feeding on him. That was a coincidence. He's just old and lethargic. If anything, he actually seems to be getting worse."

"I think you're right," I said. "I don't think that I can blame you for that. On the other hand, you *did* feed on me," I replied.

"Sorry about that," Dr. Grouchi said. "What was the coincidence that you mentioned?"

"Did you hear about the time that a hyphenated word and a non-hyphenated word walked into a bar together?" I asked.

"No," Dr. Grouchi said. "What happened?"

"The bartender nearly choked on the irony," I said.

"I don't get it," Dr. Grouchi said. "Hyphenated and a non-hyphenated words? What's that got to do with the RBG?"

"It has to do with life," I said. "Many things are not what they seem. And many become convoluted by our language. One of the biggest scams played by many political factions is that they subtly change the definitions of words. They do it so that things that they say actually mean the opposite of what it sounds like they said. This does fool lots of people. It tends to be the same people who think that socialism sounds like a good idea."

"But isn't that just propaganda?" Dr. Grouchi asked. "And can't propaganda be easily refuted with science?"

"Science can always be questioned," I responded. "But propaganda cannot."

"Are you questioning the science?" Dr. Grouchi asked.

"Yes," I responded, staring at Dr. Grouchi through my magnifying glass.

"Are you joking?" Dr. Grouchi asked.

"Joking?" I asked. I peered at Dr. Grouchi through my magnifying glass; Dr. Grouchi now a very tiny and pathetic-looking vampire with a high-pitched wheezing voice.

I put the magnifying glass down, balled my hand up into a fist, and brought it down swiftly and strongly on Dr. Grouchi: ***Splat!*** He was now a smear on the corner of my desk.

"Justice is the constant and perpetual will to allot to every man his due,[52]" I said. And then I concluded:

"La commedia è finita!"[53]

---

[52] A quote from *Gnaeus Domitius Annius Ulpianus* (c. 170 – 223? 228?) who was a Roman jurist that was considered to be one of the great legal authorities of his time.

[53] In English, this means "The comedy is over." This is the ending line of "Pagliacci," by Ruggero Leoncavallo. Pagliacco makes this somber statement after committing a double murder. Remember that this book started with the Prologue of Pagliacci.

Reviews From Readers

A great apocalyptic, intense yet humorous, and action-filled adventure that's great for avid fans of sci-fi and comedy. Here again, we witness another of Dr. Philip Emma's compelling books of the life of Mick Maux and his wife Carol. In this book, the reader will witness again the skills and the wits of this lovely couple as they solve each murder mystery and ultimately stop the pandemic. We also see Detective Danny in action. In all honesty, this book had me laughing throughout the plot. You could really tell that the author writes with humor and passion. Highly recommended!

This great convergence of zombies, the undead, vampires, and wudi-wang vampires turned private detectives, Mickey Maux and Carol Maux, into vampire hunters. They must find a way to stop the spread of the virus before the world turns into hell. Right after my very first read of the beginning chapters, I totally laughed out loud realizing that Dr. Philip Emma based the setting of the story on the real scenario of the Covid19 pandemic. I also commend the author's ingenuity for making the characters look interesting, humorous, and intriguing. Although there were many twists and turns, and characters that the reader needs to absorb in order to appreciate the whole story, every page is enthralling. I suggest reading it slowly to completely contextualize the whole plot and appreciate the book. Job well done, Dr. Philip Emma.

Unpredictable, enthralling, and engaging book to read, perfect for sci-fi, apocalyptic enthusiasts with a twist of comedy. Here again, we witness Mickey and Carol Maux for another adventure of their life. But this time, it's a different atmosphere. Instead of solving mystery murders of mafia bosses and rich commissioners, this time, their skills and ingenuity will be tested with a pandemic of RGB virus from Wuhan, headed by the one and only Dr. Grouchi. One thing that really cracked me up the whole time was learning the characters' names. Starting from our leading man Mickey Maux, to President Trompe and Slow Hidin'. It was just a whole new experience of intense, horror, and comedy. I love this book.

There's a lot to say about this book. I guess this is one of the best books that Dr. Philip Emma has ever written. From beginning to end, the author didn't fail to entertain the reader, starting from the unique plot, the funny names of the characters, and Mickey Maux's sense of humor. As a private detective and scientist, Mick Maux has another job offer from the lead scientist of Wuhan Institute of Virology, Dr. Grouchi. This time, instead of fighting criminals, Mick Maux is fighting vampires, zombies, and the undead. Personally, I love the book's unique plot and funny characters. When I got to the part where I read the U.S. President's name, I had a good laugh. This book is one of the best books on the shelf.

From start to finish, The Wuhan RBG Virus by Dr. Philip Emma is gripping, and will appeal to fans of horror, thrillers, science fiction, and comedy alike. In this new book featuring the private detective and scientist, Mickey Maux, the author brings in a whole new context of antagonists. This time, Mick and Carol are fighting zombies and vampires. But the police are skeptical of the existence of these creatures. The fun part begins when Dr. Grouchi hires Mick for a special job. I loved this book. The vampires and zombies looked believable and well-drawn. They were backed up with science and experiments. So, in order to solve the Wuhan RBG virus that could potentially turn anyone into one of the undead, they must find a way to stop the spread before it's too late. An excellent read.

At first glance at the title, I thought that this was a book about Covid-19. I totally loved everything from this book. We see Mick Maux in action once more, together with his lovely wife Carol, who unlike Mick, is filled with wit and sense. Their mission is to stop the spread of the Wuhan RBG Virus that started in China at Wuhan Institute of Virology. And once again, we see Mick using Math and Science equations to solve the pandemic. Honestly, this book is brilliant. The place and the characters' names just perfectly coincide with some names and places in real life which had me laughing the whole time. I also enjoyed the conversations, especially the many conversations between Mick Maux and the secretary of Dr. Grouchi. I am happy to rate this book a perfect five stars overall.

An epic story of a zombie and vampire apocalypse where Mick Maux's talent is once again tested by the Wuhan RBG virus. This book is a mix of humor and horror, and I loved it. When the world is threatened by a virus that can turn humans into zombies or vampires, Mick, Carol, and Detective Danny's help are once again needed in order to solve the problem. In all honesty, this book left me in awe. When Dr. Grouchi, the head of the Wuhan Institute of Virology passes away, Mick is all well and ready to give everyone the anti-virus medicine that he developed before it's too late. One of the highlights that I like personally was the names of the characters and the places. Surely, Dr. Philip Emma knows how to write with humor. This is a book that epic sci-fi and comedy fans will absolutely enjoy. I definitely recommend this one.

A book that will have you on the edge of your seat. A unique novel where everyone can potentially become undead without even knowing it. It's a virus that spreads like wildfire, and it's being kept secret. No one expected that a virus could turn someone into a vampire, wudi-wang vampire, or zombie. Every murder seemed a mystery and only a handful of people knew the real dangers of the virus. That included Mickey Maux. Dr. Grouchi, the doctor and scientist of the Wuhan Institute of Virology, reveals everything to Mick Maux. But he's feeding on Mick. And when Dr. Grouchi dies, Mick is ready to take matters into his own hands. After reading it, I came to the conclusion that this book has one of the coolest attributes of a good book. It perfectly brings you the intensity and horror that you are looking for without compromising the humor. Reading the characters' names for example is already eye-catching. I'm sure you're going to love every bit of the book.

An exciting book with engaging characters and funny names that demonstrates wit and humor, mixed with romance, horror, and an apocalyptic plot. Mick Maux, a private detective and scientist, is hired by Dr. Grouchi of the Wuhan Institute of Virology. His mission is to develop a vaccine to save the world from a deadly Wuhan RBG virus that can turn a human being into a zombie, vampire or wudi-wang vampire. Together with his wife Carol, and they have to solve the murder mystery while also developing a vaccine. Every scene is very unpredictable and will surely make you think deeply to connect all of the dots together. It's a fast-paced book that brings a whole new level of experience. In all honesty, I finished reading this book in just a couple of days. The book is nearly 300 pages long but it's one that's hard to put down.

A humorous, absorbing horror and suspense is an easy pick for the fans of sci-fi novels. Imagine being "undead" without you knowing it. When a virus breakdown spreads like wildfire, Mick Maux knows exactly what to do. But he can't do it alone. He needs the help of his lovely wife Carol, and the smart, bad-ass detective, Danny. Mick is being called by Dr. Grouchi, the head of the Wuhan Institute of Virology, with regards to the new RBG virus from Wuhan, China. Will Mick be able to save the world from the spread of the virus and provide a cure on time? Find out from this beautiful and funny adventure of Mick, Carol, and Danny. I love the idea that the author used real places and almost real people's names to bring life to the story. I totally laughed so hard reading the Slow Hidin' mental breakdown. I'm glad to recommend this book. Rest assured, you can't stop laughing while feeling afraid.

Fight wisely: sophisticated, humorous, and intelligent, with a heavy dose of horror. A virus outbreak that started in Wuhan China has been kept secret. People that get infected by the virus will either turn into an undead, a zombie, an ordinary vampire, or a wudi-wang vampire. Dr. Grouchi was the very first wudi-wang vampire who taught Mick everything. Vampires eat and suck blood on people. The fun part begins when the police get involved, and more crimes get committed unexpectedly and mysteriously. I admire the author's dedication and passion for writing such a stimulating novel as always. This book deserves five stars in total. The scenes were brilliant and funny. The plot is matched with science and math equations that would really have you think deeply, and the characters are very well developed. Overall, this book is top-notch. I'm glad to recommend it.

The more clues gathered, the more complex this case becomes. This book is not going to make you fall asleep; it's hard to put down. When threats from the RBG virus loom over our society, the well-known and brilliant Mick Maux's presence is highly needed in order to help stop the spread of the virus and to provide an anti-virus to the affected before the whole world becomes zombies or vampires. Through math equations, it's amazing how the author brings once again humor, and tests your knowledge and skills in order to find out the real culprit behind everything. I had a good laugh reading this book. It totally caught my attention, and everything that happened in the book stuck in my head the whole time. The names were also funny, and every time Mickey opens up a conversation,

I crack up every time. This book holds a perfect adventure that's surely going to fill you up with humor, action, suspense, and horror.

It's a deep horror, humorous, and romantic adventure of Mick, Carol, and Detective Danny's story as together they solve the mystery of missing people or people being murdered from time to time, and they must prove to the police the presence of vampires, zombies, and the undead. Mick Maux is hired by Dr. Grouchi in order to perform experiments, and to solve the missing pieces in order to form a sensible conclusion. This book is an easy pick for horror, comedy, and romance enthusiasts. I'm pretty sure you're going to love the conversation as much as the characters. It's really going to entertain you in the most amazing of ways.

More than a horror story, this is a story of a man who solves mysterious cases with the help of his beautiful and pragmatic wife, Carol. This time, it's a different adventure for Mick. Following the outbreak of a virus, Mick is surprised to learn about actual threats of the virus. They're far more dangerous than what's being reported in the news. Mick is determined to find a way to return the world back to normal. The element of surprise from this book is second to none. The plot is unique and the characters were very engaging and interesting. Each protagonist displays an act of bravery and courage, especially Mick Maux. The experience of reading this magnificent book can't be paid with money. It's not every day that we get to see and experience a book as good as this one. I highly recommend this one.

Brilliant! That's surely one of the best words that I could describe to this book. Reading this book had me laughing and cracking-up the whole time. Don't get me mistaken, this book is about a widespread infection of the Wuhan RBG virus that could turn people into undead, vampires and zombies. I just love the fact that Mick Maux stayed on character the whole time, and he's filled with humor. His conversation with other people is pure comedy. Unquestionably, Dr. Philip Emma knows how to be a comedian. In all honesty, I was surprised to find out that this book is about zombies and vampires. Dr. Philip Emma is a fine writer. I've read some of his books, like the "A Pair of Identical Murders," and more. But this book is simply one of the best of his works. The ending was unexpected, and Dr. Grouchi's passing had me broken hearted too. Will they be able to save the world from this pandemic? Will the vaccine suffice to cure the demands? What about the mysterious murders? It's a quick read that you owe to yourself for no other reason than a good laugh and horror experience. Surely recommended.

www.ingramcontent.com/pod-product-compliance
Lightning Source LLC
Chambersburg PA
CBHW071744190726
48292CB00003B/859